Sundown

D1557818

Sundown
John Joseph Mathews

with an introduction by
Virginia H. Mathews

University of Oklahoma Press : *Norman*

By John Joseph Mathews
Wah'Kon-Tah: The Osage and the White Man's Road (Norman, 1932)
Sundown (New York, 1934; Boston, 1979; Norman, 1988)
Talking to the Moon (Chicago, 1945; Norman, 1981)
Life and Death of an Oilman: The Career of E. W. Marland (Norman, 1951)
The Osages: Children of the Middle Waters (Norman, 1961)

To
WALTER STANLEY CAMPBELL
(STANLEY VESTAL)

Library of Congress Cataloging-in-Publication Data

Mathews, John Joseph, 1895–1979
    Sundown.

    (The Gregg Press Western fiction series)
    1. Osage Indians — Fiction.   I. Title.   II. Series.
PS3525.A8477S86   1988   813'.52   88–40214
ISBN 978-0-8061-2160-4 (paper)

Copyright © 1934 by John Joseph Mathews, assigned 1987 to the University of Oklahoma Press, Norman, Publishing Division of the University. Paperback edition copyright © 1988 by the University of Oklahoma Press. Manufactured in the U.S.A. First printing of the University of Oklahoma Press edition, 1988.

Introduction
by Virginia H. Mathews

To read *Sundown* with a full measure of understanding and appreciation, one must realize that in the times in which it is set American Indian people were at their lowest ebb. The Indian population had shrunk to about half a million, and the fervent hope of the federal government that Indian people would simply disappear entirely, following years of effort to that end, seemed likely to be realized. Until the human-rights revolution of the 1960s made such prohibitions illegal, it was possible to see a sign in a western restaurant proclaiming, "No Dogs, No Indians"; and "breed," meaning half or part Indian, was widely used language. In the 1950s a young American Indian veteran of the Korean War was denied burial in a cemetery in Iowa.

Against this background, it is understandable that American Indian young people—especially those of mixed blood—might well have had a problem with self-image and self-esteem. Of course, a few Indian people came into favorable public view: sports figures like Lewis Tewanina, a winner in the 1912 Olympics, and Jim Thorpe, a great football and track star. The United States Army and air services in World War I provided a means for American Indian men to breakthrough and demonstrate their military skill, patriotism, and heroism. Outstanding among them was the Oklahoma Osage Clarence L. Tinker, born in 1887, who became a brigadier general in the U.S. Air Force and was honored by having Tinker Air Force Base in Oklahoma named for him.

So physical prowess, which reflected stereotypical fleetness of foot and bravery, came to be expected and accepted where Indian people were concerned. But what of creativity and intellectual brilliance? As late as the 1930s white Americans had not become accustomed to thinking of Indians as educated, articulate beings, and in truth there were not many who were—an inevitable result of the confused bureaucracy relating to federal Indian policy, poor educational opportunities, low expectations, and little motivation. The few poets and writers of Indian heritage were to some extent regarded as curiosities, admired by a small elite but decidedly out of the mainstream. John Milton Oskison, of Cherokee decent, who wrote frontier romances which did not deal with Indian perceptions or issues, was married to Nathaniel Hawthorne's granddaughter Hildegarde (also a writer), and he fit comfortably into establishment literary circles. The Cherokees were one of the "five civilized tribes," and their great leader Sequoya placed great emphasis on literacy, having invented a written language for his people. This tribe also produced Lynn Riggs, a poet and playwright of the 1930s; his *Green Grow the Lilacs* burst into fame as the play from which the musical *Oklahoma!* was created in 1943.

But, as Andrew O. Wiget wrote of the 1930s, "The principal novelists of this period, however, were John Joseph Mathews and D'Arcy McNickle, both of whom established careers in writing. Mathews, an Osage Oxonian, became popular when his *Wah'Kon-Tah: The Osage and the White Man's Road* became a Book-of-the-Month Club success in 1932. In addition to a lyrical autobiography, *Talking to the Moon,* he is best known for *Sundown,* a novel about young Chal (for Challenge) Windzer, so named because his father expected the boy to challenge the white world. In the end, however, despite his making gestures toward becoming a lawyer, it is difficult to believe Chal will, or even can, make something of his fragmented, frustrated life."[1]

Later American Indian writers wrote on the same theme: of young Indians of mixed blood who return from encounters with the white world bruised, uncertain of their identity, and alienated from both worlds, white and Indian. Among the other novels were D'Arcy McNickle's *The Surrounded,* M. Scott Momaday's *House Made of Dawn,* which won him the Pulitzer Prize, and Leslie Marmon Silko's *Ceremony.*

John Joseph Mathews was in the vanguard of American Indian writers who brought their education, their sophistication, and their considered pondering on a dual cultural heritage to the service of their tribes and of Indian people collectively. As a result, for more than fifty years now, Indians have been speaking on equal terms—and often on terms of signifi-

---

1. Andrew O. Wiget, "Native American Literature, A Bibliographic Survey of American Indian Literary Traditions," *Choice* (Association of College and Research Libraries), June, 1986.

cant advantage—with bureaucrats and politicians, with historians, philosophers, and other intellectuals. Yet, as late as the 1970s, it was possible for a staff professional from the Bureau of Indian Affairs to testify before the National Commission on Libraries and Information Science that "Indian people can't read, don't want to learn, and would not use libraries if they had them."[2]

When Mathews's first book, *Wah'Kon-Tah,* was chosen to be the November, 1932, selection of the Book-of-the-Month Club, the jurors were Henry Seidel Canby, Christopher Morley, and Amy Loveman, all certified members of the literary establishment of the time. It was the first university press book thus singled out for popular distribution, and it sold fifty thousand copies in its first year in the depths of the depression. At last, an American Indian writer in the mainstream! When a paperback reprint of *Wah'Kon-tah* was published in 1986, a reviewer wrote that Mathews "consistently stressed the spirituality, dignity and humor of the Osages who grudgingly acculterated to the white man's road, adapting those aspects of the new way for their own purposes."[3] When *Talking to the Moon,* his third book, was reprinted in 1986, one reviewer wrote that "it was his evocation of the Osage countryside and of life on the old reservation (in *Talking to the Moon* and *Wah'Kon-Tah*) that made Mathews a legend for his prose-poetry."[4]

In 1980, the year after Mathews's death, in a tribute in the *The American Oxonian,* his longtime editor and fellow Oxonian, Savoie Lottinville, wrote of *Wah'Kon-Tah:* "As a portrait of Siouan people in transition, it is perhaps without match in the literature of the Indian in our century."[5] In the same article, Lottinville wrote about *Sundown:* "It was well and strikingly written, but in those deep depression years it

2. Taped testimony before the NCLIS, used in the 1974 report and recommendations by Virginia H. Mathews as a consultant to the Commission.

3. *Studies in American Indian Literatures,* Fall, 1985.

4. *Oklahoma Today,* May–June, 1986, p. 5.

5. Savoie Lottinville, in *The American Oxonian* 57, no. 4 (Fall, 1980).

John Joseph Mathews, 1977. Courtesy of Virginia H. Mathews.

had much the same fate as other first novels, but it was destined not to die." Published originally in 1934 by Longman, Green and Company, it is, as Lottinville says and other reviewers have noted, partly autobiographical. Reprinted in 1979 by G. K. Hall in Boston, this is *Sundown's* second reprint, fifty-four years after its first appearance.

Savoie Lottinville was editor, at the University of Oklahoma Press, of Mathews's two final books: *Life and Death of an Oilman: The Career of E. W. Marland,* published in 1951; and *The Osages: Children of the Middle Waters,* published in 1961. Of the Marland biography Lottinville said, "Historians have singled it out for the kind of distinction they seldom accord the work of a non-institutional scholar."[6] And of *The Osages:* "for all of us who work in the areas of Indian history and American expansion, the research-oriented writer who gives us reliable interpretation is a person beyond price. In *The Osages,* a massive history of his people, Mathews in 1961 demonstrated for us . . . what had been needed in this area of history. It combined history and ethnology, written from a sure linguistic base, for Mathews knew the Osage language intimately. His tribal oral history and white documents were on straight. We now cite him with the certainty that he was right. This book, it seems to me, joins the indispensable company of those . . . who recorded for us early the Homeric qualities of the Osage tradition, rites, and wi-gies or recitatives."[7]

Sundown, then, is the only fictional work of a remarkable writer who made literary history in an admittedly narrow area of American literature. It joins his other four books of history, natural history, and biography to create the oeuvre of a uniquely creative artist.

Because *Sundown* reflects so much of John Joseph Mathews's personal experience, feeling, observation, conflict, and complexity, it is thought of as autobiographical, and of course, in a sense, it is. But there are important differences between

6. Ibid.
7. Ibid.

the author and his protagonist. Like Chal Windzer in *Sundown,* John Joseph Mathews was of mixed Indian and white blood. His father, William Shirley Mathews, was a highly respected tribal leader who founded a trading company and a bank after moving with the Osage tribe onto the new reservation in northeast Oklahoma in 1872. His grandfather, a black-haired Welshman named John Mathews, founded the town of Oswego, Kansas, as a trading post. John Mathews married Mary Williams, and after she died, he married her sister Sarah, both of them daughters of William Shirley Williams and his Osage wife, A-Ci'n-Ga. William Shirley Williams is known to history as "Old Bill Williams," an interpreter, trader, guide, and explorer, and the only one of the mountain men known to have been literate. Williams, Arizona, and many other places, are named for him. Another interesting ancestor, also Welsh and related to the Williamses, was Meriwether Lewis of the Lewis and Clark expedition.

Although John Joseph Mathews's father, William Shirley Mathews, was of only one-quarter Osage blood, he served as a member of the several delegations which negotiated so successfully with the federal government for land payments and for mineral rights accrued to the tribe. He married an intelligent, energetic young woman from the Missouri French settlements, Eugenia Girardeau, who became the author's mother. John Joseph delighted in the conviction that his heredity was a good one, and he was fluent in the English, French, and Osage languages. He grew up the only surviving boy in a family with four sisters, and in keeping with the family priority accorded to education, Joe Mathews and all four sisters graduated from college.

Like Chal, his *Sundown* character, Mathews, born in Indian Territory in 1894, also roamed the hills and prairies with horse and dog, a boy full of dreams and wonderings. Even then the tug of his Indian heritage was strong, and he spent time in the camps of the elder full bloods, listening to their tales. Like Chal, he observed the coming of statehood in 1906, when the Osage Nation became part of the state of Oklahoma. Like Chal, he went off to the University of Oklahoma, played football, and joined a fraternity, popular because of his good looks, his brains, and his athletic skill but always feeling himself to be a bit of an outsider. Mathews interrupted his college career to enlist in the army. He chose the cavalry, but because of his exceptional night vision, he was soon transferred to the aviation branch of the Signal Corps and served as an instructor in night flying and as an aviator in France during World War I.

Unlike his fictional character, Chal, Mathews returned to the University of Oklahoma and was graduated Phi Beta Kappa in 1920, with a degree in geology. He refused the offer of a Rhodes Scholarship and went to Oxford on his own, one of the first—if not the first—of the American Indians to do so. His degree in natural sciences from Merton College was received in 1923. He loved his Oxford years, the burnishing of his mind, the discipline and personal attention of the tutorial system, the easy comradeship with non-Americans. He was invited to visit at great estates, where he felt at home with the British adoration of hunting, of horses and dogs and the countryside, with the reticence, formality, and tradition coupled with humor and friendship. He toured Europe and North Africa on a motorbike, did a reporting stint for an American newspaper, married an American girl in Geneva, Switzerland, lived in California and fathered two children before returning to his Osage hills in 1929.

In the felicitous words of Savoie Lottinville, "It was a response to the call of cultural integrity he could not withstand." He distrusted and disliked the frenetic, drifting world of the 1920s and could find no satisfaction or direction in it. In *Sundown* he reflects the purposelessness, the alcoholic haze, the lawlessness, the shrillness of the period which he found so distasteful. Chal's search for purpose is mingled with hatred of what he also longs for—the casual relationships, the meaningless chitchat of white culture—which runs counter to his Indian instincts. It seems safe to say, however, that by the time Mathews wrote of Chal's dilemma, he had already passed through his own period of alienation and self-doubt. Having found his identity at his roots, he knew that his purpose lay in preserving the tradition of his Osage culture and history—what he called "Osage culture rescue."

Professor Terry P. Wilson of the University of California, Berkeley, says: "*Sundown* is a unique evocation of Osage life and thought couched in the fine literary style of the writer's other work. *Sundown* illuminates the psychology of the American Indian during and after the reservation period as well as any novel published on that theme and better than most."[8]

Settled on his own allocated land amid his blackjack oaks, immersed once more in his Osage culture, John Joseph Mathews began to write seriously when he was entrusted with the personal records of Herbert Hoover's uncle Colonel Laban J. Miles, who for more than thirty years was the U.S. Indian agent to the Osages. When his friend Joseph A. Brandt became the first director of the University of Oklahoma Press, it was with Brandt's encouragement, together with that of his family and tribal elders, that *Wah'Kon-Tah* was written and became one of the Press's earliest and finest successes.

Inspired by his mother and sisters (his father had died much earlier), who maintained an active interest in Osage history and culture, Mathews founded the Osage Tribal Museum, which opened in 1938. It was the nation's first tribally owned and operated museum and is part of the Osage Agency complex. Mathews was joined in this endeavor especially by his sister Lillian Mathews, herself an archivist and historian of tribal affairs, who served on the Osage Agency staff for many years. He was perhaps prouder of his museum than of any other thing that he had written or accomplished, and he loved to regale visitors with funny stories of getting some of the old chiefs to sit and have their portraits painted by WPA artists in the 1930s.

After his success as the author of *Wah'Kon-Tah,* John

---

8. Terry P. Wilson, unpublished article.

Joseph Mathews blossomed out and made full use of his heritage and status as a mixed-blood bridge between two cultures. Governor Marland of Oklahoma pressed him into service as a Regent for Higher Education in the state. His geological training led to his appointment as representative of the Osage Tribe's oil and other geological interests, and in that role he made quarterly trips to Washington for a number of years. He served on the Osage Tribal Council and was often cast in the role of tribal spokesman. He used his influence and charm, as well as his high intelligence, to influence Indian policy, and he was involved in the reorganization of the Bureau of Indian Affairs under John Collier in the 1930s. He always had the greatest scorn for the (sometimes) well-intentioned do-gooders who wanted Indian people to shed their special status, their treaty privileges, and protections by the federal government.

As John Joseph Mathews grew older (he was to live to be eighty-four years old), he associated himself more and more closely with the Osage culture which he had done so much to record and preserve. He would tape the singing at the Osage dances in the spring of each year and afterwards would sit listening to the tapes, tapping the arm of his chair as the rhythm coursed through his veins. The building of his little stone ranch house is chronicled in *Talking to the Moon* (published first in 1945 by the University of Chicago Press and again by the University of Oklahoma Press in 1981). It was there that Mathews lived most of the years of his life, close to his hills, making friends with a coyote, photographing the dances of the prairie chickens—and it is there that he is buried. A second wife, Elizabeth, entered comfortably into his chosen life-style. Many visitors came to The Blackjacks, including U.S. senators, newspapermen, filmmakers, philosophers, and a rancher-neighbor or two; and there was barbeque and good talk. Inevitably, his admirers expressed a longing for the kind of simple, uncomplicated life Mathews lived, free of the "rat race" of New York, London, or Washington. "But they would not last out the week," he would say, laughing contentedly, because they worshipped the white man's symbols of success and status and cared nothing for the natural world. In *Sundown* it is perhaps significant that in the course of Chal's downward spiral two of the white business-success models that he observes kill themselves.

John Joseph Mathews left his beloved land no oftener than he could help. There were the trips to Washington, D.C., and trips to many parts of the country to do research. During the 1940s he spent several years in Mexico doing research on the Indian culture of that part of the Americas with funds from two successive Guggenheim grants. And since, almost above all else, he loved hunting, there was an annual trip to New Mexico in the fall to stay and hunt with friends there. In the evenings, following the day's hunt, there was much good "man talk"—joking and storytelling—with the likes of Frank Dobie and Roy Howard. Mathews had a great capacity for delight, and he took enormous pleasure in the good things of life: laughter, good food, a roaring fire, and good company when he wanted it. Above his giant stone fireplace he painted a phrase in Latin which pleased him so much that it almost seemed to have become his motto. He had found it in a Roman ruin during his North African adventuring. The translation reads: "To Hunt, to Bathe, to Play, to Laugh, That is to Live." To the day of his death he was able to say that he had never in his life done anything he did not want to do.

In response to a conjecture about whether one looked or did not look Indian, he would reply: "Being Indian isn't in looks, in features or color. Indian is inside you." In writing *Sundown*, John Joseph Mathews shows us that he had conquered himself. He created Chal out of what he had expunged from his own life—despair, dichotomies, the aimlessness, the uncertainties he knew when he was young—to become valuably and uniquely himself, triumphantly white and Indian.

Sundown

SUNDOWN

I

THE god of the great Osages was still dominant over the wild prairie and the blackjack hills when Challenge was born.

He showed his anger in fantastic play of lightning, and thunder that crashed and rolled among the hills ; in the wind that came from the great tumbling clouds which appeared in the northwest and brought twilight and ominous milk-warm silence. His beneficence he showed on April mornings when the call of the prairie chicken came rolling over the awakened prairie and the killdeer seemed to be fussing ; on June days when the emerald grass sparkled in the dew and soft breezes whispered, and the quail whistled ; and in the autumnal silences when the blackjacks were painted like dancers and dreamed in the iced sunshine with fatalistic patience. And perhaps on moon-silvered nights when the leaves of the blackjack were like metal and the insects chorused from the grass roots ; when from the fantastic shadows came the petulant cry of the whip-poor-will. But not on tranquil, dreamy nights when the screech owl screamed tremulously like a disillusioned soul, like the homeless spirit of a dead warrior. The screech owl carried the evil spirit.

On this birthnight the red, dim light which shone from the narrow window of the room where his mother labored, seemed faint and half-hearted in the brilliant moonlight ; faint as though it were a symbol of the new order, yet diffident in the vivid, full-blooded paganism of the old ; afraid, yet steady and persistent, and the only light in the Agency on this tranquil, silver night of silence.   Not even an Indian dog barked.

Sometimes the reddish gleam of the eye under the oaks would be obliterated as one of the people in the room moved, then shine out again in its feeble persistence.

Then a door slammed.   It was like a gunshot on the stillness.   John Windzer came out onto the little porch, caught hold of a post and looked up at the postoaks. . . An old setter came around the corner of the house and walked up to him.   Half crouching with his tail lowered, he apologetically licked John's hand.   John paid no attention to him but stood looking ; looking up at the treetops, or over them at the faintly showing stars.   With a quick movement he jumped from the porch and walked out under the trees. The setter followed him ; the rise of hope for some sort of activity, or at least some recognition, was indicated by the slight raising of his tail.

John stopped at the picket gate and leaned on it, looking out on the dusty road ; dust fetlock deep, and the wagon ruts casting long moon shadows like parallel black ribbons, cut into here and there by the ragged, black shadows of the oaks.

At the sound of his master's voice the setter brought his tail up and cocked his ear, then moved quickly and looked up into his face, eager but uncomprehending.   The master's face was still turned toward the tops of the trees, and the voice sounded in a sort of rhythm :

> "And now I'm in the world alone
> Upon the wide wide sea;
> But why should I for others groan
> When none will sigh for me?"

Again the silence. Then a feeling sprang up in John ; a pleasant, warm feeling of victory, and he felt that he had conquered, but he didn't know just what — anyway he was happily vindictive. He felt like a great orator standing there in the bright light, and that all the imaginary calumnies that had been heaped upon him were proved false, and he had emerged as a hero ; a conqueror, not only by his sword but by ringing words, and this little patch of the world under the oaks, unresisting and tranquil in this savage valley, was symbolic of the world that had ignored him and taken special trouble to persecute him. The setter raised his paw and scratched tentatively at John's leg. He looked down, then raised his hand to the silent, patient trees, and said in a louder voice with a special tone which he believed to be an imitation of William Jennings Bryan, his hero :

> "Perchance my Dog will whine in vain
> Till fed by stranger hands;
> But long ere I come back again
> He'd tear me where he stands."

He hesitated, then, "But I live as a challenge." However, his thoughts were not clear ; he didn't know what he challenged. As a matter of fact it had never been definite, and his confused mind tonight could not formulate words. This inability caused a slight annoyance. He moved away from the gate and started toward the house, stepping off the flagged walk once, but righting himself and walking on with shoulders straight and a quick animal-like movement into the house, slamming the door behind him. The door popped like a gun ; like a crack under the strain of the heavy silence.

He fumbled in the dark kitchen, then with the aid of the broad shafts of moonlight coming through the windows found the bottle of *Rock and Rye* where he had left it. His hand stuck to the neck as he turned the bottle up to his wide mouth. He set it heavily on the table and said, "Hagh." He stood a moment, then went with light but unsteady steps into the room where the dim red light shone.

The government doctor was ready to leave, and the wrinkled old woman who was John's mother-in-law was smiling broadly. The doctor said, "Well, John, a boy all right and a daisy." John looked at the hump under the crazy patterned quilts, then at the straight black hair flowing over the pillow. He could see the quilts move gently as his wife breathed.

Again the ecstatic feeling came over him, and he said oratorically as the thought presented itself for the first time, "He shall be a challenge to the disinheritors of his people. We'll call him Challenge." The doctor looked at him with a quizzical expression, then smiled with tolerant amusement, which changed to seriousness when John looked at him. The old mother-in-law padded here and there in her moccasins, her stomach and her flat breasts shaking. As the doctor put his hand on the door knob, she sat down in the only chair, and with her forefinger twisted a strand of iron gray hair over each ear, but remained silent.

"Well, good night," said the doctor. "Challenge is a good name."

JOHN was up early. He went to the kitchen and kindled the fire in the stove, brushed the shavings and pieces of bark off the top with a wild turkey wing. He went to the barn and fed the team, and his buckskin saddle-horse. When he came back to the kitchen the white girl was up and preparing breakfast. He took a glass, put sugar in it, then filled it with hot water from the kettle, then poured in some of the straight rye whiskey, carried the mixture to the front porch and sat down to await breakfast.

At ten o'clock he went into his wife's room and looked at the baby. The little fellow was wrinkled and very red, with a surprising shock of very black hair.

John left the room without saying anything to his wife. He brushed his suit carefully before putting it on, then arranged his large black cravat, and fastened in it the diamond horseshoe stickpin which Le Chateau had brought him from Washington. When he was dressed he went to the barn, saddled the buckskin, and swung up the dusty road in the crisp air of early autumn.

It was only a short distance from his small frame house to the center of the Agency where the Council House and the traders' stores were, but he always rode the buckskin, tied him to the hitching rack at the side of the store. All day the little pony stood, patiently stamping to shake the flies from his forelegs. Sometimes another pony would be hitched to the rack near him, and he would squeal his displeasure, lowering his ears flat to his skull, and showing his yellow teeth.

The benches in front of the trader's store were filled as John walked up. The red and white striped blankets of the fullbloods shone conspicuously among the drab suits of the mixedbloods. He said, "How," to the bench-sitters in general, and receiving a lazy response, walked into the store. The trader looked up from behind the counter, his hands black and greasy from handling the shiny harness which he had just hung up on some pegs behind him.

"Well !" he smiled, "Ready for them cigars this mornin' ?"

"Reckon I am."

"Sure 'nough, now ?"

"Yeah."

" 'Tain't a boy, surely ?"

"Guess so this time."

"Say, now, that's purty fine, I tell yuh." The trader went to the glass showcase, which was profusely specked by flies, and brought out a box which had been opened, in fact the only box of cigars in the store. "Here," he said, " 'bout half full, but reckon they's enough to go 'round." He handed the box to John and went over to the desk to make an entry in a large book.

Soon the smoke from the cheap cigars was curling around the broad-rimmed Stetsons, both black and light ones, and eddying around the eagle feathers sticking in the scalplocks of the fullbloods. The air was so still that the smoke hung in little clouds around the heads of the sitters. A forlorn, nondescript Indian dog got up from the cool shade at the side of the bench, stretched, yawned vocally, as though there had been some painful disturbance on his inside ; looked up at the silent men with profound sadness, then trotted dejectedly across the dusty road.

The shade in front of the store became narrower as the sun climbed over the quiet valley, and the shade of the postoaks which rose with great dignity above the dusty area, drew closer and closer around their roots.

A wagon came down the street, creaking, and with hubs knocking on the axles ; the hoofs of the horses and the rasping of the tires were muted in the deep dust. A tall blanketed figure sat straight and regal on the front seat, and in the bed a fat woman sat with a baby-board across her lap. Suddenly there was a sharp, inquisitive bark from the shade of the blackjacks across the road, then a medley of excited barking, and lean shapes of all colors and blends imaginable rushed out and ran toward the wagon. The three dogs following the wagon stopped and their hair stood erect on

their backs and along their spines. Then there was a medley of short barks, growls, whining and sharp, shrill yelps.
The fat woman shouted in a shrill, menacing voice, but her
words were drowned in the terrific din. The tall man
seemed not to notice. He drove on to a hitching rack under a tall oak, threw the reins out on each side, slowly
climbed down and hitched his team. The woman climbed
out, still scolding, although the dogs that had followed the
wagon were running for shelter across the road with the
others in pursuit.

The tall Indian came up to the group on the bench and
stopped ; his wife, who had thrown the baby-board on her back,
went into the store. A "how" was exchanged, then Charlie
Bienvenue, a mixedblood, said with shining black eyes, "How,
my little son," in Osage. Everyone laughed. This was a
joke, as Red Feather, the tall Indian, was a man of great
dignity and much older than Bienvenue. When the laughter had died, one of the blanketed figures said, "It is good to
see you." After a long silence, John reached down under
the bench and pulled out the box of cigars. As he offered it
to Red Feather he said, "My father, I want you to smoke
this — a son has come to my house." Wrinkles came to
the corners of Red Feather's eyes as he smiled. "Good," he
said. "For long time I thought that you did not have strong
juices in your body, but now since you have son I know that
you have good juices." John was slightly embarrassed as
he looked down and smiled guiltily. The others laughed.
Red Feather continued, "They say it is good that son should
come to lodge after many girls have come. I believe it is
better since these girls have gone away."

One by one the fullbloods stood up, pulled their blankets
about them, and walked off down the road. Soon, only
John and three mixedbloods were left. Bienvenue threw

the butt of his cigar away, then said to no one in particular, "Looks like the guv'mint's gonna play hell with that Frazer lease — 's talkin' with Jim the other day and he said he thought the Council 'ud have to go to Washin'ton this winter."

"Ain't the Frazer lease all right ?" asked John. "Whatta they wantta monkey 'round about it for ?"

"That's what I say," spoke up Pilgrim, and he spat tobacco juice out into the dust, as though freeing his tongue for action. "But of course the Reservation Oil and Gas is gonna try to git in somehow and — they tell me they're purty powerful — tell me the guv'mint's fer 'em, too."

Then Bienvenue said, "Hell, that 'ud ruin the Nation, if they ever let them fellas git a finger in."

Ed Caldwell had not spoken. Suddenly he reached in his pocket and pulled out a great gold watch to which a fob with an onyx ornament was attached. "Noon," he announced. "I tell yu they's a nigger in the woodpile somewhur. They's a few fellas in the Department itself actin' funny about the whole thing. I ain't gonna call no names. We'd better play clost to the chest up there. If they's any oil in the Nation, why we wantta get the benefit of it — if they ain't, well, they won't be nobody hurt."

"The guv'mint won't allow the Reservation Oil and Gas not to do only what's fair," said John. Ed got up and kicked each leg of his pants down, then winked at Bienvenue, "Jist come in from Elgin last night — let's go down to the barn and see what we can find." The sitters rose eagerly. "Ha ha ha HEY !" said John. "Ha ha ha HEY !" echoed the others, and they followed Ed's tall form across the dusty road to the government barn.

II

ONE might have said that Chal's early childhood was contemplative rather than one of action. Yet this would not be true ; it was both a life of contemplation and action. Contemplation, mostly in the form of dreams wherein he played the role of hero, whether in the form of man or animal.

Sometimes he was a panther lying lazily in his den and blinking in physical contentment, or a redtail hawk circling high in the blue of the sky. Often at night, when he heard the raindrops on the tin roof of his bedroom, he would be an animal ; an indefinite animal in a snug den under the dripping boughs of a tree. Sometimes real pain would be the result of these dream-world metamorphoses ; pain caused by the desire to fly over the green world high in the air, like the turkey vulture and the hawk. Unhappiness would descend on him as he lay on his back in the prairie grass, watching the graceful spirals of the redtail. He would get up with a feeling of helpless defiance and walk slowly to where his pinto cropped the grass with reins dragging. It was a hopeless feeling of inferiority in being earthbound, and at such times he would find assuagement in racing the pony over the prairie with the mane whipping his face ; racing as fast and as carelessly as the discreet little pinto would run ; racing until his attention was attracted to a coyote slinking off, or to some movement on the horizon.

Eventually his thoughts would flow into other channels, and later, as he rode into the barn lot erect and magnificent as a bemedalled general at the head of a dusty, victorious army, he would have forgotten his earlier unhappiness. The black surrey mares coming up to the gate to greet the lathered pinto were an escort, and the chickens the enthusiastic crowd. Of course there was a sort of "time out" as he opened the gate and spoke sharply to the black mares as they attempted to run past him ; time out until the general could climb back into the saddle. The gate just wasn't there, and the opening and closing of it had no part in the dream. The "general" would ride stiffly to the center of the lot, whirl about, much to the amazement and annoyance of the pinto, and stand like a statue for a few seconds. If he happened to remember, he looked around to see that there was no one within hearing of his voice, then he would make a high sounding speech to his trusting, brave, and victorious troops, then dismiss them with a flourish of his hand.

His final address to his soldiers was stilted and praiseful — the kind of thing which he believed would float down the corridors of time. No matter what high-sounding words came to his mind, he always ended with a note of defiance and profound warning : "Let England remember this day — let her remember that the men of America will defend their mother country to the last man, shouting, 'Don't give up the ship !' You have covered yourselves with glory, and I am proud of you, and your memory will be green to the end of time."

Oddly enough, he was forever leading charges against England. Sometimes he led gaily painted warriors ; Osages and Sioux against the mythical tyranny of an England who was taking Indian land, but most of the time he led an army of picture book soldiers, who were of course inevitably victorious. This was the influence of the stories which his father read to him from American history books, which gave to the American every virtue and to the Englishman every vice.

He was a boy of great action though he even dreamed during the playing of games. Often he would start out on the long dusty road over Cedarvale Hill toward the Kansas line, foxtrotting. Going on under the hot sun of August until his heart pumped like drum beats in his thin chest, and his throat became dry and he was in pain. But on he would run until he halted, staggering, then fall into the hot shade of a blackjack, where he would lie on his back and gaze up at the restless leaves.

He was not a little Indian boy even then, but a coyote, that had just outrun his uncle's greyhounds by tricking them. He had heard the pounding of their feet behind him, and could visualize the slavers flying back from their mouths, and the concentrated excitement in their eyes. When his breathing became regular, he would pull off his shirt which was already almost off, remove his denim pants, and with only his moccasins from which the beads had been worn, he would lie back and let the leaf shadows dance over his bronze body. If by this time he had not become something else or had not gone off on another line of dreaming, which would take him far away from the indolent summer voices, he would half rise and move the muscles of his nose in simulation of a coyote testing the air currents in quest of some trace of his enemies. In this simulation he often did no better than "make a face" with his nose wrinkled, but it answered the purpose ; he was a coyote.

Often, his role was suddenly changed by a grasshopper climbing slowly up a grass stem, with the purposelessness of all grasshoppers. Or a cicada breaking into monotonous song just above him. Perhaps the hot breeze would stir the leaves more violently and there would be a subdued roar, like a moan ; like a protest from Nature who had fallen into a soothing somnolence. A nuthatch moving like a shadow up a dark tree bole, fussing weakly, might send him into another dream world.

Sometimes he would not get home until after dark, walking or riding over the prairie and into the belt of blackjack where the density of the darkness, or half darkness of the twilight always produced other stimuli. If he were riding he would wheel his pony and dash off through the trees ; the stiff, tough arms of the blackjacks catching at his clothing if he did not manage to dodge them by lying flat on the back of the pony or clinging to its side as he raced ; enemies in pursuit of a fleeing brave. He would come to the edge of the sandstone hills and burst from the fringe of trees to look down upon the scattered red lights of the Agency ; dim red lights like the eyes of prowling animals. At such times he would become a scout creeping into the camp of the enemy ; leading the pony cautiously over the second growth oaks and slipping and sliding over the clay. But as he approached the barn and heard the restrained, inquisitive whinny of the mares, or the soft questioning of the Jersey cow, he would suddenly return to the world of reality with the thought of what his father might have to say about "mistreatin' stock."

Soon he would be back in the world of fantasy as he moved the heavy bales of hay from the loft to the mangers ; as he thrust his head into the hot flank of the cow, as she lazily swished her tail against his back.

Whether he was alone on the prairie or swimming with little Running Elk, Little Wild Cat, Sun-on-His-Wings, and other boys of the camp, these days seemed always to be a part of the life he was destined to live ; the quieter part of a stream near its source, lazy, murmuring and dappled.

But of this earlier life from babyhood, he remembered only a few outstanding things ; like impressions made in fresh cement which would remain distinct throughout the years. Behind these impressions would be the silence, the tranquillity of his home. Always he remembered the silence, and though he grew more loquacious as he learned to say meaningless things, he had a reverence for it as long as he lived ; even when he had assumed that veneer which he believed to be civilization.

His first lasting impression was when as a fat, bronzed baby sitting on the floor he was suddenly flooded with emotion ; emotion that suffused him and left an impression which he never forgot, but he knew the source of that emotion only after years had passed and he had learned the details from his mother.

There were no servants in the Agency and those desiring them had to go into Kansas and induce the daughter of some starving settler to come to them, after getting permission from the agent and duly registering the girl, who was thereafter known as a "har'd gurl."

It was thus that a flaming red skirt worn by one of these har'd gurls produced in the baby the first intense emotion of his life. He learned from his mother later that upon seeing the swishing skirt as the girl passed him, his baby hands clutched the air convulsively, his mouth flew open and he began to drool lavishly. Then his two chubby fists were placed in his mouth and his whole body quivered, and unconsciously, red became his favorite color ; long before he learned of the religion of his people, red was sacred to him ; long before He-Who-Walks-With-Stick told him that red was the color of the Sun, who was Grandfather, and of Fire, who was Father, and of the Dawn, sacred to Wah 'Kon-Tah.

Again, an isolated impression, the circumstances of which

he half guessed and vaguely learned from his mother, disturbed his whole life.   It must have been a Fourth of July celebration under the shade of the elms along the creek. The tinny music, the horns, the popping firecrackers and the sweating people he remembered.   He remembered having held someone's hand as he walked along, probably the hand of a har'd gurl ; when suddenly his hand was dropped, and he seemed to be left alone.   Then a towering, disheveled figure came toward him ; a mad woman with her iron gray hair flying, cursing as she strode toward him.   Her face was distorted and ugly and her eyes were gleaming. As she reached him she swung her great arm and knocked him sprawling.   He did not remember being picked up, but the har'd gurl in charge of him must have come immediately to his rescue.   But burnt forever in his memory was the intense emotion of that moment ; so intense and so searing that it affected his whole nervous system, and the picture of that wild white woman with iron gray hair and eyes flaming with hate and madness, had ever the vividness of a white scar.   Always thereafter, when the veneer dropped from a woman and she became excited and angered, he was suffused with that which seemed to be a strange chemical running through his veins, and he felt sick and his knees grew weak, and dejection sat on his spirit like black wings hovering.

He must have been older when the still, hot, summer evenings impressed themselves on his memory ; evenings filled with the scent of honeysuckle and wistaria, when the insects chorused from the grass roots, led and almost drowned by the katydids.   Evenings when there were no lights in the house and his parents sat for two or more hours in the silence. From his mother's lap with his head on her gently heaving breast, he could hear the singing on Wednesday evenings come from the lone frame church in the valley.   The little church to which the few white people of the Agency came from all directions along the dark, dusty road, swinging lanterns which they left by the front entrance.

For an hour or more he would lie thus, without day-dreaming, lulled by the bread and milk in his stomach and the sleepy, murmuring night. He would sometimes concentrate on the bass chirruping of the cricket, out of harmony with the rest of the chorus and much nearer, perhaps under the porch. If an Indian dog did not bark to bring him back to sharp consciousness, or the coyotes yap from Cedarvale Hill, a veil would come over his thoughts, smothering them in sensuous torpor, and he would be conscious only of a very slight squeak in his mother's corsets as she breathed. Even this squeak was soporific, and soon, under the weight of the hot stars and the heated air that often in midsummer was like the breath of a panting dog ; under the monotonous fiddling, buzzing and rasping from the grass and the singing that shrilled across the quiet valley, he would pass into sleep.

One day during the hot summer when he had been running through the house on his bare feet over the pine flooring that had begun to splinter, he ran a large splinter of wood into his foot. He remembered the smell of turpentine and the calm silence and the deftness of his mother. He remembered sitting on her lap in the kitchen. Pride in his independence must have been hurt, and to assuage it his mother was telling him that he should soon have a warm piece of the cake which the har'd gurl was baking as she hummed "Barbara Ellen." To make her argument stronger his mother had told him that screwflies would get into his foot and it would be very bad if he got down on the floor again —- and soon he would have a nice piece of cake and the screw-flies would go away and he would be well again in a few days.

For a long time he thought that hot cake, just out of the oven, was an antidote for screwflies, and he had thought at the time that perhaps the screwflies were already at his foot and that his mother, with her usual calmness, was pretending that they were not ; that his mother knew that the cake would drive them away, and that warm cake was the only thing with which to cure a wound which already had flies in it.   What a screwfly was he didn't know, but immediately pictured it with large red eyes and a proboscis shaped like a screw, with which it bored its way into fresh wounds.

It was at this time in his life that an intense dislike came to him.   There was a cousin of his father, a thin woman with graying hair, who through his father had secured a position as teacher in the government school.   For several weeks she stayed at the house and Chal was fascinated by her ; one of the few white women he had ever seen.   But he eyed her with suspicion when she attempted to get him to sit on her knees.   He much preferred standing in a corner and listening with fascination to her almost continuous talk. Her room on the north side of the house was filled with a sickening, sweet odor, but it was also filled with the strangest things he had ever seen.   There were pale little men and women made of china, like his mother's cups, and bottles of delicate pink and green shades, and one in particular with a little red rubber ball attached to a red rubber tube, which in turn was attached to the top of the bottle.   This he wanted very much, but certainly would never ask her for it ; she would probably have talked too much in giving it to him, and that would have embarrassed him painfully.

The most fascinating thing in the room was a large hat which, as far as he knew, never left the hanger on the back of the door.   It had a bright ribbon around the crown, and delight of delights, the ribbon was red.   And above this ribbon, sitting eternally asleep on the crown, was a gorgeous golden bird with red hackles and long tail feathers, and he, after spending many minutes just standing and looking at this incredible bird, desired it with all his heart. That bird flitted into his day-dreams and was many times present in the fantastic experiences one has when he is asleep. And always when he came into the house from play, he would go and with a little thrill running through him, stand looking at the golden bird with a desire so intense that it made him unhappy.

But it was from his father's cousin that he learned about Jesus and His birth ; travail and death. He thought about the story so much that the carpenter's little Son became his playmate in fantasy. He showed this fanciful Boy the place under the grape arbor where one could hide when he dreamed that he was a wolf or a wildcat. He told his fanciful playmate about a wild turkey that came into the barn lot with her brood and had taken corn from his hand but had run when his father came. But the fanciful playmate and the fanciful turkey never met, although he promised the former that he might see her some day if he could be very quiet and peek through the cracks in the loft.

One day cousin Ellen came into the house simulating breathlessness and sat down with her feet extended and her legs apart. She fanned herself with her large hat, saying that it was just as hot as it could be and that's all there was to it.

"I bet I've walked miles," she said. "But I tell yu though, it's cooler in this room, all right." For goodness sake, she just didn't know how a person could stand it if it got any hotter than this — she thought she reely would die. Chal's mother had stood with the wise, benign expression of fatalism and had said simply, "Well — it is hot," as though she would pat cousin Ellen on the shoulder and say, "Never mind," then left the room quietly.

Cousin Ellen stopped fanning herself and began to unwrap a small package, looking at Chal with a tight-lipped smile, "Guess what I got for a good little boy — something very nice — look." She drew some picture cards from the paper and began looking at them. "Come here," she said. "Here are all the pictures about the Christ child and the crucifixion. Here's the Christ child in the manger — isn't He sweet, and here's Joseph and Mary coming to Bethlehem — see Mary on the mule." She believed it indelicate to say "ass." "Now take them and take good care of them." Chal took the pictures in his brown hands and backed off, then turned and started to go. "Wait a minute," she said, and lifted a finger. "What do you say?" He muttered a "Thank you" over his shoulder as he went out into the yard. He went to the grape arbor and crawled under.

Certainly they were beautiful pictures : there were Mary and Joseph and the mule, the three wise men and a great, shining, abnormal star, about which he was rather doubtful. He had once asked his father if he had ever seen that star, and his father had said that he didn't guess he ever had and he reckoned no one else had neither.

There was a picture of Jesus in white robes, floating among the clouds with a great red heart on his breast toward which he was pointing. This was his favorite ; Jesus was certainly not bound to the earth like other things without wings. He looked long at the card which showed the crucifixion. There was the stripped, emaciated and pale body of Jesus with red wounds, against a background of clouds. At the foot of the cross were Magdalen and Mary the mother, the latter in a robe which he thought the most beautiful blue he had ever seen — a soft blue that made you happy. In skirts like women wear, only not so long, were the Roman soldiers with metal breastplates and long spears. One of them in particular he noticed ; the one who stood with upraised spear and shiny helmet ; the one with the mocking look on his face.

The picture held him. It fascinated him so that he couldn't look away from it, although he wanted very much to do so. That soldier in those short skirts, with his beautifully muscled legs and arms. The beautiful blue of that robe which Mary wore, bowed at the foot of the cross. For many minutes he looked at the picture, then a slow anger rose within him. As he looked steadily, the sardonic face of the Roman, the beautiful blue robe, and the pale body of Christ all became blurred and he felt a tear on his hand. He put the other pictures aside, then dug a hole in the soft earth under the vines and buried that picture of the crucifixion face down, picked up the others, and walked back to the house. But all day he thought of that Roman's face.

After dinner, before the long summer twilight, he went back to the arbor and unearthed the picture. He was surprised to see the same expression on the Roman's face, and his anger was so great that he said aloud the bad white man's words which he had heard a freighter use when his mules got stuck in the mud in front of their house. He walked into the kitchen and from a little cigar box in which he kept his treasures he took a stub pencil and began furiously to mark out all the soldiers in the picture. He thought of the group just beyond the cross as young soldiers, because in perspective they were of course smaller. The pencil marks didn't seem to have the desired effect and he rubbed harder, but still no use. In his anger and his defeat the tears came again.

His parents and cousin Ellen were on the front porch — he

could hear cousin Ellen talking. He took the big butcher's knife out of the drawer and began cutting the soldiers out of the picture — cutting until there was very little left. Just then cousin Ellen came into the kitchen to get a drink of water and saw him.

"Why — I never," she exploded. "Is that the way you do the nice pictures I give you !" She picked up the cards and made a clucking sound : "Where are the others ? I bet you cut 'em up, too." He reached in his blouse and took out the others and gave them to her, but remained silent. "I'm goin' straight and tell your mother," she warned, and her skirts flipped around the high tops of her buttoned shoes as she left the room, saying under her breath, "Little savage !"

His heart was broken. A queer world. Hadn't she told him with much show of anger and with sadness about the crucifixion, and the "mean old soldiers" of Rome ? Hadn't she said that when He had called for water they had given Him vinegar to drink ? And he was sure that the big soldier with the mean face was the one that had stuck a spear into the side of poor Jesus and had made Him die.

He went to the barn lot fence and climbed upon the top rail. He wanted to stop sobbing but he couldn't. One of the mares attempted to muzzle his foot, but he kicked her and she looked at him with surprise in her great soft eyes. He didn't care. He didn't care if he died.

There was no stern voice from the house — he didn't expect one. Cousin Ellen would be talking and talking, and his father and mother would remain silent, even when she would say what she had said to his mother in the bedroom one day — something about "respect," and coming to a "bad end." Suddenly he knew that he hated her, and anger relieved his leaden heart just a little, and though his sobs were less frequent they came, much to his humiliation.

Then he became conscious of the sunset. It was red ; his beloved red, with the tops of the blackjacks cutting into it. They seemed strange and far away and he felt intensely that he should like to go there ; go where the familiar blackjacks were like the strange scenes in his picture book. Above, there was a large dark cloud with its edges colored red by the sun. His uncle, Fire Cloud, chief of the Panther clan of the Big Hills, had been named for a cloud like that, his father had told him. He liked Fire Cloud, who came to eat at the house during payment time and sat talking with his father in Osage. He liked the tall Fire Cloud with wrinkles around his eyes, who patted him on the head and said he would bring a fawn next time he came to the Agency.

At the thought of the fawn trailing him, he forgot for the present the heaviness of his heart and was happy with plans for the dreamy future.

III

ONE September afternoon Chal had been out with John in the single-spring buggy to look at the cattle. On the way into the Agency, at the top of the hill, they passed the three great sandstone school buildings, as they drove along the fence that confined the grounds. Chal had seen these buildings many times, and associated them with the sandstone buildings in the valley. But these buildings seemed sinister to him. He had been for some time vaguely aware that some time in the hazy future he must go to school. He had often seen the little Indian boys leaning on the fence or wandering around the grounds, and sitting in the shade of the trees. He had a feeling that they were like animals in a cage, and certainly there seemed to be much sadness in their faces. Sometimes round-faced little girls would hang on the fence in their part of the grounds, with a very stiff looking white woman in the background. The little girls looked funny in their drab colored dresses all alike, and on Sundays in their blue skirts and white blouses. Sometimes he saw tall fathers and round, waddling mothers there at the fence talking with their children or bringing them things to eat ; their wagons under the oaks with the horses stamping flies.

But on this day the wagons were hitched to the hitching rack inside the fence by the boys' building and there was unusual activity. As the horses trotted past, he saw a little boy in leggings and breech clout following his father into the building, with his mother waddling behind ; her hand over her eyes to keep the sun out. He wanted to know what all the activity was about but he was afraid to ask his father, because he knew what the answer would be. He knew that he was going to school that fall and he would wait until his father said something about it. But he kept thinking about the little boy following his father into the dark door of the building. He thought of the door as a mouth into which they were going ; a big, black mouth, bigger and darker than a wildcat's.

The next morning he was attempting to ride the patient bird dog when his father came out of the house wearing his new Stetson, and said, "How — come get your hat." He went into the house and the har'd gurl combed his hair and brushed his clothes. His mother came into the room and looked at him. He was aware that both his parents were looking at him as though they had just discovered something new about him, but would say nothing.

When he was ready, his father went out the door, turned around and said, "Come on." He turned to his mother and she had a very kindly look on her face, and an expression that he had never seen there before. He thought it was like the dog's face when he didn't know exactly what you wanted him to do, and you had just scolded him for doing the wrong thing. She came closer to him, and his father said impatiently, "Come on." She looked down on him then looked quickly out the window, and said, "You goin' to school." He had heard her tell his father that she didn't like the way the men in Washin'ton ran that school, but when his father had plunged into a long talk about education and the Indian as a citizen, she had said nothing else, but sat impassively and listened to her handsome lord.

Chal went out to his father. He had wanted to ask his mother if he were coming back that night, but he had said nothing.

It seemed that he sat for a very long time on a chair and watched many white men and women talking much and rushing into and out of the room, like white people always did.   Then his father motioned to him and he followed him to a classroom.   His father was following a big man with very white hands and heavy eyebrows, who had a pencil behind his ear.   When they came to the door of the room, he could see many seats and many little Indian boys sitting there.   Then his father said, "My son," in a manner which he had when a white man was listening.   "My son, I hope you will be good now, and do what they tell you here. Whin school's out I want you to come straight home." Chal felt that he must have shown surprise, because the white man with the hands that looked like chalk, smiled at him and said, "Yep, my little man, you are a day scholar and you go home ever' night."   He felt that the white man with the chalky hands and the big eyebrows was acting the way his father acted when some other man was listening.   He was very unhappy.

His father pushed him slightly and when he looked up he saw him motioning to the school room with pursed lips.   He went in and sat down.   They seemed not to notice him. He sat there for some time and heard his father and the white man talking somewhere in the hall, then the floor boards creaked under the heavy tread of the white man, and his heart sank.

A change came over the white man when he entered the room.   He sat down in the chair at the desk and looked out over the faces with a frown, and Chal believed that he had never seen a face so severe except in the picture on the card which cousin Ellen had given him.   The one which had the face of that mean white man who had told a lie about Jesus when the rooster crowed ; meaner than the faces of the

Osages when they painted them for the mourning dance.

The white man looked at something on his desk for a long time, then looked out over the room again and said, "Now you little fellas 'ud better kinda brighten up — needn't look down at your desks like you're mad, 'cause let me tell yu I ain't — I'm not gonna have it. Your teacher will be here purty soon, I guess." He pulled a large gold watch from his pocket, opened the case, then put it back, continuing : "Ought to be here now. Her name's Miss Hoover, and I don't want any of you lookin' like a lotta wooden Eendians outside a cigar store when she tries to teach yu somethin'." He looked impatiently at the door with an expression of resignation, as though he realized that whatever he said would have no effect, and that he had learned long ago the futility of attempting to teach a lot of Eendians anything.

Miss Hoover came in like a breeze and the white man got up, made a meaningless movement with his hand and went out.

"Well," she said, smiling very brightly, "here we are." She seemed to be baffled by the total lack of response in the expressionless faces, but she kept smiling. She backed up to the desk and put her hands behind her. "Well," she repeated, "now we shall get started, sha'n't we ?" She stood thus for some moments, then emotion seemed to grip her ; her face became even brighter, and her eyes sparkled with enthusiasm. She stood on her toes and seemed heightened by some bubbling force within ; she almost rocked, "Now, we shall start from the beginning — and learn English. Then we shall come to know and understand each other. I am sure that I shall learn to love each one of you, and I hope you will return my love. For my part, I am the daughter of an eastern merchant whose forefathers were greeted by yours at Plymouth Rock, and we have come together on this lovely fall day to understand each other, haven't we ?" She had an uncomfortable feeling that she was addressing the wooden benches. "How many of you speak English ?" raising her hand. No response, no light in a single face. The light seemed to die gradually from her face, though she continued to smile. A series of painful disturbances went through her brain like slight waves, and the associated waves which these brought to her consciousness caused her to look down to see if she were dressed.

Miss Hoover was a Quaker and had received her position through the Board in Philadelphia. She had wanted the position very much, and on the announcement that she had received it could not sleep for several nights thereafter thinking about it. She was tallish, with black hair just beginning to gray, as though it had been frost-touched. Her face was thin and lightly lined as though through some sort of suffering, but perhaps due to the fact that she was a spirited person and had not married. Her creative urge had been turned into other channels, first as a teacher of American literature in an eastern high school and then as a reader of Poe's poems. But Poe did not absorb her and she was soon wondering why Longfellow had never written anything except "Hiawatha." Then she fell under the romantic spell of Fenimore Cooper, and after suffering under an intense bitter-sweet sentimentalism, was forced into action. "Ah, to teach little Indian minds," she once said. "To see them open like flowers on their own beautiful prairie." She had dreams of sitting with them in their teepees and helping the women with their babies — bringing to them the gifts of science, like gifts from heaven.

She got through the day but was somewhat tired and very doubtful, yet as she sat at dinner with the matrons and other teachers she still had the eyes of a zealot, and refused to believe what the others told her about the stupidity of Indians, though she nodded as though she understood and agreed with them.

After one visit to Mahshonkahshe's lodge, where she heard that there was a new baby, and into which she had blown like a warm southern breeze which blows your hat off and disarranges papers ; after a month standing before those passive faces in the classroom, she became disillusioned and sank easily into the lethargy which was standard at Indian schools. Like the others, she began talking about the East, and went back to Poe, but dropped Longfellow and Cooper for horseback riding. Finally the standardized conviction that Indians were Indians seeped into her heart. She could talk patronizingly about what this one did or what that one did, or said, from the position of one who had been among the Indians and therefore knew them. She felt the importance of all this when she went back to her merchant father's home as a poetic relief from the wild reservation of the Osages, with the delightful position of raconteur. With poetic license, she made the reservation a little wilder than it actually was, and the Osages a little more wild and at the same time more gloriously intriguing. Several times she blushingly hinted at romance — the imaginary attachment of a handsome warrior for herself — and laughed with the others at the very preposterousness of it.

THAT first day Chal kept thinking of Miss Hoover as Cousin Ellen and he immediately conceived a dislike for her. He looked at her when she wasn't looking, then when she looked in his direction he looked down. He couldn't help wondering if she had a hat with a glorious bird on it ; a bird with yellow body and red hackles, and if not, he wondered what kind of a bird she did have on her hat.

During the noon hour some older boys came up to him where he was standing alone.   One of them said in broken English :

"Shuh, look at that one — I bet he's ain't got them things like a boy, ain't it."

"Shuh," said another one, crowding up.   "Gurl, I bet." They all laughed.

"Sure, he's gurl, ain't it."

"Yeah, white gurl, that one."

"Why don' you go to gurl's buildin' like all them gurls ?"

The largest boy advanced toward him and leered in his face, "Yu say you ain't no gurl ?"

Chal thought his own voice was very feeble.   "No," he said, "I'm a boy."

"Ho — oo — ooo — oh, he says he's boy."

"I bet he's gurl."

Just then little Running Elk came up to see what was happening, and Chal had a desire to appeal to his friend, but something in Running Elk's face stopped him — he seemed to be with the pack.   Most of these boys were Big Hills, and he had never seen them before.   He looked at their faces and they were expressing contempt.   He was not afraid, but he was unhappy, and felt miserably alone.   The leader came up to him and screwed his face up so that it was almost terrible, attempting to frighten Chal as the grownups used to frighten their enemies when they went on the warpath, except that the elders painted their faces hideously when they wanted to frighten people.   The big boy came closer.   "Yu ain't little white gurl, huh ?   Yu look like little white gurl standin' there 'fraid."

Anger came up in Chal.   "I ain't afraid, and I ain't a little white gurl neither."   His voice still seemed feeble.

"Ho — ooo — oo — oh, he says he ain't no little white gurl what's 'fraid."

At this moment a big boy stepped up to Chal and pushed him, and he stumbled backward a step off balance. Then the bell rang and they all left, jeering over their shoulders. As he went along the walk behind them to the building, he kept saying to himself, "Gawdam 'em tuh hell."

In his misery he could see the freighter and his four mules stuck with a load of freight on the hill. The memory was persistent. He could see the mules straining and trembling and the driver's face red through his beard. He could hear the whip crack, and the oaths. There was something about the big hairy freighter and the trembling mules that made the words which the freighter used very effective and intriguing, and he always used them when he was hurt; always when his spirit was hurt. Somehow he felt that they were mysteriously forceful and could vindicate him. So when he remembered the towering, bearded freighter and the little mules, he felt the strength of those words when muttered to himself. He had never directed them to anyone or anything in particular, but muttered them to himself and immediately he felt that he had somewhat lessened the damage to his spirit.

For some time after he had regained his seat in the classroom, he muttered those words which his parents had told him were white man's bad words.

That evening he saw his father looking at him over the top of "Childe Harold." His father looked at him for a few moments and said, "Well, what yu do at school?" His mother was sewing, and there was nothing except the slightest change in her expression to indicate that she had heard. Chal remained silent, and his father continued, "If any of those Big Hill boys jump on yu, why yu know what to do.

They're mean that way." Chal looked at the stove. He felt his father looking at him. He wished fervently that his father would stop looking at him. John continued :

"Pick up a rock — anything handy and let 'er fly, if they jump on yu. Then they won't bother yu any more. That's the way to do it — if yu don't, they'll think you're 'fraid."

He was relieved when his father started reading again. Then he heard him put his book down and get up. John began walking up and down the room with quick steps. He was a graceful figure, with his black hair resting on his shoulders, and his quick, almost furtive glances. Chal knew he was going to talk. John gave Chal one quick look, then said :

"One time — maybe you heard your mother and I talkin' about him — Squit Little Hawk. Well, he was Cherokee, that is, his mother was Osage and his father was Cherokee, and he was one of the first boys to come to the guv'mint school. Somehow the little Big Hills and the others too, for that matter, heard he was part Cherokee and they started teasin' him, jumpin' on him. Well, he missed it there. He wouldn't fight back at 'em, and the only thing he would say was, 'Quit now.' Kept sayin', 'Quit.' In those days very few of the little Osages could speak English and reckon they thought he was saying', 'squit.' Natcherly they figured he was a coward and they didn't like him 'cause he wouldn't fight, and he had a purty bad time of it, I tell yu. That's the way of course that many boys get their names — from something they say or do or some incident like that. They called him 'Squit,' and by golly it stuck to him. Even to this day the men his age don't have much respect for him, so he fools around with the white people mostly — neither fish nor fowl, as the sayin' goes."

He paused and looked at Chal, who was looking at the
stove.   "So yu see, you got to fight an Indian — just enough
to show him you ain't 'fraid."   Again he started walking,
then went to the door, opened it and walked out onto the
porch.   Chal knew the habit.   His father never failed,
Indian-like, to go out and look at the heavens before going
to bed.   When John came back he started taking off his
coat.

"Clear as a whistle," he said, then, "and son, you don't
want 'em sayin' you're a coward — I don't know if the
Osages will still be given names when you grow up, but you
want a good one — a name that means somethin'.   Like
mine, Not-Afraid-of-Rations — that's my Indian name.   It
sounds funny, don't it ?   Well, when I was young I was the
only one that would get into the corral with the guv'mint
steers — the others were 'fraid of 'em — never seen steers
before, and the smell of 'em made 'em sick, too.   That's
what my name means translated."

John pulled off his boots and put them by the stove, then
went into the bedroom.   Chal and his mother sat for some
time longer, but neither of them said anything.   Chal sat
looking at the stove and visualizing himself as a young man
in a corral, with long-horned steers ; standing there while the
steers stood with lowered heads and pawed the earth, and
sniffed.   The burning wood in the stove readjusted itself
with a loud thud, and Chal watched the sparks through the
mica windows.   Suddenly he was dreaming.   He was riding at the head of a party of warriors, and the Pawnees were
fleeing over the hill before them, calling in Pawnee, "Here
comes Chal and his Osage Wolves."   He could see a white
girl standing there on the prairie in a long blue mantle like
the mantle of the Virgin Mary, and she turned toward him
as a savior.   The reasons for her predicament were absent,

but the dream was delightful. When she tried to thank him he frowned and walked away, but his dream-heart was full. Still filled with his dream, he got up and walked to his little bedroom under the tin roof.

As he disappeared his mother looked at his straight back. Her face remained the same but there was a smile in her heart ; a low singing there. She was proud of her men ; that tall man who talked much and said words which she could not understand, but thrilled her because her lord had said them. And that son. There was fire in his eyes, and his face was the right kind of a face for an Osage to have, and he was straight and tall and walked like a little warrior. Some day she would put paint on his face and arrange his clothes and set the feathers in his scalplock as they should be set ; she would put the symbols of her family on him, and comb his hair as he looked at himself in a hand mirror. She could see him as a young warrior walk toward the Round-house, where the drums were already throbbing and the caller was calling the dancers in a high voice that sometimes sounded like the wolf talking to the moon. She could see him as he walked proudly, as an Osage should walk, with many bells on his leggings, tinkling. The singing in her heart almost stopped and she thought of a young woman decorating her son for the dance. She must be a good woman, she thought ; she would see that she was a good woman. She would decorate her son until she could find a good woman for him.

She got up and straightened things about the room, and took up her husband's boots and began polishing them. As she polished she thought of the secret that was in her heart. Her great lord who had some of the blood of the white man in his veins and in his heart, didn't know all she knew about their son. She knew he was no coward, and she wasn't wor-

ried about him at this guv'mint school. It was only that she
didn't like white men's ways.

She knew that she had heard him ; the lone wolf that had
howled from Cedarvale Hill. Even above the distant yapping of the coyotes she had heard him. And at that moment she had given her son secretly to the wolf ; the wolf
had wanted him and she had given her son. There had
been no evil to mar that propitious night, because she had
listened ; there had been no voice of evil ; no screech owl had
quaveringly disturbed the stillness. She knew this because
she had listened all night. The white man's doctor thought
she was asleep after her son had come, and her lord thought
she was asleep, but she was listening. Her mother sitting
like a frog was listening too ; listening for a voice of evil.
But they hadn't heard the wolf ; the white man's doctor and
her mother were busy with her son's coming, and above the
creaking of the floor boards and the wordless activity she had
heard him ; she had heard him above the distant yapping of
the coyotes. Then as her lord slept, she and her mother had
listened throughout the night, but they had heard no voice
of evil.

As she went into the dark bedroom to lie beside her lord,
the singing in her heart almost dinned in her ears.

IV

DURING the summers many of the boys from the school went to their homes ; to Hominy Post, and on Salt Creek to Gray Horse Post, along the Arkansas River, and northeast on Caney River. But sometimes some of the boys would come with their parents to the Agency for the June payment, and they would camp with the Agency Indians. The boys would swim, run horse races, and play with those of the village.

It was a surprise to Chal to find that the Big Hill boys were just like any of the others, and he soon accepted them just as he was beginning to accept the little white boys who were coming into the Agency.

The long summer days were spent playing water tag. Someone, in order to start the game, had to be chosen as "it," and the others would dive and hide so that he could not find them. The boy who was "it" would swim around in circles, out of the leaf-shade into the patches of sunlight that flecked the calm water. He would realize suddenly that that which looked like dark water weed along the dark banks, was not weed at all but black hair floating there. Then he would see the nose in the middle of this floating hair, and immediately look in another direction, then dive, still looking in the second direction. But once under the water he would turn and swim to where he had seen the hair floating, and if he were quick enough, tag the boy, who then became "it."

When they grew tired of this game, they would go to the big sycamore tree where the ponies were tied and bring one of them into the deep water, and as many as could do so would get on his back and make him swim in circles. One of the boys would slide off his rump and catch him by the tail so that he would keep swimming.

Sometimes a man would come down to the swimming hole with his little boy on his back — a very small, round-faced boy who could scarcely walk. The man would smile with deep wrinkles radiating from his eyes and slowly throw off his blanket. He would take off his breech clout and moccasins, then with the naked boy on his back come to the edge of the water, holding the little one's arms around his neck. He would stand there for some time and look down the creek, and up into the trees, then turning his head he would speak to the boy with a very serious expression, saying, "How." Then he would dive into the water with the boy on his back. The man would come up immediately and throw the long hair out of his face with a twist of his head as he waited for the appearance of his son. The little boy would appear somewhere on the surface of the water ; sometimes his black hair would appear like fine roots of water weed, and sometimes it was his copper-colored bottom which appeared first. The man would rush to him, and holding him above the water with one hand, swim to the shore. The little boy made funny faces and amused Chal and his playmates very much, but of course he never cried. The father would put the little boy on the bank while he stood in water up to his armpits. Soon he would climb up on the bank and dive with the little boy again and again ; until he thought the little boy had had enough, then he would sit on the bank and let the air dry his body and his long hair. He would put on his moccasins and breech clout slowly, and he seemed to be dreaming of something very far away. Sometimes he would sit and watch the tag game, make comments, and laugh when a boy had been found through his pantomimic directions from the bank. One day while Chal and his playmates were playing tag, the agent's son and Charlie Fancher, the trader's son, with several new white boys whom Chal had never seen, came to the swimming hole. The agent's son had been to the sycamore swimming hole before, but the little white boys usually used the swimming hole on Clear Creek. There were three ponies and six boys ; the ponies carrying "doubs." The newcomers stood and stared at the game, then they tied their mounts near the Indian ponies and began to undress. The little Indian boys went on playing but Chal felt very annoyed with the intrusion, and he told little Running Elk and Sun-on-His-Wing that he was going because the white boys stared so and made so much noise. As they undressed they began to shout at each other, saying "Huh" when they didn't hear what was said. The little Indian boys believed that they said "Huh" so much because they were all talking at the same time ; talking like blackbirds bathing in a mud puddle after a rain.

The Indian boys pretended not to see them, but were so fascinated by some of the things they heard that they lost interest in their game. One of the little boys on the bank used words like a freighter, and Chal thought he used them because he wanted to show the others how big he was. As they undressed and revealed white, glistening bodies, they kept using such fascinating words as "gee whiz," and "the hell yu bawl out," and "judas priest." Chal wondered what all these things meant, and as he watched them come up to the bank one at a time and dive in, or push each other in and roar with laughter, he had a feeling that their white bodies were indecent in some inscrutable way. He didn't know why but he felt that they were a sort of sacrilege.

Soon they were shouting and splashing in the water, duck-

ing each other. One by one the Indian boys climbed out
and started to put on their moccasins. Chal and Sun-on-
His-Wings were just getting out when there was a commotion among the horses. There was an excited, coaxing,
eager whinnying, and they all looked up to where the horses
were tied in time to see Sun-on-His-Wings' pinto stallion
break loose and consummate an amorous flirtation which he
was having with a little sorrel mare that one of the white
boys had ridden ; a flirtation which they had carried on
through the agency of the little air currents.

The little white boys swam to the bank and crawled out
shouting, "Oh-oh !" and "Hot doggie," and looking at each
other with expressions burdened with secretiveness as they
gathered around. Several of them looked around at the
undergrowth as though expecting someone to come and
catch them in some crime. Two of them shouted and
hugged each other and danced in circles.

The little Indian boys after the first look continued putting on their clothes. Chal was mystified. He couldn't
understand what made those white boys act that way. He
believed that only crazy people acted that way, but he was
sure they weren't crazy. The impression of that day was
deep and he remembered the incident the rest of his life ;
that impression of the white man making so much over the
very unimportant matter of the possibility of another horse
coming into the world.

Chal rode double on the little stallion behind Sun-on-His-
Wings, having left his pony at the camp. They rode over
the high grass, out of the creek bottom toward the camp ;
a barebacked cavalcade of brown bodies in the summer sun.
Little Eagle pulled his pony back on its haunches and waited
for Sun-on-His-Wings, then he said, "I bet that colt gonna
be pintado too, ain't it ?"

"Yeah," said Sun-on-His-Wings, "maybe."

Little Cub turned and placed his brown hand on his pony's rump, "It ain't that way all time — sometimes colt, he look like woman horse — like hees mama."

Sun-on-His-Wings said as though after thought, "Will that colt belong to me ?"

Chal was quick with an answer. "No, foolish one," he said in Osage. "That colt will be colt of that white boy — it will be for him, that colt."

"Ho-hoooo," said Sun-on-His-Wings.

They could see the low, rounded lodges of the camp ; the horses grazing clumsily in their hobbles, and the inevitable smoke rising almost invisibly on the heated air of summer. As they rode along the dust curled around them.

A group of women was coming from the camp toward them. There were several old women and several girls with their heads hidden in their blankets ; walking slowly from the camp. It was a swimming party ; the old women and their young charges. When the boys were within a hundred yards of them, Running Elk looked around, smiled at his companions, and said "How." Then lying flat on his pony's neck, he put him in a dead run toward the group. Running straight at them, and causing the girls to scatter like quail. But two old women stood their ground, and when the pony seemed almost on them, they took off their blankets and waved them like signal blankets. Running Elk, of course, was expecting this, and turned his pony abruptly before it had time to shy at the blanket, clinging to the off side like a warrior with only his foot showing over the pony's back ; galloping back to join the group of boys and share in the appreciation of the joke. The old women stood and shouted unintelligible imprecations, and in the hands of one glinted a butcher's knife. The group of girls

formed again, but one old duenna stood watching the horse-
men, shrilly denouncing Running Elk.   They heard her, as
they came closer, say something about "coyote's brother."

After they had passed, Chal looked back and she was still
standing, scolding and waving her glinting knife.   He
thought of the white boys at the swimming hole and he
said to Sun-on-His-Wings in English, "Better ride back
there.   I guess we better tell them about the white boys."
Sun-on-His-Wings turned the pinto and galloped back.   As
the woman saw them coming she shouted to the others and
they waited, while she advanced to meet the boys, scolding
them.   She took off her blanket again and began waving it
in order to frighten the pony, but Sun-on-His-Wings held
up his hand as a sign of friendly intentions and that he
wished to speak to her.   She held the blanket in one hand
and let the hand which held the knife drop to her side, but
she kept scolding and frowning.

"Talk short, coyote's brother," she said menacingly.

"Grandmother," said Sun-on-His-Wings, "protector of un-
married girls, where you go there are many white boys.   I
tell you this thing.   We have come from that place."

The old woman's face changed from annoyance to a hard
expression of contempt.   "Hunnh," she said, "we will go
back."   She turned and waddled off toward the group.

Sun-on-His-Wings turned his stallion and put him into a
run toward the others, who had stopped to see what was up,
but when they saw the pinto coming they lay low over their
ponies' necks, and with the dust almost obscuring them,
raced into camp ; up to and among the lodges, causing
women to scold and the dogs to bark excitedly.   Several
women cooking food in great black pots brandished spoons
and scolded, and the children were mixed up with the dogs
running here and there.   A group of men lying under the

shade of green blackjack boughs which formed the roof of an open structure, didn't even look up from their talk. One woman stood shading her eyes, and watched the boys sliding off their ponies. She said with a scolding voice, "Now we must watch pots — coyotes have come to lodges."

Running Elk, Sun-on-His-Wings and Chal stood for a while watching a woman cut the beef into small strips and hang them on a blackjack pole lying horizontally on two cross-pieces. To one side, were two women, one on each side of a great, crawling, slimy mass that had been a steer's stomach, cleaning the intestines. The women were sweating, and their hands were bloody and slimy.

The three boys strolled around the camp until they came to old Een-Ee-Ah-Peh's lodge. Obviously, she had shared in the beef that had been killed, and certainly she was boiling some of it in a great black kettle. She was old and waddled about her work slowly, and she was almost blind, hence their interest in Een-Ee-Ah-Peh. She saw the figures approach and she squinted at them from under her hand, holding several pink strips of meat in the other hand. She couldn't make out whether those dim forms were horses or dogs. Not dogs, they were too tall for dogs, but wait — she stared more intently. Yes, one of the figures had disappeared, and the other two were certainly dogs ; they were the size of dogs now and were coming slowly up to the meat on the drying-rack. She was certain now. She left the pot and raising her spoon, waddled toward them scolding, and they crawled away as dogs should crawl away at the voice of a woman. They crawled away slowly and grudgingly, she thought, but at any rate they had gone ; at least out of her dim sight. She didn't see the two figures rise, and another figure, which was Sun-on-His-Wings, dancing and grimacing, and shouting wildly, "Yi-yi — ha hey !" as he clung stubbornly to a steaming piece of meat which he had taken from the pot during the approach of the "dogs." The three of them bent low into the long grass at the edge of the camp, then made their way to a pecan tree, where they sat and feasted.

Chal wiped his mouth on the tail of his shirt, which was always out of his denim trousers, and said in English, "Old Een-Ee-Ah-Peh is good cook, ain't it ?"

"Yeah," said Running Elk, "he cooks good and his eyes tell him we are dogs. Maybe his eyes see that which is true and our eyes see only lies." Running Elk, despite his two years at the government school, never used the word "she." He lay on his back, and with his hands laced behind his head, looked up into the branches of the great tree. Sun-on-His-Wings said :

"She is like dead leaf of the blackjack in winter — there is no more talk of summer in her. She clings to the branches of blackjack and around her are leaves of summer, but she will not fall to ground and die."

Chal thought, "If she did fall to the ground she would be too old to dance as dead leaves dance in the cold winds of autumn ; as they dance before they lie still and snow covers them, and they are still forever." Then he said, "She is too fat and old to dance like leaf that has fallen."

"Yeah," said Running Elk, "He mus' know he can't dance, and he is 'shamed to fall to ground."

The leaf shadows played on Running Elk's flat, brown stomach as it moved very slightly up and down, and he continued to look into the branches of the tree. Sun-on-His-Wings rested on his elbow and with half-closed eyes dreamed like a cat full of milk, while Chal attempted to stop a procession of red ants with a bone from the feast.

V

FAR from the screeching of the mechanism of Progress, the little Agency slept peacefully in the winter sun which seemed to have come through a layer of ice far above, or sweltered under the hot shade of the postoaks during the summer, when the heat seemed to be pressed down by a gray-blue bowl, without means of escape. The calm waters seemed to ripple just a little, as a mountain lake might ripple in a slight breeze, when the payments were made. The people came from all directions in to the Agency ; in wagons, horseback, and afoot. The mixedbloods stayed with relatives, and the fullbloods set up their lodges along the creek, among the blackjacks on the hill by the agent's residence, or among the lodges of the Agency Indians at the village.

Holagony's voice would quaver over the little valley and the wild blackjack hills, as he called the people to come get their money ; interest on the trust fund which represented the money the tribe had received from the government for their lands in Kansas. "Ho-ho-hoooooooooooooooooooooooo !" he would call. There was a promise in that long, far-reaching chant ; something which charged the atmosphere with expectancy.

To little Chal, playing with corn cobs into which he had stuck wild turkey feathers, it was fascinating. He would drop what he had been doing and in breech clout and moccasins run to the gate, and pressing his cheek against the wire, would lose himself under the spell of that voice ; leaving the imprint of the wire on his face.

As he grew older he would listen for it with thrilling anticipation, and he would know when to expect it. When he saw Indian wagons lumbering through the thick dust in front of his father's house, the husband sitting like some great lord in the high seat, and the wife, with her children around her, sitting in the box ; when Fire Cloud, his uncle, would bring his two wives and sit at his father's table, he knew it was payment time. At such times there would be no sound except a few sentences in Osage, and when his uncle and his wives had finished, they would wrap the remainder of the food in their red handkerchiefs. But even if he didn't see the wagons along the road, hiding themselves in their own dust, he would sometimes hear the drum beats like the beats of his own heart, come up from the bottoms on the still air of night, or the singing that made his heart beat faster.

After the June payment in particular did the Agency seem to fall back into sleep, not to awake until September payment, after which the days became cooler and there was some activity. And when the leaves had turned and the nights were frost-touched, Chal could hear better, too. The sounds traveled on the heavy air to the little room under the tin roof where he slept with both windows open. He could hear the wild turkeys flying to roost in the trees along the creek at sunset, and sometimes in the night the long, quavering howl of the wolf ; a call that made the tingling feeling come in the back of his neck, as though the hair were standing up like the hairs along a dog's backbone. Then there were always choruses of coyotes and the booming of the great horned owl and the barred owls from the creek bottom. And then sometimes, when he waked early in the morning, he could hear some mourner on the hill which bordered the creek, chanting the song of death, and always some inscrutable sorrow welled and flooded him ; something that was not understandable and was mysterious, and seemed especially fitting for the dense dark hours just before dawn ; the hours most fitted for that questing, that feeble attempt to understand.

Perhaps he did not put these things into words in his mind, but he felt much that way, and on the mornings when he heard the chant from across the creek he could not go back to sleep, but would lie there in the silence and cry, for no reason whatever ; cry because there was something in him which seemed to choke him and which couldn't come out, and there wasn't anything to do about it but cry until his pillow of wild duck feathers was wet and uncomfortable. He would come suddenly to the realization that his mother might discover the wet spot later, and would stop crying and wait until he heard his father moving about the house, before rising.

It seemed that overnight the atmosphere began to change. Strange white people had begun coming into the Agency, and John was excited. He talked about allotment more and more and said that in a few years there would be thousands of people in the new town of Kihekah which had grown out of the old Agency. John would walk up and down the room in his excitement and talk, telling his wife who sat quietly, putting beads on moccasins, that the Agency, counting resident fullbloods, mixedbloods, and those white people who had permits to live there, now had about twenty-five hundred people, and that the act of Congress providing for the laying out of town sites in the old reservation would make Kihekah a town, and people would come from all over to live there.

Chal had heard much about allotment and "filing" for

several years and he felt the excitement. His father would take the team and be gone for several days and come back cold and uncomfortable, to tell his wife that he had filed on something or other. Then one day, Chal went along. They drove out over Cedarvale Hill and through the black-jacks to a little prairie. His father tied a white handker-chief around the rim of the wheel, and as he drove in a cer-tain direction, counted the revolutions, then he would turn in another direction and count the revolutions of the wheel again, and Chal thought it was very uninteresting, but sat silently as his father counted audibly each time the hand-kerchief came up.

The horses would snort when rabbits jumped out from under their hoofs and ran away, and a coyote left his bed in the high grass and attempted to slink off unseen. John nudged Chal in the side and pursed his lips Indian fashion in the direction of the coyote, but no word was spoken.

Then one day, when Chal had been attending school for some time, all the subdued excitement ; that smoldering restiveness that seemed to have seized the people, burst into flame, and John announced to his family that the guv'mint had by an act of Congress provided for the laying out of townships over the reservation. John used such words as "Congress," and "provided," often in his ill-concealed excite-ment about the whole matter of allotment ; used them as often as he possibly could do so, in nearly all cases quoting the very words used in the act with a certain satisfaction and show. "If it hadn't been for the progressives on the council, they never would have been any allotment, if it was left up to the fullblood party," he would say with an air which in-timated that he had had much to do with it.

Chal, as he listened to his father's dream-talk about the future, would wonder why the fullbloods didn't want this thing, allotment. It seemed to be the very best of things and he couldn't see why they were against it. He remembered that his father had always talked about the stubbornness of the fullbloods, and he had often heard him tell the story about the people who came from Washington — a Commission which talked to the Osages at the village. They had come from all of the reservation for payment. His father would tell how Bare Legs stood up during the council, and holding his war hatchet in his right hand had said that any Osage who wished to allot the lands and the trust fund, would find that hatchet in his trail. Chal had often imagined the Osages coming along the trail, and upon seeing Bare Legs' hatchet lying across it, stop, then after some talk form a circle and make speeches about it, finally going back the way they had come. Chal would usually conclude the fancy by declaring aloud that the hatchet was sacred, and that the Osages knew it, and because of the hatchet would never go to the allotment, or whatever it was.

But now it seemed certain that the allotment was coming, and he wondered what the spirit of old Bare Legs would say about it. As his father talked and seemed so sure that allotment and the laying out of town lots were good ; with his father saying things that were not good about the fullbloods, he thought that they must be being "mean" or something. But the speech of Bare Legs before the Commission intrigued him and after one of his father's talks as he paced up and down the floor, Chal asked him to tell that story again, though he had heard it many times. Another favorite was the story of the scalping of the Wichita chief, and especially was he intrigued when his father stressed the fact that the gun with which the chief was killed could not be heard far because it was fired at high noon on the prairie ; it was fascinating to know that there were other Wichitas

just over the hill who had not heard the gunshot. And
there was the story of the Osage war party which had defeated a band of Pawnees, and a lone Pawnee having his
horse shot from under him, had run to a hill and begged
the Osages to be merciful ; crying there on the prairie.
Then his father's magic words in conclusion, "But he was a
coward, and the Osages killed him, and wouldn't even take
his scalp because he was cowardly. They made up a song
about him, too — 'member the one you hear at the dances,
about 'Pawnee cryin' on the hill ?' " Chal, with black eyes
glistening, would invariably request the song, and John in
his clear voice would sing it to him, beating the rhythm on
the wall with his hand.

One morning the government school band began playing
and Chal walked up into the center of the Agency with his
father. There were many strange people there, and standing in a buggy was a very strange white man with a large
hat and a big watch chain across his vest, with elk teeth hanging from it. He had cast off his coat and his white sleeves
gleamed in the sun. He would shout and talk incessantly,
then point at someone. He would bring out a large red
handkerchief from his hip pocket and wipe the sweat from
his face. The people standing around the buggy seemed to
be in a very good humor and laughed and joked with each
other, but there were no fullbloods there ; all mixedbloods
and many strange white people. When the man had
stopped talking in one place, he was driven on to another
place, and he would go through the same gestures and point
at people and embarrass them, but they would laugh.

At first Chal was enchanted by this tall man who talked
so much, and he followed the buggy with the crowd ; walking in the dust behind his father. But eventually it grew
monotonous, and in the afternoon he said he would stay at
home. His father said something about his "seein' history

made," but he said he would like to stay at home that afternoon. For years the word "history" was always associated
with that tall man with the gleaming white sleeves and the
dangling elk teeth across his vest ; he even remembered the
dust that had settled in the creases of the man's vest and
trousers ; that tall white man who made history and kept
wiping his face with a red handkerchief.

Several days later, John harnessed the mares and drove
them around to the hitching post in front of the house and
tied them there, went into the house, came back out and on
his way to the gate stopped and said, "Son, you wantta go
to the lot sale up at the head of Bird ?" Chal hesitated.
He didn't care about the man who made history, but he
thought he might like to go to the prairie. He could hold
his corn cobs with the wild turkey feathers stuck in the end
out of the buggy in such a way that he might pretend that
they were real turkeys flying.

On the high prairie there was not a tree in sight. Groups
of people were already moving from place to place as Chal
and his father drove up. John hurriedly unhooked the
horses and hitched them to the back of the buggy, then
brought out the lunch. After a few bites, he started off with
a segment of pie in his hand. "Come on when you're
finished," he said to Chal over his shoulder.

All afternoon Chal moved with the crowd from place to
place, but the tall white man who was making history was of
no further interest to him. As the people moved along the
prairie, stopping then moving on, flocks of prairie chickens
would rise and sail off, alternately flapping and sailing over
the low, swelling hills. Chal was soon far away in a dream
of his own. He was pretending that where the green of the
prairie met the blue of the sky was the edge of the world.
And he was busy building fantasies on the other side of that
blue wall. He pretended that the road which he could see

twisting over the green ; parallel lines lying across the
prairie, passing out of sight, then appearing again on the far
hillsides ; passing the tall posts which marked the gates
through the barbed wire fences ; would lose itself in the haze
of distance as it passed through the gate in the blue wall of
his fanciful edge of the world.

JOHN WINDZER was almost continually thrilled these days in
the atmosphere of growth and progress ; that atmosphere
which indicated that something momentous was about to
happen, something cataclysmic and revolutionary, but which
never quite happened ; that something indefinite that would
change the whole existence of people who lived at the
Agency.

He had become a member of the Osage Council and was
proud to be one of the Progressives, who were mostly mixedbloods with a few weak-spined and easily led fullbloods.
They employed all the tricks of their white brothers to get
what they wanted and had fought hard and long for allotment of the reservation, until, with the influence of the
ubiquitous whites waiting on the borders, they got the con-
sent of the Council for allotment. In reality the allotment
was forced upon the tribe by people outside the reservation
who had no particular interest in the welfare of the tribe.
John and the other councilmen took much pride in their
progressive principles and were pleased when government
officials patted them on the back and approved of their work.

Many people in all lines of business came into the Agency,
which was now the town of Kihekah. Cattlemen watched
jealously the advent of tenant farmers, and the traders dis-
couraged newcomers who desired to set up shops. These
newcomers were mostly people without means ; people who
were looking for a chance and filled with the dreams which
always influenced the Amer-European on his conquest of the

American continent. Many of these people, in all professions, had been failures in their own communities ; types who could not have gained entrance before allotment, but who started to trickle in afterwards.

In the breasts of the Progressives was the desire for riches and prosperity, but they did not have the white man's artfulness in reaching the objective, and their ideals were more sincere because their source was the pride of seeing their native country developed.

And thus the days passed for John. There wasn't much time now for sitting long hours in the shade of the traders' stores, talking lazily with the other mixedbloods and the fullbloods. There were Council meetings to be attended, and everywhere the buzz of activity.

After the act of Congress allotting the Osages and the expiration of the Frazer oil lease, the subleases were continued. Under these the tribe received one-eighth royalty on each forty-two-gallon barrel of oil rather than the one-tenth royalty under the old lease. This provision was inserted in the allotment bill by a brilliant young Sioux who had married into the tribe ; also the provision that all minerals should be held as community property.

John forgot that he had called the fullbloods "stumbling blocks," and under the tingling expectation of some indefinite, but glorious future, he read more of the poetry of Byron, and Bryan's "Commoner" became his bible. "We had to let Running Horse and his fullblood party have that provision about the minerals, so's tu git the allotment bill through," he would say slyly, as he paced up and down the room before his admiring wife and son.

Chal wondered how his father, who must be right, had made Running Horse, Fire Cloud, and Red Bird understand all this about allotment. He remembered when he went with his father to the village to talk, many of the older men were there and some members of the Council. They were lying in front of Red Bird's lodge, talking in Osage. He couldn't understand all they were saying but he could understand enough to know that his father was telling them the allotment would be good for the people. He remembered that they had all shaken their heads persistently and Red Bird had said, "We are selfish. We want our land for ourselves. We do not want to give it up." Red Bird had made a circular movement with his eagle wing fan to indicate the land of the reservation. Then he had looked at the buckskin handle of his fan for some time. Suddenly he opened both arms wide and brought his hands together on his chest. As though he were bringing all the land together in his arms. He said, "We are selfish. We want to keep our land. There is plenty land for white man, I believe. There is plenty land where he can put iron thing ; plenty land where he can kill deer to make feast for black bird with red head. We are selfish. We will stay where our grandfathers are buried, and white man can stay home and attend to his business there."

More and more people came to the town ; every day Chal would meet some new white boy. News of new oil leases would occupy the front page of the weekly *Trumpet,* and John would read aloud the doings of the Osage Council, and when his name was mentioned he would read the story with great pride. But in his heart there was jealousy of Running Horse, the great orator, the irony of whose speeches in perfect English even reached Washington.

One day John came home from the smoke-filled council

room.   He went to the old smoke-house, and after rummaging for some time in a very dusty rawhide trunk, brought out a sheaf of old letters and papers.   There were pictures of Osages, and old letters written in a very neat hand with many curlicues.   He smiled with self-appreciation, then, putting some of the letters back after carefully reading them, he shut and strapped the trunk.   He carried the pictures to the house, walked into the front room and laid them on the table, then he shouted, "Come here."   His wife came softly out of the kitchen and Chal rose and went over to the table.

"Looky here," he said, his eyes shining.   "Here's some paintin's or somethin' that your — great-grandfather, my grandfather made."   He held up each picture.   Sketches of Osages when they lived on the Osage River in Missouri ; pictures of chiefs, papooses and women.   Below each picture was written in the same neat hand that appeared on the letters in the old trunk such titles as "An Osage Chieftain," "An Osage Maiden," and "A Brave, Grand Osages."   There was one that fascinated Chal very much, the picture titled, "Payhousky, Chief of Grand Osages."   It depicted a man carrying a hand mirror with beaded handle.   He wore the old-style scalplock with an eagle feather sticking out of it and his head was shaved.   The leggings were of white buckskin and he wore a breech clout that hung to his heels. Chal thought he looked too thin and savage, and that his nose was too big, but he was fascinated.   There was something which gave the impression that he was about to move very quickly and strike an enemy with his battle-axe.   As his father and mother looked at the other pictures, he felt disappointed that he couldn't see what this man was about to strike.   Apparently something off the edge of the picture. He worried about this even after his parents and he were seated at the table, with the weak light of the kerosene lamp causing the food in his plate to make little shadows. His thoughts were broken by his father's voice.

"Well, I guess they're satisfied that I'm Osage, all right. The Commission just finished fixin' the Osage rolls today." He continued eating, then Chal saw that he straightened up and looked almost haughty. "Huh," he said, "not only found out that I was bona fidy, but by gollys they found out that my grandfather musta been some punkins." He seemed to swell. Then he continued, "The very fella that drawed those pictures you been lookin' at was my grandfather, and seems like I was named after him." He ate a few mouthfuls as though he were too modest to talk further. He raised his eyes to his wife, "Mr. Andrews said to me, he said, 'Mr. Windzer, looks like you have a little royal blood in your veins — that one-fourth white blood of yours may be royal.' Seems like grandfather's name was Sir John Windzer, and he lived amongst the Osages and drawed those pictures — kind of an artist, I guess."

There was silence, and for the first time John didn't like the Indian silence of his wife — he felt that they ought to talk about this bit of news. He felt a little annoyed and that he was not appreciated.

After dinner he couldn't read anything after he had read again the last issue of the *Trumpet ;* Bryan's "Cross of Gold" speech and "Childe Harold" were dull indeed compared with the winey feeling which filled him. He took his hat and left without saying a word. He walked up the dusty road to Fancher's store, where the dim red light shone in the window, and there would be some of the citizens of the town, loafing.

THAT autumn a private school was started which was to take the place of a public school until the town could support one.   John decided that Chal ought to attend the new school. That would be progress, he believed, and the thing to do. Chal was unhappy.   He sat in his seat like some little bronze figure while the others whispered all around him when the teacher left the room.   During the winter he sat there day after day, and after two attempts to get him to recite, the teacher ignored him.   When a question was asked he became frightened ; he knew the answer but was afraid to speak out.   The other boys and girls would raise their hands frantically, and some of the little boys would snap their fingers.

He wasn't bored but fascinated by these strange people. He had always heard that the ordinary white people who came into the reservation, the white people not connected with the Agency, were inferior.   But if they were inferior as everyone said they were, why were they so sure of themselves, and why did they always get what they wanted ?

On the third day the freckle-faced Fobus boy, who was a natural leader, began to tease him.   He and several other boys began simulating warriors and dancing round and making the tremolo.   They sang "hunka shay, hunka shay," which they believed to be some Osage word.   They jeered at him almost all one recess, but he stood like a solemn owl attacked by crows.   The pack spirit was finally set aflame by his silence and his lack of action, and the Fobus boy came close in his mock dancing, and pushed him.   There was no sudden leaping of anger, no gesture of defense, but he knew that that was the greatest insult that could be offered.   He walked to a nearby stone pile, selected one that would fly true.   The boys stopped to see what he was going to do and they began to hide behind each other in mock fear. They expected him to stand there and threaten with the rock, afraid to throw it.   But he wasted no time.   He took care-

ful aim, and being an expert at stone throwing, he hit the
Fobus boy where he intended to hit him, on the forehead.
He fell limp, with his blood coloring the sandy, bare soil of
the yard. Chal did not look at him again but walked
down the dusty road home without looking to either side.

Chal said nothing about the incident, but the next morning he did not go to school. From the way his father
walked up and down the room, he knew that he had heard
all about it. John stopped and looked down at him. "I
guess Jack Fobus is all right now. I saw his father yesterday and had a talk with Miss Allen. I told Miss Allen
she dasn't touch you if the way I heard it was true."

Chal had no more trouble with the little boys, but he
went each morning to the schoolhouse with a heavy heart,
and he welcomed Saturdays. He soon found playmates
among the white boys. He had known Charlie Fancher,
the trader's son, for some time, and Tom, the government
miller's son. After school hours he would play with them,
usually in his father's large hayloft, and sometimes he would
carry Charlie "doubs" on his little pinto, and Tom would
ride his own bay pony. They would go to the pasture a
mile out of town to get the town herd of milk cows. Tom
was town herdsman, and received a dollar a cow for the
season.

That winter the Osage Council went to Washington about
the oil leases, and each Saturday Chal would go to Fancher's
store to get the mail that had been brought by hacks from
the railroad junction. He would bring his father's letters
to his mother every week, and sometimes she would read
parts of them to him. After reading them, she would go
into her room and put them into a long pasteboard box; a
box which had a lid decorated with flowers and birds and
two little fat cupids sitting at each end with arrows strung

ready to shoot. Chal had seen the box several times when his mother was looking for something. He often wondered why those two fat little white boys wanted to shoot each other, but judging from the expression on their faces, he guessed that they were only playing.

One Saturday the snow was lying deep on the usually dusty road and Chal's breath was like smoke as he ran through the snow. Sometimes the drifts were so deep that he fell to his knees, and the old setter thinking that he was playing some new game, would rush up to him and circle, with his belly close to the snow. Chal would struggle, all the while lowering his head, much to the delight of the dog, who would bark excitedly. Chal was imagining himself a buck and the dog represented several hounds. The buck would struggle to regain his feet, circle the bouncing dog with lowered head, and dash on toward the store with the dog at his heels. He would be a fleeing buck until he arrived at the door of the store, then he would walk in with great dignity and ask Mr. Fancher for the mail. Mr. Fancher would hand him the letters and almost invariably ask him, "How's your paw gittin' along up there — a'right?" Sometimes Chal would say, "Guess so," and at other times say nothing. On the outside again, if there was no one in sight, he would resume the role of wounded buck and run home, gaining the gate before the dog.

On this morning he was standing with his head lowered and the dog was dancing around him with great glee, when his mother came to the door and told him that the agent had come back from Washington, and had told her that his father would be back soon. She told him that he had better bring the letter in to her before he got it wet.

He sat while she read the letter through. She held it in her hand a moment, then turned to him and said, "Your

father says in here that he's comin' home." Chal thought
he saw a queer expression on her face ; not exactly an expression on her face, perhaps something he heard in her
voice.   Suddenly he thought about the way the snow was
drifted at the end of the barn, and he went out there to see
what could be done about it.   After he was gone, his
mother read the letter over again :

Washington, D. C.

My dear wife :
   I guess its all off.   The leases that the Council give, I guess
will be cancelled by the Govt.   That means that the People's Oil
& Gas leases are no 'count.   I dont know why they did this cause
it seems like that ⅛ royalty to the tribe and one well on ever 160
acres is pretty good for the tribe.   Some of the boys say that its
the Reservation Oil & Gas people that is makin the Govt. do this,
but I cant hardly believe that but thats what everbody seems to
think.   I dont believe the Govt. would do a thing like that.
   I guess everthing is alright at home.   I will be home next week
some time.

Signed, Your Husband
John Windzer

   She sat for a long time thinking over these things which
her lord had written from far away Washington.   She got
up and put the letter carefully away in the ornate box.   She
thought it would be good to let him think that the guv'mint
had not done this because those other white men had told
them to do it.   She couldn't see the importance of all this
business, but it meant so much to her lord and she didn't
want to see him unhappy.   She would tell him that the
guv'mint didn't do this thing.   He was like a little boy ;
he always believed in the guv'mint.   There were only white
men up there at Washin'ton, and she knew that white men
talked from the end of their tongues and not from their
hearts.   But her husband believed that everybody talked
from the heart.

The Councilmen arrived in the Agency in three hacks from the railroad junction. Chal saw them come in. The fullbloods with their blankets drawn closely about their heads to protect them from the cold wind, and the mixedbloods with their overcoat collars turned up and fur caps turned down over their ears. He wanted to carry his father's bag for him but after one trial found that it was too heavy.

John brought his wife a necklace with an onyx pendant and he brought Chal a watch fob with a picture of the Capitol on it, saying that he should save it until some day he would have a watch. He was full of his experiences and he talked much about the trip and about Washington, but Chal believed he was worried.

The next day when he was playing in the yard his father came in at the gate and passed him without even looking at him. He seemed hurt, as he walked into the house. It was unusual for him to come home in the middle of the afternoon. Even when there was no Council meeting, he would be with the others at Fancher's store, talking. Chal believed there might be something of interest in what he might hear or see.

He slipped into the house, then to the kitchen door, and he heard his father's voice saying, "Hagh." He knew his father was taking a drink of *Rock and Rye*. He waited, then he heard his father say, "Well, I guess they're satisfied." Then silence. He heard his mother say, "Maybe the guv'mint didn't do it, maybe some — " "The hell they didn't," his father snapped back, "I jist guess they did have somethin' to do with it — who else would."

"Maybe the agent — "

"Naw, what yu talkin' about — the agent — he'd haf to do what the guv'mint asked him to do. Naw, it was the guv'mint. Looks like what they said about the Reservation Oil might be true. I kinda think Running Horse went a little too strong in his speech — it was in all the papers. We're gonna send a lawyer up there and fight the thing, all right — we'd had a meetin' and decided to do that."

Chal heard his father approach the door and he went quickly into the other room.

At dinner his father ate very little. Suddenly he looked at Chal. "Son, your father has been branded by the guv'mint as a traitor." There was a long silence. "This afternoon the agent got a letter from the Secretary of the Interior kickin' us all off the Council — 'cause we let leases to the People's Oil company, so they kicked us off the Council — they wanted the Reservation Oil company to have the leases." John looked at Chal intently for a moment, then said, "Don't you believe your father's a traitor to nobody."

John paced the floor for some time after dinner, then went to bed. Chal and his mother sat by the stove, and they could hear the springs of the bed in the other room as John turned restlessly.

For days John was moody. He would go into the kitchen often and drink from the bottle of *Rock and Rye*. He heard only half of the talk at Fancher's. He didn't defend himself, nor was he filled with injured innocence, but his pride was hurt, and the jaunty, enthusiastic man, the man of consequence which he believed himself to be, became one who acted like a dog that had been whipped. His black eyes showed disillusionment, and the dismissal from an unimportant, practically powerless Indian council, seemed tragic to him. Dismissed by a Secretary of the Interior whose vanity had been hurt by the very effective speech of an Osage Indian who had learned to use the white man's words and the involved phraseology of the period with new force.

With his natural ability as an orator, Running Horse had flayed the Secretary in the flowery words which he, the Secretary, understood. He said he was scurrilous and unprincipled ; saying that he had sold himself like Judas for the thirty pieces of silver and had betrayed a great trust ; he called him a capon with only the outward appearances of virility, which accusation was bad in both languages.

The case which the Council put into the hands of its lawyer came to nothing, but for months afterward the face of the Secretary of the Interior would twitch with anger and hate when anyone mentioned the matter of the canceled leases and the consequences.

Chal had never thought much about the Government except that it seemed always present, like an atmosphere. But its presence had been beneficent and protective, he felt. However, if it could dismiss the Council represented by such mighty men as his father, Red Bird and Running Horse, it must be very sinister and more powerful than they thought. He was glad that he wasn't going to the great sandstone school buildings any more. Even their shadows thrown across the road seemed cold and soulless now.

The word "guv'mint" assumed another coloration. He had visualized it as a great force which had overcome everything ; but a force that was just and kindly, like the picture of God on one of the cards which Cousin Ellen had given him. A great, bearded patriarch somewhere among the clouds, with outspread arms. Now he felt that it would be better to avoid it, as one might avoid the giant which the little white boy, Jack, had killed.

VI

As the years went by, the fevered expectancy seemed to increase. Nothing was certain and calm any more, but the atmosphere was a-tingle with uncertainty ; a thrilling uncertainty which would some day evolve into a glorious certainty. Each day brought more news of something about to happen. A new bank was to open. Fancher was starting a new brick building. The city council was going to pave the streets just as soon as they could get around to it. A Greek came to town and stood on the corner for several hours, with his hands behind his back, watching the activity. Then he opened up a restaurant, but it was not a boarding-house ; it had "Cafe" painted above the door in large letters. The mixedbloods of French descent were the only ones who pronounced the word correctly. And they said that some rich men had already located their businesses in the new town ; very rich men. Men who had made the run for land in '89, and had seen their stores at crossroads grow into towns. Now they were hunting greener pastures and had come to Kihekah. They said the richest one was worth twenty or thirty thousand dollars.

The mixedbloods were proud of the town. It was growing very fast and real business men were coming there, and churches began to spring up here and there in the valley. Tall derricks were erected almost in the city limits and gas was soon supplied to the residents. Across the prairie the telephone poles marched in single file and shone garishly among the blackjacks, and the prairie breezes sang sad little songs in the wires.

One day the last ties of the new railroad were laid along the creek and a locomotive screamed a long blast which reverberated among the hills, and brought everyone out into the streets and down to the tracks. A gambler's team became frightened and ran away, and the gambler was killed, but everyone seemed to think it was a sort of retribution. There was no place for the old time gambler and bandit in this community which had begun to awaken to the optimistic voice of Progress.

The citizens formed in groups and watched the engine standing there, lazily pumping water. They watched the frog-like, greasy fireman with his long-spouted oilcan, as he puttered around the high drive wheels. The steam rose as high as the hills on this cold morning, obscuring the blackjacks. The citizens stood for hours, waiting for this big locomotive to do something ; whistle again, or play around proudly on its new tracks. Those glinting steel strings that twisted crazily up the creek valley, and curved around the hills, finally losing themselves in the immensity of the prairie.

Slowly from the east the black oil derricks crept toward the west, rising above the blackjacks, like some unnatural growth from the diseased tissues of the earth. The payments in royalties to the members of the tribe on the roll became larger and larger as the oil production increased. As the production increased, the population increased.

John had almost stopped talking about the "constitootional convention" of the new state that had been added to the federation. For several years after the convention and statehood, he had talked with pride about the part the Indians had played in the making of this great, new state. He would name over the Cherokees, the Chickasaws, the Choctaws, and others, who had made what he said "was gonna be an Indian state." He had memorized Running Horse's brilliant speech at the convention and had learned the song that had been written in honor of the new state by some enthusiast, stressing the lines, "Fairest daughter of the West."

Chal remembered the day that the old reservation became a part of the new state. People had ridden up and down the streets and had fired off guns and tooted horns. The old bell in the Osage Council House which had tolled for the councilmen to gather, found the emotion of this occasion almost too much for it. Chal had thought, as he sat in the buck brush on the side of the hill, that the old bell was trying to show its appreciation since the reservation had become a county in the new state — "the biggest county," John had said proudly. It seemed to want to peal, to laugh, to shout, but its old hinges were rusted and it was not equal to this new responsibility thrust upon it by Amer-European boisterousness and excitement. It had never been called upon to do anything except toll with dignity, then rest, awaiting the tall blanketed figures who came with stateliness to grave council.

Chal felt like laughing as he sat there. To him that old bell had always had personality like Holagony's voice. Suddenly he had a picture of old Holagony attempting to skip about, laugh and shout, and slap people on the back. When it had first started, the old bell tolled with melody and feeling, but the man on the rope wanted more out of it, and in its attempts to respond to a feeling which it didn't understand, it choked up and gave out terrible noises like a wagon tire being shaped by a blacksmith. Chal was so happy about the bell that he didn't notice the excitement about him.

But he moved with the new tempo as he grew taller. He liked to watch the carpenters and the brick-masons building the two-story buildings which had begun to band the hill ; he watched the shovels excavate the hard yellow clay at the bottom of the hill, and even at home he could hear the hammers and the saws, the chuffing of the train and the rattle of shunted freight cars. He heard constantly the grumbling of the drilling wells.

It had been several years since he had heard the wild turkeys flying up to roost along the creek, and he could scarcely remember what the howl of the wolf was like. The crows going to roost did not fly raucously over his father's house any more, but sometimes, if he happened to be awake, he could hear in the ringing silence of the morning before dawn the long, quavering chant of death from the hills across the valley.

But of this constant expectancy which seemed to thrill everyone in town, he felt nothing out among the hills or on the prairie. He rode along slouched in his new saddle, dreaming, as the breezes of the prairie hissed in his pony's tail ; dreaming to the accompaniment of the rhythmic creaking of the leather. Away from the activity of Progress which had become so important, he felt a pleasure which seemed to be absent when he was in town. On the few occasions when the pounding hoofs of his pony flushed a small flock of prairie chickens, he would come to the realization that he didn't see them in large flocks any more ; that it had been years since he had heard the familiar booming carried across the April prairie. When he came to little blackjack-covered ravines that reached out like feathered fingers into the prairie, he didn't seem to miss the band of deer bounding away ; their white tails bobbing and seeming to float away among the black boles of the trees. Had he seen one lone frightened buck, he might have missed the band, but there were no more deer, and he was not acutely conscious of their absence. Sometimes as he rode along, a golden eagle would sit high on a limestone escarpment, watching him, and the redtailed hawks were always present and seemed to taunt him as usual about being earthbound ; circling low and screaming weakly their contempt.

The wild blackjacks stood patiently as before, and the cold winds still rattled their leaves sadly, like old women talking of the glories of the past. The winter prairie, copper-colored and glimmering with snow patches, was as before, only here and there scarred by a shack, a jumble of fences and barns surrounded by dark patches of ploughed ground, where dead horseweeds and cockleburrs stood rank and desolate. Here and there looming, yellow and black dams appeared at the heads of ravines, behind which the water sparkled in the sun. And now occasionally, above the murmuring and talking of the prairie wind in the grass, could be heard the distant roar of a train, and sometimes its black smoke made a smudge on the horizon.

The springs were the same. The frogs still chorused from the prairie seepages on mild nights that were soft and filled with vague urges. One didn't hear the coyote chorus from Cedarvale Hill any more, but out on the prairie they still talked to the moon ; the great, red spring moon that rose slowly out of the prairie and startled you.

At such times he had some of the old fancies of his childhood. The trees assumed personality and the hills were there to obstruct his view, to hide a fleeing coyote, or to offer difficulties to his mad racing ; to resist him playfully. He found himself still talking with the birds and animals, and held regular conversation with the old pinto.

Sometimes as he rode along or lay in the shade of a tree on a summer's day, he would think with amusement of his childhood tendency to personalize everything. He remembered the first time he had heard the word "civilization." Somehow he got the idea that civilization was feminine ; someone must have said "her civilization" in referring to the Nation, and he henceforth associated the two. Perhaps he saw a picture of a woman with a sword, standing haughtily in defiance of something. In any case, he thought of civilization as a woman. When as a little boy he had first heard that civilization was coming to the Agency, he had worried about the matter. In fancy he saw the most delicate white woman he could imagine ; a composite of all the white women he had seen. A woman with her laces, fluttering handkerchiefs, and sickening perfumery, he glorified as civilization. He used to visualize this lady drooping in the intense heat of the Agency ; wilting and growing pale when the heat crept over the valley after sunrise. That heat that made the leaves of the weeds droop, and the sandstones too hot to touch ; that made the yellow dust in front of the Council House so hot that you could feel it through your shoe soles. A heat that left no refuge, no haven, deceiving you with the ragged shade of the blackjacks which looked cool, but was breathless. Long days when the sun burst above the blackjacks on the hill to the east, and traveled slowly across the valley, fiery and pitiless, making of life a faint murmur ; the great fire-god whose priests were the strident cicada and the ticking grasshopper, worshiping monotonously.

At such times he fancied the lady, Civilization, pale and beautiful, lying on her bed and people standing around her. Curiously, he didn't see the fullbloods standing around the bed of the lady, but sad-faced mixedbloods, the traders and the new white people who had come into the town. He could work himself up over this fanciful situation to the point that tears actually started. However, at this point he usually stopped thinking about it in shame.

He remembered that the fullbloods didn't come into the Agency as often as they had before the allotment, and that they seemed to be resigned and to keep to themselves. They had made him think of the blackjacks on the hills that surrounded the valley. Blackjacks that had stood there so patiently, as they had always done, and seemed to pay no attention to all the activity of Progress in the valley at their feet. He had thought of them as being contemptuous as they stood proudly in their gorgeous red, yellow and orange in the brilliant sun of autumn. He remembered how he used to think of them as painted warriors, ready to come down and attack the town. As a matter of fact, he still had that impression of them, standing there on the hills, aloof from all the hammering, the loud talking, the swearing, and the shrieking of steel, which seemed so important to those animals in the valley.

But away from that thrill of the indefinite something that was glorious, Chal now felt relaxed, and out from under the responsibility of continually playing a role. He shouldn't have expressed it that way, but he felt it, and the feeling was something like the craving for some essential which has been absent for some time in one's food, like salt or sugar. The urge to saddle his pony and ride out by himself became imperative, usually about once a week, and that had to be on Saturdays or Sundays. Those were the only days that he could get away from the monotony of the fresh-paint environment of the new high school.

Sometimes he took a skillet and some bacon strapped to the saddle strings, and he always carried his gun. He slept out under the blankets which he carried on his saddle. He always dreaded the time when he must go back home, and never recovered from the feeling of tragedy on the approach of Monday mornings.

He had succeeded, to a certain extent, in associating himself almost entirely with the white boys, but occasionally he saw his old playmates of the village. He seemed to have less and less in common with them, and it was plain to him that Sun-on-His-Wings and Running Elk lacked the spirit of the times — lacked "get-up," as John expressed it. They seemed contented just to sit in the village and talk, like many of the other young men. However, like many of the other young men, they were now wearing "citizens' clothes," but clothes didn't seem to change them any. They hadn't gone to Carlisle, but had gone to high school with him. They made him tired, the way they acted. Everybody knew that they were football stars and could have a prominent place in the social activities of the students, yet they remained apart and said nothing. After classes, they would untie their ponies and trot off together toward the village. They didn't seem to be grateful for the frantic cheers of the girls' pep organization after some brilliant play. In fact, he had begun to feel vicarious shame for them. They danced at the Roundhouse in the village every June and September, but they would not go to the civilized dances at the high school.

But when he had been out alone on his pony, he didn't think of the high school or his friends there. He didn't tell anyone where he had been on his weekends, because he felt ashamed. People didn't go out by themselves riding on the prairie, unless they were "riding fence" or on some other business. So at times when someone asked him where he had been, he always had the excuse of having some business with his father's cattle, and there was no more curiosity.

Cattle were practical, and looking after them a perfectly rea-
sonable occupation during the weekend, and of course he
always intimated that he had to do it under parental com-
pulsion. It was the thing to say ; that the "governor" had
made you do this or that, and the high school boys always
intimated such authority. It seemed, in some inscrutable
way, to indicate the importance of your father as well ; importance as a cattle owner, banker, or merchant. With Chal
it was a means of stopping curiosity which his Indian heart
hated, and at the same time it served as a defense for his
weakness. He simply copied the other boys because he
thought it was the thing to do, and they in turn very likely
got their ideas from novels of the period, wherein "scions" of
rich manufacturers in the East were always sent away by
rugged self-made fathers to some lumber camp or branch fac-
tory, to separate them from girls or other evils.

Now, as when he was a little boy, there was that dreamy
joy of living, when one's heartbeats are in rhythm with the
pulse of the earth and waving grass blades give as much
pleasure as a flaming sunset or a silent moonlight night.
All this was there. There was that harmony wherein he
lost himself again, but during the last three years there had
been something else as well. A disquieting thing which
flooded him and urged him to some sort of action. He often
felt he should like to ride his pony at a dead run across the
prairie as he had done as a little boy. But when he was a
little boy there was not that devilish urge, like madness. As
a little boy he had liked the wind on his body and the delight of action, and he had felt in harmony with everything
about him. But now there was something within him
which was much more painful at times than his old desire
to fly. He felt that there was something in him which
must come out, and unable to find any other expression, he

took action as a means, and raced his pony wildly as before. He would race him until he felt sorry for the panting little fellow. One day he removed his saddle when the rain started, undressed, and raced naked, but even then he felt that he had not got rid of that thing which was within him. Periodically, he felt poignantly unhappy and sometimes surprised himself by breaking into an old war song, and as he sang he felt himself growing excited and gripped by this thing within which he couldn't satisfy. Sometimes he would swim until he could feel his legs growing weaker and weaker, then climb glistening and dripping onto the bank.

He watched with more than fascination the summer storms that broke over the prairie ; watched from the shelter of a limestone escarpment, and when the lightning seemed to dance over the emerald prairie and the thunder rolled among the hills, he became intensely unhappy. One day he stripped off his clothes and danced in a storm and sang a war song. Sang and danced until he was almost exhausted and his body was wet with rain and sweat ; water so warm that he couldn't tell whether it was rain or sweat.

One night he hobbled his pony and rolled into his blanket. It was a summer's night. The frogs were silent and the darkness seemed to be waiting for something. Down the creek a barred owl gave his hunting call at intervals, and he could hear his pony jump from grass tuft to grass tuft. They were the only sounds in that warm silence.

Then close by the coyotes yelped in chorus, like the staccato yelps of Comanche dancers. He heard his pony snort and he rose up on his elbow. He was startled. There was the moon, large and white, hanging in a gleaming sycamore. The coyotes stopped as suddenly as they had begun. A great unhappiness filled him, and for the briefest moment he envied the coyotes, but he didn't know why. For some time he looked at the moon, and the more he looked the more intense became the emotion that seemed to be trying to strangle him. He arose from his blankets and stood naked there in the light, then walked nervously and aimlessly about. He stopped and looked around at the dense moon shadows. The silence was ringing and broken now only at intervals by the lazy call of that owl.

He went back to his blankets and put on his shoes, then crossed the creek and climbed a little hill in the full flood of the ghostly light. He stood there, then spread his arms toward the moon. He tried to think of all the beautiful words he had ever heard, both in Osage and English, and as he remembered them he spoke them aloud to the moon, but they would not suffice it seemed ; they were not sufficient to relieve that choking feeling. The moon became smaller as it climbed above the treetops.

He tried to dance but the hill was rocky, then he chanted ; chanted an Osage song, but the feeling that he was being overpowered caused him to stop. He sat down and lowered his head, and something hot fell on his thigh. He wiped his eyes with his hand, then got up and looked around as if he expected to see someone spying on him. Only the prairie and the dark line of trees along the creek ; the prairie under the moon where the limestone boulders seemed to float.

He wiped his eyes again and said, "Gawdam it !" then descended the hill. When he reached the creek he pulled off his shoes and slid into the water. He swam for an hour, alternately swimming and floating on his back ; breaking the silvered surface of the water as though it were a fragile solid. Finally he felt sleepy, and went up and rolled into his blanket.

And besides making himself unhappy looking at sunsets,

and having the desire to make songs about everything he saw that impressed him, he liked to look at himself in pools of water, and often he found himself posturing on his pony before imaginary people. Sometimes he took an eagle feather with him to wear in his hair, and one time he took some paints and painted his face, and for a short time felt the thrill of the eagle feather spinning in his hair. But he did this only once. He had felt so mortified that he could scarcely bathe the paint off fast enough. He almost sweated when he thought of the possibility of a cowboy having seen him.

But this mysterious unhappiness came to him only at times, and never except when he was alone on the prairie. He could remember when it first came to him three years before. Sun-on-His-Wings and Running Elk were with him. They had ridden out one summer day far from the village. All the morning they had played the game of "rescue." One of them would stand on the prairie and another would dash full speed toward him, then turn his pony just as he got to the one standing. The standing one would jump up behind the rider just as the pony slowed down on the turn, and they would race back to the starting point.

At noon they had killed rabbits and roasted them over the fire, then lay on their backs in the shade for an hour. The afternoon they had spent swimming and playing water tag.

Chal had noticed a difference in Running Elk that summer. He had grown faster than Sun-on-His-Wings. And it seemed to Chal that the back of Running Elk's neck had become redder and much larger, and it was very funny to hear him talk now ; he talked like a wounded crow.

After swimming they had put on their moccasins and started running down the bank of the creek, but soon Running Elk stopped and said that he was going back, and after a while Sun-on-His-Wings also turned back, but Chal kept on going. He felt that he could trot on like that forever. He ran far up the creek, until he came to a round hole of clear water. He stopped at its edge and stood there, his stomach moving slowly in and out. Suddenly he jumped in and swam about for some time.

The sun was setting and the west looked like leaping flames that had been suddenly solidified, and the limestone rocks bordering the water were pink-tinted. He came out and stood on the rock. Then, very suddenly, that mysterious feeling came over him. A mild fire seemed to be coursing through his veins and he felt that he wanted to sing and dance ; sing and dance with deep reverence. He felt that some kind of glory had descended upon him, accompanied by a sort of sweetness and a thrilling appreciation of himself. He wanted to struggle with something. His body seemed a wonderful thing just then, and he had a feeling that he could conquer anything that might stand in his way. There seemed to be intense urges which made him deliciously unhappy.

THE black derricks crept farther west. Sometimes near the town they "shot" a well with nitroglycerine, so that the strata might be loosened and allow a freer flow of the oil. At such times the citizens of the town would drive out and watch the spray of oil as it shot high into the air, and hear the gravels rattle on the woodwork of the derrick, like shot.

Everyone was happy and almost playful. On one occasion a mixedblood rushed into the spraying oil and had his new suit and a "damned good hat — a twenty-five-dollar hat" covered with oil. He said, "Whoopee !" He didn't give a damn.

They would troop back to town, feeling in their hearts that the indefinite glory was not far off now. The mixed-bloods would stand in groups at the corners and discuss the well, some of them rattling the silver dollars in their pockets as they talked. They would shout jovially at anyone crossing the street ; some pleasantry in Osage or in English.

DuBois joined one such group, expanding facetiously, "Say," he said, "by gawd, if I had a nose like that, I'd charge people to see it." The others laughed, and the one accused felt embarrassed, and attempted not to show in his face that his vanity had been wounded just a little. He shifted his tobacco, then said, "Well, I guess it's big all right, but they's one thing, it ain't in everbody's business." The laughter was then directed toward DuBois, who went to the curbing of the new sidewalk and spat onto the pavement, then came back. "Say," he said, desiring to change the subject, "was yu out to the well they shot this mornin' — looks like it's a-comin', don't it ?" The others shook their heads in a way that would indicate that ; "Sure looks thataway." DuBois continued,

"I's talkin' with a geologist the other day, and he said he thought they's oil all under the Osage — said if they found that Carsonville sand west o' here, that he knew it was all under the Osage."

The sun warmed the corner with a beneficence that seemed only for that particular corner of the world as they talked about the future ; about that future which was sure to be glorious, though its particular glory was vague.

They moved over toward the sandstone building which had been the office building. Some of them sat on the

broad window sill which had been worn smooth by genera-
tions of sitters. There was nothing to do except talk.
Their incomes were so large now that they didn't think of
working at anything ; in fact, they had never worked except
by spurts when some enthusiasm came over them. Some
enthusiasm like starting a chicken farm and raising chickens
for a market that didn't exist, or breeding white-faced cattle
and pure-bred hogs.

But now, how could anyone keep his mind on anything
except oil, when that tingling thrill was constantly with one ;
that thrill that expressed itself in expansive camaraderie and
boisterousness ? Besides, these people were only being true
to the blood in their veins. Many of them were descendants
of French gentleman adventurers who were buried in the
Osage camps on the Missouri river, or lost forever in the
wild forests of the new land. And many of them were
descendants of laughing *coureurs du bois,* and of men who
defeated Braddock from behind trees, and had come back
with their allies, the great Osages, and married Osage women.
The mixedblood descendants of these adventurers were
usually handsome, careless and promiscuous. They had no
tendency to acquisitiveness, and their lives were made
sparkling by a series of enthusiasms. They lived merrily,
whether they were definitely sure of the next meal or not.

From the earliest days of the Agency, they had sat in
front of the traders' stores during the summer, hunted during the autumn, and sat around the big-bellied stoves and
spat into the sawdust during the winter. As the Agency
became a town they still sat and talked, and as the town
grew they continued to talk and laugh, standing or sitting
and watching the traffic.

Many of the older traders had come to the Agency out
of the spirit of adventure and profit. They were in many

cases men of some culture and family, and they developed a great respect and sometimes actual love for the Indian. Which was rather unique in that their large profit-taking was not always within the bounds of ethics, if the ethics of their religious training had anything to do with business practice.   They did not compete with each other and perhaps ethics was not necessary.

They took much credit for allowing their Indian clients to have provisions on account, and even sacrificed comfort to haul provisions to far away camps during severe winters. During the great epidemic of smallpox they had even endangered themselves to supply the Indians with necessities, driving with their provisions to a designated rock or tree near an infected camp and leaving them there.   To compensate for their sacrifices, they often added extra percentages to the bill.   The interest from the tribal trust fund was definite and sure, but these early traders always felt a certain magnanimity in allowing the Indians to have whatever provisions and clothing they needed between the quarterly payments.   Especially during the epidemic, when the desire for the continuance of the trade overbalanced their fears, they felt particularly self-righteous.   They came back from these trips with the fear of the disease in their hearts, but they felt better after they had seen that all the saucers had been refilled with carbolic acid and set in the windows of their stores.   And they kept these saucers filled in the windows at their homes, though they had sent their families out of the reservation during the period of the epidemic.   They took no chances of germs wandering aimlessly into their homes through the windows.

Now, they too watched the black derricks spread from the east with an enthusiasm that was somewhat dampened by the fact that such development would bring more competition. They worried when they thought of those riches under them and all around them going to others. The old reservation had been theirs and they still felt that the new county was theirs as well, and they felt vindictive toward all the people who were coming in to share the trade with them. The Agency was their home and the town became their home. They talked the language of their friends, the Osages, and felt sincerely protective toward them. But things were moving too fast, and they had difficulty adjusting themselves to the new tempo of Progress, having spent their youth in the hard tranquillity of an Indian nation, where a man's word was as good as his signature.

The new people who came in after the allotment were of all types, representing many professions or no profession in particular. Drifting artisans and laborers, lawyers, doctors, shopkeepers, bootleggers, shrewd and unscrupulous men who did business on the new curbs, and men and women with criminal tendencies who lacked the courage. There were representatives of oil companies, geologists and lease men, and oil field employes from the ends of the earth.

They came slowly at first as the black derricks moved toward the west, then they came in hundreds. After the war, however, when people all over the country spoke of "normalcy" and said that prosperity had come to the Federation of States, they came into the little town in swarms, and the mixedbloods stood on the corner and proudly guessed that there must be fifteen or twenty thousand people in town.

There were no factories, no mills, no industry except the cattle business which had flourished for years. There weren't even any oil refineries. These had been established in neighboring towns because the owners felt that it was too expensive to satisfy all the business men who seemed to have influence over the destinies of the town. A big railroad missed Kihekah by six miles for reasons which remained obscure.

The black derricks that sprang up among the blackjacks over night gave to the Osages and all the mixedbloods on the roll one-sixth of every forty-two-gallon barrel of oil. As more oil came out of the ground the quarterly payments became larger and larger, and as the payments became larger and larger, men's heads became filled with dreams and their lives became frenzied activity. So intoxicated did they become that they forgot to stop in their frantic grasping to point the finger of accusation at a neighbor. Still there was no keen competition. One had only to sit and think up schemes for bringing to himself more of the wealth which surrounded him.

ONE afternoon black clouds came up in the northwest and tumbled over each other in their attempts to be in the van ; tumbling as though with deliberate design, as though directed by angry gods to destroy the town in the valley among the blackjacks. Lightning played against the black mass and there was distant thunder. The outer edges of the clouds were whipped by crazy little winds, and a deep silence settled over the valley. The rest of the sky was pale green.

In the town the people began thinking of the cellars. John walked to the front porch of his house, looked at the sky for some time, then went back in and sat down, picked up the *Trumpet* and began reading. Down the street Du-Bois had just come home from Goldie's, where he had spent the afternoon with one of the new girls. He went to the door and looked at the sky, and as he looked the first heavy drops spattered on the roof of his house. He went to the bedroom where his wife was lying, expecting a new baby.

He made the sign of the cross over her bed as she slept, and did the same at each window of the room, then called the children. He led them into the cellar and made the sign of the cross again as he closed the door.

Jep Newberg, the leading merchant and general business man among the newcomers, telephoned to his wife and told her to go to the cellar. He stood at the large plate glass window of his store, and shifted his chewed, unlit cigar first to one side of his mouth and then to the other. He didn't like that sky. A raindrop spattered on the plate glass. He thought of his secretary sitting back in the office, and he went back and stood over her. She was bent over the books, adding the usual twenty per cent to the purchases of Indians made that day.

"Let that go," he said. "Leave that off." He laid his stubby finger on the page of the book. She looked up at him with a question. He said :

"Say, looks purty bad outside. Maybe you'd better go over to the Blue Front basement — might be blowy." He didn't give her time to adjust her hat properly, and she had just managed to get into one sleeve of her raincoat before he pushed her out the front door and told her to run. She wondered if he were really growing cold ; becoming tired. "Maybe the old cat has been after him again," she thought as she went to the Blue Front drug store. The druggist was motioning to her from the top of the basement steps.

Jep saw that the sidewalk was profusely covered with dark splashes. He went back to the vault, stepped inside, and left the door half open. He shifted his cigar nervously as he stood there.

Chal was on the prairie on the other side of the creek from the village. When he noticed the clouds were so menacing he put his pony into a trot, but already the big drops had begun to fall, and suddenly the tall cottonwood along the little creek began to bend with the under sides of its leaves showing gray. He could hear the wind moaning in the blackjacks along the ridge to the west ; it was like a protest.

He knew he couldn't make the village so he rode toward a hill where the small blackjack saplings were growing. He heard hoof beats behind him, and looked around. Three Osages on ponies came up to him ; an old man whom he had seen many times but couldn't recall his name, young White Elk, and Sun-on-His-Wings. He was surprised and he had to keep looking forward to keep them from seeing the surprise on his face. Their faces were painted in a manner he hadn't seen for years, and he guessed that their bodies were naked. They were covered with their blankets which were pulled up around their heads. They greeted each other and rode on as though they had been together all day.

A terrific gust of wind hit them just as they neared the saplings. Chal looked up and saw the clouds boiling above them, and the old man looked as well, and as he did so he stopped his pony and slid off saying, "How." Chal and the others slid off of their ponies and all ran to the young blackjacks, each one lying down on his belly and each grasping tightly the thin, flexible stem of a sapling.

Everything was blurred. The wind howled and the rain came before it horizontally across the prairie. Objects flew past and the little trees bent and swished, but you heard only the roar of the wind, above which the thunder cracked and the earth seemed to shiver.

The wind died and the rain, still falling, began to slacken, and the skies began to clear. They stood up and looked around. They could hear the roaring of the water in the

little creek. The ponies were gone. Chal looked at the
faces of the three and that which had puzzled him became
clear.

They had seen the storm coming and had prepared themselves for the ancient ritual of defiance and sacrifice. Though
he had heard about it, he had never seen it, and thought that
the people had discontinued the ceremony. But he could
see it all now. They had seen the storm coming and had
ridden out to the hill so that they might be visible to Wah
'Kon-Tah, and manifest their bravery by defying the storm,
but ready to die by a bolt of lightning if it pleased the Great
Mysteries. There was some reason why they had ridden
out. Perhaps it was because Wah 'Kon-Tah had mani-
fested his displeasure in some way, and they had wanted to
show him that they were still Osages and were not afraid
to die ; that they would sacrifice themselves if he wished it
for the benefit of the tribe. Chal didn't know why they
had not carried their guns with them to shoot into the storm
— they used to do that, he remembered. He guessed that
they didn't want to attract the attention of white people who
might chance to be near.

They had probably come down when they saw that cyclone coming — Wah 'Kon-Tah would not want them to
face a cyclone, with death a certainty. They would have no
chance that way. Lightning was fickle, or rather, it was
directed by the Great Mysteries to a certain spot.

Chal's clothes were wet and he felt shivery as he walked
with his companions toward the village. The little creek
was bank full, and they unhesitatingly walked into the
muddy, swirling water and swam across, climbing out several
yards downstream. The water of the creek felt warm to
Chal's chilled body.

When they had gone some distance from the roaring

creek, they stopped and listened to a greater roar; a roar that shook the earth under their feet. The old man was visibly disturbed as he looked at the sky in all directions. The roar became louder and Chal thought that the old man looked bewildered, but no one said anything.

When they reached the village, all four of the ponies were there quietly grazing among the débris of wagons and lodge-coverings. The people were walking here and there, searching for their belongings, but most of them were standing in a group talking. Chal didn't even stop to think whether any of them had been hurt. He knew that they had all gone out and clung to the saplings and sumac bushes at the edge of the village.

When his little party came up to the group, the old man asked in Osage, "That roar, what is that thing which makes ground afraid?" Charging Bull pointed toward the town, "I told my son to go see about that thing. He is back now. He says it is gas well. He says lightning struck gas well."

"Ho-hoooo," said the old man and Chal was sure that he saw relief in his face.

Sun-on-His-Wings, shivering in his wet blanket, turned to Chal and said in English, "Let's go over there to my father's lodge — maybe there's a far there." He pointed to one of the few lodges left standing.

When they were both naked and warming themselves and Chal was drying his clothes, Sun-on-His-Wings said, "That old man is Black Elk. He will say that lightning struck that gas well 'cause the Great Spirit don't want the white people to come here any more. He will say in council some time that Osages ought to see that, and run all the white people out of their land, I bet." They were silent for some time, then Sun-on-His-Wings raised his voice again above the roar, "He's an old man, though, and he don't know about these things. His body is here but his mind is back in a place where we lived many years ago."

Chal wanted to ask his friend why he had gone with old Black Elk to the hill, since Sun-on-His-Wings was now a Peyote worshipper, but he only smiled about the old man and said nothing.

Chal rode back to town with the constant roar of the fire in his ears, and as he drew near it became deafening. As he approached he could see the flame above the pipe. The derrick had burned and the flame didn't begin at the pipe but several feet above it, like a great jet.

People were standing in groups some distance from the flame ; standing on the hillside and sitting on stone walls, and some had climbed to the roofs of barns and houses. Just watching. Several men were nearer than the others and Chal could see that they had rifles. He could see them point the guns at the flame, then white puffs of smoke, but the report was drowned. They were attempting to separate the thin column of roaring gas from the flame above, but they failed.

He stood there for some time and watched ; the crowd amused him. White people seemed so helpless when they couldn't talk, and it was funny to see them so inefficient, standing there. He could see some of them move toward each other, not able to restrain themselves any longer, and attempt to talk above the terrific roar. For a moment as he sat there on his pony, he wondered if they were as great as he had always thought them to be. These doubts gave rise to confusion and he dismissed them after a moment.

His attention was attracted to some people standing around a man high up on the hill. The man was standing on a stone wall and gesticulating. Here was something strange ; some strange thing the white people were doing there upon the hill. He was intrigued.

He rode up to where the people were gathering and stopped outside the circle, but he could see over the heads of the others from his position. The thin man who was standing on the retaining wall was shouting and raising his hands to the sky. Chal thought he was one of those people who sell medicine at first, but he was not selling anything, that was plain. His face was distorted and his eyes had a wild light in them. The roar was not so loud here and Chal could hear some of the things he said :

"Come to Jesus, come to Jesus, come you sinners and repent ! Jesus loves you — arms — I shall come — far — Jesus is good, Jesus is — square — " The words would come indistinctly, and be lost as the little breeze that had sprung up carried the roar back over the hill. But Chal was fascinated by this man. He was fascinated by the veins that stood out his neck and the way he moaned and shouted when he couldn't think of any more words. But eventually he would break into words again. Chal looked at the people around the speaker and he saw that they stood with their mouths open. On the outside of the circle some high school boys giggled and an older man turned and frowned at them.

The man would get down on his knees on the wall and lift his hands into the air, saying that that flaming gas well was a sign, and that everybody ought to make peace with their God. Then he would get up and pound the palm of his hand with the fist of the other, and point to the people in the front of the circle with a finger that shook.

Chal was surprised to see a man go forward and fall on his knees at the foot of the wall. Then a young girl and two women rushed forward and fell on their knees, weeping and groaning. He was startled by a cry close by him ; like the cry of a rabbit caught by an owl, and a woman, scratching and clawing her way through the crowd, made his pony snort. Her hat was on the side of her head and her iron gray hair had fallen about her shoulders. She rushed forward to the wall and fell on her face shrieking.

Chal felt that a knot had come into his stomach, and the blood in his veins seemed to have turned to water, the water carrying some sort of poison. He turned his pony and rode away, shaking slightly.

He was glad to see that his father's house had not been disturbed by the cyclone ; and he noticed that outside of a few trees and several houses some distance from the business district, very little damage had been done. He smiled to himself when he thought of what interpretation old Black Elk might put upon the fact that the village had been in the direct path of the storm, and that the town had been left intact.

After dinner he went back to the burning well with his father. People were still standing there, fascinated. He and his father stopped by a group of mixedbloods. They seemed to have doubts about the ability of the men running around below to put out the flame. DuBois shouted that they were "crazier 'n hell if they thought they was gonna put it out with rifles."

As they stood the flames lighted up the whole country-side, and the light could be seen for many miles that night. The terrific, ground-shivering roar and the light that spread over the whole valley ; the light that made the blackjacks on the hills look like ghost trees, appeared to the mixedbloods standing there as a symbol of that indefinite glory that was coming. That light that you could see as far away as the old Cherokee country, and that roar that drowned all other sounds, gave them a feeling of vague greatness and importance in the universe. Here was the manifestation of a power that made the white man stand and wonder ; a power that came out of their own hills, and that light, in which you could "pick up a pin a mile away," was certainly the light of glory.

Turning away from the spectacle, with a facetious remark in Osage, DuBois went home. He found one of the new doctors there. He had had a misunderstanding with the old government doctor, because he had forgotten to pay for former services rendered. He walked into the room where his wife lay, full of the emotion which had suffused him as he watched the fire. The doctor held the baby up to him and he saw that it was a boy.

"Well, Doc, he's already got a name," he said proudly, "Osage Oil DuBois."

VII

In the autumn Chal set out for the University. There was a small party from Kihekah. Running Elk and Sun-on-His-Wings had decided to go, despite the young man from the University who appeared in town that summer and talked of the many allurements, not the least of which was football. Most of the things which this young man said did not appeal to them, because the young representative had, "talked from the teeth," they agreed after his visit. A thing they both saw and felt, but which never would have been expressed had not Afraid-of-Bear, who played tackle at Carlisle, come up to them one day at the village, very drunk. He had smiled vacuously, and after several attempts to get his arms around Running Elk's neck, kept repeating, "Yu ma frien', yu ma frien', ain't it ?" Running Elk had looked over at Sun-on-His-Wings and said quietly, with amusement, "He talks from teeth — mus' be from the University." They laughed.

The representative from the University had slapped each one of them on the back and held one of their hands in his as he said, "Sure glad to meet you men, and we wantta see you down at the Varsity — we need you men down there — sure do, and we'll sure treat you right." He had used the word "men" consciously, as though to indicate that "fellas" or "boys" lacked virility, and were words dangerous in a society where the manly virtues were scrupulously kept — where certain words in salutation and assumed mannerisms were defenses against softness.

As the train rattled toward the University, Running Elk and Sun-on-His-Wings sat silently watching the land that slid by the windows grow flatter and more reddish. They were thinking of this decision to attend the University, and fear of the unknown came up in them ; the fear that tradition puts into the hearts of those who have a feeling of adjustment with their environments ; the unconscious fighting against change. The promises of the young representative from the University were ignored, and they had no anticipation of the glorious opening of a new life. There was only the little thrill that fear incites and the resentment against the young man who had slapped them on the back and had "talked from the teeth."

In talking with the others the young man had assumed a different attitude. He had patronized them, as the sophomore ever patronizes the unfortunate ones who have not yet entered the glories of higher education, and the superiority he felt in his heart was greater because he himself had come from a town even smaller than Kihekah, in a much less populated part of the state. From his position as a man of parts he felt a slight contempt for these small-town "men," but he allowed them to believe that they were on the same plane with himself, yet he did not go so far with his insincere good fellowship as he had with the Indians. He had almost strutted before what he assumed to be Indian ignorance and stupidity, and he mistook their placid silence for fearful admiration of himself, and had responded to this silence with sickening energy.

Charlie Fancher had thought that the young man was a sort of god, and couldn't say "yes" and "that sure is fine" often enough or with sufficient emotion, while Chal had felt the same emotions of disgust and resentment experienced by the Indians, and he was flooded with nausea every time he thought of that exuberant, soulless hand on his back. But he had smiled, showing white teeth against his bronze face, and had attempted to drown his feelings because he thought them to be wrong. Simply out of step again.

As Chal listened to the enthusiasms of Nelson Newberg and Fancher, he had a queer feeling that he had cut the bonds of the old life. The red prairie with the thicket-filled ravines, and the already browned, short grasses, he watched closely in panorama from the train window. He could not help thinking of the rounded, still green hills of home ; of the serene blackjacks on the ridges under the September sun, and the scent of the crushed weeds under the hoofs of his pinto came to him, making his heart beat faster. Yesterday when he had gone for one last plover hunt with his father, seemed years ago. How fat they were — so fat that some of them had burst open when they struck the ground, and the greases had spoiled their breast feathers. He thought of the clumsy young prairie chickens they had flushed accidentally ; clumsy in the takeoff, yet they had sailed across the prairie, across the intervening valley profusely covered with yellow daisies and prairie goldenrod, disappearing over the limestone ridge.

But the Red Beds were not unbeautiful, he thought. In the distance there was haze, and the red of the earth showing along the edges of the ravines was not out of harmony. Pleasing, until some farmhouse came into view surrounded by outhouses and wire fences ; houses that looked like excrescences and tinted by the red dust ; houses lonely in the midst of space and listening resignedly to the song of the wind. Sometimes a pond would pass the window, filled with thick red water, and the white hogs rooting with concentration near a drab house were tinted with the ubiquitous red.

The train passed little towns with red streets and red-stained houses ; even the loungers at the stations and the loafers on the shady sides of the buildings were red-tinted, and the wheels of the wagons hitched to the racks, and the wheels and bodies of small cars were spotted with the dried, red mud, and colored by the dust. Chal thought that they were sad little towns that had been disillusioned after a short dream of glory. They had been built with thought-less exuberance of frenzied settlement ; their builders chafing at the delay of material. Now, they seemed to lack courage, sitting there on the open plains of the Red Beds.

Chal did not know the reason for this ugliness ; this ugli-ness which white men seemed to produce. He did not know that these buildings were expressions of a race still influenced by an environment thousands of miles across the ocean, and that these foreign expressions were due to the fact that the race was not yet in adjustment with the new environment. He felt simply that these things were not beautiful. He would not have dared suggest his thoughts to anyone ; it would have been like a sacrilege and certainly unpatriotic. One believed in his country and his state, and accepted the heroics of the race for land in the new terri-tory, and all the virtues of the Anglo-Saxon ; the romantics and righteousness of their winning of the West, as taught by his history. He almost despised himself for the feeling deep within him which feebly remonstrated. He kept this feeling subdued ; kept it from bubbling up into the placid waters of his consciousness, so that nothing would disturb those waters to keep them from reflecting the impressions that ought to be mirrored, if one were to remain in step. He certainly didn't want anyone to know that he was queer.

Disturbing his flow of thoughts and taking him from the sliding panorama of the plains were the voice and activity of Nelson Newberg. Nelson always held the most conspicuous position wherever he went, and as he talked under the influence of a kind of intoxication that had come to him in the anticipation of attending the University, he demanded and received the deference of Sylvester and Charlie. They sat and showed their appreciation on their beaming faces.

Nelson's position was assured in Kihekah because his mother had come from Massachusetts, and this fact was sufficient. She was the social leader of the little town among the blackjacks. Besides this, his father was the richest business man in town and was considered "purty smart" because of a rather admirable shrewdness in business ; a shrewdness which was really not necessary in a community where the greatest and almost only source of wealth were the oil royalties paid quarterly to the Osages ; money which they handled with Olympian indifference. But Jep Newberg's shrewdness allowed him a greater field for operation, and inspired him to greater daring than any other business man. When Jep made a statement people listened, and he assumed a sort of gruffness and dramatic good fellowship, and walked and talked with invulnerable assurance.

Naturally, when the son of Jep and Mrs. Jepworth N. Newberg became whimsical, effusively friendly, morose, or obviously and bluntly ignored one of the other citizens' sons or daughters, they conformed to the nuances of every mood, and he was dramatically aware of it. He talked brightly and arrogantly as the train rolled along. His vanity had been fired for so long that he was glazed to the extent that he was impervious to irony, reason, or weary indulgence.

Nelson had met nearly everyone in the car and of course had told each one that he was going to the University ; he told them this with an assumed nonchalance which had in it a touch of boredom. He told them with authority about the University and the activities there — things which he had gleaned from a prospectus and from one visit at a track meet. He intimated that the University would not really do much for him academically or culturally, but that he would spend some time there as a sort of interlude to the business of life, which would be the gradual taking over of his father's affairs. He hinted that these affairs were colossal. The conversation that had caused him to come back to his admirers with an expression of injured innocence, was one with a heavy man who looked at him from under a black Stetson hat and overhanging, black eyebrows ; eyebrows which had made him nervous in the first place. The man had said after a few minutes of Nelson's insufferable monologue, "Yu say you're from Kihekey ? What's your old man do — skin Injuns ?"

Nelson hadn't been able to think of an answer until many minutes after he came back to his seat, then of course it was too late to give it. But the glaze showed no lasting impression and he was soon talking with animation.

"Say," he was saying to Charlie when Chal again became conscious of the talk about him, "you gonna wear that hat down there — ha ha ha, look at that hat — here, let's throw it out the winda." He pretended to grab it, but Charlie ducked and laughed good-naturedly, though he almost sweated in the realization that his hat was not the thing.

Then with an expression which indicated, "that's enough of that," Nelson turned to Chal. "Wake up, Chal, yu been asleep ?" Chal smiled. Chal had always been inscrutable to Nelson, and he was ever careful in his relationship with him. He thought him queer, just as everyone else thought, but he felt an impulse to be serious when he talked with Chal ; his dramatic instinct urged it as the best way. He felt sure of friendly response if he were serious, though their relationship had never been strained in any way. They had been associated for a long time with a kind of mutual toler-ance. Nelson had never paid much attention to Sun-on-His-Wings and Running Elk, but he was sure that they were stupid and unresponsive ; stupid because they didn't talk much. But Chal talked just enough to be worthy of his notice, and Chal had that "Japanesey smile," and you never knew what he was thinking. This made Nelson feel un-easy ; uneasy to the extent that he took careful pains to be very serious.

"Say, Chal," he said, assuming a very grave expression, "d'yu think you'll make the team next year ?"

Chal smiled and felt a slight embarrassment. "Don' know."

"Well, I think you'll make it — now there's Shorty Sla-back and Kerr — both lighter than you. I know Freddy likes light backfield men. I'uz talkin' with Goat Bergman, he's captain, yu know, and he says they're gonna build the offense 'round a light backfield." Charlie interrupted,

"Who's Freddy ?" Nelson stared at him as though he had committed *lese majesty,* then he roared with affected merriment. "Haw ! Haw ! Haw ! He don't know who Freddy is," and again long and affected haw-haws. "Why he's the coach, rummy." Then he laughed some more, un-til Charlie seemed to be sufficiently punished, judging by the flush of his face and the feebleness of his forced smile. This interruption changed the direction of Nelson's thoughts and actions, much to Chal's relief, and soon he was lost again in the fascinating monotony of the plains, and the talk about him seemed far away.

The Red Beds had begun to intrigue Chal, and he noted carefully every detail of them as the little inter-city car squeaked and rumbled the last miles to the University. He began to anticipate a strange land. He wondered if one could see the University from some point on the way, but he didn't want to ask and he appeared as though he were not the least bit excited. Sun-on-His-Wings and Running Elk sat solemnly, as though they were not in the least concerned, but Chal knew that much was going on inside. As he looked at their expressionless faces he felt a little annoyed with them for acting like Indians. He could understand what was going on in their minds but he was afraid that they would be misunderstood by other people, and he wanted them to be liked and appreciated.

The car came to a sudden stop and already, with a black shiny bag in his hand, and an expression of extreme gravity and importance, Nelson was standing on the platform. The gravity hid tingling excitement and his actions were successfully impressing Charlie and Sylvester. Chal knew that he would soon frown and take command of the little party, directing and commanding with deep seriousness which was his idea of *savoir faire*.

A party of "men" from the Chi house came up and introduced themselves, took the bags, and the little party was soon gliding up the street in a long, shiny car. The "men" from the fraternity house were being very pleasant and constantly smiling. They pretended to listen to Nelson, who was inquiring about matters pertaining to the University, as though he had been absent for several years and had a desire to check up on the activities once familiar to him. Charlie and Sylvester sat subdued after their somewhat diffident, "Glad to meet yu's," while Running Elk and Sun-on-His-Wings sat like wooden images, replying "yes" or "no" to attempted conversation by the "men" from the fraternity house, who were apparently interested in every detail of their lives, and seemed to have heard of them as important personages. They inti-

mated that they were happy to have at last had the great honor
of meeting them.

The driver of the car, Jack Castle, was not so well dressed
as the others. His trousers were shabby and loose, and he
wore a cap on the side of his head, and let a cigarette hang
from his lips as he looked dreamily down the street. He had
a nonchalance which Chal almost admired. Even the Administration Building, which loomed at the end of the avenue, thrusting itself abruptly from the endless red plains,
seemed insignificant to the nonchalance of Jack Castle.

If he did not wear the uncomfortably tight trousers and
short coats of the other immaculate brothers, and despite the
fact that he had come from a town which was not even a
county seat, Jack was important. He owned the only car
available to the fraternity during the period of pledging activities, and he was by far the richest man in the University.
Hence, his carelessness was overlooked, and the fact that he
had all the characteristics of a "scissor-bill" was ignored. As
he drove dreamily up the avenue with this load of prospectives, the faint smell of new varnish and the shine of the
interior of the car, the smooth silence of the motor, gave him
assurance ; but he was thinking of the half-finished quart of
whiskey in his new wardrobe trunk.

The long car drew up in front of the fraternity house.
Jack climbed indolently out and walked slowly up to the
door and entered without saying a word ; in fact, he had
not spoken all the time. He had remained seated in the
car when the brothers escorted the others solicitously from
the station.

As the group approached the porch, Chal's knees were almost shaking, and he had a sudden feeling that he could not
stand to be slapped on the back again, and he was worried
about what he should say to the obvious insincerities, and

how he should react to the effusiveness of the brothers. The other brothers who had been lolling on the porch, arose as if by some signal, and came to meet them with outstretched hands and faces covered with mechanical smiles. They came down the steps in a body and pressed around Chal and his companions, all saying the same thing in the same way. Running Elk and Sun-on-His-Wings were taken up the steps with a brother on each side of them, and Chal saw that they were looking at the pavement in their humiliated embarrassment. Nelson was talking as usual ; something about cars, while Sylvester and Charlie were silent and happily unsure. They were ready to accept an invitation to join the fraternity ; this wonderful fraternity in particular.

The party was to stay there that night, but Chal, Sun-on-His-Wings, and Running Elk were to go to another house for dinner, and almost before they were washed, two "men" appeared in the parlor. Two of the brothers came up to the room, shut the door and passed a few trivial remarks which were obviously just a prelude to that which they had come to say. Brother Harmon lit a cigarette, sat carelessly on the table, pulled his trouser leg up just so, then blowing a cloud of smoke through his nose, said very pleasantly :

" 'Course you men are goin' over to the Megs for dinner, and I tell yu those birds'll give yu a good sweatin' — 'at's all right, all in the game, see, but — yu see, that's what they do, but yu gotta look around a little. 'Course, I know you men won't do anything until yu talk to me, like you promised — kind of an understandin' among friends, see. Yu know I told you what would happen when I'se down to Kihekah last summer. You men go on over there, but don't promise anything — yu know you promised me you wouldn't decide until you talked it over with me."

The other brother got up from the edge of the bed and

walked up to the mirror after Chal had finished.   He looked at himself, rubbed his face, then picked up Chal's comb and began to make more distinct a parting in his hair which had been plastered to his skull with a patented grease ; hair which shone like varnished, yellow leather.   Then still regarding his handsome face with approval, he said, as he worked with patience at the already perfect parting :

"Tell yu what I'd do — I'd take — I'd give 'em those buttons, Harmon, that you got in your pocket, and let 'em just carry 'em over in their pockets, so that if they get to sweatin' 'em too hard they can just feel of those buttons and they'll be all right."

"Yeah," said Harmon as if the thought had just occurred to him.   "Fine, just take the buttons over — you won't be pledged, see, just carry 'em over in your pocket."

He offered one to Chal, but he refused to take it, saying that he'd rather not.

"It's no obligation, see — "   But Chal insisted that he'd rather not, and the others refused by simply shaking their heads.

"Oh, well, it's all right, you fellas be sure and don't let 'em sweat you into anything, that's all."   The brother with the leather-like hair ran to the door and shouted down the hall, "Answer that phone, somea you birds."   But he backed in and was talking with someone at the door.

"Yeah, sure, they're here, just gettin' ready — come on in — er — Mr. Sun-on-His-Wings, Mr. Running Elk, and Mr. Windzer — Mr. McCullough.   Yeah, Mack, that's all right — sure, they're ready to go."   He turned to the three guests.   "This is one uh the Megs men — where you're goin' tuh eat."

Chal felt tired and full of misgivings as he walked to the door to cut short any more conversation.   Running Elk and

Sun-on-His-Wings followed. A naked brother, dripping and glistening, almost ran into them as they turned a corner. He looked at Harmon with an apologetic expression, then hurried on, leaving great, wet tracks like a bear on the polished floor.

That evening at the Megs house seemed hazy to Chal. The songs in praise of the fraternity before they sat down to dinner, and the conversation of the varsity football guard who was placed on one side of him for the express purpose of talking football, made little impression on him. He refused to worry about Running Elk and Sun-on-His-Wings — he didn't care if they disgraced the whole tribe. They would accept everything with silence and people would think they were stupid, but he couldn't do anything about it.

For three days he went from house to house — to dinners and to luncheons, and each time he felt more ashamed of himself. The feeling that he was out of step never had been so intense. He felt alone and unfortunate. He did not know what to talk about with these "men" of the University. Some of them he recognized as football men, whose names he had seen flaring in the headlines of sport pages, but he couldn't even talk to them about football. He drew more and more into himself when they patronized him or pretended an interest in him which he knew they were far from feeling.

Nelson had already pledged himself to the Chis, and of course Charlie and Sylvester had followed him. Chal had begun to envy Nelson's ability to adjust himself, even though the brothers said some very nasty things to him after he had put on the pledge button. But Chal noticed that these things affected him very little, and he had already begun to ignore his companions from Kihekah ; believing himself to have ascended into another stage of magnificence ;

another magnificence deserved by the son of Jep Newberg.

After a week, most of the prospectives had been pledged by the several fraternities, and Chal had begun to believe that he wanted to go home. He met Running Elk and Sun-on-His-Wings coming from classes with large shiny buttons on their coat lapels ; buttons with strange devices on them, symbolic of things hidden in ritual.

The three stood at the Varsity corner for half an hour one morning. They stood in silence for some time, then one of them said that it sure was hot. Running Elk pursed his lips in the direction of a girl and boy pulling and pushing each other, as they came down from the campus. The boy had one arm full of their books, and the girl, thus free, carried a little stick. She seemed conscious of her skirts swirling gracefully around her ankles, and the fact that her hair looked nice. The three found the actions of these two people very interesting, but they looked away quickly. They spoke no word of their attitude, or of the intensity of the last week ; they gave no hint to each other of their hopes or fears.

That evening Chal had dinner with the Megs again, and it was this dinner which caused him to pledge to the Chis the next day, mostly through weariness of the whole thing.

During that evening he stood by himself, as usual. People never talked with him for long, he guessed, because he didn't know what to say, and people always grew tired and went away to join other groups where there were talk and laughter. He asked the next brother who came out of duty to talk with him, where he might find the bathroom. When he started to shut the door, the knob was pulled from the outside, and several of the brothers came in and surrounded him.

The little room was hot and he was in a near panic.

Those standing around him were the pick of the fraternity, those known as "silver-tongues." Apparently the fraternity had decided to make one more try on this solemn, stupid fellow from Kihekah — probably because of his record in high school football and the fact that he was showing up well on the freshman team. Behind the "silver-tongues" stood the five Indians of the chapter, three of whom were on the varsity football team and the other two well known campus politicians.

The spokesman pulled out the fraternity's pledge button, and advanced toward Chal, saying soothingly and consolingly that he was sure that Chal was tired and wanted this thing over — he knew how it was. When Chal refused, he referred to the solemn Indians behind him ; to the guard and the end, and the all-conference halfback. He said Chal could see that the fraternity had some of the most famous names on the campus — kind of a Indian fraternity, in fact.

Chal felt the perspiration tickling his spine and he kept applying his handkerchief to his dripping forehead. If he could only see something sincere on those faces about him. Within, a voice kept telling him that he was out of step ; that this was the University, and that these men were the representatives of civilization. For an hour he endured. He looked helplessly at the stolid faces of the Indians — they were suffering as well, he could see that, but not for him. They wanted to be somewhere else, like everyone else in the room. The varsity guard kept shifting his great sweaty body from one foot to the other. Everyone had loosened his collar, and each of the "silver-tongues" had had his say, and the original one was still talking, but Chal had not heard him for several minutes. He was suddenly seized with obstinacy, unshakable, unreasonable obstinacy. He said, "I can't," and before they realized it, he was through the door, and was descending the stairs with the others behind him. Downstairs, the brothers disappeared, except the one who offered him his hat. A hot wave of bitterness came over Chal, and he felt very awkward as he said good night. He was scarcely down the steps when his host disappeared within the house. On every other occasion some one, or perhaps two of the brothers had accompanied him to his room or to another fraternity house.

The night was cool, and a faint September moon made long shadows, and there were patches of moonlight on the grass of the campus, let through by the branches of the locust trees ; patches that seemed material, like spilled milk. The ivy on the Administration Building glistened in the feeble light.

Chal walked past the group of buildings, dark and deserted to the soft night except for a light in one of the windows high up under the tower of the Administration Building. Screechy strains from a violin came floating down to him like a desecration. He walked down a dusty road behind the buildings into the equally dusty highway, then followed it toward the river. This was the first time he had been free since his arrival. He believed that he should be able to think the thing out if he were free, but tonight he just walked with a rapid stride toward the river, as though he would leave all the confused thoughts behind him. He passed a tall, ugly farmhouse rising out of the sand ; a dark, silent house. He wondered what the people were like who lived there ; they were farmers, he knew, but they were a part of all this. Probably they didn't go to the University, but they were not out of step. They must be like the people whom he had seen in the little town last Saturday. People with red-tinted clothes, as though the Red Beds had marked them and were claiming them as their own ; coloring them so that they would not be noticeable against the things which surrounded them. He knew from history that they had not been here long, but they were certainly a part of things now. He had seen them draped over dilapidated cars which were spattered with red mud and stained like themselves with the red dust, and he guessed then that they were talking about the price of hogs and about crops. They had things to say to each other, and they were a part of the life of the country, and this fact seemed to give them assurance.

His thoughts were disturbed by the sharp barking of a hound which changed suddenly into the most mournful howl he had ever heard. The howl sounded more natural, as though the hound's flap-eared breed had been placed on the earth to howl but through the interference of men were attempting to bark.

The thin stream of water which flowed sluggishly over the sand in threads was silvered by the moonlight ; flowing steadily through and over the sand of the river bed, but imperceptibly. The river was an historic stream and along its course much of the drama of two contending races was enacted. But, burdened though it was with such memories, it never boasted. Chal was impressed by its quiet purposefulness. He had always thought of rivers as being boastful.

He sat on a log near the water in a moon-silvered space and watched. At intervals cars rumbled over the bridge upstream, and nearby the September insects chirruped. When the cars had passed, above the chirruping of the insects, he could hear the faint, apologetic murmur of the water. For the first time in a week he felt pleasantly alive. He just sat there in the spell of the light-flooded night with no thoughts to disturb him.

He got up, went to the edge and felt of the water ; it was warm — about the temperature of his blood, because he couldn't tell just when he had touched it. He looked up the river at the silvered streams of water and the waste of sand which was almost intangible in the moonlight. He threw off his coat and unbuttoned his collar, but his hands stopped. He felt an unpleasant suffusion of blood that seemed warmer than blood. He decided he wouldn't go into the water — what if someone should see him. Of course there was only the remotest possibility, but if someone did see him, they'd think he was crazy. The faces of some of the men he had met during the frenzy of the last week came up before him and he could see the expressions on their faces. He knew that they wouldn't think of doing such a crazy thing. In the first place, it would be humiliating to have anyone know that he walked out here by himself, but to undress and float around in the water, that would be too much — they'd know he was crazy, and he was not quite sure that they wouldn't be right. He wasn't a boy in the Osage hills any more. As he buttoned his collar and drew on his coat, he decided that he was going to be like other people, and perhaps some day people would form groups around him and listen to what he had to say.

He walked through the deep sand back to the highway, and spoke aloud to himself, as though to allay the fears in his heart, by expressing to the silent night the acknowledgment of his frailty. "I'm a damned fool," he said.

It was still early when he came to the Chi house. Three of the brothers were playing bridge and a fourth was reading the sport page. He stood for some time before going up to the room which he shared for the length of his visit. They didn't seem to notice him, and he wanted especially to be noticed tonight. He wanted someone to come up to him, lay an insincere hand on his shoulder, and ask as though intensely interested, about the dinner at the Megs house. No one came near him and he went upstairs, believing that he was lost ; convinced that his queerness had finally resulted in disgrace.

There were several brothers in the room when he came in. They spoke and he returned the greeting, then went to the other side of the room and sat down. He had an intense desire to talk ; to say something in the way of conversation to these brothers holding a "bull session," but he couldn't — he just sat, and the others went on with their talk.

When they left, he went to bed with a heavy heart. To-morrow his visit at the Chi house would end, and if they did not ask him to join again, he must arrange for another room. For hours he heard the noises of the house. Doors were opened and shut. He could hear laughter and occasionally the low hum of conversation, until the sounds died slowly and the big house was silent. He went to sleep in tragic loneliness.

THE freshmen sat upstairs and waited. Down below in the mysterious room, behind the door which was always locked, the members of the chapter were in solemn meeting. Chal sat with the freshmen and a heavy load was on his mind. He knew what pledge court was, but he also knew that Sun-on-His-Wings and Running Elk didn't know anything about it. He knew that he could go through the humiliation, but he fervently hoped that the members would not find anything real or fanciful against Running Elk and Sun-on-His-Wings. He understood that it was only horse-play, and that you had to be a good sport and take it laugh-ingly, but he was sure that their dignity would not tolerate a paddle wielded against their sacred persons.

He wondered if he ought to go and tell someone that Running Elk and Sun-on-His-Wings would not understand

this sort of thing — that to touch an Indian's body consti-
tuted an insult, and they wouldn't understand this thing
called pledge court.   But he saw how hopeless it would be
— the brothers would only laugh at him.   He looked over
at Sun-on-His-Wings sitting on the divan, smiling as Smutts
talked to him about football.   Running Elk was sitting by
the window.   Running Elk always sat by a window — it
was instinctive.   Chal always thought that it was funny that
he should be influenced that way by heredity, because he was
sure that it was an hereditary instinct, and every time he saw
Running Elk take the chair closest to a window he always
thought of the story which his father told him about some
of his mother's relatives.   They had come to the Agency
during payment time and had stayed for several days.   It
was Tah He Kah He and his two wives.   They had put up
their lodges in the postoaks back of the agent's residence.
A blizzard had come and John had asked them to come into
his house and sleep in the kitchen — to bring their buffalo
robes and sleep on the floor in the warm kitchen.   John said
that the wind had blown a gale that night, and he had to
get up several times and grope his way to the barn to see
about the stock.

The next morning Tah He Kah He was up early and decided to build a fire in the stove.   Soon the kitchen was
filled with suffocating smoke and he and his wives were
running from window to window then back to the doors, but
were unable to get out.   In the confusion John had appeared.   He turned the knob of the door and they walked
out as though nothing had happened, but they would not
come back into the warm room, even after John had demonstrated to them how to turn the knob of the door, and the
way the lids fitted on the stove.   They had never slept in a
house before, and they had done so this time because

the wood in the camp was wet and the wind was very cold.

As Chal looked at Running Elk he thought there must be some lingering fear in his heart ; fear of being shut up in a house.

Brother Harkins came to the door and leered. He was a sophomore by the grace of a lax system. His desire to use the paddle on freshmen might have indicated sadistic tendencies, but it was only his way of impressing others, especially freshmen, with the fact that he was a sophomore, and he enjoyed all the prerogatives. His delight in pledge court was perhaps in vindication of his deficiencies in his status. He stood for some time with a satyr expression and enjoyed the effect of his sudden appearance. He looked from face to face, then he said slowly and with deep meaning, "Come on, you birds — little party downstairs."

The brothers were seated in a circle, each with a paddle. Chal's heart grew suddenly heavy. Not out of fear, but from the humiliation of the thing ; vicarious humiliation. Running Elk and Sun-on-His-Wings could not understand as he did. The freshmen stood in a row, and one brother after another got up and preferred charges. One said that a certain freshman had not come when he had called him to borrow a dress tie from him ; another said that a freshman had gone to the game last Saturday without his red cap, and what was more, he had taken a girl. Then Harkins got up, brandishing his paddle, named each freshman present, and preferred a charge. Chal heard his own name. "Windzer didn't go to the freshman meeting, and I find — er — that 'Blanket Running Elk' and 'Blanket Sun-on-His-Wings' didn't either — the Kihekah delegation, it seems like, are kinda campus shy." He came to the center of the room and leered at the Kihekah delegation.

"What's the matter with you men from the hill country ? I'm gonna do a little rear end work to see if that won't help your memory. Out here, Fancher — bend over." He raised his paddle and looked around, "Any other brother got anything against this man ?" On hearing no answer, he hit Fancher very hard several times, and Fancher turned very red and forced a smile. A man by the name of Tucker was next. He had been to military school, and had boasted that his "west end" was like leather. He took the paddling with good nature. "All right, Windzer."

Chal grew hot all over and thought he was smiling with good humor and sportsmanship, but he noted that Harkins looked at him in a queer manner, as though he saw something strange on his face. They both hesitated, then Harkins seemed to regain his assurance, waved the paddle and said, "Come on." Chal went to the center of the room. Because he felt that he was showing what he felt, he was annoyed with himself. With his head down looking at the floor, he thought he would have time to regain his composure, like a boxer gaining his wind between rounds. It wasn't what you felt, it was showing it to others that was so terrible. The paddle stung him. He went back to the place where he had been standing with a broad, teeth-revealing smile, and he was pleased with the knowledge that he had revealed nothing else. He had the Indian way of smiling when he was angry, masking the gentler and kindlier emotions with an unreadable expression ; sometimes even a surly expression. But he was not angry now ; he was afraid for Running Elk and Sun-on-His-Wings, and something like a shock went through him when Harkins called, "All right, Running Elk, guess you're next."

Running Elk stood still. There was nothing on his face, and he said nothing. Again Harkins called, "All right

Running Elk — we can't stay here all night." The room became very quiet. You could hear Stub Bailey's adenoidal breathing. Then Harkins stood looking at Running Elk, who in turn stood looking at nothing in particular. Harmon, who was chairman of the meeting, scraped his feet on the floor, and someone coughed. Chal saw both Harmon and Harkins look at Running Elk's face, then look away. He knew that they saw nothing there, and he could see that they didn't know what to do about it. Harkins was fired with anger. The idea that anyone, a freshman in particular, should defy him, a sophomore, was more than his pride could stand. His lip quivered and he advanced toward Running Elk, but stopped a few paces away and looked again to see if he could tell what was in that expressionless face. There was nothing ; Running Elk seemed unaware of him. This put him into a rage, yet there was something confusing in the situation and he had a feeling deep down that he would like to extricate himself without damage, if possible. But he couldn't find a way out — he must go on, and he wasn't sure that the brothers were behind him.

Chal, in his intense uneasiness, thought of a pack of wolves and an old buffalo bull ; an old buffalo bull with lowered head, the lead wolf afraid to advance because he was unsure of the courage of his mates. He was well acquainted with the pack instinct in all animals. He had been with the gang who had run the little freckle-faced Callahan boy to his own door, simply because he had red hair. He remembered his first day at the Indian boarding school, and as he thought of that day he knew that Running Elk would not let himself be paddled. If he did so he would consider himself a coward. Chal thought he ought to try to explain it to the brothers. Just as he was about to speak out, Harmon's feet scraped again and he said with authority, "Guess you

better let pledge Running Elk go this time — he didn't
know he was supposed to go, I guess." This was what
Harkins wanted. "All right," he said, "but he ought to be
paddled — if you wanta spoil these pledges, it's all right with
me." He felt a great relief and a warm gratitude toward
Harmon for saving his face. At any other time he might
have argued the question, but now he pretended that Harmon as chairman represented a rigid authority.

CHAL noticed that Running Elk and Sun-on-His-Wings were
absent from football practice the next afternoon. Red Can-
ton was running at right half in Sun-on-His-Wings' place,
and Kayovitch was in Running Elk's place at end. From
his position Chal watched the stocky, sweaty figure of Rusty
Carson calling the signals, bending, unbending, looking half
around and walking with short steps that gave the impression of latent power and speed. He kept looking at the
back of Carson's freckled neck, which looked like thick
leather. He watched him look up to see where the coach
was, then spit an amber stream before calling signals.

Carson was one of those hard, stocky, unimaginative people who grow up in smoky, clattering districts of a city ; the
districts where fires spurt out of high chimneys all day ;
where the air is full of the din of belching trains, the shrieking
of steel against steel. Where the air is a mixture of coke
smoke and the unmistakable odor of packing house. Chal
was fascinated by him. He was a natural leader, and even
in the University had attracted a following of his own kind
— young roughnecks whom he had probably led on stealing
expeditions or against other gangs of boys in the city.

As he watched the back of Carson's neck, Chal wondered
what would happen if he were to cut it with a sharp knife ;
he wondered if there would be blood coming out of the

wound. The more he thought about it, the more he doubted it. He couldn't imagine that neck bleeding.

When he was dressed, the coach came up to him and said, "Say, Windzer, maybe you better go and see about those two 'Blankets' — first time they've missed practice."

Chal went down the street and up the stairs to the room which his friends shared. He went in. He noticed that the trunks were packed, but he didn't say anything about it. Running Elk was lying on the bed reading a magazine, and Sun-on-His-Wings was combing his hair. He sat down and lit a cigarette. Sun-on-His-Wings smiled and looked over at Running Elk, pursed his lips toward Chal: "Big University man, ain't it? Smoking cigarette." Chal smiled, and indicating the trunks with his lips, said, "Quittin'?" Sun-on-His-Wings finished combing his hair, put the comb carefully in his pocket, and picked up a time-table.

"What does it say there about trains on the Katy?" Chal took the time-table, held it in his hand, then smiled, "Don't hafta look — one at ten tonight and one at noon tomorrow. The one tonight gets into Goodwater pretty early in the morning." Sun-on-His-Wings looked at Running Elk. "That one tonight, huh?"

"Yeah."

Running Elk put his magazine down and looked out the window into the densest branches of an elm, and Sun-on-His-Wings scraped something off the cuff of his trousers. Then he sat on one of the trunks. For some time the three of them sat thus, then Running Elk spoke, "I b'lieve that fella Rusty is sure good — he'll play next year."

"Yeah, he's fast," said Chal.

"I bet they will have chance to beat Nebraska this year — whatta they call 'em — Huskers, ain't it?"

"Yeah."

"They call Missouri 'Taggers,' ain't it ?"

Sun-on-His-Wings said, "Ain — haven't got any elephants."

The other two smiled. "Oughtta have elephants," he continued. "I bet that would be big enough — elephants." The three of them smiled.

Somewhere downstairs a dinner bell tinkled, and there was a sudden commotion in the hall ; the sound of feet descending the creaky stairs to the dining room. Chal got up and went to the door, then turned and said,

"Comin' to the house for dinner — I'm hungry." Sun-on-His-Wings answered for both. "Not comin'." Chal said, "I'll be back and go down to the station with you."

He cut across some vacant lots, then walked down the avenue to the fraternity house. He arrived just as the cook's moon-faced son was ringing the dinner bell.

THE three of them sat in the dim light of the interurban station on three of the four suitcases, waiting for the eight o'clock car. They had not spoken when Chal came back from dinner, and they had said nothing as they drove down to the station in a jitney. They sat silently for some time afterward. Sun-on-His-Wings was drumming the rhythm of an Osage dance song on the side of a suitcase, as though he were dreaming. He stopped suddenly, and the corners of his eyes made crows-feet as he turned to Running Elk, "Say, purty soon we gonna hear about old Chal. Eat-'Em-Alive Windzer, they gonna call him, I bet. I bet we read in the papers about Windzer Crushes Elephants — we gonna read that in the paper. He's gonna be a bad man, I bet." Running Elk smiled, and Chal looked at his feet and smiled feebly.

He was suffused with a pleasant feeling as he sat there. The world seemed natural again, sitting thus, but he sure didn't want to see his friends go home. He believed they ought to stay, all right, but they had decided to leave and there wasn't anything he could do about it. He didn't know what had contributed to the decision; everything, he guessed.

He knew as well as if they had told him in detail, that their hearts were very heavy on leaving the football practice. He knew also that they were confused about almost everything which had happened to them. He recalled the day they had gone in to pay their fees to the Y.M.C.A. secretary. The way they had looked when the secretary had slapped each one of them on the back, and had stood with his arms over their shoulders, telling them that he hoped they would be happy here. He recalled the way the secretary had looked at two other freshmen who came in with their red caps clenched in their hands, as he talked with Running Elk and Sun-on-His-Wings. Chal was sure he was thinking as he talked, of those other two freshmen who had come in to pay their fees.

There were many things, he guessed, which had caused their decision. In a way, he was glad they were going; their going would relieve him of much responsibility, and the fear which seemed to be with him always; the fear that they would do something wrong. He had enough to do to adjust himself. He felt a little angry with them, and with all the others at home because they were so backward about taking up civilized ways of talking and acting. He knew he was gonna stick it out.

The hoarse whistle of the car put an end to his thoughts, and he became slightly nervous. What if they made a mistake in getting on the car — climbed into the wrong door and caused people to laugh at them ?

Sun-on-His-Wings held out his hand and dropped the two pledge buttons into Chal's palm. "Better take these back," he said. Chal put them in his pocket. As the car was being unloaded and turned, they stood there without saying a word. Three tall figures in the feeble light of the single lamp over the station door ; casting elongated shadows on the platform.

Before they climbed aboard, each extended his hand in turn and placed the fingers lightly in Chal's palm, without pressure, barely touching his hand with theirs. As they climbed the steps, Chal felt something in his throat. He didn't mean to say anything, but he said in his emotion, "How." They did not turn around, but entered and were lost in the interior of the car.

VIII

It was the night of the homecoming dance ; the Chis always gave a dance during homecoming.

Chal was in his room thinking about the fifty-five yard pass which had won the game, first visualizing himself in the role of receiver and then in the role of passer. He couldn't decide which one he should like to have been, though in his dreaming he had a tendency to favor the passer. He was just attempting to word the headlines with his own name appearing, when Chick Talmadge came in with a towel around his middle, the soap still in his ears. "Say," he said hurriedly, "where's your powder ?" Chal pointed to it, and Chick began to use it copiously, the drifting flakes making the hair on his chest look frost-covered. Chal admired Chick's physique, but he wouldn't admit the fact to himself, and he thought that Chick had too much hair on his chest.

Chick finished the powdering, then took up Chal's comb, but before using it advanced his fresh-shaven face close to the mirror and examined with intensity a small red pimple. His hair was shiny, as though veneered. As he ran the comb carefully through it again, he said, "Say, frosh, got a date, I trust ?" He liked to use the word "trust" and always employed it when speaking to a freshman.

"Yeah."

"Who'd ya ask ?"

"I don' know, Clarence got the date for me."

"Oh, hell, he got you a Pi — he's official doormat at the
Pi house.   Who is she, do ya know ?"

"Said she was a pledge."

Chick was still attempting to improve the perfect parting
in his hair.   "Yeah, I know — looks like Theda Bara, got a
shape like Venus and ya hafta tie her to the floor when she
dances to keep her from floatin' off.   Probably one uh the
cellar gang, makin' her first and only dance uh the season —
mention her name ?"

"I think he said Blossom somebody."

"Wasn't Blo Daubeney ?"

"Yeah, that's it."

Chick turned from the glass in mock surprise and looked
steadily at Chal, "Say, frosh, that's too rich for your blood
— say, lissen, that little fairy can put her shoes under my
bed an-ee time."   He walked over to the table and picked
up a package of cigarettes.   "These your cigarettes ?"   He
lit one, then kept the package.   "Future all-Americans can't
smoke cigarettes.   Lissen, frosh, you come sweetly up to
future Brother Talmadge and offer him about half the dances
on the old menu, see.   Why, Blo Daubeney's one uh my all-
American harem — captain, see."   He turned toward the
door, then looked back.   "Lissen, Redtail, don't forget — it's
the old paddle, see — I can swing a mean one."

CHAL stood against the wall with Clarence.   There were
several chairs in the room, but no one was sitting.   Several
of the "men" spoke to each other rather carelessly and with
a touch of nervousness.   Clarence, all stiff in his "tux,"
watched the stairs and kept feeling of his tie.   Stub Classen
came in and immediately assumed an air of familiarity and
proprietorship.   It was said that he was engaged to the
president of the sorority.   He looked at Clarence and Chal

in their black-and-white, then at the others ; several others from various fraternity houses in lounge suits, for this was date night. Stub threw his hat carelessly on one of the chairs. It was below the dignity of the squadmen to go bareheaded, as such flouting of conventions indicated, at least hinted at doubtful virility.

" 'Lo, men," he said with graceless carelessness, as he flopped himself into a chair with the arrogance of one who is someone. He was a varsity man and the name of Stub Classen meant something on the campus. "Why don't you birds sit down ?" he said as he waved a broad stubby hand around the room. He looked at Clarence. "Havin' a shin-dig over at the old club, Clarence ?"

"Yeah."

Chal looked at this great football player. Everyone had heard of him, and Chal had expected to see a god, but he was disappointed. A passage from some Persian poetry he had read in translation, about someone having that grace of the hind parts of an elephant, came to his mind. He couldn't help thinking about that when he looked at Stub. There was something about Stub's arrogance and self love ; something about his naïve assurance, that made the thing even more applicable, Chal believed, and he wasn't accustomed to seeing such broad feet and thick ankles ; ankles that looked like a what-you-may-call-it, an iron wahdonska that had been left unfinished. The black silk socks made the ankles look exactly like iron. There was the least bulge just above his waist, and the vest buttons strained when the bulge moved up and down as he breathed. In the silence, the slightly nervous, slightly charged silence, Chal thought he could hear Stub breathe. He knew that this was only imagination induced by Stub's heavy shoulders ; his heaviness and thickness in general, but he couldn't see how Stub could breathe any other way but audibly.

The president of the chapter came downstairs. She was tall and she moved with that particular assurance which indicated that she had everything well in hand. She looked capable ; just the kind of person who would be president of a sorority. She wore a blue ribbon around her hair, a white waist and a blue skirt. There was steadiness in her tread ; practicality even in her walk. She was the kind of person who made good grades because it was the practical thing to do. She smiled at Chal, but he saw immediately that it wasn't deep ; she was smiling from the teeth, and he thought she must have assumed it at the head of the stairs. She shook the hand of each one, and when she came to Chal she looked at him, then at Clarence, and the latter immediately said, "This is Chal Windzer, one of our pledges — Mr. Windzer, Miss Kayser." She looked patronizingly at Chal, "Well, that's fine — congratulations — you're in a fine bunch of boys." Chal was able to say, "Thank you," only after she had passed on to one of the others. He put his finger in his collar to let in some cool air, and he wondered if he looked all right. At the last impression of his face in the mirror that evening, he had seen a bronze face in black-and-white ; the white making the bronze stand out, and he had wondered if he wasn't too dark. He had often wished that he weren't so bronze. It set him off from other people, and he felt that he was queer anyway, without calling attention to the fact. It was embarrassing to attract attention, and when people looked at him he became shy. He thought he still might have black eyes and straight black hair that shone like patent leather when he put grease on it, if his face were only white.

Stub stood holding Miss Kayser's coat with that air of importance ; that smiling assurance of his own worth. His thick, stubby-fingered hands were even clumsy holding the coat.

Then three other sisters came down the stairs ; all three smiling from the teeth, although the one behind was a little late in turning her smile on, Chal thought. She must have caught her heel in the ragged carpet at the head of the stairs. One waved her handkerchief as she descended, in a gay salute. When they made their rounds saying, "Hullo, there," he was ready for them this time. He was introduced by Clarence as "one of our pledges." He waited until each one had said, "congratulations," then he said, "thank you," and bowed slightly. While they were preparing to leave with their dates, Chal suddenly grew hot and felt sure that he shouldn't have bowed. He wasn't sure why he had bowed, because he had intended to say simply, "thank you," and remember to smile. He hoped that Clarence had not seen it, but he guessed perhaps it was all right to bow a little. He was feeling a little better when he was suddenly aware that he had given them a limp hand, with just the three middle fingers touching their palms in a salute ; Indian fashion. He grew hot all over again. Why couldn't he remember to grasp other people's hands with conscious pressure ? He had had his hand hurt enough since his arrival at the University to have remembered this. Tonight the four girls had gripped his hand with conscious and special pressure ; almost too much pressure for their strength. Since his arrival he had watched the men shaking hands, and he had noticed particularly the special thought which they seemed to give to the formality, as they waited with feigned eagerness while the introducer finished his sentence.

Chal couldn't see how they could hurt his slim hand by

natural pressure, so he was sure they were conscious of how hard they were going to press someone's hand while awaiting the introduction. He thought it must be something like slapping people on the back ; it must indicate heartiness, sincerity, and above all it must be done to indicate strong character. He thought that if people had not noticed his limber-fingered salute too much, he would in the future attempt to show character in his hand grasp. He guessed that must be the right way to show other people that you were forceful, sincere and able.

Eventually there were only three left ; Chal, Clarence, and Sparks from the Megs house. They sat down, and Sparks and Clarence began talking about things which Chal didn't understand, though he listened carefully and noted every mannerism of both. He heard them say something about running someone for May queen.

Upstairs, Blo was dressed, all except her shoes. She was sitting on the bed with her flimsy, flowing skirts up over her knees, showing several inches of very round, white legs. She was rolling the tops of flesh-colored stockings around pieces of rubber bands which she had just found after a search in many rooms. Her roommate, Gladys, stood by in a faded blue dressing gown, tied around the middle with a string, watching the deft fingers as they rolled. Occasionally she moved her hand forward a little, as though she would assist, but let it fall limply back to her side. Blo was frowning. She was unaware of the way the light made her hair look like rich taffy in that position. For once, she was not admiring her glorious self. But she was thinking of herself ; thinking of how every darned thing had gone against her this evening ; the long hunt for rubber bands and having to lie about the reason for wanting them, especially if there were any of the older girls present. The bathroom had been occupied from six o'clock until late, and her name had stood far down on the list of bathers that was tacked on the door. She had felt injured at that; seemed like special meanness on the part of the others. They knew that she was goin' to the Chi dance, and they did it a-purpose — maybe not a-purpose, but it 'ud be just like 'em, she thought.

There was a footstep outside, and Gladys made a quick movement as though she would detain the intruder with her hand. Blo pushed her skirts down around her ankles and put her hands to her hair, looking at the door. It opened and Clara Parsons came in, wearing a red evening gown, with her shoe bag over her wrist and her hair veil already adjusted. "My goodness, Blo, aren't you ready yet — gracious — hurry up, we're late already." She left the room and the quiet air of the room stirred a very little with her passage, and bore a scent almost too sweet.

Blo pulled her skirts up again and began to adjust the improvised garters; she almost jerked them up this time, and her frown deepened. Gladys made a motion of resignation with her arms. "The old gal would 've hit the ceilin' if she'd seen you — goin' to a dance without your corset." Blo held out each silk-encased leg and scrutinized it carefully; with approval. She saw that the seams were straight up the back, gave another turn to the roll of her stockings, stood up and let her silver clothes that resembled a bell in shape, fall to her ankles. She caressed her skirts carefully, then looked up at Gladys. "Say, what did the cats say about my shavin' under my arms?" She turned, picked up her shoes, and put them on while Gladys told her how the chapter had had a special meeting about it. "T' hell with 'em!" said Blo. She got up and went to the mirror, thrust her face very close under the light, and applied lipstick; very carefully and lightly. She didn't want it distinct, the old cats might see it. She picked up the mirror and looked steadily at the back of her head. The frown left her face and she smiled softly, and her eyes sparkled. Into her stomach came a feeling, that which she thought of as a "hurty" feeling ; a bitter-sweet feeling that surged all over you after it left your stomach, and you couldn't do anything about it but just smile ; smile because you couldn't help smiling. A smile that seemed to make your teeth whiter, your hair more shiny, and your eyes more sparkling. Her cheeks tingled a little as she looked at her reflection. She never used the word "glorious," but as she stood there she thought, "I'm a dream," and that meant the same thing. Full of this mood, she put on her hair veil, picked up the silken bag which contained her dancing shoes, and swished out of the room, with Gladys admiringly at her heels. She came to the head of the stairs and stood for a moment. She took one last look at her glory in a little mirror out of her bag. She stood a moment longer, as though waiting to be announced, then looked up at Gladys and said, "All right, Glad ?"

"Fine."

She picked up the front of her skirt, threw her head back, and seemed to float down the stairs. Clarence and Clara were talking. Chal was being left out of the conversation, as freshmen are supposed to be left out of conversations, and he was just sitting when Blo appeared on the stairs.

She came down smiling. Her teeth seemed to be shining in the stairs' light, and from that moment Chal remembered her very big brown eyes and her shining blond hair. The breath-taking impression of radiant silver floating, brown eyes above a smile that dazzled, gave him a queer feeling in his stomach. Something warm flooded him, seeming to come from his stomach, and suffused with that something warm, every thought was drowned and he stood paralyzed.

There was no quick appraisal, no thought at all. If he could have run out of doors, he would have done so, and probably walked and walked, not knowing where. Blo approached lightly, with a graceful swing, smiling. She looked intently at his face, and the light of her smile seemed to blind him, and he felt that his hands were hairy paws and his feet were glued to the floor. The something in his stomach turned to tingling suddenly, and his throat became dry and his knees felt as though they were becoming very weak.

There was the introduction, and conversation, of course, but the first thing he remembered was the humiliating way his hand shook as he held, what he believed to be the most wonderful, rustling garment he had ever seen. Blo smiled over her shoulder as he took his hands from her cloak, and he choked. Then he remembered with a flush; a flush that burned his cheek, that he had choked that way some time during the introduction. As he stepped forward with haste, he almost bumped into her and came very close to stepping on that wonderful, silvery gown.

All the way down to the dance in the jitney he thought of the brilliant lights which he must face with this shining, glorious, silvery girl with big eyes. A delicious fear came to him; almost the same sensation you have when a quail is about to rise, as the dog stands rigid with front legs shaking slightly.

They were talking, Clarence, Clara and Blo, but he didn't know what they were saying. He was sitting with the driver and they were in the back seat. He found himself hoping that they would be a long time getting to the dance, believing that in the meantime, some sort of courage might come to him.

He waited with Clarence until Clara and Blo came out of the dressing room, smiling teeth-revealing smiles. Again that breath-taking something came into his stomach as Blo advanced.

"Given the programs yet ?" she said sweetly, widening her brown eyes.

"No, not yet," he almost whispered.

They stood, and the music began. Already several couples were on the floor, when he felt Blo's hand on his shoulder. "Le's dance," she said. He thought that he'd lost control of his feet ; he couldn't get into the rhythm, but she didn't seem to notice. She was smiling over her shoulder and speaking to people. Chal heard someone shout, "Third ?" and she nodded. At the end of the room there were several shouting at her at the same time. The music stopped and two of the pledges came up and handed Chal two programs. It seemed that he had scarcely time to look at them when he was overwhelmed by men wanting dances, and he just managed to save three for himself.

As he dragged around the floor with other partners, he was simply passing time until the next dance with Blo. When it did come, he could dance only to the first encore, as someone claimed her immediately. As he walked back to the line of stags he felt better and mildly possessive now. It was kinda like football, he thought. After you had handled the ball once your nervousness left you and you felt good again.

When the second dance came along he thought he ought to talk about something, but he couldn't think of anything to say, and she didn't seem to want to say anything, anyway. She just danced and smiled that smile where you saw nothing but gleaming teeth and brown eyes, and when she looked up at you you almost lost step. She laid her head lightly against his shoulder, as though she were tired, and he had a feeling that he would protect her ; protect her against a shadowy thing which might harm her ; protect her against the world, with his life if necessary. There semed to be something personal about the way she let her head rest against his shoulder ; and appealed to his protective manhood.

Suddenly Blo nestled closer, and Chal noticed that she had suddenly forgotten to smile over her shoulder at other men who were watching her over the heads and shoulders of other girls. It seemed to Chal that she merged with him in the rhythm of the dance, and it occurred to him that all this time she had been thinking of something else ; thinking of the other people on the floor, even though she was light and graceful and responded to the lightest pressure of his hand on her back. But now she was lost in the rhythm, and immediately he was transported into other realms, and there was something indefinite but sacred about this dance. He could not definitely hear the music, but he was conscious of the drum beats and his feet seemed to touch the floor with the drum beats, and even his heart was in rhythm. That was as it should be, the drum beats, and he began to feel a religious fervency, as though this delicious semi-oblivion were a prayer. But this was a new experience, merging with someone in such fervency ; someone like the Moon Woman, who, like many things beautiful, lived briefly. Like the Moon Woman of his childhood who reigned over the forgetfulness of the night ; over the tranquil world of dreams ; the world of Wah 'Kon. But these thoughts were hazy, like flitting dreams, and he could not recall them later. He only remembered a supreme fervency, a beautiful fervency that passed like the physical sensations of a dream. They did not stand out, clear and sparkling, like the sensations of the day.

He couldn't remember when the music stopped. He found himself standing with Blo, but it was not until after-

ward that he remembered she had left her hand on his arm
for a moment.   He didn't see it that time, the new something which had come into her eyes ; a fleeting something
that had made them more beautiful ; but which passed as
quickly as it had come.   Then he seemed to wake up, and
he noticed forms and faces and the murmuring of voices
around him.   He was afraid to look at Blo and there was
something like singing in his heart.

When the music started for the encore, he got only three
steps before he was tagged.   He walked to the back of the
room without seeing or thinking.

The third dance with Blo was the next one.   He had
been standing at the back of the room watching the dancers,
waiting ; following that silvery wonder as she swirled among
the other dancers.   A delightful, quivering eagerness had
taken the place of the fear.   Chick Talmadge came up to
him with his program in his hand, "Gotta dance ?"

Chal was startled.   "No, full up," he said.   Chick
looked at him severely, and Chal could smell his alcoholic
breath.   He said :

"Say, stand aside, freshman, what d'ya mean, no dance —
full up — le's see that menu.   Here, what about this one,
the next one ?"   He wrote his name over the cross that de-
noted "partner" and handed it back to Chal, "No trade, see,
I'm a stag — you c'n go smoke a pill, see — no encore stuff,
see."

"I'll ask her if — "

"If what ?   Say, lissen freshman, you don't tell her anything."

Chal stood at the back of the room.   From that moment
the dance was a drab monotony.   The music droned on, and
the scraping of many feet was in his ears.   He saw Blo, rosy
and white, dancing a few steps with one partner, then turn-

ing to glide into the arms of another, without changing her smile. He watched men struggle with their partners, some of them facing forward with set expressions, and with feet scraping. He noticed that everyone's shoes were gray with the dust that the dancing stirred up. He could hear the laughter of girls as they passed him, and he noticed the intense expressions of other men standing with him, their minds and eyes and ears too occupied with the dancers or with some particular figure in someone else's arms, to talk. They did attempt to carry on conversation, but it was half-hearted, and was more a gesture toward that which they believed to be sociability than from interest in the subject.

At the door of the Pi house they said good night. Blo squeezed Chal's hand and said, "I sure had a good time," and as she looked up into his face in the semi-darkness, his heart almost stopped. He realized that her hand was squeezing his, and he was allowing his fingers to remain limp in an Indian salute. He was almost too late but gripped her hand just as it was about to leave his, and to his surprise he felt her hand tighten on his again. He felt with a thrill that some message had been thus conveyed, but he didn't know just what; some understanding which he didn't understand.

The door closed behind the girls and he walked up the dark, elm-bordered avenue with Clarence. Clarence was silent, as though the thoughts of a junior were too sacred to be conveyed to a mere freshman. Chal couldn't have heard him anyway, as all the way to the Chi house he was dreaming and thinking of the things which he should like to have said and done. Things which would have indicated to Blo the important, manly, courageous sort of person he wished to be, as well as a nonchalant man of the world.

The Administration Building stood dark against the stars,

with the locusts, sycamores and elms hiding its feet, and the
Science Building gleamed even in the darkness ; a careful
pile of limestone, aware of its strong foundation. Across the
campus, the Fine Arts Building seemed diffident and resigned, as though that which it symbolized had been hopelessly outdistanced by the progress of a people. From the
first time Chal had seen it, it had in some inscrutable way,
reminded him of a bookcase with leaded glass ; a bookcase
containing books which no one ever read.

The light was very dim on the stairway as Clara and Blo
walked almost droopingly up the stairs. At the top of the
stairs, Clara said, "Goo'night," stopped, and took off her
shoes, then walked down the hall to her room. Blo went
into her dark room and fumbled with the light. There was
a hump under the bedclothes, and at the top of the hump
Gladys's dark hair. Blo was suddenly inflamed to think
that Gladys was there sleeping when her feet hurt so. She
stooped and pulled off her shoes, and as she did so a sharp
pain shot through one of her feet. This was too much ; too
much to suffer this way in silence, with Gladys sleeping there
peacefully and comfortably. She frowned as she looked at
the hump. She picked up a burning foot and rubbed it,
then wriggled her toes and felt them come unstuck.

Her thickish red lips were parted slightly, with the lower
one drooping, and the frown on her face narrowed her eyes.
She limped toward the closet to get her nightgown, but as
she passed the mirror she stopped to look. She caught sight
of her face, which seemed distorted, and she came closer and
held it up to the glass. She began widening her eyes and
the face softened. Approval came into her eyes, and soon
she was smiling. She stood back a little and let the lids
of her eyes droop, narrowing them to almost a slit, then she
widened them again and smiled, turned and looked at her-

self over her shoulder. Forgetting her feet, she swirled about, still watching herself, then she put her hands on her hips, lifted one of her feet and stood that way a moment.

She went back to the closet, rummaged there a while, then came out holding a red shawl which her uncle had sent to her mother from Panama. She undressed as she looked at herself in the mirror. When she was quite naked except for her stockings, she stood for some moments and appreciated the beauty of her hips and her rounded thighs. She knew she was perfect — the only thing that ever bothered her was her bowlegs. When you had bowlegs the seams of your stockings were always awry. She liked to look at herself this way — the stockings made it look daring and — and — kinda — it gave you a queer, ticklish feeling.

She pulled off her stockings and spent some minutes draping the shawl around her, leaving one breast only half hidden, and drawing the shawl tight around her middle, the tassels dancing with every movement. Just as she was about to change to another position, she heard a sound at the door. The smile left her face and she frowned at the crack under the door. When she was sure of the movement outside the door, she let the shawl slip to her feet and caught up Gladys's old dressing gown, just as the door opened and May Severin stuck her disheveled head into the room. May then slipped in, turned, and with her back to Blo carefully closed the door. She tiptoed to the trunk and sat down. Blo fumbled for the string that answered for a belt to the dressing gown. May crossed her legs so that the lace of her nightgown and the edge of her dressing gown touched her thin ankles, and with a cigarette dangling from her mouth, struck a match on the frayed sole of one of her mules. Having lit the cigarette, she held it clumsily between her forefinger and thumb, and reached into her dressing gown pocket, pulling out a package of cigarettes which she offered to Blo.

She looked at Blo through a veil of smoke and said, "How's the dance ?" Blo walked over to the door and stuffed a little piece of paper in the keyhole, then after lighting her cigarette, replied, "Lord deliver me — Biff Bach thinks he's broken-field runnin', and — oh, I don' know."

"Who'd yu go with ?"

"Chal Windzer, a pledge from Kihekah — not a bad dancer, but he never says anything — stands around like a — he's an Indian."

"I saw him th' other day — kinda handsome."

"Something Japanesey about him when he smiles."

"Yeah. Y' know, I reely think he's handsome — say he's got rocks."

"Yeah, just a few oil wells in his back yard, I guess."

Blo began to look around for her nightgown and mules, and May sat and puffed as though the thing to do was to smoke the cigarette as quickly as possible so that she might have the pleasure of lighting another one. There was something pleasing about the lighting of cigarettes. The frown came to Blo's face again and she was filled with injury — she couldn't find that darn' gown. She looked over at the hump on the bed with the hair spread all over the pillow, and the frown deepened. Dammit, there was Glad, asl — "Glad," she shouted, and took the hump by the shoulder. Gladys's head came up suddenly, as though she had been caught asleep at the post, and blinking into the frowning face of Blo, attempted to focus her sight and her mind.

"Stupid," said Blo. "Don't look so stupid, where in hell is my gown ?" Gladys pushed down the covers and sat on the edge of the bed. She threw her hair back, then got up and walked unsteadily to the closet. She reappeared with the

gown in one hand and mules in the other.   Blo took them
from her and said, "Thanks."   Gladys stood for a moment,
threw her hair back again, and blinked in the light.   Then
she saw May for the first time.   "Oh — hullo, May."

"Hullo, have a pill ?"

"No, thanks.   Have a good time at the dance, Blo ?"

"Rotten."

Gladys stood blinking as though she felt obliged to think
of more of the amenities, but failing, went over to the bed
and sat down.   Blo stood in front of the glass with the
cigarette dangling from her lips, and tied the blue ribbon
around the pink nightgown, studying her image carefully.
Then she went over to the other edge of the bed and sat
down.   They sat in silence for some time and then May
said, "Goin' to the Meg formal ?   Course you are, though
— ole popularity."   Blo pretended modesty.   "D'ya think
so ?   Guess I'm goin', but I think I'll wear boots and spurs,
or it'll be Varsity, 20 — Blo, nothin'."

"Those football cows oughtta be barred," May suggested.

Blo yawned and Gladys fell into bed again with a sleepy
grunt.   May got up and carefully put out her cigarette,
went to the door and peeped out, then passed through the
door, raising her hand in salutation.   Blo rose and went to
the glass again, and looked at herself intently.   She let down
her hair and tied it back with a string, then was occupied for
several minutes applying cream to her face.   After one last
pat at her face, she turned out the light and went to bed.

The springs had scarcely stopped creaking, when Blo said
in a petulant voice, "Glad, for heaven's sake, get your
big — "   Then a grunt as if she were pushing something,
and a sleepy sigh from Gladys.   Then silence.

But Blo's thoughts moved on.   After all, she was thinking, Chal was good lookin' and rich too, she guessed.   She

had heard that Osages were rich. Her date book was filled with library dates, Saturday morning and Saturday afternoon dates, dances on weekends. And each Sunday was filled. There were breakfast dates, church dates, dinner dates, afternoon dates, "sandwiches" dates, and Sunday night dates. As a matter of fact, her date book was filled until Christmas, almost filled for the second semester. Chal would call, she thought, and when he called she could arrange a date for him. She could give Hank's date — Hank was always hanging around and he wouldn't care — he'd come back.

Far away a dog was barking. That was the only sound in the still night except for the ticking of a cheap alarm clock on the dresser. Her thoughts became slower ; maybe Chal had a big car at home and would bring it down next year. Thinking of cars a warmth came over her. She thought of Jack Castle and the way he looked at her at dances, when he didn't know that she had seen him looking. His careless way of doing things and his assurance intrigued her. The word "assurance" was not in her vocabulary, but Jack's manner appealed to her even though she couldn't give it a name. "That way of his," expressed to her the same thing. "That way of his" radiated that mysterious thing which great wealth gave — that thing that made you drive a great shiny car as though you were unconscious of the car, and gave you the privilege to be careless about your clothes, abrupt and crude. He had never spoken to her and of course he had never danced with her. And that fact alone was enough to intrigue her. But some day he would dance with her. She was sure of that.

Her thoughts became sluggish and indistinct, and just before she went to sleep, there was a hazy vision of herself, a very attractive self, in cute clothes, waving to people from Jack's long, shiny car.

ONE morning Chal came out of the fraternity house with his books under his arm. The autumn air was icy, and at the same time the rays of the sun warmed his body through his clothes. The air was still and the leaves of the elms and locusts were not even quivering. The sun induced a supreme, profound peace over everything, and he felt that he wanted to do something about it, but he was not sure what. As he neared the Geology Building for his ten o'clock class, he saw students streaming up all the approaches to the campus. Some were in pairs, dawdling along, men and girls unconscious of everything except each other's presence. A great hulking fellow came slowly up the walk with a girl ; a small girl, who kept looking up into his face and smiling. The big fellow was utterly unconscious of the grass, the trees, the buildings, the lazy autumn sunshine and golden, red and brown leaves of the campus. There was a thick smile on his face ; a face that was ready to please, yet proud and in some inscrutable way, possessive. Chal thought of a dog, but yet he believed the fellow's expression was not the expression of a dog when he looks at his master, but more like the tail of a dog expressing readiness to serve ; expressing love and obedience by the simple wagging of his tail.

The fellow loomed. He wore a great sweater with the varsity letter on the front, and he had the girl's books as well as his own under his arm. Behind them and in front of them streamed the others, but of them, of the impossible colors, of the cottonwood leaves falling silently to the green grass, these two were oblivious. When they were opposite Chal, the towering halfback pushed the girl off the walk, and she came back and charged him with delicate fists which he dodged in mock fear, then they both laughed and sauntered on.

Girls and men came by singly, some with very serious

looks in their faces and very efficient quick steps, as though they had but a little time to live and accomplish that which they were supposed to accomplish. Chal thought it was rather as though they were going somewhere to make money. A girl came by with set face, her neat skirts flopping around her shoe tops, and she was eating an apple. Fewer and fewer passed him, and finally the most peaceful sun imaginable beamed down on an empty campus.

A bell rang upstairs and Chal put out his cigarette, hesitated, then went upstairs to the lab, opened his locker and placed his books in it. He walked quickly past the door where his class was being held, and down the stairs.

He walked past the buildings of the University, then out into the road leading toward the river. There was a tingling in his fingertips as he walked faster, then suddenly he had an impulse to trot, but before he did so he looked back to see that no one was in sight, then he broke into a trot down the road. He felt the cold air in his face and a fierce kind of well-being came up in him. Unconsciously he crawled through a barbed wire fence and trotted across a pasture, then down a ravine. Soon he was dodging about and bending low as he ran. Then he stopped suddenly. He looked around to see if anyone had seen him. Three cows lifted their heads as they chewed and looked at him steadily with stupid surprise. He sat down, panting slightly. He felt his face grow hot as he realized that for the last few minutes he had been imagining himself a coyote. He said, "Ho-ho-hooooo," as though to drown the realization as he attempted to think of something else. The cows looked up again and he said to them, "You think I'm a damn' fool, I guess." The thought that he had reverted to his old childhood game humiliated him so that he became almost miserable. Then he said aloud, "I guess I am crazy, all right."

But the peace there among the vines, the elms and the persimmon trees soon flooded him and drowned the disturbing thoughts. He just sat and thought of nothing in particular. A cardinal flitted like a flame through the undergrowth and balanced on a grape vine close by him. As he did not move the bird wondered what sort of an animal he was. The bird lowered his head then raised it and chirped with a voice as clear as a whistle, then flew jerkily away down the ravine. Two red-headed woodpeckers began chasing each other around the bole of an old half-dead tree, raucously scolding. Chal thought there must be a nut tree close by, as occasionally he could hear the thud of a nut falling.

He got up and walked noiselessly down the ravine, working his way through the thicket-choked bottoms. He could feel the sun on his back and the sand trickling into his shoes. He stopped and looked around, then pulled off his sweater and tied it around his waist the way the Osages tied their blankets. He came to a fence and climbed over. The fence made him think of the last Saturday afternoon when a party had walked to the river and had eaten persimmons on the way. They had climbed this very fence, and he remembered Bess Judson's white thigh which she had exposed as she climbed over. When he thought of this, a queer feeling came in his stomach. Then he thought of Blo and he felt his thoughts were sacrilegious about Bess. Anyway he couldn't think that way about Blo. But Bess — Bess had a sort of careless way about her. And he believed that she knew her leg was showing that way.

Blo was not with the party, and he had been glad. He and Bess had been thrown together on the way back. He felt that he had been a bore on the picnic ; they had all walked down the river road jabbering, and they had jabbered all the time they were roasting "wienies," and he had not known what to say so he had remained silent. On the way back they had paired off and he had been left with Bess, and he had been glad to get back. He had endured the picnic, but he remembered that there had been a little wind that day, and even now he felt a little surge of emotion when he thought of the way that wind had picked up the sand from the river bed and had carried it along in little clouds like smoke. He remembered too the way the water-fingers of the Canuck crawled along over the sand and gleamed in the sun.

As he walked slowly through the thicket, he felt the sand filling his shoes at every step and he was saying to himself that he would not go on any more picnics like that. He didn't like girls when they wore riding breeches, anyway — they looked clumsy and thick, and when they stooped they were ugly from behind. He guessed they were kinda sensible in a way, but he sure didn't think they looked nice.

When he came to the river he stood for some time and looked at the silently moving water. He looked up-stream, hoping that the sand might be blowing like smoke coming out of the earth, but there was no wind — today the water didn't even sparkle like diamonds. Then as he stood he thought he could hear the faint murmuring of the water, and there was no other sound in all the flood of autumn sunshine, except the occasional tapping of a downy woodpecker. The river, the trees, and the earth were not dreaming peacefully, he felt, but seemed to be expecting something. They had that peace, that listening and that tenseness which precedes something drastic. The activity of the insects and the birds indicated that something was imminent. He guessed that must be the reason why he had been so restless.

He tied his sweater into a ball and lay down full length on the sand, using it as a pillow. As he looked up into the branches of a big elm, a racial instinct came to him. He raised up and looked around for something to drum on; something, any kind of a wahdonska that would sound like a drum. There was nothing in sight, so he fell back again and began dreamily to hum a social song of his people. The song which he liked best of all the songs was the one with the beautiful rhythm; the one with the rhythm almost as beautiful as the planting song. He cleared his throat and sang softly to himself:

> "Pawnee standing on hill,
> Pawnee standing there on hill.
> Pawnee crying on hill,
> Pawnee crying there on hill.
>
> "Pawnee shot by Osage arrow,
> Pawnee shot on hill by Osage arrow.
> Pawnee gives his heart to fear,
> Pawnee falls by Osage arrow."

He hummed on and on under the spell of the rhythm, under the peace of the sun and the thrilling sadness of autumn. His eyes closed, and he was with a party of Osages; the same party who had chased that last Pawnee of a war party to the hill, where he cried out to be saved; cried like a woman. Chal, in the dream, was the one who fired the arrow into the heart of the Pawnee because he was a coward.

He felt the sun on his eyes and he stopped humming and opened them. The sun had climbed to mid-heaven, and he got up and moved over into the shade again. He sat there looking dreamily at the water and the yellow waste of sand, and again he believed he could hear a faint murmur like the murmur of life. A thrill passed through his body, almost like a chill, and he wished that he were among his hills again. The blackjacks would be painted like warriors, and like painted warriors they would care for nothing except their own glory and that which was in their hearts. Even the scents of his hills came to him ; the acrid odor of weeds crushed by his pony's hoofes, and the fascinating odor of the hickory after frost.

He began dreaming again. He was riding over the prairie where a diffident, autumnal breeze played, and he could feel it against his bare chest. But he was not alone. Blo was with him, riding across the prairie. He could see her hair shining in the sun and he watched the breeze play with wisps of it. She seemed to be looking ahead at the place where the sky and prairie met. He could see what was in her great brown eyes, and he knew that which he saw there came from her heart. On and on they rode in silence, with only the talk of their faces, and he felt like a protector ; that he could die for her.

Suddenly she became the dream woman of his childhood ; her blue mantle hanging on each side of the pony and her hair on her shoulders. She looked at him and he was startled. The dream woman's face had never been distinct, but now he saw it was Blo's face. The emotion which the dream brought, brought him back to reality.

He felt a kind of ecstasy thinking of nothing for a while, then he wanted to dream some more. He made himself visualize the hackberries and the elms in the deep canyon at the head of Buck Creek. He saw the tops of the trees as they showed above the limestone rim of the canyon; the tops of those trees that had never failed to thrill him from the first time he had seen them. Miles and miles of blue and green, or blue and copper, then suddenly that thin line of darker green, or slate color if it were in winter, appearing suddenly, gave a never failing mystery to that wind-swept space. In fancy he was riding toward those trees again, when suddenly he heard a loud sniff.

He turned and saw a small herd of cattle approaching the river down the trail that led to a water hole. He felt very foolish and said aloud, as though to prove to the staring cattle that he was there on some practical business like any sane person : "Well, what th' hell d'yu want ?" The word "hell" always seemed practical and forceful to him. He got up, pulled on his sweater, then started along the edge of the river. He looked at the sun and saw that the shadows were growing long and that already there was a chill in the air.

When he came to the football field he looked through a crack and saw that practice was still going on. He watched for some time, then he saw that Bill Ralls was running in his place in the backfield. He circled the field carefully, went by the lab to get his books, and went to the house. The large house was vacant. Everyone was out watching practice or strolling along the walks with girls.

He became unhappy. He sat down in his room by the window, and he could hear every sound in the heavy air. He could hear Freddy bawling someone out and the signals being called, and occasionally he could hear the impact of a foot against the ball. He sat thus until the shadows lengthened and merged in the twilight. Noises came up from down-stairs where the brothers were coming in for dinner. The dinner bell rang, and he went slowly down-stairs, but he hesitated, then went out the front door. He would eat somewhere else ; he didn't want anyone to say anything to him. He was disappointed with himself and he felt that he had somehow reverted. He was dejected and felt distinctly that he was out of step, and he believed that on this particular night he knew the truth about himself ; that he was hopeless.

IX

CHAL found it difficult to enter into the conversations at the
fraternity house. He liked to hear the brothers discussing
football. He liked to talk of records on the track, and about
the possibilities of the basketball team. But he had a feeling that the others found little interest in the things which
he had to say, and naturally he became silent. On these
subjects which he understood and about which he might
have talked he forced himself to listen only. In the case of
conversations about other matters he was completely at a
loss to understand their attitudes and their philosophies.
The secretiveness behind some of the allusions and stories
concerning women he could not understand. He had never
been able to see anything strange or unusual about mating.
He had seen it all of his life among the hills, and to him it
was a part of nature ; a part of the scheme of things which
he had always thought was beautiful. There were certain
things which were natural ; certain laws. Though these
things had never been handed down to him as laws, everyone he ever knew had accepted them as such ; as a part of
the nature of things.

But he found that life at the University was just a pro-
jection of the strange attitudes of the white people who had
come into the Osage to live. He had learned about this
strange attitude toward sex from the little boys, but it had
never been clear to him. Little Indian boys never talked
about girls because girls were not a worthy subject for boys
who expected some day to be warriors. He had always

heard that girls and boys must live apart until they were old enough to be married, and that their marriage was arranged by their parents, and that's all there was to it.

But here at the University he heard jokes about marriage and about girls, and he couldn't see the point to them. He couldn't see why there was so much importance attached to such natural things, and why the brothers laughed and looked as though they were secretly enjoying something that was forbidden. When they talked about "chickens" he knew that they were talking about professional women, and he knew that they differed from "nice" girls, but he couldn't see why they talked so much about it. One time he attempted to take part in a conversation by commenting that he thought a certain coed had beautiful breasts in her evening gown. One of the older men who was "dating" this particular girl took exception to the remark and paddled him unmercifully at the next pledge court. After that he had remained absolutely silent during the conversations, and he felt more miserable because such things made him feel apart.

One time during the winter when the weather had changed temperamentally from balminess to severe cold, the ponds in the neighborhood of the University were frozen over. He had gone with a party of people, skating. He had been skating with a flushed-faced girl who seemed to enjoy the smooth gliding and the cold wind against her face as much as he did, and he was very happy that he could see so much in her face of the joy of speed and rhythm. She had stopped occasionally and had looked into a small mirror in order to fluff her hair and run a powder puff over her face, then resumed skating with more assurance.

They had been skating along at a terrific pace when she caught her skate on a small twig that had been frozen into the ice, and had fallen and slid for some distance. He re-

membered that she began fumbling with her skirts even before she stopped sliding, and had quickly pulled them down
and had begun to repair her hair before he could turn.   He
had skated up to her and remained silent.   He had felt
helpless and had begun cursing himself because he had nothing to say about her fall ; no words of regret or inquiry about
her disaster.   He had pulled her up and had felt that he
ought to express to her that he was very sorry, but he hadn't
been able to say anything.   Her face still had traces of her
furious blush, and he had misinterpreted that blush.   He
had believed that she was hurt, then he had a happy thought
and had smiled a little because he had thought that after all
he could be of some help.   He had smiled at her and said,
"You ought to wear heavy pants."   She had looked at him
quickly and he was still smiling ; then he remembered her
eyes seemed to have sparks in them as she looked at him
defiantly.   Then suddenly, after she had turned her attention to where the others were building a fire, had skated off
to join them.   And there she had remained the rest of the
afternoon.

He had wanted to skate with her again ; her grace and
the pleasure which she showed on her face, as she had sailed
along at his side gave him deep pleasure, but he understood
that there was something wrong and he humored her whim.
At least he supposed it was a whim ; anyway, he did not go
near her any more.

So he had remained silent when conversation turned to
girls.   The girls of the University were referred to as "nice"
girls and he preferred silence rather than make a mistake
about them.   But all the time he was attempting to be like
the others, and he was unhappy when he felt that he was
not like them.   One time he even ventured a remark when
the conversation in the smoke-filled room of the fraternity

house was on safe ground — conversation about "chickens," but he was miserable to find that his joke was pointless and that it fell heavily in the dead silence.

He could appreciate humor — the kind he had heard around the camps of the Osages. The manner in which they told jokes was not burdened with a sort of secretiveness, and they talked about such things just as they talked about anything else. He had heard many jokes about women and men around the camps, and he thought they were funny because they were about men of great dignity who, through amorous action, became ridiculous. Any joke about dignity made ridiculous was always funny and the plain language in which it was told seemed quite natural to him.

There was a campus tradition about a girl named Stella. The brothers at the house referred to her and the sorority to which she belonged was ashamed of the fact that she had been a member. Chal knew this through a sort of undercurrent of innuendoes, and he wanted to know what Stella had done, but he wouldn't ask anyone. He only knew that she had been expelled by her sorority and had gone back to her home on the plains in disgrace. Perhaps she had said things which were not approved, or had slipped out at night, or smoked cigarettes. He often wondered about this girl Stella, even though her expulsion had occurred several years before he came to the University.

He thought that the coeds were glorious creatures when he first came, but after a while he began to notice mannerisms which he didn't understand and he gradually lost interest in most of them. The older girls of the University held no fear for him as they did for other freshmen. In his simple, inherited philosophy, a woman who was not pretty or graceful in some physical way, was not to be considered, and he couldn't help feeling that ill-favored women were on the plane with all women and less important in the scheme of things than men. However, he worshiped beauty.

The activities of the University soon fell into routine. The football season came to an end, and then there was Christmas vacation. After that there were long hours of sitting in classrooms, listening to the drone of his instructors or sensing the weariness in their attitude toward the students. His grades were just good enough to qualify him for initiation, and he couldn't understand why the brothers warned him about them. He guessed that the instructors expected people to talk as much as possible, whether they knew anything about the subject or not, and he knew that he ought to have gone up to the instructors after class and talked with them. He didn't know what he might have talked about, but he had seen other students doing it and he supposed that it was the thing to do.

He couldn't see anything wrong about it and he would gladly have done the same, if he could have made himself do it. He tried to force himself to do it several times, but there was something about it that was not natural to him. He had inherited a definite appreciation of deception. His people had practiced deception in exactly the same way all life of the earth practiced deception ; in order to survive, either in war with enemies or for the purpose of food-getting. But the trouble was, of course, that he couldn't see the importance of pretending when the purpose was not important. He thought it was important to use deception in a game of skill, or war, and he might have practiced deception if he had ever become hungry. He couldn't see the importance of good grades, and it was quite the same to him whether he received good ones or very bad ones, and this, of course, only made the chasm deeper ; that chasm which divided him from the others.

Outwardly at least he attempted to live the life of an undergraduate to the full, but these attempts only made him more aware of his uniqueness. There was an organization on the campus which was called a "pep" organization, its purpose being to make demonstrations during football games. They called themselves the "Iron Men," and affected that which popular fancy was led to believe was the raiment of dock wallopers or stevedores, in varsity colors. Chal joined them after he stopped playing football, because the older brothers in the house had urged him to do so. Since he was not going to shine in football and bring honor to the fraternity, then he must go into campus activities and clutch with ever ready hands any honors that might be floating about the campus. To be an Iron Man was an honor and one had his picture in the yearbook. The fact that one belonged to such a patriotic organization as the Iron Men, one could list among the other honors scraped up for himself at the end of his senior year ; a list of honors that went under your picture in the yearbook.

The Iron Men were in evidence on the days of football games. They formed into long lines and carried paddles, and with hands on each others' shoulders, did a sort of prison lock-step as they repeated monotonously, "We're hard, we're mean." This demonstration with flashing paddles was supposed to fill the freshman who had forgotten his symbolic cap, with fear.

Chal marched with the Iron Men listlessly, and he could never bring himself to repeat the formula. The other members wondered what he was doing in their ranks, but their wonder was not greater than his. He couldn't understand what it was all about, much less get into the spirit. The student just in front of him on several occasions was a thin-bony-shouldered fellow with spectacles, and Chal could hear him repeat the words with a sort of sacred fervor and he wondered about this man. He watched his shoulder blades work under his tight fitting sweater, and he was fascinated by the back of his neck, which seemed too small to hold up his large head. Chal thought of him as a sunflower with its great bloom and thin stem. Sometimes when he looked at that thin neck closely, he had a desire to put his hand up and choke this fellow. An overwhelming impulse, which he hurriedly put out of his mind — perhaps it was like the desire some people have to jump from high places. One time he almost sweated, the desire was so intense, and he immediately looked away so that he wouldn't be tempted. He had nothing but the friendliest feeling toward this fellow, though he had never spoken to him.

Of course the campus had begun to talk of Blo. Blo Daubeney became a by-word, and Chal caught glimpses of her occasionally. He saw her dawdling about the campus, nearly always surrounded by several students, and at such times she was always the embodiment of vivacity. Every minute of her time was taken, he knew, but he had no desire to call her. He was not acquisitive, but possessive, and he thought of her as his own in the land of fantasy and let it go at that. She flashed into his consciousness at the oddest times, and at such times he felt tingling, even in his finger-tips, but he was satisfied to worship from afar, as though he had placed her with the Great Mysteries of his people. To his Indian mind there was little difference between the dream world and the world of reality, and he knew that beauty was usually in the dream world. Here was beauty and he worshiped it in the same way he had always worshiped the beauty which surrounded him, but this attitude was now confused with desire, and he became clumsy and sometimes unhappy. He had only to think of her, to hear her name, or see her, and his heart would sing but his face became a little more wooden, and no one could have guessed what was going on inside.   Sometimes the mere sight of her had the effect of sending him on a long walk to the river.

Sometimes the older boys at the house made him attend dances, and he usually saw her there.   Sometimes she was like silver, and sometimes she was like the Moon Woman in a blue mantle.   One evening he was waiting at the Pi house with one of the older men.   He was looking across the hall into a room where a girl and boy sat.   A fair-haired boy and a dark-haired girl.   They just sat and looked at each other, and smiled, talking intermittently in whispers. There seemed to be beauty there, and Chal was fascinated. The girl was not pretty, and her feet looked very big in her white shoes.   So big and white were her feet that they seemed to demand his attention.   Then he noticed that her ankles were thick, and her waist and the upper part of her body thin, but his attention was always drawn back to those white shoes, as though nature wished him to appreciate a whimsicality.   The girl's face shone with something that came from the depths, and the boy's face shone as well, and soon Chal forgot everything but the beauty he saw there. It gave him a strange happiness.   There was no insincerity, no boasting, never the expression of a face-going-somewhere-to-get-money, or eyes made cold by duty.   In his interest he almost forgot that he sat in the house where Blo lived. At first he had felt her presence, and had been a little nervous, but that had passed when he saw the faces of those two in the next room.

Then there was something like electricity in the air of the room where he sat and he felt the queer feeling in his stom-ach, and a great fear came to him, and he knew he had to fight something powerful within himself.   He would not look at the stairs, but watched the face of a boy who was standing and looking up, and he saw on that boy's face that Blo was descending. He watched the boy attempt to button a button on his coat that was already buttoned, then he saw him advance nervously. Chal arose with the rest of the people in the room. There was a communal force in the concentration of all eyes on the stairs, and he looked. There was Blo, advancing toward the boy who was her "date," and with widened eyes and her teeth gleaming, she reached for his hand. Everyone was standing now, and Blo made the rounds, speaking to everyone in the room, and her eyes seemed to say to the men, "How wonderful and virile and handsome you are." She approached Chal and he saw that her gown was red ; red, the color of the dawn, and to him came the picture of fire dancing. Then he seemed to lose all consciousness of everything about him, but suddenly he realized that she was looking back over her shoulder and smiling as she said, "Goo'bye." She said this to no one in particular, and Chal saw that her date had a fixed, ecstatic smile which he was probably attempting to subdue.

THE one telephone at the Chi house, in use constantly during the afternoons and evenings, rang imperiously for Chal. He heard Blo's voice. "Hello," it said, "this Chal Windzer ?"

"Yeah."

"Well, look, the girls are having some fraternity men over to dinner Sunday, and I wondered if you'd come — there'll be several others from your house."

"Yeah, I guess — certainly, I'll be a — glad to come — I — "

"Well, good, how are you — don't see much of you, still goin' out for football ? But that's no excuse for high-tonin' me, is it ?"

"No, I uh — I quit football — ah — "

"Well, that's too bad, maybe you were too good for 'em. Ever'body says you're good."

"I — it's not — "

"You'll come, won't you — Sunday — 'bye."

Chal slowly hung up the receiver, then went up to his room. He sat down by the window and it seemed that several minutes passed before he could subdue the queer feeling that suffused him. He got up, picked up his pencil, and said, "Dammit." He lay down on the bed and looked up at the ceiling.

There it was again. He had talked like a fool — guess she thought he was a fool, all right, talkin' that way. Why couldn't he talk like the others — the way they talked to girls over the phone — kid 'em along with cleverness. No wonder people never paid any attention to him — never formed groups with him as the center — never included him in anything. What the others did and said seemed easy enough, but try as he might, he couldn't imitate them. The things which were so important to other people and seemed unimportant to him, were difficult to imitate. He believed that they talked about things which were obvious.

Blo left the telephone thinking that she had done well, and and she had a sense of self-righteousness. The girls of the house had urged her through her well known popularity, to get more of the Chis to come to the Pi house, and she had done her part. She had done her part without the possibility of offending any of her admirers. Chal never had dates, and everyone would know that she had been asked to have him over. Thus they would know that she was not show-ing favoritism. As she prepared herself for an afternoon date, the thought came to her that she might have called

Jack Castle, but she knew that he would call eventually and it would be better to let him do it. The girls thought that Jack was not as nice as he ought to be. There were stories about Jack's big car being seen in front of a drab house on a dark street in the city. A house with stairs leading up to a closed door from the outside. To Blo the stories about Jack made him all the more thrilling and she thought she would like to have dates with Jack just to spite the old cats, if for no other reason.

At the dinner, Chal was Blo's special care. She hovered over him even more than the girls had set as the standard for the entertaining of guests. But he wouldn't talk. Of course, he was not completely silent, but he didn't talk as other people talked, and to this fact was due much of Blo's solicitude. She wanted him to have a good time, not only to please the girls, but she felt that his silence was a kind of challenge to her effectiveness. He might also be added to her list of admirers, and everyone knew that a girl couldn't have too many admirers on the campus. You sensed that other girls deferred to you, and you knew instinctively that the girls of your own chapter were secretly proud of you in the house and openly proud of you on the campus or at dances. The unit which was the sorority, somehow over-coming instinctive jealousies, and indicated either a step forward in the organization of society, the individual losing himself in the unit, or else just the influence of the herd instinct.

After the first clumsiness and the men had got seated without disarranging the fancy little gadgets on the table, they watched the president to see what utensil she was going to use first. The conversation began to flow with more freeness and with less consciousness, led by Classen, the football hero, who was recognized in the Pi house. There was soon a hum of conversation around the table, then the vying for the center of attraction between Nelson Newberg, who knew his own value, and Stub Classen, who was assured of his. Classen was certainly winning, and Nelson had to resort to loud laughter over a most trivial remark by Henny Sears in order to draw attention from Classen. Nelson's laughter was loud and he slapped his thigh in his forced merriment, not stopping until someone said, "What's the joke over there ?" But he paid no attention to the question and tapered off his laugh, pleasantly conscious that Classen was looking at him with interest and that he, Nelson, had the attention of the table.

Blo's presence, like an incipient intoxication suffusing Chal, he had forgotten himself for a moment. Of course Blo had kept up a constant chatter and this had relieved him of the burden of conversation, but he sensed that she was becoming tired of devoting herself to him alone, and had already begun to look about the table for her usual homage. About this time, Nelson had started his laugh.

Chal knew Nelson very well and he envied the ease with which he met people ; his glibness, even though it was just blackbird talk. But that long, forced laugh which was the signal that the limelight had been switched made Chal uncomfortable. He was filled with vicarious shame for Nelson and he wanted to look away and think of something else. He looked up when he heard other voices, and he noted that Nelson had won the attention at the table. He was smiling at Henny as she looked at her plate in mock embarrassment, while the others watched them.

"C'mon," Nelson said, "shall I tell 'em what you said ?"

"Nelson Newberg, I'll — " She raised her hand as

though she would strike him and he dodged in an exaggerated manner.

"Henny said — " continued Nelson, then looked at her and smiled.

"It's no fair — now — I didn't even say it."

Nelson went off into another sustained fit of laughter and again Chal wanted to be somewhere else, but he noted that none of the others seemed to mind Nelson's histrionics. In fact, they seemed to appreciate them.

Nelson tried hard to keep the attention of the table and Henny was not displeased, but the others soon tired of the show and turned to those beside them and began talking of other things, and Classen finally managed to get his end of the table back under his spell. Before the dinner was over, the men were getting back some of the usual assurance of the young male. Interest came back into Blo's face as she realized that her responsibility of entertaining Chal would soon be under the influence of the after-dinner environment. She began to feel that the center of interest had remained too long away from her glorious self, and she knew that she didn't have to resort to such crude maneuvers as those employed by Nelson and Classen to get it back either. She didn't even have to become vocal ; there were hundreds of little ways that were as instinctive as the manner of a female bird during the mating season, but more effective in Blo's case since they were under absolute control.

SPRING came to the campus with a warm softness that seemed to whisper. The days became drowsy and scent-filled, and couples appeared on the river road, strolling aimlessly. They carried sticks and played as they walked along ; as though time was not and there was nothing important in all the world. The freshmen who were qualified were duly initiated into the mysteries of their respective orders, and beamed with the consciousness of shining emblems on vests and shirtwaists.

Chal was filled with a vague but insistent yearning for something. In the classrooms he listened to the droning, soporific voices of the instructors but didn't know what they were saying. He dreamed most of the time, and looked out of the windows. His clothes became burdensome, and he felt sticky and uncomfortable. When he became too uncomfortable, he would walk out into the country by himself, but was ever careful to take paths leading through the pastures ; cow trails mostly, where he would not be seen. He didn't want people to know that he walked out into the country. He walked through pastures where the first green grass had begun to push up through the soil, and the redbuds begun to show along the ravines. The cardinals had begun to whistle cheerfully, and men, almost hidden by red dust, followed along the plowed furrows of their fields, their voices coming over the warm earth as they cursed listless mules. The words were unintelligible, and for that reason were a part of the pulsing of the earth, but Chal knew that these men were referring to their mules as descendants of female dogs, and telling them that they were crazy and damned and cockeyed.

Sometimes as he walked, the urge to pull off his clothes and trot came to him ; the desire to play the role of coyote, but he dismissed such desires now with shame, and when they were most disturbing he would murmur aloud to drown the unconventional thought, and he would dismiss the thoughts of his first months at the University in the same manner. He was more civilized now and more knowing, and he was ashamed of his recent past. Anyway, his mind

was occupied with dreams of another nature now. He was
not some animal or another person, but himself as he walked
along. He was himself in a land of fantasy wherein the
stupid things he did and the clumsy things he said in the
presence of Blo were forgotten. In this world of fantasy he
was an elegant man of the world and she was as he saw her
in reality. He could see her laugh in that devastating way
of hers at his sallies, and he always said the right thing and
did the right thing. Other men would come up to him
and stand in a circle while he talked. In this fantastic realm,
he had been chosen on the all-conference football team, and
had been mentioned for the all-American, and everyone said
that he carried his honors lightly.

Sometimes as he walked, oblivious to the trees, the scents
and the voices around him ; crawling through barbed wire
fences, climbing hills and crossing ravines mechanically, he
visualized himself as the outstanding star in a very important
conference game, and he saw his name in large black headlines. He couldn't dream fast enough to visualize all the
honors that came to him. He even visualized a great feast
and dance held in his honor by the Osages when he arrived
back home for Christmas. They had made a song and invented a dance especially for him, and they gave him a name,
but he couldn't decide what the name should be. As pleasant as the dream was, he decided to leave the Osage part of
it out. He didn't want to call attention to the fact that
most of his blood was of an uncivilized race like the Osages.
He believed that they didn't have any backbone, and he certainly wanted to make something out of himself.

His thoughts would become practical sometimes, and at
such times he was sure he was going to major in economics,
to prepare himself for business. He decided that he would
be a business man and amount to something in Kihekah.

It wasn't an Indian agency any more, but was growing into a thriving town and they said that the oil leases were becoming more and more exciting, as people came there from all over to bid for leases at the sales. Chal believed he wanted to be a substantial citizen in that community. Nelson need not worry because his father would put him into some sort of business, and Charlie Fancher would go into the store with his father, and Chal was sure that if he didn't go into some kind of business he would be like the other Osages.

Sun-on-His-Wings had gone back to the blanket, he had heard, and Running Elk was still wearing citizen's clothes, but loafed around the Oil Exchange pool hall. When he saw Running Elk Christmas-time, he was pretty drunk and had been drinking for some time they told him. But Chal knew that he wouldn't be like that ; he would be a business man and amount to something.

During these day-dreams he would lie on his back for hours. He could feel the chill still in the ground but he didn't notice it until the hour grew late, then the growing chill always served to remind him of the hour. On his way back he could see in the distance the bastard Gothic of the Administration Building thrusting itself out of the plains, and the white of the Law and Science buildings barely indicated by the gleaming among the green trees. There was something abrupt and startling the way the tower of the Administration thrust itself out of the low, curving Red Beds, and yet the distance gave it a certain harmony with the gentle curves of the landscape.

As the sun descended the Red Beds became more attractive, and in the distance the low hills became violet, just like the hills at home. The red became more vivid and beautiful in the last rays of the sun, and the red-tinted water of the ponds reflected the sun. The near landscape became rich and tranquil as the cold air crept slowly up from the valleys.

One evening when Chal got back to the house it was dark and the brothers had had dinner. He started up the stairs to his room but Chick Talmadge stopped him, "Say, Redtail, I wouldst have speech with thee." Chal stopped. "Say," said Chick, coming toward him, "I gotta date with the queen uh Sheba this sweet night, and methinkest, by God, I must hie me to the city that hath no heart and leave my flower to wilt, if I cannot employ thy friendship and brotherhood." Then Chick became serious.

"Say, no kiddin', I gotta date with the glorious Blo to-night, and damned if my guv'nor didn't call me and tell me to come pronto. May be back, see, and in that case you step out and I step in, but if I don't get back tonight, why — you know, show the little lady a good time."

Chal didn't answer and Chick went on. "You'll do — matter of fact, I want you. I don' want any uh the others — you're the only safe one around the house — not afraid of ole Redtail fleeing with the future Mrs. Talmadge." He passed on up to the telephone, then shouted back, "I'll call 'er and fix it up, and you're due at seven bells, hear?"

Chal undressed without realizing it, and was in the shower when Chick stuck his head in and shouted above the splashing, "It's all right — fixed it up," and disappeared. Chal's heart was singing. As he dressed he looked at his watch and saw that he had plenty of time, yet too much time, and again not enough. He wondered why he had a feeling that was something like a religious emotion when he thought of Blo. Of course it never occurred to him that it might be the tribal heritage of religion associated with beauty and dreams.

He walked past the Pi house five times before he got up

enough courage to go to the door and knock. As he stood at the door he kept whispering to himself the word, "extravaganza." There were certain words in English which fascinated him and he whispered them to himself occasionally when deeply stirred. He didn't know why he said words aloud to himself unless it was because they served as a kind of weight ; something practical and of the earth, to keep his spirit from floating away on the currents of his emotion. He liked especially the word "extravaganza" and as he waited he kept saying it to himself. He didn't know what it meant, but he didn't want to know — it was beautiful and satisfying and that was all he required of it.

The door was opened and Blo came out quickly, and taking him by the arm, said, "Howdy, how are you ?" Not giving him time to answer, she said, "I wanted to get away from the house. I saw you comin', so I thought I'd just come down." Chal was conscious only of the odor of sandalwood as they walked up the elm-bordered walk. He didn't know that she had cut this date with Henry Comstock and had given it to Chick ; that Henry was coming over to date one of the other girls and might see her, therefore knowing that she had lied to him.

They walked slowly up the walk in the soft spring air. Someone was playing a ukulele and the strains floated out across the street. A group of men passed and Blo raised her hand and said, "Howdy," and the men returned the greeting with eagerness. When they came to the Varsity shop corner, Chal knew that he ought to ask her to have a coke. When he did so, she refused, sacrificing the thrill of being seen and admired by everyone. Someone might tell Henry that they had seen her with another date, and she sure didn't want to make him mad at her.

They kept walking until they were on the road leading

to the river, but Chal had not realized that they had gone so
far until she said as though defensively, "I can't go to the
river." Chal stopped, then she added, "Oh, but we can go
on a little farther."

They walked along without talking. Chal was not
thinking, nor was he dreaming. For some time he was in
a trance, then he suddenly felt pain and was chagrined with
the realization that he wasn't saying anything to her. He
ought to talk to her, but he couldn't think of anything to
say. He looked at her face in the darkness and it seemed
to be calm and reposed, but even in the darkness he felt that
the expression which she usually wore was not there ; there
were no sparkling eyes and half-opened mouth. He wished
intensely he could say funny things to make her laugh, and
because he couldn't he was unhappy. He believed he could
talk with her tonight, all right, but he couldn't say the funny
things which people always said. He believed he could tell
her how the wind made the dust in the river bed look like a
smoke cloud ; about the moonlight on the tongues of water
crawling over the sand. He could talk about the Administration Building rising out of the plain, and making you
happy just to look at it, but he guessed, in fact he was sure, that
such things were not the things to talk about. He had never
thought of talking about them to anyone else, but for some
mysterious reason he wanted her to know about them. He
guessed she'd sure think he was crazy if he said anything
about them. Just walking along a sandy road in a mild
spring night was sufficient anyway, he finally concluded.

Blo wasn't aware of the spring night, nor was she aware of
Chal. She was wondering if that darn dressmaker would
make 'her red dress too short. Just like her — she'd be
willing to bet that it would be too short. It was the only
thing she had to wear to the Psi spring formal, and Walter

would be proud of her and the whole Psi chapter would re-volve around her.   She hoped Walter would give away most of the dances, as he sure couldn't dance, and her heart pained her as she thought of her silver slippers that he had ruined. Thinking of the silver slippers she remembered the scene with her father when she bought them, and how her mother had come to her aid.   Her father had said that they would "all go to hell in a hand basket."   Then her mind came back to Jerry and she wondered if he would tell Henry about her cutting a date with him.   She guessed he wouldn't.

She realized suddenly that she'd better come alive if she wanted Chal to make another date some time — he was a good dancer.

"Beautiful night, isn't it — penny for your thoughts," and she turned the full power of her smile up to Chal's face and raised her eyebrows, forgetting that it was quite dark. Chal tried not to smile, he too forgetting that it was quite dark.   If he smiled, she might see what was in his heart, but his happiness was too great and he turned to her and smiled a little, "Oh, I don' know — guess I wasn't thinkin'."   He felt that now was the chance to carry on with some trivial chatter, but he couldn't, and it seemed that Blo couldn't think of anything to say either.   Most of her conversation was based on the remarks of her many male companions, and was made up of what were known as "comebacks." When this base was lacking, she couldn't talk at all, espe-cially when she was so far away from the inspiration which the presence of other people, especially men, gave her.   Her silence annoyed her and she found herself not caring whether Chal made a date with her or not.   She had begun to be-lieve that she was in some way mistreated, but suddenly she had an inspiration and asked the time, "Oh," she said when Chal told her, "we gotta get back."

As they passed the Varsity shop on the way back she looked longingly at it and spoke gaily to some students lounging on the outside. When those students stared at Chal he became angry, and almost forgot to ask her if she wanted a coke. She refused again, but when they had gone a little way she said, "You know, I b'lieve I do want a coke now." And she thought, "I don't care if Henry does see me."

The room was full of students sitting at the tables. They pretended to be talking with each other, but they were really waiting to see who might come in, especially what girls might drop in with their dates. As soon as Blo and Chal entered, all eyes were upon them, and Blo's soul touched the heights. She greeted the room with a wave of her hand and walked toward a table in the corner which some students had just vacated. All eyes followed her to the table ; some with simple adoration, some with appreciation, and Chal, saw Carrington's eyes following her closely, and he thought they looked greedy.

Chal was embarrassed to be close to so much attention, and he knew that some of the eyes were upon him as well, but he didn't turn his gaze and his face was quite blank. He knew several of the students in the room but he failed to recognize them, and they immediately thought that they were being high-toned, because he was out with Blo Daubeney. This event added nothing to his popularity, but they might have had a different attitude had they known that he was manifesting the simplest, sincerest kind of embarrassment and shyness, attempting to remain as inconspicuous as possible. If he had stopped at several of the tables and had slapped backs and said in a booming voice, "Howdy, men, sure glad to see you !" and waved a genial hand to the people in the room, they would have accounted him a "good scout."

As they sipped their cokes, Blo glowed and Chal was almost happy again, but he was annoyed with himself because he had been too shy to speak to the people in the room. He hoped that Blo would not think him a "stick."

In her presence he did not think of his actions during the evening, but after he had said good night to her and had come into his own room he grew very bitter with himself. He did not go to sleep for hours that night, damning himself with the accusation that he would never be as other people were, and that he would never really be civilized. He was hot and uncomfortable under the covers as he tossed about in the bed, and just before he went to sleep he said to himself aloud, "I wish I didn't have a drop of God damn' Indian blood in my veins."

As the spring wore on he thought much about going home, but there was something which kept telling him that he must stay. The very atmosphere of the campus became lazy. Students loitered about the Varsity shop in groups and some of them cast off their coats and sat in the sun in their glaring white sleeves. During the afternoons, couples strolled up and down the walks, dropped into the shop for drinks, then loitered on their way home.

The brothers at the fraternity house sat on the porch and talked or played catch out in the yard. However, there was more studying than at most times of the year, and at night lights burned in windows around the campus until midnight and sometimes until morning as the time for final examinations approached. Mockingbirds came and sang persistently all day ; balancing on the top branches of trees or on telephone poles. Sometimes when Chal sat up studying his Latin, a mockingbird would sing from the tree outside his window and he would invariably become homesick. He would walk to the window and dream until he couldn't get his mind back to the dead world of Rome, no matter how interesting it was ; no matter how the words intrigued him.

The weather grew warmer ; almost too warm for comfort. The girls came to and from classes in cool ginghams and Chal liked to stand at the corner and watch them walking down the walk from the group of buildings. Almost daily he watched for Blo in her blue linen ; Blo coming from an eleven o'clock class, but invariably as she approached, always with some student or often with two or three, he would leave before she saw him, and walk slowly home.

In June he went home. Everybody seemed to be doing something. Charlie Fancher worked in the store and Nelson had a job in his father's office. He assumed a very important air, crossing and recrossing the street with a pencil behind his ear and papers in his hand. He would have a coke at the Blue Front, then pretend that he had to be some place immediately, but Chal knew of course that there was no rush about his going.

There were several dances and he attended, but he noticed that Sun-on-His-Wings was not there, and of course Running Elk didn't care for that kind of dancing. One night Chal asked Marie Fobus where Running Elk was and she said that she didn't know and added that they didn't invite him any more because he drank too much.

Everyone talked about oil. There was talk of anticlines, Carsonville sand, Mississippi lime, and the lease sales that now reached hundreds of thousands of dollars. There were many new faces in town and many new stores, and it seemed to Chal that almost every other man was a doctor, a lawyer, or an automobile salesman.

The summer was very hot and Chal was restive. He finally found Running Elk. He found him in the hospital after Running Elk had wrecked his very expensive roadster, and had been confined to the hospital for several weeks. He was just recovering from a case of delirium tremens and Chal thought that he had never heard anyone talk so crazy. One morning he went out to see Sun-on-His-Wings at the village but found him very uninteresting too. He stayed at the village and did very little outside of taking part in the dances and in the Peyote ceremonies. He just sat at the village all day, talking, except when he went down to the creek to water his horses. Chal was disappointed in his friends because it seemed that they didn't have any ambition. Their incomes were large and were getting larger as the oil production increased ; he couldn't see why they didn't have some ambition and get into some business.

Chal thought the little town was very dull and backward after the University. There was no one to talk with. He was the only person not doing something except the mixed-bloods and the fullbloods, but he believed that there wasn't much interest in them — he certainly didn't want to be like them. He knew that he ought to be doing something. Of course he had never in all his life done anything. Not even as a little boy when the little white boys were delivering papers or telegrams, or working in their fathers' stores and offices. It seemed to him that it was a disgrace to sit around and do nothing all summer. His ponies were out in the country, but no one rode horseback any more except the Indians, and many of them were buying cars.

Cars were the thing now. Jep Newberg had a new, shiny one, and Nelson was always boasting about it, and its possession in the family gave a certain new prominence of which he was actively aware. The Fanchers had a car as well, and several of the mixedblood families had bought very large ones.

The newcomers didn't have much of anything ; those who had come since Chal had left. They lived above stores and went about with expressions of incredulity in the midst of wealth and prosperity. They flocked around their hero, Jep Newberg, laughing at his most trivial jokes. Chal thought they were forever planning something ; some way to acquire some of the wealth which they saw on all sides.

John still drove the sorrel mares. He said he was 'fraid of gasoline and if he ever had the money he would buy a steamer — that was the car — no danger. He was very busy these days, too. He was excited about the way the town was growing and kept saying that the Osage council was not the council it used to be. He said they were too wishy-washy now, and the first thing they knew they were gonna do some damn' fool thing and tie up some of the oil royalties.

Chal talked with his father very little since his return, but for the first time in his life he began to see his father as something less than a hero. The first morning after his return his father had called the University "your school." The University wasn't a "school," it was a university, and was called the "varsity" by those who knew, and if anybody called it anything else it just showed they were not in the know, that's all, and not worthy of much attention. John had wondered if Chal had joined a "debatin' club," and if his "marks" had been good. Chal felt that it wasn't much use tryin' to explain to him.

However, with his father's wish in mind, he had gone to one of the meetings of the Solon society at the University. But he had gone only once, partly because of the attitude of people toward such societies, and because he had found the meeting very uninteresting. For instance when he had mentioned that he would join such a club, some of the brothers at the house had laughed with derision, but others had said that it would be another activity for the old frat. They used the word "frat" with derision, because everyone knew it was passé. The evening he had gone to the meeting he was introduced to everyone, his introducer making him uncomfortable by keeping his hand on his shoulder all the while. Then he had sat and listened to the debate between the Blues and the Reds. He attempted to understand what it was all about but he was quite confused and a little annoyed with himself. This attitude soon changed to disgust when he thought of what Jack Castle had said about such societies.

Serious-faced debaters arose and talked ponderously with their chins stuck out consciously, he thought, and made every statement as though the existence of the world depended upon its self-evident truth. Then they walked with dignity off the stage as though they had said the last word on the subject.

One morning he and his mother were alone. They were sitting together in the front room, and after a very long silence she said, "You go back next fall, don't you?" He looked up at her. She looked so fresh and sweet sitting there, with the deep lines in her dark face, and her large eyes that were black and moist, like the eyes of a doe. He hadn't seen her with her blanket and moccasins since he had returned, and the ugly beads which she used to wear around her neck were absent. There was a great change and he wondered why he had not noticed it until now. Her room was different, too. He noticed that she had hung his pictures, taken when a little boy, on the walls. On her table were two books and a University bulletin. He didn't remember that she had ever read a book before, though she had been graduated from the Osage Mission. He noticed that the bulletin had been used more than the others. It all came to him very suddenly as he sat there. She was doing this for him. She was attempting to be what he might desire her to be, silently, in her Indian way. She had read that bulletin carefully, he would bet, so that she might know about this place where her son had gone.

A wave of love came over him and he had a queer feeling around his eyes ; that distinct feeling that always presaged tears when he was a little boy. He looked away quickly so that she couldn't see his face, but she was looking at something before her ; or perhaps at nothing.

They sat for some time thus. Then she spoke softly, looking straight ahead :

"They talk of war in the white man's — in the papers."

Chal thought, "Has she started reading the papers ?" He said, "I don't guess the guv'mint will fight the Germans — just talk, I guess." He wondered why he had used the word "guv'mint" in the old way of the reservation. He guessed it was because that word had always been associated with authority outside of the reservation ; that potent thing which controlled the destinies of Indian agents, of school children, and controlled the payments. He knew he ought to say "our government," or "the United States."

His mother continued : "Your father says that Mr. Bryan will see that there is no war with — those — other — "

"The Germans ?" Chal supplied hastily. He wanted to say that he thought that his father was silly, making so much of Bryan ; thinking he was a great man because he said a lot of pretty things. He didn't know why he thought this, as he didn't know much about Mr. Bryan except what he heard his father say.

"Your father says this thing," his mother said, still looking in front of her, "but I believe that Mr. Bryan cannot stop a war with his tongue."

Chal was surprised. Here was his mother really having an independent opinion. He gave her a quick look. He would soon hear what she really had on her mind.

She spoke again : "You can ride good, and your father says you have a good eye with guns, and your horses are good too, I believe."

A peculiar kind of pride came up in Chal and he felt quite important suddenly. Then he remembered the brothers at the fraternity house had said that probably there would be no cavalry in the war if the United States went in. He enjoyed a deep, hereditary emotion, and he forgot his mother's naïveté in the thrill that came over him. He got up and walked a few paces, then stood and looked down at his mother, straightening himself and throwing out his chest, "I shall fly in the air, like a bird," he said with assurance. Up to that moment he had not thought much about the war, and had thought of flying as a very desirable thing but not with any hope of ever doing it. As he stood there, his heart swelled as he visualized the papers with his name among the other heroes of the air.

X

OUT from town about ten miles were the remnants of a ranch. One which John had started during the time when there had been great enthusiasm among the mixedbloods about cattle. Cattlemen leased large areas of grassland from the tribe and brought in cattle by the thousands, and this inspired some of the mixedbloods, and they also had made leases and stocked the grass with cattle. Like John, however, there was that certain touch which was necessary to make the business profitable, and they failed.

There were a few buildings left, surrounded by fields, which during wet years produced corn, but during dry years produced nothing more than horseweeds and cockleburrs. The three-hundred-and-twenty-acre nucleus of this ranch John had filed on as his and his wife's homesteads. It was still called "the ranch," though a tenant farmer year after year plowed the sandy fields, planted corn, made a hay crop from the natural grass, then sat in the shade until the corn was ready to gather.

Chal kept his horses here now. One morning when he was very restless he decided to go out and see his horses. He could walk out very easily, but he was ashamed of walking; people might think he was crazy walking out to the ranch, and someone would be sure to see him. He didn't want to ask his father to take him out with the team and buggy. After several days of pacing up and down the room, he decided this morning to go out and stay at the ranch for a few days. His father, who had been talking about oil and the guv'mint as usual, looked up when he heard Chal's statement, then resumed talking.

Chal set out afoot, but he did not take the road. He slipped into the postoaks back of the house and went out across the hills. When he had climbed to the prairie through the blackjacks he suddenly had a feeling that this was what he had wanted. On his way the blackjacks caught at his clothing and he remembered how he used to play that they were the enemy ; how he had run through them, dodging and whooping to scare them, and occasionally gashing one with the hatchet which he carried in his belt. As he walked, the thought of his boyhood didn't disturb him to-day ; he wasn't ashamed and it didn't seem so crazy after all.

Standing there at the fringe of trees where the prairie began, it seemed that the world was filled with meadowlark singing, but he could hear the weak, persistent voice of the dickcissel, and could see them swaying on the tops of weeds.

He stood for a moment, then backed up against a great postoak. It was an unconscious action and he didn't know why he had done it. For some time he stood there absolutely motionless, thinking of nothing in particular but looking out over the emerald prairie. A coyote came trotting down the ravine that led through the blackjacks, stopping occasionally to test the air currents. "I've got the wind," Chal thought. Then he realized that he had on a white shirt and became slightly worried. Then he smiled to himself to think that he placed so much importance on the possibility of a coyote's seeing him. It occurred to him that he was being very silly, but he was enjoying the whole situation immensely.

It was an old dog coyote and remnants of his last winter's coat hung ragged and matted from his neck. He stopped and nosed in the grass then sniffed the ground like a setter.

He started to trot off, then changed his mind and came back to a tuft of grass and re-examined it. This time a meadow-lark flew up, then fell to the ground and made a queer little noise, and started flopping as though helplessly. The old coyote stood with front legs apart and watched the apparently wounded bird, then nosed in the grass tuft with care and energy. His nose found the eggs and he was busy for minutes eating them, then he turned the nest over and examined it with vague hope of finding more eggs. His pointed nose was yellow from his meal and Chal laughed silently. He gave his nose two ineffective swipes with his tongue, then trotted toward the place where the mother bird had made her stage fall. She flopped and made a sound like a young bird, but the coyote knew the trick, and she flew off on sound wing.

The coyote half turned and looked intently across the prairie, then fell to his belly in the grass and Chal could see only the tips of his ears, made translucent by the sun. Chal watched the horizon where the coyote was looking. He saw an object moving along the prairie ; the crown of a Stetson hat. The rest of the hat appeared, then the head of a rider, and later a horse and rider came into full view. The horse was foxtrotting, and the cowboy sat with his hands on the horn. They passed within a few yards of the coyote and Chal but the rider was looking straight ahead.

When they had passed, but not quite out of sight, the coyote became nervous, got up and trotted down the ravine looking back over his shoulder. Finally he stopped and looked back just as the horse and rider went out of sight over the next swell in the prairie. Chal stepped out from the tree and the coyote ran into the canyon looking over his shoulder. Chal was suffused with happiness, and he felt that he should like to make up a song about that coyote.

As he walked along he kept thinking about that coyote and the song that one could make about him. For instance, when he was nosing the eggs ; that could be indicated by single drum beats, and when he was hiding, foxtrotting, and running, different rhythms would indicate these actions, and he believed that the song certainly ought to end with a whoop indicating the coyote going out of sight. He believed it would make a good song to dance by.

He found his pinto with a "grass belly" ; round and sleek — round as a barrel. When he caught him up and rode him he sweated all over, and was flecked with sweat-foam ; covered with sweat-foam from just going a mile at a trot.

The next morning he saddled up and told the tenant that he was gonna see if there was any fence needed fixin'. He didn't have any intention of riding the fence. He had learned long ago to have a purpose, and that a practical one, to hide his purposelessness. He rode out over the prairie and he could feel the springiness of the ground through his pony. He put the pony into a gallop and he was soon sweating. The acrid odor of the sweat and the sweat-wet leather, with the creaking of the saddle, filled him with emotion and he wanted to do something about it, but it just bubbled and wouldn't flow over and leave him. He put the pony into a run, but he seemed very slow with his great grass belly, and his breathing was labored.

Chal stopped under a tree and allowed the pony to blow, then got off and stretched himself on the ground, lying on his back. Everything seemed so quiet. He couldn't even hear a meadowlark or the distant cawing of a crow but he guessed it was because the pinto was making too much noise with his breathing. The sun seemed to go out like a candle suddenly, and he was enveloped in a lavender shadow ; the shadow of a cloud above. The clouds were moving across

the very blue, sky, and their whiteness, their cottony whiteness, made the sky seem bluer.   As he looked at the blue
of the sky he thought of the blue mantle worn by the ma-
donna on one of his old holy cards.   Then he thought of
his dream woman — the dream woman in the blue mantle
who used to lead him by the hand into regions of fantasy,
who guarded him from danger, and snuggled his head on her
breast when he was a little boy.   As he thought of his boyhood dreams he wondered why he used to call her the dream
woman.   He didn't know even now, since he had sense
enough to analyze things.   He smiled — he sure must have
been crazy when he was a kid.

He shut his eyes and began to think of the conversation
with his mother about flying.   He didn't visualize the ships
he would fly nor his companions, but thought of himself as
a great hero.

The pinto snorted and Chal opened his eyes but remained
motionless ; the dream vanishing like a cloud shadow.   He
was suddenly alert.   The pinto was looking intently toward
the west with ears forward and without moving, and Chal
sat up and looked in that direction.   He saw a man walking
across the prairie and he was as surprised and mystified as
the pinto.   He wondered who could be walking across the
prairie with all those Texas steers on the range.

The figure was tall and carried a stick, and little puffs of
smoke came from a black pipe.   A man walking across the
prairie was an unusual sight, and Chal felt that everything
alive within sight must have stopped whatever it was doing
to watch this strange thing.   There was something pre-
sumptuous about it ; something outside the conventions, and
the prairie world seemed to be caught at some sort of dis-
advantage, and didn't know exactly what to do about it.   A
band of steers stopped grazing and gazed, and high in the

air a red-tail hawk circled over this strange, horseless figure in this immensity of undulating emerald.

The man came up to the tree and said, "Hello," then Chal recognized him as Mr. Granville, of the University. Chal was embarrassed as though this tall, thin-legged man striding across the prairie had known about his dream-thoughts. He had a feeling that he had been caught.

Mr. Granville sat down and took off his hat and Chal felt uncomfortable. He felt that he would be expected to say something and because he knew that he wouldn't know what to talk about he felt vindictive toward this man. He had studied geology one and two under Mr. Granville at the University, but had never spoken more than a half dozen words with him, though he was one of the few instructors who really interested him. In fact, he fascinated Chal with his beautiful words; English that flowed softly and was almost lyrical. At least Chal thought it lyrical when compared with the voices of other people. Because of this and because of Mr. Granville's reticence and his queer actions, Chal had been drawn to him. They said at the University that he was queer because he took long walks by himself, wouldn't accept dinner invitations, and lived by himself in an old stone house with just an old housekeeper. Students laughed at him because he was an Englishman, and they didn't know what he was talking about most of the time. He wore short pants like the old knickerbockers the boys used to wear, and gay stockings, and his shoes were thick-soled things. Students thought he was crazy because he rode a bicycle to classes. In fact, everyone on the campus made fun of him except the advanced geology students, and they seemed to defer to his opinions.

And of course there were all kinds of stories about him. Some said he had been in the war and was a deserter, and others said he was an English slacker. And finally the story got about that he was some kind of a prince or dook or somethin' incognito. Inevitably, there was the talk that he might be a spy.

He and Chal sat in the shade of the lone blackjack for some time in silence. Mr. Granville looked intently across the prairie to the hills across the creek, where there were several oil derricks, apparently unaware of Chal's presence, and Chal sat wondering what he should do ; what one of the brothers at the University would do in a case of this kind ; he wanted to do what he thought ought to be done. But there was nothing forced upon him and they just sat. The pinto having recovered his breath, started cropping grass, trailing his reins but careful that he didn't step on them.

The red-tail hawk circled down closer as if he would make sure about this unusual animal that strode so arrogantly across the open prairie. He circled even closer and gave a weak scream, as though he had made up his mind to resent that strange animal's presence. Mr. Granville looked up, watched the circling bird for a second, then said, "I say, Wendzah, that is the buteo borealis, — the red-tail, is it not ?"

A thrill came over Chal. Certainly it was his beloved buteo borealis, the red-tail, but — but — who would have thought that anyone else could have been interested in the fact besides himself. And that was the way to pronounce "borealis," was it ? "Yeah — yes," he said, "that's the red-tail." He was filled with pleasure and he wanted to go on talking about the red-tail hawk ; about his habits, and about the things he himself had seen him do, but he remained silent. He expressed very badly this feeling by getting to his feet, and moving aimlessly forward as though he would get a better view ; by putting his hand in his pocket and taking out his knife, then putting it back again. He wanted to tell Mr. Granville that the biological survey didn't know what it was talking about when it said that the red-tail ate only field mice. But he felt ashamed of the disturbance on his inside and sat down again. Mr. Granville was the first person he had ever talked with, except the Osages, who hadn't placed all big hawks under the title of "hen hawks," and all smaller ones under the title "chicken hawks." He wanted Mr. Granville to stay there, even if they didn't say a word.

Mr. Granville, still looking at the graceful circles of the red-tail, said, "Graceful beggar — dare say we shall be flying without motors some day — taking advantage of the air currents, sort of thing."

"Turkey buzzar' — that is, vultures are even more graceful," said Chal, "and they can fly for hours without moving their wings. I've seen them — " He was talking too much and he became embarrassed again.

"Really. Yes, I think I've noticed that. Pardon me, you have seen them do what ?"

Chal was reassured. "I was goin' to say that I've seen 'em rise from fence posts without moving their wings — into the wind, of course."

"I say, that is flying, isn't it — or rather, one should say sailing, really. Yes." Mr. Granville lit a match, inverted his slender-stemmed, round-bowled pipe, and sucked audibly until smoke came, then he righted the bowl and clutched his bony knees again.

Chal was more fascinated than ever. Mr. Granville didn't have that attitude instructors usually have toward undergraduates. The thought that there was any distinction was not even in the back of his mind, he believed. He hadn't asked a single question — personal question, and in turn had made no explanation.

Mr. Granville waved his stick. "Those hills remind one of Devonshire a bit, yet there is something here which Devonshire hadn't got — this is wilder." He looked at Chal to see if he might have misinterpreted the word "wilder," then continued, "Perhaps more natural ; in the primal state — I — I — don't like the word virginal when applied to nature — dare say one should say 'untouched.' "

To Chal's mind came a picture he had seen of English countryside but he didn't know where Devonshire was. He liked the name as it sounded quite foreign, but he didn't want to be embarrassed by not knowing anything about the subject. He had been embarrassed many times by people talking about subjects which he knew nothing about ; people who finding that he knew nothing about the subject, assumed almost insulting attitudes, explaining to him in detail when he didn't want to hear about it at all. But Mr. Granville said no more about Devonshire and they sat saying nothing. The shade of the tree moved in closer and closer from the northwest and was soon circling its feet. The sun was very hot and the pinto began to stamp flies and throw his head in desperation.

Chal arose. He didn't know what to say about the noon meal at the ranch house, though he certainly wanted Mr. Granville to come over. He saw Mr. Granville take out his watch and look at it, then he turned to Chal, "It's noon, and I had no idea what the time was." He pointed his stick toward the derricks across the creek, "One might go straight across from here to reach the house, isn't that right ?" Chal stood silent. He didn't know what house he was talking about. Mr. Granville looked at him and then explained,

"You see, the I.R.O. people have a little house over there which I believe they call a clubhouse — I'm stopping there. I'm doing a little work for them during the vacation — sub-surface." He looked at Chal as though he felt he had done all the explaining necessary by one geologist to another. Chal thought this would be a good time to warn him about the cattle, but he decided to wait, and instead he said, "I'm going back to the ranch, and I certainly would like you to come and have dinner with me — we call the noon meal dinner." That fine point of etiquette as to which meal was to be called dinner had not yet been definitely settled in the blackjacks by civilization's representatives.

"Why, yes, how jolly — which way do we go ?"

Chal caught the pinto and started over the hills to the ranch, leading him by the reins. Mr. Granville fell into step with him and said, between the frying and bubbling in his little black pipe, "These pintos," raising his stick to indicate Chal's pony, "but after all, I believe you call them paints, are quite beautiful. I was just wondering if the white ancestor — and they must have had a white ancestor — was not quite a well-bred Arab."

Chal thought, "This fellow certainly thinks of everything — sees everything." No one had ever wondered about the pinto, as far as he could remember — he was just a pinto. Then he said, "I guess he is," then he had an inspiration, "most of the mustangs came from Spanish horses and I s'pose Spain musta had Arab stock."

"Quite." They walked along in silence for some time, then, "Your people got their horses from the Spanish or from Spanish-speaking people, I imagine."

Chal wasn't sure that he liked that "your people," as though Mr. Granville were placing him in a different cate-gory ; identifying him with that which he had begun to believe was backward and uncivilized. "I think they did," Chal said. "They have two names for horses : one name from the word 'caballo' and the other from the name 'Kiowa.'"

"How interesting. Possibly their first horses were got from the Kiowas, and they called them, naturally, by that name, and very likely they heard the Kiowas call them 'caballo.' Very interesting." He stopped and picked up a handful of sand. They had come into a road where the wagon and buggy wheels had cut deep into the sandstone, and the ruts were filled with sand. Mr. Granville looked intently at the sand in the palm of his hand then he said, "I say, this must be Elgin sandstone here." He looked around at the hills. "Yes, I'm quite sure it is." Chal noticed that he made the "g" hard in Elgin.

As they approached the ranch house, Chal grew a little nervous. He had always been clumsy about introducing people — he had always thought of it as a rather silly formula. When you walked into an Indian lodge or house, you said "how," saluted by touching hands, and sat down. Every time someone said "glad to meet ya," it made him want to look at the floor.

They walked into the front door and Mrs. Carroll came in from the kitchen wiping her hands on her apron. It seemed to Chal that she was forever wiping her hands on her apron. Color came to Chal's face as he went through the formality of introduction : "This is Mr. Granville — he's a professor at the University — Mrs. Carroll." Mrs. Carroll looked at Chal apologetically, as though she very much wanted his support. "Mercy, Chal, I didn't know you was gonna bring a stranger home, er we mighta had somethin' differ'nt." She approached Mr. Granville, shook hands, and said, "I'm gladta make your acquaintance," and Mr. Granville said, "How do you do." She straightened a little lace thing on the back of one of the chairs and drew it up. "Have a cheer, and make yourself t' home, if yu c'n find room." The room was a large one.

Cal Carroll came in and Mrs. Carroll withdrew. He purposely ignored Mr. Granville. "Chal, want y'r pony t' have some corn?"

"Yeah, guess so — oughtta be hardenin' up a little."

"Verge 'lowed you would — he's done fed 'im."

"Mr. Carroll, this is Mr. Granville from the University." Mr. Granville smiled and nodded his head, and Cal advanced and shook hands, saying, "Gladta meet yu, Mr. Canwell." Cal took off his hat and hung it on the rack, then sat down heavily. He looked up at Mr. Granville, "Whur didja come from this mornin'?"

"I walked over from the I.R.O. field."

" 'Lowed maybe ya had — didn't see no horse, an' they hain't been ary buggy along the road this mornin'. Didja come along the south fence?"

Mr. Granville looked at Chal, then he said, "I came straightway across the prairie." Chal knew that Cal was going to warn him about walking across the prairie and he was glad to be relieved of the responsibility, even though it might indicate that he had been careless about not having told him before.

"Reckon Chal's told you about crossin' the prairie 'mongst cattle, thataway?"

Chal spoke up. "I meant to tell you that it's dangerous, walkin' across the prairie."

"Oh, really, how stupid of me. Yes. Of course, fools and angels, you know." Cal looked at Mr. Granville intently, then got up and started toward the kitchen. He looked back over his shoulder and said, "Yu fellers'll want

to wash up a little, reckon — the woman's about got somethin' fixed."

The table was full of food ; very good, rich food. The
"meat" which was the fat bacon of last winter's kill, lay in
yellow grease, and the mashed potatoes still had their eyes,
looming in the flaky whiteness. Cal fell to work, but Mrs.
Carroll seemed too solicitous about the company to eat. The
smaller children and Verge, the shifty-eyed son, ate with
their heads lowered, just above their plates, while Emma, the
sixteen-year-old daughter, handled the plates with unaccustomed tenderness and an assumed grace. She swished back
and forth between the stove and the table. Chal saw that
she had run upstairs to put on her shoes for the occasion, but
they only accentuated the chigger-bitten, thick legs, and evi-
dently she had made a hurried pass at her face with some
cheap powder, while looking into the cracked glass upstairs.

When the sharpness of hunger had been dulled, the heads
rose from the plates ; the eaters began forking at segments of
apple pie in the center of the table, and passing the sorghum
jug. Emma took a long hickory stick with ribbons cut
from a newspaper tied to the end, and began waving it over
the table to keep the flies away. Chal became nervous. He
knew what was on the minds of the Carrolls. They would
scarcely refrain from starting a barrage of questions as to
Mr. Granville's past, present and future, and he knew exactly what the first question would be. Cal would say,
"Whur d'yu live whin yer at home ?" and from then on a
regular series of questions, prefaced with "I reckon," "I 'low,"
or "thought mebbey." There would be many questions
with wearisome obligations attached. He felt that they
usually showed more than ordinary respect for him and
might refrain from asking many questions, as Mr. Gran-

ville was his guest.   But Mr. Granville's English and the fact that he had walked there that morning across the prairie, besides the fact that he was "kind 'ee a furrin feller," would be too much for them.

Chal had never felt this way about other people he had brought out to the ranch, as they could usually take care of themselves and really liked it ; liked talking about themselves and strutting what they believed to be their superiority. He remembered the time that Nelson Newberg and Charlie Fancher had come out quail hunting with him and he had had a difficult time getting them back to the field.   But Mr. Granville was the kind of victim he felt himself to be on many occasions.

He watched the progress of the dinner and he decided that as soon as the inevitable apologies for the food were made by Mrs. Carroll, he would say that they had to go — that they had to do something or other.

Then Cal stacked his knife, fork and spoon on his plate and pushed it from him, took a toothpick out of the hob-nailed container, looked at Mr. Granville and said, "Whur d'ya live whin yer at home ?"   Chal was surprised at the easy manner with which Mr. Granville accepted the question.

"Oh," he said smiling, "I am an Englishman — I live in England."

"Weh-ull," said Mrs. Carroll.

Cal knowed he was right.   He knowed that feller was a furriner the minute he seen him — couldn't hardly fool him.   He said, pushing back his chair, "Le's go in th' other room."   In that one sentence Chal read the beginning of what he had feared, and he saw that the words "Englishman" and "England" had so affected Mrs. Carroll that she had completely forgotten the apology about the food.

As they sat in the front room, Chal's nervousness grew. He knew they couldn't leave for a while yet — not until the men went to work, and it was only just past noon. Cal pulled out some chewing tobacco, cut a piece off with his knife, rolled it around in his mouth for a second, and said, "Raise purty good crops whur you live ?" Chal almost sank in his chair and he was afraid to look up, so he kept looking at a knot-hole in the floor.

"Fair, I should say, though you know that we should starve if you people of the United States, Australia, and Canada didn't feed us."

Mr. Granville anticipated Cal's next question. "You see, England is a small island, and we can't raise enough food for our people, so we must import it. Of course we have no maize — corn, you know — at least, very little."

Cal felt a little superior because he was an American, "Reckon mebbey your people is lawyers, or somethin' thataway." Mr. Granville smiled, "No, I'm afraid that my people are not much at working."

The talk went on and Chal began thinking of something else. He was resigned, and he felt some relief as well. Apparently Mr. Granville could take care of himself — much better than he could in such circumstances. As the conversation droned on, he thought of Devonshire ; he thought it must be a very nice place, but the Osage was untouched, and Devonshire wasn't. He guessed there must be a lot of farms, like there were in Kansas. His thoughts jumped from place to place, and the conversation became only a sound, then suddenly he became conscious of it again. Cal was talking, and he knew that Cal had been talking for some time. That was clever of Mr. Granville to get Cal to talk rather than answer questions. He looked up at Mr. Granville's face and saw that he was interested, then he looked at Cal's face and noticed that he was moved by his own recital.   Mrs. Carroll was sitting there with her bosom curving out over her stomach where her rough hands were folded, and her feet, in a manure-stained pair of her husband's offcast shoes, barely touched the floor.   Cal was saying :

"But an Injun won't hardly never tell you no lie.   If he says he'll do somethin' er other, he'll do er.   Harris didn't have no contrac' er writin' of no kind, cause he knowed he could trus' ole Sassy Chief.   Uh course, ole Sassy Chief putt up the money, and they's to go halfs.   Got the money th'ough the office somehow, reckon — they was a split som'urs.

"I'se a young feller that had jist come over into the reservation and found me a job with Harris.   They's about six of us boys, ridin' an' doin' one thing another 'round th' ranch. Ole Sassy Chief come out oncet or twicet lookin' 'round at the cattle doin' the summer.   Reckon he was th' first Injun I'd ever saw.   He was kind'ee a proud-lookin' feller when he forked a hoss.   He allus had a eagle feather a-stickin' in the top uh his head an' it made 'im look about seven foot tall.

"Well, it come August an' Harris called us boys in : 'Boys,' he says, 'I wantcha t' go out tomorrow and cut out about two hunderd steers and take 'em off down som'urs in the strip country and lose 'em.'   I seen 'im wink at the foreman.

"Well, we'us ready t' ship and ole Sassy Chief comes out with a little banty-legged white feller from th' office, and we strung 'em out and uh course counted only eight hunderd. Whin we got 'em rounded up, Harris an' ole Sassy Chief come a-ridin' up, and the little white feller from the office set in tuh doin' some figgerin'.   Harris lit into us, a-cussin' us about they bein' only eight hunderd head instid of a thousand, but uh course we kep' our traps shet. The ole Injun didn' say nothin', but jist sat his hoss lookin' at the cattle.

"Well, we drove to Elgin th' nex' day, and they brought a good price, though I heer'd Harris say that he wasn't gonna ship tell the nex' month — he said that t' the little white feller, so's the Injun could hear 'im. Then was th' high price — see the p'int? 'Cause nex' month, in September, the price went purty low — too many cattle on th' market. But Harris went intuh the Agency and give ole Sassy Chief his share of th' market price for September, on eight hunderd head. Uh course, we shipped the whole shebang in August — one thousand head. Reason why I think they musta had it fixed some way er other, them sales musta showed on the bill uv ladin' er whatever it is that shows about th' time shipped an' how many.

"Well, sir, ole Sassy Chief never knowed the differ'nce. But next year Harris went intuh business by hisself.

"Now, thatsa way Daniel Webster Harris got 'is start, an' I reckon now he's wuth a million dollars. He's in th' oil bizness now too. I seen him th'other day whin I'se in town, and I walked right up to 'im and shuck han's with 'im. He was makin' some kind uh p'litical speech on thuh corner. They's lotta people 'round 'im, but whin he seen me he called me Cal, 'Hello, there, Cal,' he says, 'you ole dog coyote, you,' he says. We stood thur and talked — him a-holdin' mah arm. Reckon he's one uh the smartest men in thuh country, an' shore would like tuh see him git to be guv'nor."

Chal grew hot all over and he wanted to say something. He was on the verge of saying something, but after all he supposed that it was smart of Harris. That was business.

But in this case he knew the rest of the story, and that was what he wanted to talk about. He didn't want Mr. Granville to be under the impression that Indians were so stupid. He knew they didn't have any backbone about business, but he knew they sure weren't stupid. He remained silent and was afraid to look up from the floor. He remembered the story. Wolf had told it at the village many times, and even though Wolf was the type of Indian who was always against everything and hated all white men, Chal knew that the story was true. Saucy Chief knew how many cattle there were and he knew that they had been hidden. He also knew where they had been hidden, because he had followed the trail afterward. He had not been suspicious before the count because he believed that a word was sacred, and the word of Harris had been given him. But after the count he had returned and followed the trail, and had come upon the cattle. There were two cowboys guarding them, but of course they hadn't seen Saucy Chief. Saucy Chief had sat on his horse, hidden by the blackjacks on a hill north of Pond Creek, and had watched the herd on the trail to Elgin the next day.

But Saucy Chief was a chief — that's what Chal wanted to tell Mr. Granville. It was below his dignity to talk like a woman to the agent, and it was against his religious beliefs as a Peyote worshiper to seek revenge. But he knew all about the matter. They said that Mr. Harris came to the village and had urged him for hours to continue the partnership the following spring. But he just sat and listened, looking at the hills, then had said "No."

Chal came back to the conversation again, and Cal was telling Mr. Granville how old Saucy Chief was later burned to death in his house in the village, because some white settlers had heard that he had much money there. As Cal talked he looked at his wife significantly. "En' I got a idee that I knowed one uh them fellers what had a hand in it too — useta work with 'im, but I ain't callin' no names."

"This has been a very interesting — I — I — thank you for the pleasant afternoon," Mr. Granville said as he arose. Chal arose and they left the house. Cal got his hat and started out the door to the barn. "Purty nice feller," he said to his wife, "fer a furriner — kind'ee a slow feller — he didn't say nothin'.'"

As Cal walked to the barn there was an unaccustomed spring in his step. The tobacco in his cheek had a sweeter taste. That feller had sat there and never opened his mouth — lettin' his pipe go out, listenin'. Cal felt that there had been something romantic about his obscure life after all ; he felt distinctly that there had been somewhat of glory in it.

Many white men who came into contact with the Plains Indian had felt that glory in the very contact ; reflected glory which had set them to strutting. Cal was not the least important of these as he went to the barn to hook up the mules.

Chal walked with Mr. Granville, leading his pinto. They were silent. Mr. Granville kept inverting his pipe and lighting it with distinct sounds ; a bubbling, a frying, and the sound of air passing through his nostrils. He would forget that he had lit it, and strike another match, place it to the bowl, discover that the pipe was lit, then throw the match away, never losing his long stride. Chal felt pushed to keep up with him, especially in his high-heeled cowboy boots, and he could feel a blister coming on his heel.

They went along the south line of fence ; along the fringe of blackjacks. When they were almost to the creek, Mr. Granville stopped. "I say, Wenzah, you know it is not really necessary to go along with me — that is, I hope you don't feel obliged — of course I shall be glad to have you."

"Oh, that's all right — I can ride back and I don't mind the walk."

"If you really want to, of course. I should like to have you stop with me a little while at my digs, if you'd like."

Chal wanted to be alone, yet he liked Mr. Granville's company, but he wasn't sure that Mr. Granville wanted his. He seemed to be thinking about something and Chal guessed it was about the conversation with Cal. Again the urge came to tell Mr. Granville about Saucy Chief. He felt that he ought to let him know that Cal hadn't known the whole story, and that white men never had been able to see both sides. Of all men, he wanted Mr. Granville to know about it, but he couldn't bring himself to tell him. They walked on toward the creek in silence.

XI

Cool weather came slowly to the campus that autumn. The leaves of the elms had turned pale yellow, shriveled, and had fallen long before the cold frosty mornings came. The coeds who had bought dashing autumn suits were disappointed, and had to go about the campus for two months after the term began, wearing gingham.

The football season opened, but the usual autumn activity was dulled a little by the warm weather. Lethargy came over Chal and yet, buzzing slightly inside him at all times, was a sort of tingling like the tingling you experience when you are expecting momentarily the setter to come down on a covey of quail. He read the papers and followed the talk of war. He believed that he was soft and unfit and he had an urge to put himself into condition. He had the idea that an individual, like a nation, ought to be prepared for war. He would get up in the mornings and look at his tall, darkish body in the glass, and each morning he thought he would do something about it. Apparently he was in good condition, but he felt that he wasn't at all. He went to the gymnasium once but only stood around and watched some people do acrobatics. He should like to exercise in that manner too, but he had never done any exercising on bars and on the rings and he certainly didn't want to attempt it when there were people there, watching.

He got a suit one afternoon and went out to the football field to practice with the scrubs. He stood around for some time and no one noticed him. Then he started passing a ball with another unnoticed man. He had just started for the showers when the old freshman coach shouted to him. He stopped. The coach came up to him, and Chal could see that he wanted to ask him why in the name of Mike he hadn't come out sooner, and to make him feel that he had missed his chance on the varsity, but something in Chal's face stopped him. He shook hands instead.

"How yu making it ?" he said.

"All right, I guess."

"Gonna come out regular now ?"

Chal had an inspiration. He didn't know exactly what he ought to say to this coach, but he felt he ought to have some good excuse, so he said, "I'm gonna enlist."

"What with ?" Chal wanted to tell him that he was going to fly, but he felt that this would sound too much like boasting, so he said, "Ambulance corps, I guess."

The coach turned at the sound of scrimmage close by and shouted out to the fullback of that autumn's crop of freshmen who were scrimmaging against the varsity :

"Hey, there, Noble — that ain't the way to run interference — why'n'chu do what I tole yu — get in there an' blast that man out — git your shoulder into his guts and take him outta there."

He and Chal stood and watched the freshman attempt to go around end again. The coach shouted, "Tha's better," then turned back to Chal, his eyes squinting in the bright sun. He squatted on his heels and picked up a stick, and Chal squatted as well. Chal thought the coach was going to say something, but he just squatted and made marks in the dust, then he arose and said, "Yu wanna go in a little while and git up a sweat ? — yu haven't even got up a sweat." He felt of Chal's dry jersey. "You're out for a little exercise, I guess."

"Yeah, thought I'd come out for a little exercise."

The sun shone down relentlessly and Chal was glad to go to the showers. His clothes were dripping wet. He had a feeling that he had been neglecting himself and he believed that he was very much out of condition, and there was something which kept telling him that he ought to be in condition for that which was coming.

By late winter the atmosphere had become so charged that Chal stopped studying and walked about the campus, or sat listening to the boys at the house discuss the war and the possibility of the United States entering it. He got into condition again by scrimmaging with the varsity and running along the river road with the track men.

They said at the house that all college men would be officers, all right — they were pretty sure of that, and they said that when the United States got into the war it wouldn't last long. Those brothers who had attended military schools became the center of interest for the first time. They took great pleasure in making the others feel unaccustomed and ineffective.

One afternoon Chal was walking along the campus. He saw the tall figure of Mr. Granville striding along with his stick and pipe. His tweed coat with the big pockets hung loosely from his bony shoulders. He passed Chal as though he didn't see him, then turned and said, "Oh, hello, Wenzah."

"Hello."

"I say, should you like to have a little walk — I've only just set out."

They walked along together down the road to the river. They walked for some time without talking, then Mr. Granville stopped and pointed his stick at a vine that was crawling up the stem of a weed. "Curious thing about that vine. I mean, it's literally choking out the gardens of Cornwall and Devonshire, and here it is really a rahther diffident thing."

Chal waited while he bent over and examined the little vine. "Yes," he continued, "the seed must have come over in a boat from America, and got started in Devonshire. It hadn't got enemies there, and throve like anything. It's really a menace." Chal felt that it wasn't necessary for him to say anything, to say for instance, "Well, well," or "How strange," when he talked with Mr. Granville.

They walked on for some distance and Chal said, "Kinda like the English sparrow here." Mr. Granville looked at him. "Yes, that's right, the English sparrow is a nuisance here — in England one seldom sees him — for the same reason I dare say — no enemies ; none of his traditional enemies here as in England."

"Yeah. He was brought over in eighteen and fifty."

An hour later they were back in town. Mr. Granville pointed his stick at an old stone house. "Here are my digs, should you like to come in ?"

They entered a room which seemed to Chal to be cluttered with all the small objects imaginable. Trivial things, which one would not ordinarily keep. On a table in the corner were hand specimens of limestone, sandstones and shales, and bottles of sand. The fire in the fireplace had almost died. There were little strings of tobacco on the floor.

Mr. Granville didn't ask him to sit down but went over to the fireplace and locked his hands behind him, puffing at his pipe. Chal sat in the only chair by the fireplace. The landlady came in. "I guess you want your tea now, and I got some of the cakes you like."

"I say, that's capital — splendid."

As Chal sat drinking tea he was wondering what the men at the house would say if they could see him having afternoon tea with "Goosie" Granville. During the silence he kept looking at a piece of propeller on the mantel.

When they had finished, and after Mr. Granville had lit his pipe after the usual struggle, he arose, talking through the pipe. "I notice you are interested in that bit of souvenir." He went over to the mantel, picked up the piece of propeller and handed it to Chal. He stood by while Chal examined it, then he took it up and placed it carefully back on the mantel, and smiled back over his shoulder at Chal. "It's Hun." Chal wanted to know how he happened to have a propeller from a Hun ship. Maybe what they said about his being a spy was right after all. Mr. Granville said, "Your country has decided to get into the show, I see."

"Yes," said Chal, remembering the headlines in all the papers that morning. Then it seemed that Mr. Granville became very awkward, standing by the mantel. He attempted to light his pipe when it was already gurgling and frying beautifully. His face became red and he began with difficulty and embarrassment, "I say, Wenzah, one might — that is — I may assume the prerogative sort of thing of a — your — an instructor, and ask what you intend to do about the service. I — as a matter of fact, it seems that you are rahther the type for the air service. I wondered if you had given the matter any thought."

Chal had a definite feeling of happiness, and when he answered he did so as though he had planned the thing for months. "Yeah," he said, looking at the floor, "I'm going into the air service."

"Capital. I dare say you will be going soon." He turned and sat down at the desk. He wrote for a short time, and his pen scratches seemed very loud in the silent room. He arose and handed Chal an envelope, "Simply a letter of introduction to my friend Captain Lloyd, who is in the — the city, as a sort of adviser about examination of potential air pilots. I simply say there," he said, pointing to the letter, "that I should be glad to have him meet you, and of your desire to go into the air service."

When Chal went back to the house, he had a desire to tell everyone that he was going to fly. He wanted to make a startling announcement, but he remained silent. That night he wrote a letter to his parents and packed his bags. He hoped that no one would see him go — he couldn't stand to have all the boys say good-bye to him. He waited the next morning until nearly everyone had gone to classes, then left a note for the president of the chapter in which he told him that he was going to fly. As he wrote the lines, "I guess I am going to fly," his heart seemed to be beating a little faster.

He came silently through the six-weeks' ground school. He was practically unnoticed among the others who were living every minute with profound fear of not obtaining their commissions, in an atmosphere that was charged with tenseness and fear. Every Saturday afternoon the cadets crowded around the bulletin board to see whether or not they had failed in radio, motors, reconnaissance, or something else. The course was concentrated into a few weeks, and the fact that it was very difficult was due to the short time.

In the Junior Wing, they drilled all morning, forming fours, company fronts, and column of squads. For hours they drilled in the brilliant sun of those first two weeks. Chal hated it. The terrible routine almost drove him to the conclusion that he should give up and go back home, but he could see that the others wouldn't have given up the chance of gaining a commission for anything. He believed the thing to do was to stick it out, but the monotonous drilling was very difficult for him and somehow depressed him. He would execute the commands in a mechanical manner as he dreamed. He dreamed almost constantly of Blo, but he did not dedicate his unhappiness to her. He didn't want her ever to know that he had gone through such humiliation. He wanted her to know only about the future which would possibly be glorious.

When at night he sat on his bunk waiting eagerly for "lights out," he could see the others bent over pads writing to their girls, and he felt a little lonely and out of things. He believed he wanted a girl to whom he could write letters nearly every night, then he would not feel so much out of things.

No one noticed anyone else very much, and when someone left an empty bunk to go home ; having failed in motors or some other examination, no one seemed to care. When the cadet major, who had been an all-American, failed for the fourth time in motors, everyone knew about it. He had been given two extra chances on account of his national prominence. His failure had the effect of inspiring dejection, and the usual expressions of worry which the cadets carried became more pronounced. If they could "kick" Sullivan out, they could kick anyone out.

That Saturday afternoon Chal saw the cadets crowd to the bulletin board, and watched them read their names and grades. He was fascinated by the expressions on their faces, and in his fascination almost forgot his own grades. Some looked as though something had stuck them as they walked away from the board looking neither to left nor right. Others couldn't control the smiles that crept softly over their faces, and were unaware of the touch of color that crept back. Chal waited until the last. This was the first afternoon he had stayed to look at the bulletin board, as he hadn't cared whether he failed or not — at least he couldn't worry about it, no matter how hard he tried ; no matter if it was the thing to do.   But this was the fourth week, and he had begun to care a little, since he had decided that it would be the wrong thing to be sent away on account of grades.

He hung back until the others had gone, then he saw Sullivan go guiltily up to the board.   He looked at Chal and hesitated, but he couldn't refrain from knowing the truth any longer.   Chal stood back when he saw the expression on his face, as he did not want to embarrass him. Chal thought that his face certainly indicated that he knew what the board would tell him.   He looked at the board for some time and his face became almost pale, as he looked around as though in search of help.   He looked again, then turned away.   He stopped and looked back.   When he started away again Chal walked up to the board.

The yard was empty now and the cadets had caught the cars into town for the brief afternoon off.   Chal saw that his grades were all right, and started to walk away when he noticed that Sullivan was standing before the board again as though fascinated.   He saw him turn and sit down on the bench and put his head in his hands.   Chal wanted to go up to him and do something.   He felt a great sorrow in his heart for this man because he felt that he was not a white man any more.   He knew that his heart could hold no more and the overflow was coming out his eyes, as the Osages said.   As Chal started for the gate, he wondered what the girl looked like ; the one Sullivan wrote to every night.

Then it came to him that he had actually seen a white man cry and he wondered about it.   He had seen many Indians cry, but he didn't know that a white man ever cried. As he walked toward the cars he looked at his newly shined shoes with satisfaction.   He wanted to look back at that figure on the bench, but Sullivan might be looking and that would be very embarrassing. He couldn't believe that he had actually seen a white man cry.

As the car wound its creaking and screaming way down into the town, he knew that he was very sorry for that big white man sitting there crying ; hulking there on the bench with his big broad shoulders moving with his emotion. Chal felt that his great, powerful body and his football glory was all he had had to offer that girl. He knew that Sullivan couldn't talk ; couldn't express himself, and he guessed that he must be very helpless and forlorn sitting there, because he couldn't laugh either. Sullivan thought that all this was very important. Chal knew that he thought it was important from the way he acted as cadet major — he had been very proud as cadet major. He concluded that it was the right thing to consider it very important, but Sullivan didn't have a sense of humor. Everyone else thought it was very important, except that fella Wood from Chicago. He was so frightened that he was not going to get through that everything became a joke to him, and he said some very funny things inspired by his fear, and made the others laugh when they didn't even want to laugh. It seemed that when they laughed they felt a little more fear than before, as though they had committed some crime against the realities.

On the last day of the Ground School, Chal stood with the others and heard his name called when the adjutant finally got to the "W's." He was not worried. He knew he had passed and would be sent to a flying school. Some time that morning a member of the graduating squadron had placed the squadron's symbol over the door of the school. It was a large sign which carried the picture of a United States bombing plane flying above Potsdam. Potsdam was represented by a round tower, above which could be seen a bomb falling from the ship.   As the adjutant called the names, Chal looked intently at this symbol.   Instinctively, he felt that it was the usual boast of the white man, then he believed that he had been unfair, and was being an Osage who believed that the white man boasted in everything he did.   But he didn't want to think that any more, and he believed that it was pretty clever.   But later, he found that he had to keep telling himself that the slogan of his squadron was really clever.

A VERY much rushed War Department had caused many acres of sagebrush and cactus to be cleared, so that the flying field might be constructed.   There was a long row of hangars facing the field, and behind the hangars a long street. On the other side of the street were the quarters of the cadets and the officers, the mess-halls and the hospital, gleaming in the brilliant sun.

Chal was assigned to a tall instructor who had civilian status.   He was physically unfit for military service and the War Department had hired him as an instructor, until it could develop a military instructor to take his place.   He was a languid man with a humorous twinkle in his eye, and he took the work of instruction as calmly and carelessly as he lived.   He had been an exhibition flyer for some years and Chal felt sure that he had heard of his exploits.

Each day Chal went up with Metz for his instruction. Metz flew the dual-control ship from the front seat and Chal sat behind.   When eventually he was allowed to take over the controls, Metz would sit and use the hand signals agreed upon.   If Chal insisted on letting his nose down, flying nose high, or if he allowed either wing to drag, Metz would signal gently with his hand without looking around.   Sometimes he would turn around and point down to some interesting thing on the ground, and though Chal could not see the twinkle behind his goggles, he knew it was there — he could feel it.

In some strange manner Chal came to have a great admiration for the back of that thin neck topped by a helmet which made the head look like a leather-wrapped egg. He remembered for years the back of Metz's head and his thin neck. And every time he saw someone slowly fill a cigarette paper, roll it with a half smile, then light the cigarette and smoke with contentment, he would experience a warm feeling and remember Metz.

Before Chal left the field after his instructions each day, he and Metz would stand and talk, waiting for the next cadet to appear. Metz would stand with his goggles raised and the red mark on his forehead which his helmet had made would be quite distinct, as he slowly rolled a cigarette. Before Chal left for the barracks Metz would sometimes say, "Yu wanna get that right wing up more, see — 'member to get that right wing up more." Chal always walked away with the determination to keep that right wing up.

One morning when he came to the station he found a small man with a first lieutenant's bars, and bright new wings on his tunic, just under his flying coat. As Chal approached, one of the other students of the flight had just finished his instructions and passed him without speaking. The lieutenant looked up from his wristwatch. "This Windzer? Say, why in the hell don't you get out here when you're s'posed to?" Chal looked quickly at his face. "Salute an officer when ya see one — wheren'tha hell did you get your trainin'?" Chal saluted. Then the lieutenant stared at him and said :

"How many hours yu had?"

"About eight."

"About eight — don't you know how many you've had ? And say, what about sayin' 'sir' ?   About eight, huh — that don' mean anything.   About eight — might mean between seven an' eight, or between eight an' nine.   I guess you know you're in the military service, and there's no such thing as about — it is or it isn't."   He looked at Chal as though he expected him to say something but seemed a little at loss when he saw him standing there stiff at attention with nothing on his face which might indicate that his words had been heard.   He wanted to see on Chal's face defeat and submission as well as appreciation of his status as first lieutenant in the flying service of the United States army.

He walked over to the ship and climbed into the cockpit, adjusted his safety belt, then shouted to Chal above the noise of the idling motor, "Come on."   Before he lowered his goggles he turned to Chal in the back seat and said, "I guess you know that Metz was killed last night — I'm takin' his place."   When there was no response he looked around to see if Chal had heard him, then he shouted above the motor, which was now racing and straining at the blocks, "I said Metz was killed yesterday — some student of this stage froze the controls on 'im."   He pulled the throttle back and allowed the motor to idle, then turned in his seat, slid his goggles up very deliberately, and looked at Chal as though he would like to choke him.   He looked steadily into what he believed to be an absolutely wooden face.   It seemed to Chal that he was about to swear but thought better about it.   "Yeah," he continued, "that fella from your stage, Kerns — Kerns, that's it — that's the man who froze the controls on Metz — on your stage, know 'um ?"

Chal felt compelled to answer.   "Yeah."   Chal remembered the tall cadet with the curly hair who had been very nervous ever since he had arrived at flying school.

The lieutenant turned again and fumbled in the big pockets of his flying coat, then he pulled out a leather filled with shot and faced Chal again with a cynical smile, "If any uh you birds freeze the controls while I'm instructin', I'm gonna use this, see." He held the leather up so that Chal could see it, then put it back in his pocket. He shouted back to Chal without turning around this time, "You ready?"

They climbed up over the hangars, then circled the field with the traffic, and Chal waited for a signal which would indicate that he should take the controls, but none came. They landed and the lieutenant turned around and looked at Chal with his goggles up. "I'm gonna turn 'em over to you this time, and I want you to fly like you ought to, er I'll ground you for a week, see." Chal didn't respond. "God-damn-it! If you hear me, say somethin — don't set there with your finger in it."

"Yes, sir," Chal snapped. He felt that he should like to kill that fathead. In some strange way he connected him with Metz's absence. The lieutenant turned and looked at him through his goggles, then said, "All right, take it off."

Chal climbed into the traffic and circled the field. He had been getting too much altitude with Mr. Metz when he was allowed to take the controls, and he saw with satisfaction that he was not too high this time and that his wings were all right, and his nose on the horizon. Just then the lieutenant began to motion almost frantically with the black-mitten of his right hand. He was giving the signal for Chal to bring his right wing up, which he did immediately, then he received the signal to bring his left wing up, then to lower his nose. Immediately he saw the black mitten waving frantically, and making the motion which was the signal to raise his nose. Chal had begun to sweat under his helmet, but he was not excited about all these frantic directions from the front seat. Just as he was banking to come into the field, he felt the controls almost shaken out of his hands, and he allowed his instructor to take them. He was not given the usual signal for control release, and he believed that it was because the lieutenant was excited. They glided down into the field with the wires singing, and the lieutenant was so upset that he made a very bad landing. When the ship had stopped and the motor idled, the lieutenant turned around, raised his goggles and looked at Chal with utmost contempt. "Well, I'll be God-damned," he said. He attempted to give the impression that he was too disturbed to say anything more, and he just sat and stared. Chal felt uncomfortable at first, then he felt angry. He believed that he had flown that ship well, but that man staring at him that way was what made him angry.

The lieutenant climbed out of the cockpit and stood by Chal. He had unhooked his helmet and raised his goggles, and the backwash of the idling propeller played with the loose ends of his helmet. "All right," he said, and he attempted to sneer, "go on, break your neck — I'm through. Give 'er the gun." Chal shoved the throttle forward and took off. As he made the first turn he looked back at the field and saw the lieutenant standing down there, like an insect. In front there seemed to be hundreds of ships, and he had the impression that every plane on the field was ahead of him, and he had a fear that he could not get around without hitting at least one of them. He watched with alertness, but as he was making the second turn there was another dual-control making the turn as well. The fear that he might do something wrong caused him to curse the pilot of that ship. He was flying faster than the other ship, so he throttled down, but still it was too close to him. When he saw it bank and glide down to land, he gave his ship the throttle and went around again. This time there were not so many ships — at least it seemed that way, and he flew around this time with more confidence. He could see the lieutenant standing there on the bare field, exactly like some strange animal of the grass roots that had been caught temporarily out in the open. He felt that he should like to hit him if he could — at least make him run when he landed.

He cut his motor and glided down and he could see the lieutenant grow bigger and bigger just over the nose of the ship, and he hoped fervently that he might make the lieutenant run for his life. However, he shot past him, and he could see the great shadow of his plane moving along the ground, and saw it pass over the lieutenant, then he gave all of his attention to landing. Before he was aware of it he had made a landing and was running along the ground with the tailskid groaning.

When he stopped, he sat in the cockpit and waited for the lieutenant. He came up with a ragged cigarette half blown away by the wind, sticking out from the corner of his mouth. "Well," he said sarcastically, "ya made it." Then he looked up. "You did the right thing up there when that other ship was landin'." Chal had forgotten about the other ship, but somehow he was surprised at the commendation.

The lieutenant climbed into the cockpit and they taxied to the station. The cadet next on the list was waiting, and Chal could see that he was very nervous. The lieutenant returned his nervous salute as though returning salutes was a tiresome thing, but Chal thought that he enjoyed it very much. After returning the salute he looked at the list, then at Chal, and said,

"You, Windzer —"

"Yes, sir."

"Well, you can report to the solo flying stage tomorrow — through with you here."

Chal was happy. One of the delightful cries which rang down the cadet barracks these days was, "I've soloed."

THERE was more social life and more time in which to enjoy it than there had been at Ground School. In the city near the flying field there were dances and parties. Girls and young married women came out to the field in large cars and took the cadets to the city on Saturday afternoons.

Things seemed upside down after the great disturbance that entrance into the war had caused, and the enthusiasm with which people attempted to manifest patriotism, seemed to be without control or reason. It seemed to Chal that everyone was enjoying the change immensely. Here was something new, like a new vogue, and people, especially women and girls who had nothing to do, came under the spell of this great, new adventure. Under the guise of patriotism they called at the field for the cadets.

One day Chal was walking out of the entrance of the field. A large negro chauffeur approached him, cap in hand. "Ah beg yo' pahdon, suh, de lady what Ah drives fuh says, could she take you to town?" Chal looked up and saw a woman sitting in a car, smiling. He was too embarrassed to say anything but walked over to the car and as the chauffeur held open the door he climbed in and sat down. The interior was filled with the odor of some very strong scent; the definite kind of thing which seems to shout at you to notice it and its wearer. Chal and the lady were silent for a short time as they drove along, then the lady spoke. "I think it's a shame you fellows have to ride in the street car." Chal didn't know what he was expected to say to that, then he thought of a smile, and he smiled at her. They drove on silently for a time, and he knew that she was watching him as he looked straight ahead. He wasn't displeased. He had looked at his right profile many times and had always thought it very good, especially in the military cap.

"Are you Spanish or something ?" she asked, looking up at him from the corner of the seat to which she had shifted. He had forgotten that he was different from the others with his dark skin, but he wasn't annoyed with his skin now. He wished for a moment that he were Spanish, inasmuch as that was what she wanted him to be. That would be real romance, and he felt that here was certainly a romantic situation. He didn't want to destroy the thrilling situation, so he said, "Yes, Spanish." He should like to have indicated that he had a title, as well, but he thought he had better not.

She settled snugly into the corner and put a foot tentatively on the folded seat in front of her. Chal guessed that she wanted him to appreciate the small foot and the neat ankle encased in expensive silk, but he saw them only out of the corner of his eye. He was afraid to look around because he knew that she was watching his face intently.

As they drove through the main part of the city, she drew herself forward and looked out the window. "Oh, let's go into Abbenard's and get a hot choc'lit." Before Chal could say anything she changed her mind, turned to him and said, "Are you expected anywhere ?" Then, before he could answer, "I thought if you weren't, we could go out to my house, then back to the dance tonight." He didn't answer, but looked around at her, then straight ahead again. Some strange, powerful influence came over him and he had a feeling that he didn't want to leave this woman. But he didn't want her to see it in his eyes. The feeling was so intense that he felt she would be able to see it on his face and in his eyes.

They drove out through the residential section and into a region where the massive houses stood among green lawns and shrubbery. They stopped at one of these houses and the tires ground on the chat of the long, curving driveway. The grass was mowed and every bush was in its place. Chal felt that all this was very artificial ; like pictures one sees of trees and landscape.

When they entered the house the lady shed her very expensive fur coat, and as Chal lifted it he felt its great weight and wondered why one should require such a heavy coat in this sub-tropical climate. It was midwinter and the sun shone down genially, causing one some discomfort. A servant brought in some brandy, and even about her there was something artificial, and he sensed that she was there just for a short time. As she placed the tray on a table she wore an expression which seemed to say, "I'm as good as you are." The pictures and the furniture, the expensive hangings and carpets, seemed to be there for some other reason than for the purpose of adding atmosphere and comfort to a home. Everything in the room was cold and formal and exact.

The hostess reappeared from upstairs. There was an air about her as though she had made reparations, but Chal couldn't see just what she had done. There was an expression on her face which indicated that she had found her face all right, and that she generally approved of herself and in consequence was quite ready for anything. Her manner seemed to say, "Am I not all right ?   What now ?"

She curled up in a chair, sitting on her feet. The edge of a pink underskirt trimmed with rich lace escaped from the hem of her dress, and fell along her silk-clad leg. Chal wanted to keep looking at that pink skirt. There was something about the intimacy, the pinkness and the lace that gave him a delightful feeling ; made him feel that he should like to stay here indefinitely. He attempted to look elsewhere so that she could not see him looking at that pink skirt. He had a queer feeling ; a tingling insistence that he should like to have this woman very much, and that nothing else mattered at present.

She jumped up from her chair and stooped with outstretched arms as a ludicrous little dog came trotting into the room. His toenails made a ticking sound as he padded across the bare spots between carpets. "Oh, mumsy's little Fidelis," she said, rising and holding the little dog up to her neck. She sat down and held him on her knees, then his bright little eyes found Chal and he began to bark. The hostess laughed, showing very white teeth. "My, my !" she said. Chal laughed as well, but he decided that he didn't like that dog. She allowed it to jump down and it came over and sniffed at Chal's boots. The hostess sat forward with her elbows on her knees. "Don't you think he looks cute ?" she said, smiling at Chal. "Got him in Rome. Supposed to be what they call *loup de Rome* — you know, wolf of Rome." Chal smiled.

"I guess you've been in Rome," she said. He wanted to say "Yes," in a manner which would imply, "Of course," but he said rather feebly, "No," then added, "Never have," as though he would say, but I have been other places. He was very glad that she didn't go any further with the conversation about Rome.

As they sat he felt he ought to talk about something, but he couldn't think of anything to say, and she didn't seem to want to talk anyway. They just sat, looking covertly at each other. She got up and held out some cigarettes. He was trying to subdue the feeling deep within him, that the most important thing in the world was to have this woman. He was ashamed of his thoughts and he wanted sincerely to hide them from himself. He believed he was being very primitive, but the feeling persisted, and he couldn't do anything about it. Everything she did seemed to associate itself sweetly with his desire, as well as everything she wore. There was something provocative about the locket around her neck which swung out on its long gold chain as she bent over to pet Fidelis.

As they sat he hoped that she could not read his thoughts, but the tingling all over his body was so intense that he was sure she could see that there was something wrong with him. She kept smiling at him in a manner that seemed to indicate that whatever he chose to say or do would be quite all right with her. Her silence seemed to be expectation and approval of herself, of him, and of the situation.

If only she would stop sitting on her feet in the big chair, and that margin of pink underskirt were concealed, he felt he could subdue that warm thrill which suffused him. He thought he ought to be going. She got up and walked to the table. The gold chain swung as she picked up the cigarettes. He had never seen a woman smoke a cigarette before, and he knew that it was considered daring and not quite the thing. She lit her cigarette as though she expected it to explode, then looked at him and smiled.

"I tell you, le's go to dinner, then we can dance on the roof." He wasn't sure whether he ought to call for her later or stay until she was ready. She started for the stairs and smiled back at him. "Be down in a jiff."

When she had gone upstairs, he walked to the mirror over the ornate fireplace where flickering, blue gas flames played over imitation logs. He felt in the breast pocket of his tunic and found his comb, carefully combed his black hair, then adjusted his collar. His hands trembled slightly.

During dinner he felt calmer, and later, during the dancing, he forgot about the earlier thrill. The music was good and she danced very well, and there was a pleasing rhythm in the drum beats. He was pleased to see the other cadets and officers look at them as they danced. Sometimes she danced too close and he couldn't dance so well. He believed that she did it consciously.

When he helped her out of the car she put her hand on his and smiled apologetically. "I can't send you back to the field in the car — you see, Fred's home and I — he would wonder. There's a car stop at the corner."

He took off his cap and started to say good night, but she interrupted him.

"Listen," she said, looking slyly at the chauffeur, "I can't see you next Saturday." She turned to the chauffeur. "Better put the car up, Bill." She watched the tail light move away in the darkness, then she smiled up at Chal. "I tell you, I'll drop you a note, hear?" She squeezed his hand and laughed. "But who are you?"

"Cadet Windzer."

"I'm Lou Kerry — I'll send a note, hear?" She ran up the walk, then waved to him from the door.

During the long taxi ride to the field, Chal was exhilarated but even the fact that he felt his thoughts had been very primitive did not interfere with his happiness. He wondered what she would say if she knew how he had felt, and he wondered what other people would say. He was pretty sure that you weren't supposed to feel that way about nice women. But she smoked cigarettes — what did that mean, he wondered. But he was too full of himself to have the old feeling that he was out of step. He didn't feel out of step in the least, and he wished he would hurry up and get his commission and his wings. He lit another cigarette without realizing what he was doing, and had to throw almost half of the unsmoked cigarette away. He pictured himself in shiny boots, with glittering spurs rattling, and wings shining on his breast.

When he got out at the gate he felt very proud, and very important as he walked past the guard. The University seemed to be far in his past and he felt a little contempt for the people of the University, and certainly for the people in Kihekah. He thought of himself as being separated by a great abyss from Sun-on-His-Wings and Running Elk, and from the village with the people moving among the lodges.

XII

For some time the cadets in Chal's barracks had been talking with awe about a British ace who had come to the field to instruct in acrobatics and aerial combat. They said he was a V.C. and had any number of other decorations.

Because of the tenseness of the atmosphere and the daily excitement rumors floated over the field continuously. One day the cadets would hear that someone had told someone else that they were going to fly at the front as sergeants and not as second lieutenants, and that the new commandant was another cavalry major who had never even been in a plane. It was rumored that he ordered cavalry drill for the cadets every afternoon. Someone said that he had heard at headquarters through a friend, that they had calculated that the deaths of cadets on the field averaged one a day, and that that was the average of every field in the country. There was even a mystery about Peyton Parson's death. Someone had said that someone had heard in a roundabout way that Peyt's struts had been sawed so that they would give way in the air.

Peyt's empty bunk was next to Chal's, and Chal had liked him very much. He was a dark-eyed boy who had run to the barracks window the morning after the squadron had come to the flying field, and had shouted to the others with eyes gleaming, "They're up already." Of all the cadets who had thus far been killed, Chal liked Peyt best, and when he looked at Peyt's bunk there with the bedding taken from it he thought that he had liked Peyt much better than he really had. It seemed that he now thought much about Peyt, since he had gone. Perhaps that cold, bare floor around the bunk made him feel unhappy.

As he sat one day on his bunk thinking of that cold floor, he received orders to report for acrobatics the next morning. That meant that he would finish the course and get his commission. He knew that he could pass the test. He had been doing tailspins, immelmans and loops every time he left the field. He liked to do acrobatics in the still air just before sunset, watching the green earth with its white roads and geometrical fields of yellows, grays and brown change place with the sky. There was something about this time of day which caused him to go into a frenzy of looping ; doing one after another until he had lost altitude or had grown tired.

Thus when he reported the next morning, he was self-confident. A tall man with large pockets on his tunic, and a black tie in his shirt collar, came toward him. When Chal saw his stride and the little black pipe he knew it was Mr. Granville. He came to attention and saluted and the tall figure raised his hand carelessly, the fingers of which did not come within five inches of his cap.

"I say, it's Wenzah, yes — well, look here, I dare say this is our crate." He pointed his stick at a nearby ship with several mechanics standing around it. He walked up to it, fumbled about in the front cockpit, then turned to Chal again. "We shall fly over to the meadows, then I believe I am supposed to get out and watch you do acrobatics. Are you quite ready ?"

Chal watched him get into the front cockpit, then climbed into the rear one. The backwash from the idling propeller carried to him the strong scent of Mr. Granville's tobacco, though his pipe was out and in his pocket. They landed on a meadow dotted here and there with haystacks. Major Granville climbed out and came around to Chal. "Do whatever you're supposed to do — the usual thing, you know." He smiled, and Chal felt that the smile which came to his own face must have flowed up from the bottom of his stomach, as it seemed to warm every vein in his body. As he took off he waved his hand to Major Granville and the thought came to him that he had not seen the V.C. on his tunic.

He climbed up to three thousand feet above the meadow and immediately executed three loops in succession. At the top of the last one his motor conked for a second and he thought he could feel the plane sink on its back. For fifteen minutes he went into immelmans, barrel rolls, loops, wing-overs, and stalls, then spun the ship down to within a thousand feet, leveled off and made a beautiful three-point landing among the haystacks.

He left the motor idling and climbed out. Major Granville was gone. He looked around, then the thought came to him that this might be part of the examination. A trick to ascertain what he might do in this situation. Just as he was attempting to find some reason for such a trick, Major Granville came toward him. His pipe was going and his boots were muddy. He approached Chal with a flower in his hand. "I say, this the *Yucca elata* thing I've been wondering about. I had a letter from Allenby and he said he was sure one might find it here. I have found it, you see — I found the little rotter." He mistook the expression which gave Chal's feeling away for surprise that one might be corresponding with the great general unofficially, and he added, "Yes, Allenby is writing a book on the flora of Palestine, and he has some very queer theories about the Yucca. I am gathering notes here and we are exchanging data."

Major Granville put the flower tenderly away in his note case, then sat down with his arms around his thin knees. Chal thought his pipe gurgled with happiness. Chal sat down by him and lit a cigarette. The propeller of the ship turned lazily in the sun ; the sun rays glinted on it and the whole ship seemed to be animated. The light wind that had arisen rocked the wings slightly. Chal said,

"I didn't know you were in the service, Mr. — Major Granville."

"Oh yes, quite. I was in the show for some time — invalided here so as to be available when your people should come in." He laughed. "Almost a spy, you see."

"There was excitement in our barracks when we heard you had a V.C."

"Yes ? I'm very proud — it is a great honor." He arose. "We must be going — we shall be short of petrol." He took a little book from his pocket. "Let's see, you went through everything — fifteen minutes. All right, shall we be off ?"

A week later Chal received his R.M.A. He sported his shiny new boots and his new wings in the city the next afternoon. When he got back to the field he found that he had been ordered to the new night flying school.

At least one of the many rumors became a fact. The new commandant instituted cavalry drill on the field, but there was only one horse and Captain Baker rode him. Chal was excused on account of his night flying but the cadets and the officers of his barracks cursed the commandant and the War Department and the hot sun. As the ships roared at intervals over the barracks, they sat on their bunks and talked and swore. They all agreed that it was the goddamnedest thing they had ever heard of. One day when they came in hot and resentful from drill, Wood, still a

cadet, came in laughing as usual. He had somehow held
on, though always on the verge of being expelled. Perhaps
fate had decided that he must fly that bomber over the lines
during a heavy fog and smash into a tree, the day before
the Armistice. Chal liked Wood and watched him, ever
ready to hear what he might say. He came in with his face
wet with perspiration and began to stamp the floor and imitate the whinny of a horse. He jumped and pranced down
the aisle of the barracks, hitting his drill shoes hard against
the flooring and kicking out at the bunks as he passed, at the
same time making a noise like a horse with his closed lips.

Chal thought this was the funniest thing he had ever
seen. He could understand that kind of humor. He sincerely hoped that Wood would get his commission before
they expelled him from the service.

WHEN he had finished the night flying course, Chal was
called to headquarters and ushered into the office of the officer in charge of night operations. He saw Tad sitting at
the desk with his brow wrinkled as though he were making
a great decision on a paper which he held in his hand. He
knew Tad from ground school days and had seen through
his posing. He stood there and waited. Soon Tad looked
up, but instead of saying hello he said, "Lieutenant, have you
quit salutin' superiors?" Chal was about to smile, but he
saw Tad was really in earnest, and he saluted with exaggerated stiffness.

Tad was the grandson of one the richest men in the United
States ; a man with international fame. Tad had been a
little slow in ground school and Chal had helped him secretly with an examination. He knew that Tad didn't really
care to fly ; he simply wanted the glory which he believed
belonged to flying. As he stood there it occurred to Chal

in that instant that Tad had been appointed to this position through some mysterious influence, and that the silver bars on his shoulder ought to be brass ones like his own. Everyone in the barracks had known about the sudden promotion and Tad's appointment to this safe job, but there hadn't been much talk about it. They had taken it as a matter of course and Chal had heard some of the young officers express sincere envy of Tad. Chal had taken it for granted as well, but as he stood there at attention waiting for Tad to speak, he was smiling inside. This was also a humor which his Indian soul could understand — Tad was assuming the dignity of a great man and that was very funny.

Tad raised his head, then rang a bell on his desk and an orderly came in and saluted stiffly. He handed him some papers without looking up. "Orderly, take these papers to Captain Boag," then looked up to see whether the orderly had saluted properly. He looked at Chal, then with the assumed seriousness on his face which made Chal smile within, said, "Lieutenant, the commandant has seen fit to appoint you as an instructor of night bomb raiding — because of your excellent ability as a night flyer and on my suggestion. You will take up your duties tonight." He raised his hand carelessly to his head and pretended that he was interested in some papers on his desk. Chal stood a moment, then said, "Tad — Lieutenant, I hope this appointment won't keep me from goin' across — I want to get across as soon as I can." Tad looked up at him with scorn. "Lieutenant, we don't reason or question in the service of the United States army — we *do* — you are now an officer of the post — good day."

Chal walked out of the office with a heavy heart. "Stuck," he thought, " 'cause I helped that bird with his reconnaissance paper." The sun was hot and the glare made him

want to shut his eyes for relief.   Flying wires sang as the
ships glided over the hangars into the field, and high up in
the hot sky the motors roared.   A figure passed him in flying coat and goggles, then he heard a voice call to him.
The figure said, "Come here."   He went back and looked
at the man's face, wondering what he wanted.

"Don't you know a superior officer when you see him ?
Why didn't you salute ?   What's your name ?   I'm gittin'
tired uh you fellas tryin' tuh run this field."   He glared at
Chal with what he thought must be hatred, and Chal was
so startled by the incident that he didn't think the figure's
oil-smeared face was funny.

"Now, salute."   Chal brought his heels together and
saluted.   "All right, the next time I catch you not salutin'
in a military manner, I'm gonna put you on the ground for
a month, yuh understand ?"   Chal was silent.

"Well, d'yuh hear what I'm sayin' ?"

"Yes, sir."

"That's better."   The figure turned and went on up the
company street.

Chal was hot all over and his collar seemed too small for
his neck, and he felt that there was poison in his veins.   As
he continued along, he muttered the words of the old
freighter.   He muttered them several times but they didn't
do any good, and the sense of deep shame and humiliation
persisted.   He felt that he should like to go back and tell
that fellow to go to hell, even if he were a superior officer.
He began to think of the things he might have said ; things
which might have been to the point and showed his contempt in return.   Another figure in flying coat came toward
him carrying his goggles, but he didn't hear or see anything
because of his burning shame.   Red stopped him.   "Hey !"
he said, "Where yuh goin' ?"   Chal looked up with a forced

smile. He could always smile best when he was disturbed or very angry ; a smile that put anyone off the track as to what was in your mind. A smile that hid any traces that your face might show, indicating that which was on the inside.

"Jist had Colonel Beggs up," said Red, pretending he thought it very trivial. "You know, Chal, I bet that ole bastard had never been in a ship before, the way he acted. He was so God-damned scared he cussed hell outa me when we got down, and I didn't do a thing but straight flyin', neither. The ole kiwi would uh ruined his collar if I'd uh looped." Chal liked this talk. He smiled encouragement, and Red, instead of continuing about how scared the old kiwi was, started to cuss him for his cavalry drill idea. When Red got on this subject his humor left him and he couldn't do anything except swear.

That night, after flying hours, Chal lay on his bunk and thought of Major Granville. He thought of the day of the acrobatics test. He recalled Major Granville striding up to him carrying a flower, and about General Allenby studying the flora of Palestine in the middle of the greatest war in history. Then his thoughts came back to Colonel Beggs and to Tad and he mumbled as though he would drown the thought. He turned over on his bunk with the vague idea that if he turned over the thoughts might leave him, but they persisted. He thought for some time of these things, and he finally came to the conclusion that England must be a kind of slow country without any "get-up-and-go" like Americans. Americans were too busy doing things to waste their time on flowers. He guessed the reason why he had liked Major Granville, and the idea of a great general writing a book on flora, was because he was queer himself.

ONE evening as he was getting into the sidecar preparing to go to the field for flying, a note was handed to Chal.   It was from Lou Kerry.   She wanted him to come down to the coast, indicating that she would be at the Spanish Main hotel for a week.

The night was warm and calm, with the moon silvering the whole world.   So intense was the moonlight that the floodlights from the hangars seemed dim, and the flyers were landing by the moon's light at the edge of the field.   You could scarcely see the wing-tip lights and the tail light, but you could see the planes themselves, roaring high above.

After the evening's flying was over, Sergeant Meyer had all the ships taken in from the line except one.   Chal climbed in and took off for his nightly ride.   He climbed lazily, circling up to six thousand feet.   There was no one else up. At about five thousand feet he left the bumpy air and flew along in air that was so smooth that he scarcely realized he was flying.

Far below he could see the lights of the field and far in the distance the moonlight glinting on the sea.   Under him were the lights of the city with a central cluster indicating the business center.   The radiating lines of light blinked like stars and they seemed small and insignificant.   Occasionally he could see a light moving along one of these lines ; moving along like some phosphorous-nosed bug.   He was soothed by the drone of the motor and the perfect stillness of the air, and his heart was filled with contentment as he made great circles like some nocturnal bird, hunting.

He was lulled into dreaminess by the roar of the motor, the scent of castor oil and the smooth air.   Then he noticed the moonlight on his wings ; the beams attempting to penetrate them, making them almost transparent.   The translucent wings against the dark earth six thousand feet below seemed intangible and ghostly. He thought of himself as a spark of life in a ghost-ship, flying through the still night that was silver-flooded. Then he thought with his heart beating fast of the fact that over the whole moon-silvered continent at that hour, he must be the only living thing at that altitude. He was sure that the field far below him was the only night flying field in the United States. He had a feeling of superiority, and he kept thinking of the millions of people below him as white men. When he became conscious that he was thinking of them as white men he smiled to himself.

The emotion grew and soon he was suffused with it and wanted to do something. Flying calmly along was not sufficient, he must do something about it. He turned the ship into a steep bank, then looped it, but at the top of the loop the motor sputtered and he could smell fresh gasoline. He was sorry he had looped, especially since it had given him no satisfaction. He wanted to fly along in the moonlight like a ghost above the dark world, until his gasoline was exhausted. But his motor was missing now, and he was sorrier than ever that he had looped. He wanted to express himself in some kind of activity, but he had to descend to the field, limping. Meyer was waiting for him when he landed, and he told him that there was a cylinder missing.

He walked through the obsidian shadows which the hangars made and down the quiet squadron street to his room in the barracks. The moonlight came in the windows and gave on his cot. The papers on the table which he used for a desk were glaring white. He went to the window and looked out, but he saw nothing but the other barracks and the officers' mess waiting for the day's activity. They were startling white in their new paint, and severely efficient. He walked back to the desk and sat down. He knew he couldn't sleep and he had this deep urge to do something. He paced up and down, then sat at the desk again, picked up his pen and held it over a piece of paper for some time. He thought he should like to write about the night ; about the fact that he had been the only living thing up there in all that immensity. He wanted to write poetry — write poetry because he didn't have a violin. He couldn't play a violin, but he felt that anyone ought to be able to play one who felt as he felt tonight ; anyone so full of something which was actually painful — something that almost choked you. He sat for some time, then pushed the paper away and got up and went back to the window. As he stood there he thought that if he could only paint, he could express what was in him. He didn't visualize the picture one might paint, but he felt he could do it if he had brushes in his hand. As he looked out at the gleaming white barracks, he felt that he was going to cry, and he became very much ashamed of himself, and his body felt hot all over.

With a quick movement he picked up his cap and went back across the squadron street to the hangar, and his thoughts seemed clear and precise now. There was a light in the hangar. He almost laughed at the surprise on Meyer's face as he slid the heavy door back. Meyer was standing on the ship replacing spark plugs. Chal walked up to him and looked up. Meyer said, "Lieutenant, I guess she's all right now, kinda fouled a plug — musta been loopin'." He smiled good naturedly. Chal didn't answer, but walked toward the door, then back again, and said, "Where's your time sheet ?"

"Over on the bench."

Chal looked at the sheet for some time. "Look," he said, "I'm gonna take this ship out for another spin. Barrett here — see, we can blur that time in a little bit. You and I don't know he's in, see — we'll hunt for him now."

Meyer had always admired this dark-skinned officer who seemed so careless, and who didn't have the air that he was better'n you just because he was a lieutenant. Meyer smiled, "Probably gonna see some jane," he thought.

They rolled the ship out, and Meyer got his helmet and goggles. Chal warmed the motor up, then took off and immediately flew away from the field, as he thought it better not to make too much noise. Soon the sea was sparkling before them, and they circled out over it for a while, and Chal thought it might be fun to keep flying; keep flying into the distant haze caused by the moonlight. Then he decided to fly as close to the calm water as possible and dip his undercarriage just a little. He had to do something. He turned back to Meyer and pointed down, and Meyer nodded, although he didn't know what Chal meant to do. He thought Lieutenant Windzer must be crazy, but he was in for anything — after all, the lieutenant was the one responsible.

They descended slowly in a wide spiral. On one of the turns, Chal saw the great mass of the Spanish Main hotel, sprawling and white in the moonlight. He thought of Lou. He thought of her being somewhere under that tiled roof that was in the shape of a maltese cross from the air. When he thought of her, he felt his fingertips tingle, and he felt that the emotion which had dominated him for some time was slowly being transformed into action, although the action was vague. He thought he might be flying too low over the little sea town, so he spiraled down some distance from the hotel and the town. He leveled off and flew in to the beach from the sea. He could see almost as well as in the daytime. The moon lighted up the white sands that had been blown into little hummocks out of which dwarfed trees grew. They looked like ragged urchins scattered out over the brilliant sand, looking for something.

He set the ship down on the hard sand close to the water, cut the switch and climbed out. "Meyer, you watch the ship — I'm gonna go down the beach a little while." Meyer smiled and crawled out of the cockpit. He was standing by the side of the ship when Chal looked back from down the beach.

Chal didn't know what he was going to do, but he didn't care very much, and he certainly didn't want to think definitely about anything. He walked along the edge of the water. The waves rolled up nearly to his shining boots, then swished like silk rubbed together and retreated, leaving little silver pools. The moon made a path straight across the sea to Chal, which kept up with him as he walked along, as though it were a great cord of a circle having its center somewhere on the other side of the swelling water. The sea was calm but the path undulated just a little, and Chal attempted to imagine someone walking along that undulating path.

The great white hotel cast its moon shadows across the graveled walks, and as he approached the sweet scent of honeysuckle was carried to him. The shrubbery at the foot of the sprawling building seemed to add to the silence with their deep shadows. A mockingbird was singing ecstatically.

Chal almost shook as he walked into the immense tiled lobby. There was no one there. The light over the desk was dim, and the shadows were so thick in the great place that you imagined there were silent figures ready to appear from them at any time. He wondered why he had come, after all, and he smiled to himself. Then he heard the

slight squeaking of leather, and the night clerk raised a
sleepy head from a chair in a dark corner. He arose deliberately and came forward. Chal was startled, but he
straightened himself and looked very formidable as he had
seen other officers do. He looked at the clerk as though he
were an insect. He was embarrassed and he was defending
himself in this manner. He said to the clerk before he
could ask what he wanted, "I want to leave a note for Miz.
Kerry."

"Yes, sir." He pushed some note paper over to Chal,
and he wrote deliberately :

Dear Lou :
    Just flew down from the field to make a call. I received your
letter. Better luck next time.

Then he thought it would be prankish to leave the time.
He looked up at the clock, and on the corner of the paper
wrote, "Time, 3:15 a. m." He handed the note to the clerk,
said, "Thank you," and walked out, as though the simple
leaving of a note had been the definite motive of his visit.
It might really have been that, as the motives for his activity
had certainly been vague.

The leaving of the note, and the start which the clerk
had given him, in some way relieved his emotion, though
he still felt a need for some kind of action. He stopped
and looked back at the hotel, which was partly hidden by the
curve in the beach, then he walked up the beach until the
hotel was completely hidden and he could not yet see the
ship. He began taking off his clothes, without thinking,
and stood naked in the moonlight. He listened to the
swishing of the waves and thought that the musical gurgling
of the water along the edges of the ponds among his own
hills was much prettier.

He trotted up the beach, jumping the waves as they rolled in on the hard sand. He trotted until he came into sight of the center section of the ship above the scrub growths and could smell Meyer's cigarette, then he stopped. His stomach was moving in and out slowly, and he was sweating. He turned and trotted back, following the receding waves, then advancing as the waves advanced, attempting to keep the water from touching him ; playing a little game. Suddenly he wondered if by any chance Meyer might have seen him. He looked over his shoulder, but the center section of the ship was hidden by the shore line and the hummocks. When he got to his clothes he was breathing fast and he sat there for a while. He had heard that you shouldn't go into water until you cooled off. Then he remembered the time that some of the young Osages had run a foot race into the Agency from Sand Creek which was ten miles distant. They were very hot, but he remembered that some older men had punctured each one of them with a sharp knife so that the blood oozed out, and some other men standing about had poured cold water over them. He guessed cold water wouldn't hurt him, and he got up and walked to the edge of the waves. The moon path came to his feet again. He stepped in and swam out in the path of the moon. He swam so far out that the shore line seemed hazy. He turned on his back and floated and wondered why he had not thought of doing this oftener. As he floated in the brilliant moonlight, many thoughts passed through his consciousness, some of them not connected with anything in particular. He thought of the people in bathing suits on this beach, actually playing in the sand or sleeping in the sun. One day he saw a fat man covered up with sand by a girl much younger than himself, who was painted like dolls he had seen. The fat man had a bald head, too, and he must have been important — in some kind of business, he guessed. He was surprised when he first saw people playing on the beach without many clothes on. White men usually took life so seriously in the hills, making themselves appear very important.

He felt much better when he got back to his clothes. He was delightfully weak and drowsy, and he regretted that he couldn't lie there on the sand and sleep. When he reached the ship, Meyer was lying on the sand, asleep. His stomach sagged just a little under his web belt and O.D. shirt, and he had one hand thrown out carelessly and ineffectively on the sand, like a child. Chal smiled as he stood over him. He stood there for some time in the pulsing night, with the rhythm of the swishing waves in his ears, and he thought he could hear the mockingbird.

Meyer roused himself with an apologetic expression on his florid face. Chal climbed into the cockpit and Meyer went around to spin the propeller. When they were ready, they took off down the beach as there was no wind.

THE next day he was sitting on his bunk just awakened from a sound sleep, and was wondering whether he should dress and go to the mess for lunch. Lunch was the night flyer's breakfast. An orderly handed him a note from Lou, in which she urged him to come down that night after flying hours. He read it over several times and felt the old tingling over his body. She just wanted to see him and maybe go bathing in the moonlight, and here he was thinking something quite different. As he combed his hair before the glass, he guessed it would be a long time before he became really civilized, but the tingling sensation was pleasant.

That evening as he arrived at the field, Sergeant Meyer

handed him a note. It was a second note from Lou. There was something in the lines and the neat rounded letters of this note which thrilled him more than the first one.

"I forgot about the hour when you'll be through flying, so I guess you'd better just come around to my room. It's over the honeysuckle arbor, and I'll have the light on. You can just climb up and we will have a nice visit. You see, it wouldn't look very good, you coming up through the lobby at that time, would it?"

Chal assigned the ships on the line to cadets thinking of the adventure, then about midnight an idea came to him. He called Meyer and looked at the time book. "We'll keep 62075 down, and you and I will take it up to check alignment." He smiled at Meyer.

The sergeant walked away with a smile. He didn't think they'd be any trouble about it. They went up often to check things when cadets reported wing heaviness or somethin'. He didn't think they'd get caught. That fella was purty smart. That was a smart one all right when he blurred the time in on Cadet Lloyd last night. It made him laff the way they went around to Lloyd's barracks and woke him up, askin' him where he'd been, and they had been out lookin' for him. Then the Loot smilin' at him and sayin', "Guess we was on a wild goose chase." It 'uz funny the way the chuckle-headed cadet was standin' at attention in his pajamas, when the Loot was tellin' him that his time in was blurred so they'd had to make sure that he'd come back. That was coverin' up tracks purty fine all right. That fella sure wasn't anybody's fool. Then tonight this here alignment business.

At midnight 62075 roared out of the moonlit field into the sky, its wing-tip lights and the taillight like three dim stars.

The hotel seemed calm and deserted among its shadows, but in the little town there was more activity ; more insects with phosphorous eyes crawling down there. There were several windows lighted against the glaring white of the hotel, and from five thousand feet Chal attempted to single out the honeysuckle arbor. He circled far out over the sea and spiraled down and came in to the shore low, landing in the same place as the night before.

As he walked along the shore he didn't notice the moon path, nor was he aware of anything except his tendency to run instead of walk. He was ashamed of himself. It was the first time in his life that he had desired to get some place in a hurry, and the first time he had been absolutely devoid of native caution. That caution that made him reticent, that made of his face a mask when he was with strangers, and caused him to miss no movement about him in the sky or on the earth.

Even when he arrived at the hotel and came up into the shadows, he stopped only because he made himself do so. His tunic collar was rubbing his neck and he felt a drop of sweat roll down his back. He crept in among the shadows and found the arbor, then saw the lighted window. He could scarcely stand still. He looked all about him, then he heard murmuring. It came from under the arbor, and it was low talking that lovers use with each other. Disconnected phrases that are softened and intriguing. He moved stealthily forward and he saw a couple sitting on the bench under the arbor so close together that they looked like one. A light shone feebly on the man's face and he saw that he was from the field ; one of the non-flyers who were really glorified clerks, and called by the pilots, kiwis. The man drew the girl's face to his and remained in that position for some time. As Chal watched, he was suddenly suffused

with the most extraordinary feeling. It was half anger, a
wild anger which urged him to run up to this man and pull
him away, and choke him if he resisted, causing him to run
away among the shadows. He had never seen the girl before, but his blood seemed to pound through his veins and
his heart thumped. Then the tendency left him as quickly
as it came, and he crept back into the shadows of the shrubbery to wait.

For some minutes he waited there as the whispering was
carried to him. Then a light went out in the third story but
the light in the first-floor window above the arbor shone
on. He became calmer under the spell of the night and
began to think of the mystery of a light in a window ; its
warmth in the cold wind's howl, and its cheerful assurance
on a summer's night. He remembered how as a little boy
he was fascinated by the dim red lights of the Agency, and
how he constructed stories about the people in the rooms.
Happy little stories, because he could never think of heavy-
heartedness in a room from which a light was shining.

He was soon completely lost in his memory of lights.
He thought about the light across the snow, shining from
the narrow window of the agent's residence, and a rabbit hopping into it and freezing to appear like a piece of sandstone ;
freezing because he had suddenly hopped into the light and
was afraid. He had laughed at that rabbit, and tonight
the memory of him brought a smile to his face. A gentle
happiness came to him as he remembered those lights of the
Agency like a dozen pairs of red eyes under the oaks, as he
came riding over the hill after a day on the prairie. He remembered how they would invariably change his dreaming
and become the eyes of panthers lying there in the valley
waiting for him. There were the lights of the ranch house
in the snow — . A figure darkened the window over the

arbor for a moment, then disappeared. His dream was broken.

He lay there with his heart pounding for a while longer, then the girl on the bench got up and brushed her skirts, and the conversation became louder as though a spell had been broken, and Chal felt sorry that he had had such wild thoughts about that officer. The girl started toward the front of the hotel and the officer followed. Reluctantly, Chal thought.

He arose and stood in the shadows for a while, then walked toward the arbor. It was easy to climb, and mixed with his eagerness was a delightful pride in his stealth and noiselessness, as it occurred to him that this was also a great game which required deception. He was just reaching for the white sill when the light went out. He must have made a little noise, and he felt a brief disappointment, but he thought she must have been watching.

He climbed over the window trembling in spite of himself. Lou stood by the foot of the bed in a dressing-gown. His thoughts were quick and sharp and his impressions vivid, but there were only two impressions. The face in the shaft of moonlight, and the white V which was Lou's neck. He stood inside the window. He expected her to say something ; she was always able to talk. He looked at her face and saw that her smile was nervous ; she couldn't smile the way she wanted to smile, and she wanted to have a coy, inviting and playful expression, he was sure. But her attitude reminded him more of a hen prairie chicken when the cocks are dancing in the spring.

He said feebly, "I got your note." He thought she said, "Oh, yes," but he wasn't sure. He knew that his voice was not loud when he spoke, but he began to wonder if he had spoken at all. The delicious trembling left him suddenly, and in its place there was an eager intensity and everything around him seemed to be charged with electricity, and a primitive understanding came to him.

As the summer wore on, Lou became more insistent and became quite possessive. She drove out to the field at all hours, and every morning he received a note from her. He felt that he ought to treat this thing as important, but he couldn't. Other people seemed to think such things were important, and Carl Sandeson, who was engaged to a girl back home, had suffered visibly after a weekend on leave in the city, because he believed that he had done something wrong. But Chal's life was not disturbed by his adventures, and he couldn't understand why Carl felt the way he did, and why the others strutted and boasted about their conquests. But there were so many things which he felt he ought to consider important, which seemed natural to him, that he stopped trying to understand. Mating had always been a part of the life of the earth about him as he grew up. Those activities that sometimes came with spring and bird-song, always inspired an especial beauty, and a special ecstasy in the life of his People and their brothers. When everything on earth seemed to want to sing about being alive.

It was the beauty that came from mating activities, nuptial plumage and fur, the manifestations of that life athrill, which disturbed him. The importance lay in the fact that it inspired beauty. A cardinal flashing through the spring woods, and the azure of the bluebird were symbols of that beauty. It was a time of extravagant expression when all life attempted to show in various ways the beauty of its existence, with the assurance of a shiny-haired, swollen-necked buck stamping his graceful feet unafraid, in the season when he knew that you would keep your bow at your side and give him the trail.

Lou couldn't understand why he avoided her, but she must know that he did.   She could not understand that there was no beauty now outside the beauty of that moonlight night.   That adventure when there was zest in deceiving the authorities at the field and the people at the hotel.   To Chal the breathless ecstasy of that night was the expression of something which often pained him, but the arranged meetings, though still on the sly, grew monotonous and he tired of them.

He had more assurance now among the other officers of the field.   He felt that he was one of them and was happy in the thought.   His vanity was fired by their allusions to Lou's visits, and he attempted to act in the matter as one of them might act when he assumed carelessness and reticence rather than naturally becoming boastful.   They became more interested in him and admired his indifference which they thought was cleverly assumed.   "Say, that sure is one good-lookin' woman," they would say of Lou, and at such times Chal felt his importance.

The way the girls at the dances looked at him and the way they acted when he danced with them, filled him with self-assurance and he felt that he had begun to be gilded by that desirable thing which he called civilization.   He was becoming a man among civilized men.   He realized that his bronze complexion was one of the reasons why girls and women seemed to be attracted to him and he appreciated it as an asset.   He kept his Indian keenness, though he could never make himself look at people except covertly.   He saw many things in people's faces which they didn't know they were showing.

WHILE rumors were flying around the field that Germany was having internal trouble ; that the Kaiser had been murdered ; that the Germans had manufactured a new super-armored ship, and had shot down Lufberry from such a ship, Chal received orders.   He was quite happy to leave the field, where rumors seemed to absorb all interests.   There were rumors about poison gas, and about the Battalion of Death winning back Russia for the Allies ; Russia who had filled the officers with injured innocence when she had so inconsiderately let them down.

Chal and three other officers took three ships off during the night and flew toward a field on the Atlantic seaboard, stopping here and there along the way to get gas and have their ships inspected.   He was glad that he had escaped saying good-bye to Lou and to the officers at the mess.   The last time he had seen Lou her eyes were like the eyes of a hungry animal when she looked at him, and he was sure he couldn't stand to say good-bye.   Thus, as he roared through the night, he was happy.   Clusters of lights sparkled far below in the darkness as they passed over towns.   During the long hours he watched Captain Anderson's lights rise and fall in front of him like the lights of a ship at sea. Growing tired of watching the ship ahead of him, he amused himself by watching for the clusters of lights 'far below him like a galaxy, which indicated cities and towns. Flying over cities there would be lights running out from the central cluster, like radii, losing themselves in the surrounding darkness.   The hum of the motors was soporific, and he became too lethargic to dream.   Captain Anderson's ship would sink suddenly and he would feel instinctively that he ought to nose down to remain on his leader's level, but his ship would suddenly sink down to that level without any activity on his part.   Then the lead ship would rise like a spectral bird above him and he would have the instinct to climb, but immediately he would be carried up to the level of the leader. There were impressions of the fields where they stopped for gas. The mechanics running out and taking the ends of their wings in order to help them turn. At one field a sleepy officer standing with his hands in his pockets, his attitude seeming to say, "You can't fool me with polite words — I'm onto you." An orderly with hot coffee, and Captain Anderson, his goggles up and his eyes blinking over the cup, saying, "Hits the spot." Then the three ships lined up, and the sputter as the propellers were being turned, then the even roar of the motors. The feeling for the buckle of your safety belt in the darkness, and then the blocks taken away from Captain Anderson's ship and the cloud of intangible dust which hides his taillight for a moment. Then his own ship running over the ground, then off again roaring into the darkness.

Three months later the Armistice came, and a flight in formation of all the airworthy ships on the new field celebrated the event. Some said there were a hundred and fifty ships up over the flag-bedecked city, where the citizens looked like ants whose hill had been disturbed, streaming through the canyons which were the streets. It was a great formation, led by the white hospital ship which had a big red cross on the side.

Three pilots were killed during the demonstration, and Chal felt very sad when he heard that Captain Anderson was one of them. They said that the white-coated assistants who rode out on the "Meat Wagon" to the scene of the crash, had to bring parts of the motor back to the hospital. They said that Captain Anderson had lost a wing at six thousand feet.

SUNDOWN 233

CHAL decided to stay in the service. For a year he was an
officer of the post at the new field, but life became monotonous. There was very little flying as the War Department
was trying out new motors and ships. He made long trips
ferrying ships from one field to another but always over the
same course, and he came to know every city and town on a
route. The monotony of the thing made him unhappy.

He received letters from his father ; short letters telling
him about what the guv'mint had done or was gonna do, and
these letters told him with pride that he wouldn't know the
town now. It had been recognized as a city of the first
class, and the oil sales were larger and larger and would soon
run into millions of dollars. His father nearly always mentioned the fact that he and Chal's mother were proud of
their soldier ; that that was the life for a man.

But the long hours grew heavier and the routine flying lost
its edge. There was nothing new. Up in the morning to
fly for a few hours then back to the barracks to sit and
watch the other officers play bridge or poker. He had never
learned to play either game and he was ashamed to admit
the fact, so he pretended that he didn't like to play. Sometimes he found himself dreaming of the wind on the prairie
and as the autumn approached, he began to grow restive.
He dreamed of the blackjacks and the way they would soon
be standing in the sun in their abandoned glory. When the
first geese flew over he became almost homesick.

One night Lieutenant Bergh brought in a jug of corn
whisky, and several of the officers sat in a smoky room, drank
it, and told stories. The glasses were kept full and soon a
warmth came over Chal. He didn't know how the subject
came up but he found himself talking about his hills. He
talked of them as though they were a paradise on earth, and

he felt with intensity that particular night that they were. He must have described them with feeling, as everyone in the room listened to him ; listened to him until several of the officers caused a disturbance by talking with loud voices when they thought they were speaking softly.

The next morning his head pained and he felt that he should like to make a loud noise and drown all he had said the night before. He realized that he had talked too much and he was embarrassed.

At mess that day Captain Hackett said, "Say, Windzer, you're quite a talker. I don't believe I ever heard you say five words ever since I've known you, and here you were last night just layin' it off."

"And it was interestin', too," said Lieutenant Stubbs. "Gave me an idea about that part of the country I never had before. I thought Indian reservations were full of cactus and rattlesnakes — and — "

"Tourists," added Captain Hackett.

"Yeah, and tourists — sure gave me a new slant."

Chal was so embarrassed that he wanted to leave the table, but he smiled and said, "Guess I was feelin' pretty good."

But the hills came oftener to his consciousness and he spent much time attempting to banish a vague feeling of unhappiness. He remembered that his father had said that an Indian was not a wanderer — that people said they were nomads, but that no one loved his native soil more than Indians, and that they were always unhappy away from it. His father used to quote the old men. "The old fellas always told us," his father would say, "that an Indian had to stay on the earth that made him because he believed that he had come out of a certain soil like the trees and things."

It seemed to Chal that these things influenced him more

and more, especially since the excitement of the war was over and the spirit of conquest had gone out of flying. True to his heritage he couldn't tolerate monotony and routine, and duty with a capital "D" had never meant much to him. He attempted to dismiss these thoughts because he believed that he had gone a long way from his former life.

One morning he received a telegram that his father had been killed. He got leave and went home.

He was sitting in the front room with his mother. She would sit silently for several minutes, then she would make a statement that seemed to have no connection with the one that had gone before. "They found his pistol in his hand," she would say proudly. Then another long silence. "The agent said that white people in town could be guardians for young Osages and they will not have their money long, I believe." She sat looking straight in front of her with her hands lying in her lap. Chal thought there was a kind of fatalism in the very way her hands lay in her lap. "Your father said that the guv'mint would not let these white people cheat Indians, but they have done it all the time." There was another silence.

"That Congress that your father talked much about, made a law that little children and orphans would be looked after by that new state. There were not many guardians wanted to take care of little children then, 'cause that was when you were a little boy and the Osages did not have so much money. These guardians would say that to that new state, and the new state would say that everything is all right, but the new state didn't care, I believe. Now since you were a soldier, the agent said that that Congress made a new law — that — the — office Indians — "

Chal looked up quickly at his mother, "You mean restricted Indians."

"Yes, office Indians," she persisted. "They will have guardians, too, and many white mans made the agent say that they could be guardians of these office Indians. There is lots of money now and these white mans like it 'cause they are guardians for these Indians. When they was not much money there were few of these guardians, now there are many." There was another long silence and the sound of the clock ticking in the other room seemed very loud. Chal saw one of his mother's hands move slightly as though through some emotion, as she continued :

"One day I was in new car which your father bought, in front of agent's office. I see many white mans comin' up the hill. They had red faces and sweat was on their faces and they rubbed their hats with their handkerchiefs. It was a very hot day and they walked very fast, these white mans, and they do not know that their cigars did not have fire on them. When they went into agent's office you could see that their thoughts were far away and their eyes saw nothing. They did not stop and talk to each other like white people do. I thought, 'That is white man goin' to tell agent that it will be good to let them be guardians of office Indians,' and they were wondering if agent would say yes." Her right hand moved and she twisted a strand of hair back of her ear. "Your father says there is no law for this, and he was very sad, because he knew many of these white mans. He always said that guv'mint would not let white mans that is lawyer and white mans that sells clothes and houses, and white mans that is doctors, cheat Indian. But I believe your father did not believe this. I believe his tongue said this so that his heart could hear it.

"He said that guv'mint would not let white mans come here, but white mans did come here. He said that this civilization was here now. He said that bad white mans

would not come here now, 'cause this civilization is here
now. I said here is your pistol, but he said, this is not a
wild country no more. But I said, you read in papers every
day that bandit comes here to hide in hills. But he said,
no, it is a civilized country now. He took that pistol,
though. Now he is gone. Those white mans took that
new car. That pistol is here. He had that pistol in his
hand and one of those white bandits is not here, either."

They sat silently while the clock ticked, then Chal saw
his mother draw herself up proudly. "When they found him,
they said he had that pistol in his hand."

Chal remained in town several days after the funeral of
his father, talking and loafing. He had been embarrassed
during the ceremony of the burial because some of the older
Osages had come to the grave, and turning their eyes to the
sky, had chanted the song of death. He had been deeply
moved by it, but there were so many new white people in
town now, that he thought they shouldn't have gone through
the primitive ritual after the Christian burial. He pretended to himself that his father had been an important man
in the building of the new state, and he often intimated that
his father had had quite a bit to do with the constitutional
convention, by molding opinion with his oratory. He was
not so ready to boast of his father's activity in behalf of the
Osages in Washington, but he liked to believe that he had
been a figure in Washington as well.

He was proud of the new paved streets and the tall buildings that had been built in his absence, and he took great
pride in the number of cars to be seen in the streets. Nearly
all of the mixedbloods had cars now, and many of the fullbloods had at last given up their horses and had bought cars.

One day he met some young school teachers who had
come in from towns all over the state and he talked with

them over drug store drinks.   He appreciated the fact that
he was in the flying service and the fact gave him an assurance and a facility in conversation that pleased him very
much.   Nelson Newberg came in and suggested that they
all go for a ride.   When they were rolling slowly down the
street attempting to be very witty, and all naturally alive to
each other, Nelson pointed to Chal's house and said, "There's
where Chal lives."   He wasn't ashamed before all these people.   It was a large house with a pleasing yard and tall trees
and one didn't notice its ugliness, and its size was the important thing after all.

Afterward, he believed that Nelson had known and had
pointed out the house with a purpose, because just as they
were passing, two tall, blanketed Indians came out.   One
was an old man and the other was still in middle age.   They
came quickly, regally out of the house, and behind them was
Chal's mother, watching them leave.

"Ha ha ha ha ha ha," laughed Nelson, "look, who's that,
ole Kick-a-Hole-in-the-Sky and Rain-in-the-Face — come to
see you, Chal ?"

It seemed to Chal that all the warmth of importance and
all the sweet juices of appreciation left his body like sap
leaves a tree ; down through his feet and through the floor
boards of the car, leaving nothing but water behind.   They
were across the bridge and moving slowly along the black
road before he recovered sufficiently to think.   Nelson and
the very blond girl were pummeling each other in the front
seat, Nelson putting up his hands in defense was crouched
halfway under the steering wheel, laughing.   They didn't
seem to notice that Chal had been uncomfortable and he
immediately took courage, but he was annoyed.   It would
happen that Circling Hawk and his Uncle Fire Cloud should
come out of the house at that time.   Every time they came

to town they came to the house ; came in without knocking
and walked back to the picture of John hanging in a large,
ornate frame which Chal knew to be very bad taste.   Standing there looking up at the picture, they would chant the
song of death.   He wished they would stop it, it made his
mother very sad, and when he heard it he felt as though he
wanted to cry.   Besides, they might come some time when
he had someone there visiting him.

CHAL returned to duty at the field but stayed only a few
months, then resigned his commission.   It was not difficult,
as the War Department had not decided exactly what lines
they would follow in the development of the air service.
When he returned home, the town seemed larger and noisier,
and a new brick building had sprung up in his absence.

The black derricks had now passed on to the west ; out beyond the blackjack fringes onto the high prairie, where they
stood like sterile forests against the sky.   Everyone talked of
the Salt Creek field.   The oil world had turned its eyes
toward Salt Creek, they said.   People from the town drove
out to the end of the pavement, then over the dusty roads
that twisted into ravines and climbed the prairie hills from
all directions, and entered the forest of black derricks where
they became lost in the maze of roads crossing and recrossing each other.   A near-sighted Sunday driver from Kihekah, taking his family out to see the greatest oil field in the
world, would lose himself hopelessly.

He would eat lunch with his wife and children at the
doubtful cafe "Quick Eats," where Conny served food, "Like
You Like it" amid the clanking, screaming of steel, groaning
bull wheels and rasping cables ; amid the chuffing and coughing of operation ; amid the rumbling and roaring of passing
trucks loaded with tools, which shook the frame "Quick Eats

Palace" like a diffident earthquake.   The driver from Kihekah would pay a dollar for a plate containing a pallid potato,
a piece of beef sunk almost irretrievably in grease, and the
usual side dishes, with coffee, the latter splashing over the
cup rim in transit.

Hundreds of people would bump over the holes made by
heavy trucks, suffer the fine dust in their throats, in order to
visit this great field.   They would drive back to Kihekah
wondering if they were getting their share of the wealth
which was being poured into the coffers of the Osages.   As
they drove along they might consider raising the price of silk
stockings and making the profit an even two hundred per
cent.   They would probably dream of the time when they
could get back to civilization — back to Ioway or Pennsyl-
vania or Tennessee.

AFTER his father's death, Chal came into thousands of dollars.

"Why, you're rich," Jep Newberg told him one day.
"Yeah, you're rich," he said, putting his hand on Chal's
shoulder.   Chal didn't mind people putting their hands on
his shoulder so much now — it seemed the thing to do —
but he was relieved when they took their hands away.

"Say, whatta yuh figurin' on doin', now ?"   And Jep
moved his chewed, unlit cigar to the other side of his mouth.
Chal could see the juice stain glisten on his thick lower lip.

Chal knew it was not particularly an honor to have
money.   Nearly everyone had money.   The poorest new-
comer of a year or two ago now drove about in his own car,
and besides his or her particular business, many of these
people were guardians for one or more restricted Indians.
Yet there were no refineries, no factories, nothing made and
nothing produced by the citizens of the little town among

the blackjacks. The oil was carried out of the old reservation, now a county in the new state, through large pipe lines,
and long trains of tank cars rattled away from the hills every
day. Theoretically, out of every forty-two-gallon barrel of
oil produced in the old reservation, the Osage tribe received
a sixth. Everyone else sold things or rendered services.

When Chal answered Jep's question, he did so with embarrassment. "I'm not doin' anything," he said. "I uh —
I'll — uh — probably go into something, though, I guess."
Chal believed that if you weren't in some business you didn't
have the respect of the community.

"Come in," said Jep. They went into the large store that
had been practically rebuilt from the primitive frame store
of the old Agency. They walked down a long aisle, between rows of pink, yellow and orange lampshades, ornate
iron work, overstuffed furniture, showcases of hose, and piles
of Indian blankets, back to Jep's office, which was a kind of
bank. Everyone who had been in business before the oil
boom had such an office. Here they did a banking business
as well as the business of their particular trade. A banking
business that grew out of the old trader days, when the
trader talked with Indians and advanced them money until
payment time, and charged whatever interest might strike
his fancy. But there was no risk, as the payments were as
sure as death.

Jep pointed to a chair. "Set down," he said. He pulled
a pencil from his vest pocket and tapped the desk. "Say,
I got a proposition here that you oughtta have. I'll jist lay
the cards on the table. Curry owns some stock in the Oil
National, see — only he don't own it, see. He's in a tight
place and he's gonna hafta git rid of it. It's a buy — it's
like stealin' it. He's pressed, and you c'n get that stock
f'r a song. Lemme show you." He held the pencil in his

stubby fingers and made figures all over a white sheet of paper, shifting his cigar as he talked. Chal looked at the figures — they fascinated him, but he didn't even attempt to understand them. Soon his thoughts were far away, but he kept the expression of interest on his face, so that when Jep looked up he could see it.

"You see ?" Jep said finally. "There y'are. Now I tell yuh, I'd take this offer, but I jist can't handle it, havin' stock in the other bank too. Nelson's jist gettin' started here in the store. I think you oughtta have it. I wouldn' tell ever'body about this, but you're a young man jist gettin' started, an' I knew your father, too — ole John an' I were purty good friends."

Chal made a movement as if he would rise. "You don't hafto take my word for it. We'll go over an' talk to Fancher — he'll tell you the same thing. Look, lemme show yuh here." He made some more fascinating figures on another sheet of paper. "Payin' twenty per cent — can yuh beat that ? Hell, boy, it's an investment, and you c'n handle it. I could help you out a little, but you c'd handle it with idle money. Tell yuh what I c'n do — I c'n get that stock for yuh for twenty-five thousand, today."

Chal winced. His mother had just told him that morning that he had twenty-five thousand dollars in the bank. Jep looked at him, and Chal didn't know what else to do, so he smiled. Jep became encouraged, and went on about the advantages of this investment. As he sat there Chal was almost ready to say yes in order to regain his comfort, and he was also urged by the desire to get into something, but he thought of the coincidence that the price of the stock should be the amount of his deposit. He didn't know that most of the prominent business men knew almost every bank account, why it was there, and its source. They knew about every important transaction and the reasons for the transaction. This knowledge was self-preservation.

There was only one cloud in the clear sky of optimism that curved so brightly over the frenzied little valley, and that cloud never disappeared. It hung in the sky threatening to become a dark cumulus cloud which might be the source of a storm powerful enough to destroy the economic system of the little town. That cloud was the threat of an investigation by a senatorial committee. Osages and Osage oil were national news, and nearly anything was possible with such close association with national prominence. The Department of Interior, represented by the office of the commissioner of Indian affairs, had always seemed to the people of the blackjacks a very whimsical and at times unreasonable power. They knew little of the conditions in Washington and in their isolation were never sure what to expect.

The business people of the town were ever conscious of that cloud, and almost everyone was a business person, whether they bought things for eight cents and sold them for fifteen cents or for three dollars, or rendered professional services. The habit of selling merchandise at a tremendous profit had become a tradition, and the habit of selling things twice, once for cash from the beaded bag of an Indian and again on the books in the office, was still practiced. The Indian never lost his Olympian indifference to money, although he was aware of these practices. Thus, with one eye on that little cloud, the business people watched each other closely, but no matter what might happen they would stand together.

Chal didn't know that the cashier of the Oil National bank owed Jep money. As he sat there wishing he could summon up enough courage to leave, he felt that he was glued to the chair. But finally, attempting to smile, he arose quickly and left, with Jep following him to the door and urging him to think it over.

The next week as he sat at home lazily, with one leg over the arm of an overstuffed chair, he read a story in the *Trumpet* about the Osage Indians becoming civilized, about many of them going into business and making investments. The *Trumpet* pointed to Buffalo Head as a shining example. It was glad to report that Buffalo Head had just recently bought stock in the Oil National bank. As Chal read, he wondered if he had missed a chance.

A month later the town talked about the sudden leave-taking of the cashier of the Oil National bank and the county treasurer, and everyone talked about the closing of the bank, but the *Trumpet* didn't seem to know anything about it. It was just street talk ; the talk of bridge and poker tables.

XIII

THE years went by fast for Chal, though he did very little except ride around in his long, powerful red roadster. He attended all the dances, and became a pretty fair pool player, betting a dollar on the side. He drove out onto the prairie sometimes, but seldom left the new paved roads. Sometimes he picked up some of the girls of the town and circled the Newberg building, down the street, then back, and made the circle again many times. Or he sat long hours in the Blue Front drug store and dallied with other young people. The fact that he wasn't doing something still worried him, but not so much now. He took great delight in clothes, and was very careful to wear the right thing. He never walked anywhere and his saddle hung spanned by cobwebs out in the barn at the ranch. During the summer he spent many weeks at some resort in the high mountains, playing golf, drinking, and driving his red roadster over mountain trails.

Sometimes he went with a party of young people to one of the mushroom oil towns, where they sat in a little shack and bought whisky for a dollar a drink — just for the hell of it, under the impression that they were sophisticated people from Kihekah and were slumming.

But life was full. You could get the most expensive orchestra in the state to play for the dances, and though you sometimes had the discomfort of losing the interest of your partner to the slick-haired orchestra leader, the corn whisky flowed and you could always have a good time.

Nearly every day brought news of a new oil well ; a new

gusher in the Salt Creek field. Nearly every week brought news that the local bandit and his gang had robbed another bank, and you could stand and listen in the Blue Front drug store, while someone who had had the honor of not only seeing the bandit but actually talking with him held his listeners spellbound. Sometimes the *Trumpet* would scream with black headlines that another citizen had become an oil millionaire, and seemed almost ecstatic with the honor of telling it. There would be a short résumé of this man's life, in which his acquisitive struggle was stressed, and his virtues recounted. And the fortunate citizen had the admiration of the other citizens and immediately almost everything he said became oracular. They boasted of him for only a short time, as he almost invariably moved away to a larger town.

During the competitive bidding at the oil lease sales, you could stand and watch the auctioneer auction off a-hundred-sixty-acre tracts and sometimes stand within a few feet of a nationally known oil magnate whose name screamed at you from billboards along the highway. You could stand near and watch him raise his finger to the auctioneer ; a movement which meant hundreds of thousands of dollars. The postoak by the new Agency office building, under the shade of which the great would sometimes lie informally, waiting for the auction to begin, was enthusiastically called "the million dollar oak" by the citizens of the town.

After the lease sales, everyone felt pretty good. Some of the citizens worried a little, wondering if they were going to get any of the "gravy" after all, but the atmosphere was one of optimism, and they felt that glory had come. But everyone knew there was no end to it. There would be a greater glory, and many of the citizens dreamed of the time when they would be rich enough to move away ; dreamed of the time when they could visit again the sleepy little towns which they had left, with a chauffeur and an expensive car.

MARIE FOBUS came back to town.

Chal saw her walking down the street holding the hand of a little girl whose hair had just been set in a beauty parlor. The little girl could scarcely keep up with Marie's long strides, and her short silk frock was flapping midway up her fat little thighs. Chal noticed that Marie's skirts were shorter than any of the skirts in town. He wondered how they could become any shorter.

"Hello, Chal," she shouted, dragging the little girl along. Chal wanted to smile, he thought the little girl was so funny. They stood and talked for a while, then Chal said, "Le's go in an have a drenk." They found a table at the Blue Front and he thought he had never seen anything so ungraceful as Marie when she sat down. She backed up to the chair, put her knees together with a quick movement, and sat down with her knees together and her feet slightly apart. They smoked cigarettes and talked. Nearly everyone smoked cigarettes now, but Marie lit one right in the Blue Front, and only the faster girls in town did that.

Marie had married a Princeton man during the war, and had gone East somewhere. Chal had heard that she had been divorced. He bet she couldn't stand her husband after he got into citizen's clothes again, and that was the reason she had divorced him. He wanted to ask her if she had been down to visit the University recently, as a prelude to asking about Blo. He didn't ask the question.

She sat and bit little pieces out of a straw. "By Gawd, this town's back-woodsey, how do you stand it here?" The town seemed quite civilized to Chal. Everyone knew it was the fastest growing little town in the state, but he 'said, "Ah — I dunno." She turned to her little daughter and said, "Darlin', go look at the dolls up there — see 'em." The little caricature of her sophistication frowned and stuck out her lower lip. Marie pushed her gently and said, "Go on, now." She watched the little girl go toward the front of the store, then she turned back to Chal, "Lissen, for Chrissake, get me a drenk." Chal smiled knowingly but he was shocked on the inside. He didn't know why he felt shocked. Everyone carried a flask of corn whisky now, and all the girls of the town drank, but the idea of Marie Fobus of the Pi's, the strait-laced, intolerant, virginal Marie Fobus asking for a drink was a surprise to him. He got up and went to his car around the corner, took out a silver flask, looked around, then put it in his hip pocket and went down the block to a stairway. At the top of the stairs he knocked at the door.

A frowzle-headed girl stuck her head out, and her very red mouth broke into a smile. "Hello, Chal, come in. I thought maybe you was the law." Chal pulled the flask out of his pocket and handed it to her, and she called back to the other room. A girl in a faded wrapper came in and took the flask.

"What's the matter with you and the law?" asked Chal.

"Well, you know I'm straight — I ain't no cheap chicken — you know. I been sellin' stuff, see, snow, you know, to all these Osage boys for a long time, and I been square with 'em — you know that. Well, someuh these new doctors that has been comin' intuh town are commencin' to take my trade away. It was gettin' pretty bad, see, so I goes over to a certain doctor and I says to um, 'Looka here,' I says, 'Le's kinda split this thing — it's only fair,' I says. He looks at me and swells up like a toad, see, 'What d'yuh

mean,' he says, and I says, 'I mean that you been takin' my
trade,' I says.   An' I named over at least seven Osage boys
and five girls I know he tuk away from me.   Well, I wish
you could uh seen the bastard.   He puffed up and says,
'Get outta here, you — ' you know.   'Get outta here,' he
says.   'I'm gonna see that you go to the pen for this.   If
y'ever come around here again, I'm gonna see that you go to
the pen,' he says.   I was madder'n hell, but I kept the ole
trap shut, see, 'cause I thought maybe he might do it.   I'se
talkin' to Tug, y' know, the man on this beat, and he says
not to worry, but you know I can't pay off — I ain't got
the money, see.   An' y' know, that's why I been layin'
low.   We keep what little we got stashed, see."

   The girl in the faded dressing gown brought the flask
to Chal and he gave Sadie five dollars and walked out.
These kind of people were always thinkin' the worst of people, he believed.   Who ever heard of a respectable person
like a doctor sellin' dope.   Just talk, he guessed.   Running
Elk said he got his dope from a doctor too, but he was
drunk most of the time anyway.   Chal believed that most
of the things he heard were just good stories.

   They drove by Marie's home and left her little daughter
with the grandmother, then drove out of town.   They
turned into a dirt lane, bumping over dried mud ruts, then
turned out of the road among the trees.   Chal opened the
soda water bottle as he handed the flask to Marie.

   They lit cigarettes and talked, alternately taking a drink
from the bottle until it was quite empty.   A warmth came
over Chal and he felt that the most imperative thing at that
time was to get more.   He started the car and backed into
the road.   "Maybe we better go to the field — I know a
place there," he said.

   They sped out through town, along the paved highway,

then over the dusty road among the derricks, and stopped on the main street of Salt Creek. Chal went into one of the frame buildings, then reappeared with a hump under his coat, climbed in behind the wheel, and they drove off across the prairie.

Chal felt that he should like to have a beautiful spot in which to drink. The warmth in him made it imperative that they find some beautiful spot along the creek. They drove along lanes but when they started to turn in they found themselves stopped by barbed wire. "Le's have a snifter now," suggested Marie. "No," said Chal, "I wantta find a certain spot." The warm feeling also made him obstinate. He remembered how he used to ride to a round hole of water with elms arching above it ; elms in which the prairie breezes talked eternally. That was the place he wanted to find now. Marie thought he was stubborn and was about to tell him so when he said, "That — that sycamore, that's the place." They turned out of the road and drove down to the creek. Several black wells stood about on the prairie above the trees and from each a path of sterile brown earth led down to the creek, where oil and salt water had killed every blade of grass and exposed the glaring limestone. Some of the elms had been cut down, and the surface of the water had an iridescent scum on it.

Chal stopped the car and with his hands on the wheel looked. A feeling of unhappiness came over him and the alcohol that had warmed to inspiration, to obstinacy, to remembered beauty, now caused him to feel a deep anger ; a helpless anger which became bitter, injured innocence as he looked.

"Well," said Marie, eagerly, "Whatta we waitin' on ?"

He pulled the bottle from the car pocket then uncapped the soda water.

Chal drove home carefully that night. He could remember the black derricks against the red afterglow, and he could remember the glazed look in Marie's eyes. He remembered her cigarette-stained fingers and that she seemed to be constantly looking for a cigarette she had dropped. He remembered that she was careless about her skirts, but the rest of the time they spent there was a haze.

He did remember, however, coming into Kihekah and stopping in Main Street, when the red stop light flashed. He remembered how proud he had been because he had stopped, and how he had looked over at Marie for approval, but she was asleep with her head hanging over on her shoulder, and he had felt annoyance that she had not seen his skill and alertness. He didn't have any idea how long they had sat there by that oil-polluted pool of water, nor when they had started home, but he did remember that he had taken unusually large drinks out of the bottle with a vindictive feeling that he could compensate for the unhappiness which that spot, so dear to his boyhood memories, had caused him.

The next morning, for the first time in the experience of his hip-pocket flask, dances, and drinking parties, he wanted more whisky. He felt that he must have a drink. Every nerve in his body called for alcohol, and his head was bursting. For three days he stayed half intoxicated, cowed by the craving that suddenly came upon him ; without courage to face the terrible mornings after. Each night he made sure that there was some whisky in a bottle under his pillow before he went to bed.

MARIE called Chal on the telephone.

"Got a friend uh mine visitin' here and I want to show her a good time if I can, wonder if you couldn't help me ?"

"Sure."

"Well, look. She's never seen an Indian dance, and I thought we might take her out today."

The arrangements made, Chal didn't know whether he liked his responsibility or not. He knew how the dancers felt about people coming out to stare at them, yet they did nothing to stop or discourage it. They danced because they felt it impossible to give up that last expression of themselves, and though these dances at the village were only social dances for their own amusement, they adhered closely to the ancient form. They did not charge an admittance fee and because of this the dances were not swamped, perhaps because of the theory held at that time that anything free was not worth while.

As the party drove out to the village, Chal was pleased with the closeness of his companions. He liked the stiff fragility of their summer frocks and the vague scents wafted to him. He could see that Jean watched him out of the corner of her eye, seeming to be constantly aware of him. He had become accustomed to this interest in girls whom he met and he was slightly disappointed when it was not present.

He found seats on the benches behind some waddling old women and several old men. The earthen floor was hard and a little uneven, and surrounding it were benches ; making of the dance floor, an oval. The Roundhouse was built of pine and had poles supporting the rafters. It had taken the place of the old blackjack bough-covered open structure, but had been built for some time and was becoming gray with weathering.

They were early. Chal grew nervous sitting there with these immaculate girls. Jean's fingernails glinted in the light that came down through a crack in the roof and her white shoes were still spotless, though it seemed impossible that they should be, since the party had had to wade through thick dust. The girls sat and waited for something to happen ; watching every Indian who came into the room as though they expected him to whoop suddenly or climb one of the poles and hang by his toes from a rafter. Chal felt annoyed with them and with himself. He felt annoyed with them because he knew they would not be able to understand the spirit of the dance, and he was annoyed with himself because in some vague way he felt that he was not worthy of that spirit. Yet he remembered having seen a Russian dancer sit through one whole afternoon, fascinated by the dance of his people, and ever after that he had had a very warm feeling toward that particular dancer. He knew, however, that most people came to be entertained and were ready to go after a few minutes of what they thought to be monotony ; leaving the Roundhouse somewhat disappointed, but boasting thereafter, "Yeah, I've seen 'em stomp-dance." As he sat there he felt vaguely that he was betraying his people ; even though he had thought them backward and uncivilized, he sometimes had the feeling which he was experiencing this afternoon.

He told his companions he wanted to see his friend Sun-on-His-Wings as an excuse to leave them for a short time. The sun was brilliant but although it was becoming hot, it had not yet sapped the vivid greenness from the grass, and the air was fresh and filled with the voices of dickcissels. The dust in the road that led up to the Roundhouse was ankle deep, and he watched with amusement some citizens from the town helping their families through the dust. He noticed a chalky-faced young man wearing pince-nez. He had his hand under the arm of his well-dressed wife, whose weight Chal immediately guessed at two hundred pounds. The man's feeble gallantry made Chal feel happier inside.

An evil white man with a white apron around him was standing at a hot-dog stand decorated with red-white-and-blue cheesecloth. The man was shouting, "Git 'em while they're hot, boys — they're ready, they're hot." Some round-faced Indian children stood around the stand drinking strawberry pop, laughing and playing. Under the open, bough-covered structures surrounding the Roundhouse, the women were decorating their men for the dance.

Chal walked about with his hands in his pockets. A large car stopped and the dust swirled around it, and Little Flower climbed out from under the driver's wheel. Chal saw that the left side of her face had a great spot of misplaced rouge, and that the spot on the other side of the cheek was smaller and too high on the cheek bone. He noticed that her legs seemed too small and bowed in her short skirts. Her long, bronzed arms seemed very thin, and her fingers long and thin, seemed too weak to hold up the cluster of diamond rings. When she saw him, she smiled and he saw that her eyes were very bright and large, like the eyes of a doe. She made her way toward him through the dust, and as he watched her approach he had the thought that a white girl would have called him to the car. He disliked people who honked their auto horns to summon you.

She gave him her thin hand. "Hello, I haven't seen you for a long time." She tottered, and her breath was fume-laden.

"No," said Chal, "I don't see anybody any more."

"Oh, I don't either." She waved her hand unsteadily around in a semi-circle. "All this makes me tired."

"That's not the reason I don't see any of the people here any more — I'm pretty busy." He wanted to defend the village to her, and he always liked to appear that he was busy. He thought of how he had often admired Nelson

Newberg's ability to appear busy with a pencil behind his ear and paper sticking from his pocket, hurrying across the street.

"Well, I don't live here, you know." She said this as though she didn't want him to get the wrong impression. "Well," she smiled, her teeth very white, "I just thought I'd say hello." Chal walked with her toward the car, but when he noticed that the car was full of people, he stopped.

In the front seat was one of those doubtful nonentities from a large city. He affected what he believed to be the collegiate cut in clothes ; with the cheap clothes and his swaggering, the effect was a bit bizarre. Chal could see that he felt his own importance as he sat nonchalantly in the car, and he knew instinctively that he was traveling with a toothbrush and an extra shirt at the expense of Little Flower. His pal in the rear seat was the same type. By his side was a very blond girl, who sat comfortably in the corner of the seat as though she never, never wanted to leave soft cushions again.

Chal stopped when Little Flower said something about meeting her friends. Then she said, "Birdie and the rest wanted to see the dance — are they goin' to dance ?" Chal thought, 'Bad enough as it is,' then he lied, "No, they're just gonta give away a few presents — not much dancin', I guess." He allowed her to cross the dusty road alone, then after a short consultation, she climbed in and drove away in a cloud of dust.

The People had begun to gather. There were old men Chal had not seen for several years, women and children ; those who were coming to watch the dance. Some saluted with the fingers of their hand the palm of his, and to all of the men he said, "How, my father," and they replied, "How, my son." An old woman, almost blind, came waddling along with a cane.   When she saw Chal she stopped and said, "Huhn — John ee shinkah — he is man now."   She went away toward the Roundhouse mumbling, "Huhn-n-n-n-n."   Chal was glad that no one of his friends had ' seen him talking so intimately with this old woman.

Girls came in twos and threes, giggling, as Indian girls had always giggled, he remembered.   But these girls had rouged their lips ludicrously, and Chal felt that they certainly looked barbaric ; girls attempting to imitate white girls always seemed barbaric to him, and he didn't like their short skirts bobbing around their bony knees and their crow-black hair bobbed "windblown" style.

He heard the tinkling of many little bells and Yellow Horse came across the road, gorgeous in his paint and his scalplock.   Then from all directions came the tinkling of many bells, and the proud dancers approached the Roundhouse.   As Yellow Horse came close an enthusiastic photographer maneuvered in front of him and attempted to take his picture, but Yellow Horse placed his eagle-wing fan in front of his face and passed on into the Roundhouse.

Before Chal got back to his seat the singers around the kettle drum had begun to sing and beat the rhythm, TUM, tum, tum, tum — TUM, tum, tum tum ; but before he reached his seat the old rhythm in which most of the songs were sung was begun ; TUM, tum, TUM, tum, TUM, tum, TUM, tum.

Marie said, "Oh, Chal, I'm glad you're back ; Jean wants to know so many things, and I can't tell her — I feel 'shamed of myself."

Chal answered most of Jean's questions ; why the visiting Poncas wore the little round thing behind ; was that reely underwear that that fat fella had on ; who was that — that tall good-lookin' fella ; what's he doin' that for.   But she grew tired of asking questions, and soon the girls grew tired of the monotony of the thing.

The singing leader led off in a high falsetto, then as he lowered his voice the others joined. The dancers rose one by one or two at a time from their benches and danced toward the center of the room, then around the singers. When the music stopped, the dancers would jingle back to their benches, sit in rows and fan themselves with their eagle-wing fans. Sitting there with gravity and dignity. Then, after an interval, the same thing.

Chal sat watching and listening. He had almost forgotten the effect which the dancing had on him, and as usual, he had a desire to join them. He had always felt that by joining them he could express that thing which came over him at times ; that something which had to be expressed, but which he couldn't possibly put into words or actions. He sat there today with that feeling almost choking him, and he knew that he would not be able to express it, and that had the effect of making him slightly surly.

He watched the tall form of Sun-on-His-Wings dancing with religious gravity in his gay trappings ; his scalplock quivering as he danced ; his eyes looking neither to right nor left. He watched Walks Alone rise from the bench, feel behind him and straighten his beaver skin breech strap which hung almost to his heels, then dance upright toward the singers. He watched him bend with a quick movement and look intently on the ground, first on one side and then on the other, moving his head with quick jerks. As he circled the singers he touched the ground in front of him with his quirt, as though tracing footprints. Then he saw Sun-on-His-Wings put his head down like a cock prairie chicken in the spring and imitate the nuptial dance. Then he straightened a little as he danced out to the edge of the room, where he turned and danced back toward the singers, swaying and moving his head slowly from side to side like a foraging eagle. Spirit Iron seemed to grow excited as he raised his war axe and yelped, then danced, bent far over, looking for the trail of the enemy. A visiting Indian, a Ponca, by the characteristic circular mirror, encircled by turkey tail feathers placed just above his buttocks, danced frantically in his dyed long underwear. He stamped and twisted, and jerked his head fantastically ; he did the black bottom, the Charleston, and other clownish tricks until Chal looked away in disgust, but he could hear murmurs of approval from the visitors on the benches. The Ponca had been on the vaudeville stage, and he knew how to please white people. Chal knew that his People didn't like to have visiting Indians desecrate their dance, but they retained their ancient courtesy and would say nothing to the Poncas about it. However, this particular Ponca had lost his ancient courtesy and continued to come to dance with the Osages.

Old Black Bull, one of the visiting Sioux, danced like a great god, with his height, his hard, thin body, and his eyes smiling ; his great Siouxan scalplock quivering with the jerks of his head. They said he was eighty years old, and Chal could see that he was dancing one of his last prayers.

Chal had a desire to laugh at poor old Spoiler-of-the-Spring as he danced around the singers with his fat belly shaking like jelly.

As he watched Sun-on-His-Wings dancing there, he thought of Running Elk and their boyhood together. Running Elk was always the one to get into trouble ; the lovable trouble-maker. But he was dead now. They said he was shot in the head and left lying in his car in the Big Hill country.

This thing which welled in Chal again as he watched the

dancers and listened to the pulse-beats of the drum, increased his surliness with the increase in the intensity of his emotion. When Marie said, "Le's go," and began powdering her face with a large powder puff as she looked into a little mirror, he was almost angry, and he said,

"You wanted to see the dance, didn't you — well, why don't you watch it — you — le's wait a minute." He wanted to explain to Marie the importance of that which was happening before them, but he believed there was no use. These girls wouldn't understand, and they'd think he was sentimental. Then as if to temper somewhat the severity of his words to Marie, he said, "We'll go in a minute." Then he couldn't refrain from adding, "You wouldn't go in the middle of an opera." Then he thought he ought to smile.

As he forgot the summery girls at his side with their subtle scents ; as he lost himself in the dance of his people, he was not aware that Jean, grown tired of watching the dancing, was looking intently at his profile, and had decided that she liked this fellow.

After one of the songs, several figures rose and walked over to some visiting Indian, or some old man or woman sitting on the benches, and presented them with gifts. A tall dancer gave a beautiful blanket to Black Bull, and Yellow Horse put clinking silver into the hands of one of the singers. Members of the family whom the last song had honored gave some gifts to several other people.

After the next song, Spirit Iron led a beautiful bay horse into the Roundhouse and gave it to Spoiler-of-the-Spring, whose embarrassed son led it out of the room.

"This is what they call 'smokin',' " Chal explained to the girls. "You see, this is the third day — the last day of the social dances — and this is the time when the singers sing songs which honor the deeds of ancestors. The people

whose ancestors are honored make presents not only to the
singers but to other people — 'specially visitin' Indians.
You see, they say they 'smoke' you a horse, or some stroud-
ing or money, 'cause their ancestral song has been sung."

"Oh, how nice — wish they'd smoke me something,"
said Marie, gaily.

"A jug of corn ?" questioned Jean, raising the thin line
of her plucked eyebrows.

Then Chal's heart sank. He was suddenly flooded with
emotion that felt like needles pricking him, and he thought
that he could not stay any longer. The singers were singing the song of his own ancestors. The song of the "Pawnee
crying on the hill." His ancestor had killed that Pawnee,
and they had made a song about it in his honor.

Chal had an almost uncontrollable urge to go down on
the floor and dance as the singers sang that song. But he
had never danced with his people. When he was old
enough to dance he was in high school, and he hadn't wanted
the people at the high school to think that he was uncivilized.
Sun-on-His-Wings had always danced with their people, and
Running Elk had danced with them as well, until he started
drinking so much and taking dope. But Chal had never
danced with them.

He saw a tall figure rise from the bench across the floor,
let his blanket slip behind him to the bench, and begin to
dance in the rhythm of the song, remaining where he stood.
It was Fire Cloud, and a pain came to Chal's heart. Then
Old Circling Hawk rose slowly, and holding his eagle-wing
fan in front of him, danced, standing before his seat, but
soon, as though the memories were too much for the old
fellow, he moved slowly out to the middle of the floor,
dancing with great gravity, his old body as straight as a pine

tree. But Fire Cloud remained in the one position, dancing throughout the song before his bench.

Chal thought he must get out. He felt that his emotion might take the form of tears, and he knew that he could never live down that disgrace. He arose, saying, "Le's go," and helped the girls down the benches.

When they had descended from their seats, he hung back as the girls left the Roundhouse. Then as the singers stopped, he walked up to Old Black Bull, handed him a five-dollar note, shook hands with him and said, "How." He liked Black Bull.

Jean had been watching him. He had hoped that the girls had not seen him, but as they walked through the hot dust to the car, he had to explain his actions. The girls said it was romantic.

XIV

CHAL didn't know what to do with himself. He flung himself into an overstuffed chair and sat with his legs apart, then arose and walked to the window with a cigarette hanging from his lips. The cars were parked along the curbing across the street, and there were some parked in front of his father's house. Those cars parked there annoyed him. People didn't care whether they parked their cars in front of your drive or not. He believed that his mother ought to sell this property for business, though. They were too close to the heart of town — no wonder people parked their cars in front of the house. He believed they ought to sell this lot and buy one on the hill, where all the best people were building ; build a big house on the hill.

He heard his mother moving about in the next room, and the fact that they lived down in the valley in an old house seemed to be an injury, and he felt in his annoyance that his mother had something to do with it. That his mother was injuring him intentionally. He frowned as he watched the cars pass up and down along the street. His mother's soft tread continued. He wished his mother would go out more in society — go out with the society people of the town. He never saw her name among the select people who gave dinners at the new country club on the hill across the creek. He wished his mother would go out more and for pete's sake, say something — talk like other women. She just sat, and when she did talk you could tell she didn't talk English very well. She didn't talk like other people, but like the books she read. He thought it was a wonder that she had ever stashed her blankets, shrouding and leggings, but even yet when she had to go outside the house into the yard on a cold day, she threw her blanket over her shoulders instead of a coat. Threw that loud Indian blanket over her nice blue dress with the lace down the front.

He turned away from the window and sat down again in the overstuffed chair, and threw his leg over the arm. He wished he had something to do — some business, but there wasn't anything for him to do. He couldn't get a job. No one would give a job to an Indian. Certainly he wouldn't have any chance to run for a county office, 'cause the voters always said that an Indian had too much money and didn't need the job. But anyway, he felt that he could get more respect if he had a job or was in some business for himself. He knew in his heart, however, that he wouldn't go into business or get a job if he had a chance. There seemed to be another dignity somewhere that would be hurt if he worked. Then he had a thought that made him smile : he guessed he must have two dignities, one tellin' him to do something, and one tellin' him not to do anything.

He paced the floor for a few minutes, then went into his room. He uncorked a bottle of corn whisky which had little specks swimming about in it. He looked at the door ; he didn't want his mother to see him. Funny how it was now — he had to hide his whisky, and he could remember when the *Rock and Rye* used to stand on the front room table with glasses about. Of course it was against the law to get it then, but everybody had it and no one seemed to think anything about it. But now you had to hide whisky and go out into the country to drink it, and everybody thought it was smart to drink.

He turned the bottle up and took a big swallow. He went back into the other room, paced up and down the floor for a while, then went back and took another drink. He knew that it would be several days or perhaps a week before he could sober up, but he didn't care — there wasn't anything else to do anyway.

He went back to the chair in the front room. He felt warmed and contented as he sat there, and he certainly wasn't the young man who had doubted himself a few minutes ago. He felt quite important now. Suddenly he felt sentimental about the dance out at the village the other day, and he made up his mind that he would dance next time. He pictured himself in breech clout and moccasins, as the most graceful dancer in the Roundhouse. Suddenly he felt very important. He was so full of the dream that he went to the window and looked out, then began to day-dream that he was dancing alone at the Roundhouse, the drum-beats became faster and louder, and the spectators suddenly became horrified when they realized that Chal was doing a death dance. He saw Blo's face among the spectators. He saw both horror and admiration in her eyes, and he danced faster, thrilled with the idea that she would be very sorry when the end of the dance came and he killed himself as a sacrifice.

He had never heard of anything like this, but his fume-exhilarated brain was indulging in fantastic acrobatics. As he stood there looking out, he saw only the pictures in his day-dream, and he was experiencing a bitter-sweet happiness, which grew to the extent that he suddenly came back to realization, so sweet and intense was the thrill.

He turned from the window, went back into his room, put the bottle in his hip pocket, then went out to the garage to get his red roadster. He suddenly decided he would go out to the village and see Sun-on-His-Wings. He drove very fast, causing the dust to rise in a cloud which floated out over the fields.

There were no more lodges in the village now. In their places were houses ; some small, and some rather large ones, and behind each house a lot for horses. Many of the houses had drying racks for meat, and open structures covered with boughs around them.

Chal drew up in front of Sun-on-His-Wings' house and called a slovenly negro to him. The negro said that Sun-on-His-Wings was out to the old man's. Chal looked at him, then said, "You mean out to his father's ? You mean out to Chief Watching Eagle's ranch ?" Chal didn't like to hear the older men referred to with disrespect, and it was particularly distasteful to him today. He sat looking at the negro as his motor purred, and he said, "Looks like you'd have more respect for a chief, at least — I don't wantta hear you call him 'the old man' any more." Fear came into the negro's face. "Yes suh," he said. Chal's sense of injury became almost intense. "You know you're treated better when you work for an Indian than when you work for white men in town — why don't you appreciate it ?" The negro had become quite frightened, and he said, "Yes suh, Mistuh Chal, Ah knows 'at — Ah sho knows 'at." Chal felt better as he drove away.

As he sped along he thought of that black man's face and he realized how very funny it was. He smiled, but his emotion of humor was intensified by the fumes in his brain and he lost control of it and laughed out. There was something in him which magnified the humor inspired by that fear on the negro's face. He could control the ridiculous urge to laugh for a moment, but it kept returning.

The old men of his people always said that the Great Mysteries had sent the Black Rears to their people to make them laugh and forget their troubles. They came with the white man who brought trouble ; they said the Black Rears had come for that reason ; to make them laugh and forget those troubles which the white man had brought to them. They said the Black Rears came from the South ; from the direction of Good.

There was activity around Watching Eagle's ranch. The women were cutting up meat and they had erected a sweatlodge just east of the conical Peyote church. Chal stopped on the hill overlooking the houses and took another drink from the bottle.

The main house was a large one and built on top of a standstone hill, and it was surrounded by the smaller houses and the Peyote church stood apart. Most of the older Indians, those who were influenced very slightly by that which they called the Great Frenzy, lived their daily lives as the fathers had lived, dressing in their leggings, blankets and bandeau. The only change being that they now lived in houses with modern conveniences ; radios, telephones, bathrooms and modern furniture. They were now Peyote worshipers, which was a mixture of the old religion, Christianity, and the new belief in passivity and retribution.

Chal drove up among the houses and stopped under a tree. They were glad to see him. Bird Feather, the wife of Sun-on-His-Wings, looked at her neat shoes when he spoke to her. Sun-on-His-Wings wore citizen's clothes, as did all the younger men present. The older men lay in the shade of the trees in their native blankets.

Sun-on-His-Wings waved his hand to where the meat for the feast was being prepared. "You will eat with us," and he smiled. "But you must wait until tomorrow — we gonna have sweatlodge tonight." The last drink had warmed Chal considerably. He smiled at Sun-on-His-Wings and said, "I'll stay with you tonight." He didn't want Sun-on-His-Wings to know that he had been drinking.

"All right, you do not believe in Peyote — but tonight you will go to sweatlodge with me. Purty soon now, when sun sets."

They walked toward one of the small houses, went in and began stripping off their clothes. Chal was buoyed up by his drinking and he believed he wanted to see the Peyote ceremony. Sun-on-His-Wings pointed to a blanket, and Chal threw it over his shoulders, then followed his friend out of the house. They walked slowly toward the sweatlodge.

The lodge was made of cedar saplings, stripped and peeled. They were stuck in the ground in a circle, then bent over and the upper ends were tied together by rawhide. This framework was covered with canvas in place of skins. On one side of the entrance were four buckets of water, two hot and two cold, and on the other side was a small pile of limestones and a pile of wood. Near this a fire was burning, and some of the limestones were being heated there, while two attendants stood watching the fire. The fire had been lighted by Watching Eagle with the sparks from two flints.

Chal and Sun-on-His-Wings entered at the east entrance. The lodge was steaming from the hot limestones piled in a pyramid in the center of the room, over which attendants poured water. Chal cast his blanket to one side, following every movement of Sun-on-His-Wings, and they sat down together.

There were several other naked figures in the lodge, sitting in a circle, but no one looked up ; they seemed to be thinking profoundly, with their heads bowed. The sweat dripped from their foreheads and rolled down their bodies, dripping from their fingertips.

Near the center of the lodge was a small kettle sitting over a fire. An attendant came in with a quart cup full of buckeye root and poured it into the hot water in the kettle. He stirred the mixture a few moments, then filled two cups and handed them to the left around the circle. Each man supped as much as he wanted, then passed the cup to his neighbor. Chal noticed that Sun-on-His-Wings chewed some of the root as well, but he only drank of the liquid.

He wanted to see everything that was going on, but he felt that he might be ill-mannered if he watched too closely, so he kept his head bowed like the rest, but covertly watching the Road Man who sat at the west end of the lodge. On each side of the Road Man sat an old man — the Fire Chief and another old counselor.

As Chal sat, the sweat began to ooze out all over him, and he had to keep his hand to his forehead most of the time, but when he noticed the others let the sweat fall, he did likewise. Then a terrific pain came into his stomach ; it seemed that many little live things stirred there. He could scarcely keep from groaning softly, and he looked up with an expression of silent appeal to the motionless, bowed figures in the darkening lodge, but they were unaware of his pain. Sweat came faster as the pain became more acute, and he knew he must get out of the lodge very soon ; must get out and rid himself of that terrible working in his stomach that was like many live things attempting to roll themselves into balls.

Just at the moment when he thought he could bear it no longer, Sun-on-His-Wings looked over at him. His face was covered with sweat drops. Sun-on-His-Wings then spoke to the Road Man and asked permission to go out. He got up, threw his blanket around him, and started for the door. Chal followed his example quickly. Outside, a little way from the lodge, they turned their faces to the north, the direction of Evil, and emptied their stomachs.

Sun-on-His-Wings smiled, "That is the evil that has come into your body," he said.

They accepted the dipper of warm water handed to them by the attendant. Chal's blanket stuck to him and made him want to take it off, as they stood for a moment longer facing the north. As they stood there, Chal saw Runs With Cow come out of the lodge. He turned to the north, but seemed to be having trouble. An attendant, seeing this trouble, brought him the wing feather of a crow, which he used as an aid by tickling his throat.

They went back into the lodge and Chal felt suddenly quite well, and pleasantly weak, but his head was clear. They took off their blankets and took their places again in the broken circle.

One by one the worshipers asked permission, got up and passed outside, then returned to resume their attitude of bowed prayer. A dipper of cold water was passed around the circle, and it seemed to Chal that the water went to the very bottom of the stomach.

It seemed that they sat there for several hours, and it seemed odd to Chal that he could sit thus, silently and without moving. He was fascinated and calmed. There was a complete absence of urges, and his thoughts were light and left no impressions ; like sycamore leaves dropping to the surface of calm water, not even making concentric ripples, but riding away on the imperceptible current ; riding on into eternity.

He thought he heard a sound, but he didn't look up. Then he was sure, and he sat many minutes listening to the intermittent sobbing. He heard a movement, and he felt compelled to look up then. White Deer rose from his place and went over to the Road Man, who was sitting at the west end of a line running east and west through the circle. He was weeping as he sat down by the Road Man.   He picked up a cigarette paper and slowly filled it with the ground-up, dried sumac, which had been prepared in a little box for that purpose.   He rolled the cigarette slowly as he wept.   He lit it and handed it to Watching Eagle, who was the Road Man.

The little fire under the buckeye kettle made their faces the color of dawn.   Watching Eagle placed the cigarette in his mouth, and the smoke rose like a thread to the top of the lodge.   Watching Eagle took several puffs from the cigarette then waited.

White Deer said, "Road Man, my heart is heavy.   Evil surrounds my heart."   He made a motion, rubbing his body downward, passing his hands over his thighs, then he continued, "This evil which surrounds my heart is like mud that clogs the hoof of a horse when it has rained for many days.   Many times I have cried, and this evil around my heart comes out my eyes, and I say it is gone, this evil, but again it comes.   I close my heart and keep what is good there, but hate comes into my heart like the frost comes on the inside walls of a closed lodge.   My heart is cold and I say I ought to kill these white men who shot my son, Running Elk."

Chal felt a slight shock at the name of his friend.   So they knew who was killing those Big Hills one by one.   He listened intently.

White Deer continued, "They have put this dynamite into house of my cousin, those same white men.   Sometime I say I shall go to agent and tell him this.   Sometime I say I shall go to sheriff and tell him this.   I don't know what to do.   Thoughts pull at my shirt like little children and I do not know which one to follow ; I do not know which direction is good road."

There was a long silence and the prayer smoke climbed to the top of the lodge in the heavy, steamy air. Watching Eagle looked straight ahead, then he spoke softly, and slowly, using many words of which Chal had to guess the meaning : "My son, this evil in your body comes out now from your body. This evil in your heart comes out through your eyes. This evil cannot stay in your body forever.

"Long time ago there was one road and People could follow that road. They said, 'There is only one road. We can see this road. There are no other roads.' Now it seems that road is gone, and white man has brought many roads. But that road is still there. That road is still there, but there are many other roads too. There is white man's road, and there is road which comes off from forks. The bad road which no white man follows — the road which many of the People follow, thinking it is the white man's road. People who follow this road say they are as the white man, but this is not white man's road. People who follow this road say that road of Indian is bad now. But they are not Indians any more, these People who follow that road.

"The road of our People is dim now like buffalo trail across prairie. We cannot follow this road with our feet now, but we can see this road with our eyes, and our hearts will go along this road forever. Even if our bodies are carried by our feet on this road that is not Indian road. There are few of us whose eyes can see old road of our People, I believe."

The attendants came no more to pour water on the hot limestones, and the worshipers had stopped sweating. White Deer stopped crying and remained motionless. The silence that came over the lodge rang in Chal's ears. He wasn't aware of how long the silence lasted, but he was happy and contented, sitting there. Soon he became detached from this covered lodge, and he began dreaming.

There was nothing about him but the gray-blue bowl of
the sky and the prairie.   He was walking along a twisted
trail that lay crazily, like a lost lariat rope, across the
prairie.   He began running and held out his arms, then
suddenly he was flying.   He would be lifted on an uprising
current from the hot prairie, then would drop into a pocket,
and he felt that he couldn't get his breath.   He began to
fear that he might fall, but just as he thought he might hit
a hill and be crushed, he would rise on a current and be lifted
to dizzy heights.   But he couldn't get down.   When he
folded his arms, he would drop like a plummet, then when
he opened his arms, he would catch and sail off, rising suddenly on an upward current with the intense fear that he
should never come down again.

His dream was broken.   Someone moved, but nothing
followed, so he sat listening to the silence.   He wondered
what the others were thinking about.   He knew they were
thinking and praying, and he felt that he ought to be very
fervent about something too.   He decided he would ask
Sun-on-His-Wings later what you were supposed to think
about during the long silences in the sweatlodge.

He began to think again about White Deer and Running Elk.   He was impressed by White Deer's story about
the white men in the Big Hill country, and their killing of
Running Elk.   He wondered if White Deer imagined this
or if white men were realling killing the Big Hills for some
purpose.   He had been absent when Running Elk was
killed, and when he heard of his death he was very glad that
he was not at home because he knew that the relatives
would have asked him to help paint Running Elk's face for
the last ride to the Happy Hunting Ground.   Now he was
sorry that he had not been present.

He recalled instances of their boyhood together ; the twinkle in Running Elk's eyes and his dare-devilish escapades. Chal had always thought that Running Elk had been born too late ; that he might have been a great warrior in the old days. He remembered that he was ever in trouble and had gradually become a drunkard and a dope addict, and believed that he was being a white man. Chal thought of the times when he walked the streets in a queer dream, and of the times he had visited him at the jail or the hospital. Some of his dreams had been very funny, but they hadn't been funny to Running Elk, as he told them to Chal from a hospital bed or from a jail cot.

He often told Chal the story of the fat white man who followed him. He said that he would wake up in the night and that fat white man, completely naked and glistening, would stand at the door of his room with a spear in his hand. One time at the hospital that fat white man had appeared and Running Elk said he was so frightened that he jumped out of bed and ran down the hall, down the stairs, and into the basement, and hid behind the furnace until the nurses and the attendants had made the fat man go away. He told Chal that the white man's belly shook like jelly when he ran ; that that naked white man shook like a woman.

Chal had laughed at these stories when Running Elk told them to him with a very serious expression, but tonight as he thought of them he was very sorry that he had laughed. As he sat there he was sorry that he had avoided Running Elk. His thoughts were cut short by the voice of Watching Eagle, who had begun to talk to White Deer again.

"Your son and those People who have been killed by these white men, followed that road which they thought was white man's road. Your son married white woman. You have children of your son, but they are not your children. They can never have a name among their people. They have no people. Your son drank white man's whisky. He stuck his arm many times with that thing which brings bad dreams to white man. Take this son out of your mind. Take these children who are not your grandchildren out of your mind. Let this evil flow out of your heart through your eyes. Let this evil flow out of your body in sweat. Think no more of these things. These white men who kill these people will be punished. You are Indian. Here are graves of your grandfathers. You came out of this earth here. The life of this earth here comes out of ground into your feet and flows all over your body. You are part of this earth here like trees, like rabbit, like birds. Our people built their lodges here. That which came out of the ground into their feet and over their bodies into their hands, they put into making of their lodges. They made songs out of that which came out of ground into their bodies. Those lodges were good and beautiful. Those songs were good and beautiful. Thoughts which they had were good because they came out of ground here. That ground is their mother.

"White man came out of ground across that sea. His thoughts are good across that sea. His houses are beautiful across that sea, I believe. He came out of earth across that sea, and his songs are beautiful there. But he did not come out of earth here. His houses are ugly here because they did not come out of this earth, and his songs and those things which he thinks, those things which he talks, are ugly here too. They did not come out of earth here. He killed our brothers because they were not his brothers.

"We can do nothing. But we are Indian, we are not white men. We live in white man's houses now, and our feet go along another road, but our hearts are on road that is dim.

"White man's god.   He came from across that sea too. Every Sunday he comes back.   Maybe he is good god.   I do not know this thing.   Maybe he is same god every-where.   I do not know about this thing.   This Jesus brings dreams that are good, and they said that this Jesus knew how to die.   He comes back every Sunday, they say.   But I do not know about this thing.   It is Wahkon ; it is spirit mys-tery.   We are only men."

There was another long silence and Chal began to be cramped.   All this seemed to be as a dream to him and he wondered if time were actually going on outside in the night. He wondered what time it was.   Then far off down the creek he heard a rooster crow, and he thought it must be about three o'clock.

Watching Eagle moved slightly as though to ease his position and White Deer took his place in the circle.   Then Watching Eagle began again :

"We are clean now.   Evil has flowed out of our hearts and evil has flowed out of our bodies.   Soap and water will make outside clean, but evil may stay on inside.   I cannot say what you shall do.   You are men like me.   It is better if your sons marry among our people.   We have no time for troubles, and we must not make troubles.   We must keep all of these things out of our minds.   We must have time to keep our place on earth.   If we have many troubles we cannot fight to keep our place on earth.   We cannot stay here all time.   Our children must keep our place on earth.   If we think all time of these troublous things, we will not have time to think of other things.   We will not have time to keep our place on earth.   Everything that comes out of earth here must fight to keep its place on

earth.   That is good, because that way it will always be
strong.   We cannot fight white man, but we are Indian ;
we cannot be white men.   We must use our time to fight
our troubles.   To fight that evil which comes on inside
of us.

"We must go within our hearts.   Let northeast wind
blow upon us.   Let southwest wind blow upon us and find
what is in our souls.   Let that sadness around our hearts ;
that sadness which becomes evil, break and flow out through
our eyes."

A heaviness came over Chal and he felt very sleepy.   He
scarcely heard the last words uttered by Watching Eagle,
and the abrupt ending wakened him.   He wondered what
would happen now, though his drowsiness made him indifferent, and he felt that he should like to go to sleep.

He must have dozed off.   There was a movement in the
lodge, and the Road Man was standing before White Deer.
He put the palms of his hands on White Deer's forehead,
then made a motion of passing his hands over White Deer's
body.   He placed the palms of his hands on his own forehead, then passed them down over his body, then he went
back and sat down.   The Fire Chief rose and left the lodge,
then one by one the worshipers left, Chal following close
behind his friend.   Last of all to come from the lodge was
Watching Eagle, the Road Man.   He stood in the line
facing the east with the rest of them.   They stood there in
the dawnlight, silently facing the east.   They stood for
many minutes, then the sun appeared on the horizon.   They
all placed their hands on their foreheads, then extended them
to the sun, and brought them back to their foreheads.   They
stretched their hands to the sun again, and this time brought
them back to their chests, then out again and then back to
their stomachs.   Then they moved their hands down over

their bodies, over their thighs, as though laving themselves with the rays of the sun. Chal watched Watching Eagle very closely and copied every movement he made.

The worshipers then turned to the west and faced the Peyote church, holding their hands out toward the church. After they had held their hands out thus for a moment, they brought them back to their bodies, and made a movement as though laving themselves.

After this ceremony, they went back into the lodge, picked up their blankets, and dispersed. Chal drew his blanket closely around him as the morning air was quite cool. He followed Sun-on-His-Wings back to the little house. Sun-on-His-Wings threw his blanket down, went into a little room, and stepped under a shower of cold water, then came out smiling very amiably. When Chal came out from under the shower, he felt a keenness that he had not felt for days ; an exhilaration that made everything interesting. He looked around for a towel, but he noticed that Sun-on-His-Wings was allowing himself to dry without the aid of a towel, so he didn't say anything.

As they stood in the little room, Sun-on-His-Wings seemed to be enjoying himself hugely. He said, "Chal, maybe you will think about church now. I am goin' to church today, but you can't go — you do not belong. You better go to sleep, and after while we will have feast." Chal could smell the meat broiling, and he became very hungry.

He watched Sun-on-His-Wings walk toward the main ranch house with the end of his blanket trailing. He knew he was going there to put on fresh clothes ; he didn't want to touch the clothes he had taken off before the ceremony of the sweatlodge. Chal felt in his clothes and found his cigarettes, lit one and lay down on the only bed in the room. Despite his hunger and drowsiness, he was still moved by the happenings of the night, and he wanted to lie there and recapitulate. But he was too sleepy, and he was soon sound asleep. His hand slipped off the bed, and the cigarette fell to the floor, where the first morning breezes, the awakening breath of the summer morning, played delicately with the blue smoke.

XV

FOR two days Chal walked around in a sort of pleasant trance. He was dreaming a pleasant, indefinite dream, and he felt that he was going to do something definite about something ; that something being quite vague. He remembered with pleasure the night in the sweatlodge, and the feast where everyone seemed to be so happy ; in fact he was so absorbed in the pleasant feeling that he scarcely spoke to anyone. He bought cigarettes without thinking of what he was doing, and saluted acquaintances in the street without recognizing them.

He went into the Blue Front drug store one Saturday afternoon. There were several men standing there, and as usual they were talking about oil. "Hell," said Brick Stagg. "The Dolomite dropped a string uh tools, 'n'en they had a fishin' job all summer."

"Yeah, I had an interest in that lease south uh them — could uh sold out before that for twice what we paid," said Doc Lawes.

"Yeah, I know," said another, "I sold that lease — bought it at the sale last summer. Guess I didn't hold it long enough."

Chal stood and lit a cigarette. He liked to listen to the talk that went on when men gathered at the Blue Front. Such talk sounded fascinating and prosperous, and the men had a generous, hearty way about them which made money seem trivial. They were sure of themselves, like Ed Fancher and Jep Newberg, and seemed solid and practical. They seemed to see things as they were without any sentimental drivel.   They were hard headed business men.   It was this type of man that everybody was beginning to say ought to be president of the United States, or governors of the states. Everyone was saying that the states and the nation ought to have hard headed business administrations.

The smoke floated up from the expensive cigars as the men stood with their heads back, leaning against the showcases.   They listened while one of the number told of some deal he had made or about what one of the representatives of the large oil companies had told him.   Doc Lawes' large diamond flashed as he raised his hand to his cigar to take it out of his mouth so that he might spit into a large brazen cuspidor.   The movement of his face downward, and his pursed lips sufficing as a warning to Jim Bergman, who kept his foot on it during the conversation.

Chal left the Blue Front after the talkers had left.   He thought of how sentimental his thoughts had been since the night in the sweatlodge.   He felt that he had been silly, mooning the way he had, and he felt ashamed of his emotions.   He knew that he ought to be more practical about things.   The talk he had just listened to was the talk of the strong, practical men who did things, while the Osages dreamed silly things in a mystical dream-world.   Men like Doc Lawes didn't sit and dream ; they got out and did things.   Chal could even remember when Doc had first come to the town.   He drove an old gray horse to a ramshackle side-spring buggy, and the harness was patched with bailing wire.   Now look at him — with the exception of Jep Newberg and a few others, he was the richest man in town, and people respected him.   Respected what he had to say, not only about oil but about everything else.   He lived in a big house on the hill and knew both senators from the state by their first names, and always referred to the governor as "old Charley." Chal heard that when he played billiards or poker at the club, he won most of the time by talking the others out of it. People considered themselves quite lucky just to stand in a group which invariably formed around him when he was in a genial mood and wanted to talk. When he deigned to talk to anybody they felt flattered, and stenographers and girl cashiers giggled appreciatively when he thumbed them in the ribs and made suggestive remarks.

Chal wished fervently that he could be more like Doc and the others. He wished that people might smile about some deal which he had "pulled off," and say with admiration, "He's purty smart, all right." But even if he couldn't assume a boisterous good humor and say things which people appreciated ; even if people never formed little groups around him, he could at least be more practical and less sentimental.

Of course, no one knew how affected he could be over things. The people of his crowd would certainly smirk and say things that would cut if they knew. People were always talking about the younger generation nowadays, but there wasn't any foolishness about them. They were practical. Though sometimes, he, with a sort of alien keenness, saw that they bluffed. He believed that they wanted to shock other people, especially older people, but often shocked themselves in their attempts to do so. But he wished he could be like them. He wanted to be identified with that vague something which everybody else seemed to have, and which he believed to be civilization.

He walked along the street. He wasn't very happy after coming down to earth again. He heard a car horn honk, and he looked up and saw Marie Fobus at the wheel of a large car.   There were two people in the front seat with her and the back seat was full.

"Chal," she shouted, "Chal, you ole blanket."   He went over to the car and he could see that the occupants had started on a party.   "Chal," said Marie, "been lookin' for yuh all afternoon.   Come go along — we're goin' places and do things."   She opened the front door, and one of the girls in the front seat stood up, Chal crawled in, and she sat back down on his knees.

Marie backed away from the curb, and the man coming down the street who had swerved to avoid bumping into her car, looked angrily at her, and shifted his chewed cigar to the other side of his mouth.   "God, what a look," Marie commented.   She put her hand out and turned against traffic.   "Cop lookin'?" she asked of the back seat.

She roared down the street in second speed, and stopped in front of Chal's house where his car was parked.   Two of the party got out with Chal and they crowded into his roadster and followed Marie out of town.

On the main street of the blazing little oil town of Salt Creek, was a large building where prize fights were held. It had one large room which was profusely decorated with faded crepe paper.   The orchestra was at one end and the cloakrooms at the other, and there were some hard benches against the walls.   Back of the orchestra were the rest rooms, over which a large hand pointed to the inner doors.   Beneath the hand was the sign, in large letters, "Here It Is."

After Chal had taken three drinks on the way over and had gone into the men's room three times, standing amid empty bottles and cigarette stubs, and drinking with Bert Lawes, he was glowing.   The atrocious hall, the tinny music were the setting for romance.   He believed that even the member of the party whom he thought of as the funny

little girl, could dance well, though she stumbled more and
more as the evening progressed, and danced closer and
closer until he could scarcely dance with her at all.   But he
didn't mind.   He was lifted into the realms of romance,
and he felt that he was in perfect harmony with the rhythm
of the world.

At the little cafe after the dance, Chal could eat nothing,
but he felt expansive and took great pleasure in paying the
check.   There was such a glow over all life that when someone dropped a nickel in a music machine, he found that the
waltz that escaped from the grinding, tugged a little at
something inside him, though he was not aware when the
music stopped.

Two men who had been sitting at a table in the back of
the room with a girl, a tired, transparent kind of girl with
bleached hair and eyes that were made owlish with mascara,
stood up and struck at each other.   They clinched and fell
over their chairs.   They were soon separated by the other
people and one of them was led out of the room with blood
covering his face, saying, "I'll get 'em."   The fight seemed
to have given the girl animation ; she stood for some time
over the other man, consoling him with delicate pats and
encouragements that were maternal in their love and sym-
pathy.   As she consoled the man, she swore over the incident in such a manner that Chal, who had been fascinated,
forgot the words and wondered at the paradox ; the paradox
of such words coming from so pale a body.

After eating, the party went over to Lawes' ranch, accord-
ing to plan.   There was no one there, and they had the
house to themselves.   Peggy held the jug of newly acquired
corn whisky between her feet, and Chal raced at seventy
miles an hour over the dirt road to the ranch house, slightly
annoyed by the fact that the other two people in the car

had not commented on the fact that he was going seventy miles an hour.

THE next day Chal came downstairs. He didn't have any idea about the time. He felt on the rack by the front door and took down a fishing rod and a box of flies. He could hear members of the party cooking ham and eggs in the kitchen. The bed in the front room was full of relaxed, sleeping forms, in many postures. Bert Lawes sprawled in an arm chair, asleep, with his mouth open.

Chal walked out of the house and into the hot light of the sun. The weeds caught at his trousers as he walked toward the creek, and as he brushed the weeds a dust rose from them. He made his way to the great sycamore which stood higher than the other trees and gleamed among the dark boles of the elms, the oaks and the walnuts.

He sat down where the roots of the great white tree had been laid bare by successive floods. They curled and twisted like serpents in their attempts to hold to the soft bank. He remembered this tree from the time he was a little boy and used to visit at the La Rivier ranch just across the creek. This tree had been fighting to hold its place ever since he could remember, but now a few more sinuous roots were exposed, and he wasn't sure, but he believed it was inclined over the water just a little more. He remembered how as a little boy, he had given it a personality. To his little Indian mind it was not a soldier, a rugged old man, nor a fair, virtuous woman resisting the yellow-brown floods which tore at the soil around its roots, but just a tree ; that was sufficient. A tree which had personality and was fighting against the enemy ; the evil-smelling, gurgling water.

One day the water was very high and had crept even into the barn lot, like a skulking animal, noiselessly ; so noiselessly that no one from the house suspected it until Ben came to the house from milking. When Chal had heard of the flood, he immediately set out through the alluvial mud to the tree. The swirling water was forming little whirlpools among its roots, and he saw — or was it imagination — the tree trembling with fear. He had not really thought that it was trembling with fear but he liked to believe that it was. He liked to believe that it was calmed when he put his graceful brown hand on its white bole, to assure it that he would protect it against its enemy. He smiled as he thought of his boyhood, and those days which he spent along this very creek were happy ones. It seemed to him as he sat there that they were particularly happy days.

The water was lifeless. At the end of the hole a green scum appeared, and when he had flicked his fly in that direction his line had made a little thread-like path as he drew it to him. For several minutes he flipped his fly, then began to worry the little water striders, but he found this uninteresting ; they were too quick, skating contemptuously out of the way of the little black gnat with the little red tail. He stood and gazed at the dull surface of the water for some minutes. Then reeled in his line, put on the lead sinker, took off the black gnat and put on a hook, then walked back up the bank among the dusty weeds. He came back with a handful of grasshoppers, put one of them on the hook and sat down again ; silent and motionless against the white bole of the tree.

A lone cicada started his song ; later there would be a deafening chorus. A cuckoo croaked far down the creek. Chal's thoughts were lazy, like moving cloud shadows ; light and leaving no impression. He was a part of the somnolence of the afternoon, and in harmony with the life about him. His thoughts were not dreamy ones, and neither pleasing nor displeasing, just running idly on like a motor out of gear. A panther, stretched along a limb with the leaf-shadows making even more effective his protective coloring, his eyes closing and opening and his ears lazily twitching, might think in this manner. No pains of hunger and no thought of tomorrow or of yesterday, an interval in the game of survival when the spirit is being recharged so that the mechanism may be ready for self-preservation.

But Chal's senses were dulled, and he was not acutely aware of anything. The cicada singing above him, and the persistent calling of the cuckoo, seemed a part of the somnolence.

A dragonfly buzzed in a zigzag fashion and finally settled on his rod, big-eyed and iridescent. Motionless they stared at each other, and still Chal's thoughts did not rise above the dreaminess which possessed him. He simply thought that the dragonfly looked like a beautiful ribbon tied on his rod for decoration. The dragonfly buzzed off down the stream and a bullfrog splashed into the water. The squirrel that had lain full length on a horizontal limb across the creek sat up, turned and ran up the trunk of the tree, then like a shadow disappeared behind it.

Chal became suddenly conscious and he remained very quiet. He had never outgrown the ability to sense the approach of things. He felt that there was something or someone near, and he guessed it must be another fisherman. Suddenly there was a crashing of weeds and a call : "Chayul." He was intensely annoyed and he remained silent. There was more crashing and a second call, and he answered, "Here by the white tree." He arose and stood still until Peggy appeared at the top of the bank. She was guarding her face with one hand and separating the tall weed stems with the other, then catching sight of him, said, "Oh, there you are — whatcha doin' ?" She did not wait for an answer but looked around at the creek, then frowned at the steep bank. "How the devil d'yuh get down, honey ?" He came part way up the bank and extended his hand, and Peggy slid down into his arms, threw her arms around his neck and bit his ear. She stood aside and looked dubiously at everything around her, then concentrated her attention on the bare roots of the tree. "Snakes ?" she asked. "No, roots," said Chal. She looked up at him as though she didn't understand what he was talking about. She reached behind her and caught her skirts up around her knees and sat down on the white roots. She took off her shoes one at a time, shook the dust out of them and replaced them, circled her knees with her arms and looked doubtfully at the gay-colored floater-cork. "Catchin' anything ?" Before Chal could answer, she said, "The kids are all up, and we wondered where you were."

He looked at her. "Don't look like you got a head."

"Who, me ? Don't you believe it — I never have a head. But was I tight or was I tight last night. Bill's mad at Cissy — she was sittin' out in the car with Ralph all night, nearly. Gosh, I wouldn't be in her shoes."

"Where was Bill last night ?"

"Well, I'm damned — he slept with us. Don't you remember ? Gosh, honey, you weren't that blotto, were you ?"

"Where is Bill now ?" He said this as though he hadn't heard her.

"Took your Lincoln and went to get some cigarettes — to some little one-horse store in the field — can yuh get cigarettes there ?"

"Of course."

They sat for some time. Chal was thinking how he

wished to be far away, but he didn't know exactly where. Somewhere away from here ; away from this gray day of disillusionment ; a disillusionment more acute after the piti- ful gesture toward romance of the night before. He felt a pain in his head and slightly enervated. If he could only lie down somewhere under the elms in the creek bottom and go to sleep. He watched his cork as though he expected a strike, thinking that if he seemed to be intent on his fishing she might go away and leave him.

Peggy arose suddenly and said, "Come on, honey, let's go — the kids were throwin' 'em together when I left, and I was told to find you and bring you back." He hesitated.

"Come on, handsome. Say, who was that funny little girl who kept sayin', 'Let's haul off and have another one,' ? And boy, did she pass out !"

Chal stood up and dismantled his rod. He walked up to Peggy and said, "You look sweet an' fresh this afternoon." Then after noting the appreciation in her face, lifted her in his arms and climbed the bank. He carried her on through the weeds and set her down on the trail.

They entered the house with cheers from the others and several remarks alluding to what they might have been do- ing out so long. "What about a little drenk ?" someone shouted, and someone else said, "Yeah, come on, le's get goin'."

Peggy smiled with an expression of proud proprietorship as she stood by Chal with her arm hooked in his. Marie raised her dishevelled head from the bed where she had been lying, and seemed to have trouble in focusing her gaze, then with a feeble wave of her hand, said, "Hi, Chief 'Fraid-of-a- Bear—ole 'Fraid-of-a-Bear in person." She sat up and slid to the edge of the bed. Her skirts were tight around her knees, and the calves of her bare legs bulged against the edge.

There were circles below her eyes ; deep circles, that seemed very blue. There were stains under her arms as she lifted them to brush her hair back, and she seemed very soiled. Chal had a feeling of disgust when he looked at her. He took the glass which someone held up to him and drank it down.

"Look at that boy drenk," said Marie. "What a man !"

"Gosh, I can't take it without makin' a face," said the funny little girl, who had risen on her elbow on the other side of Marie. Chal looked over at her. She was lighting a cigarette and frowning as she held the match. He remembered her as the girl who had become so very drunk the night before — so drunk that her partners had had to hold her up, and at intervals before she fell into heavy sleep in a corner, she would shout, to the amusement of the others, "Le's haul off and have another one !" Today her eyes were bleary, but otherwise she seemed not to have suffered from her heavy drinking.

When she got her cigarette lighted at last, she raised her voice and said, "Le's haul off and have another one." Everyone laughed, and she seemed to appreciate herself very much.

Chal sat in a big chair and looked out across the prairie. He could see the heat dancing over the limitless green, and beyond, on the highway, dust clouds were being formed by passing cars. He noticed the veins standing out on the backs of his hands, and he was growing warm, but things didn't seem so bad now. As Marie got up from the bed and walked wearily across the room, she seemed beautiful again. A glow came over him and though he didn't take part in the conversation he was happy ; vaguely pleased with things as they were. His head didn't hurt any more, and the cigarettes had a delightful taste.

Someone fell or was pushed over the chair next to Chal

but he didn't think it was necessary to look around. He got up and walked over to the table, picked up the jug of corn whisky, and took a long drink. Cissy suddenly materialized and flung her arms around his neck. "Hullo, han'sum, le's go places and do things." He stood still. She dropped her head on his shoulder, and he could feel one of her legs give way. He could see that she was going to make a day of it, all right, after the quarrel with Bill. Chal guessed she intended to spite Bill in some way, but had already become too drunk to carry out her plans effectively.

They were standing thus when Peggy came up. Her face was flushed as she laid her hand on Cissy's shoulder, "Whatta yuh doin', neckin' my boy friend?" Cissy stared at her uncomprehendingly, then flushed with anger. "Hell, I do' want your boy friend — I — uh — " She moved away and supported herself against the table, swaying a little.

"Gimme a cigarette," Cissy said, as she began to feel in Chal's pocket. He placed one in her mouth, and lighted it for her, then Peggy took him by the hand and said, "Come on."

"Where?"

"Le's go outside."

Chal felt that someone was imposing on him; that someone was attempting to tell him what he should do; someone who believed he was drunk and was using the same methods that one uses with children. He suddenly decided that he wouldn't do anything that anybody wanted him to do, and he became very angry and shook her hand off his arm. "Go on outside if you want — I'm gonna — I'm gonna go up and go to bed." He decided that he had no other desire than to go to bed, and he had a vague feeling that he might be injuring Peggy if he did so. He pushed her hand away again and walked off to the stairs, unsteadily.

He found a room on the east.   The breeze played with the bed clothes, and that was the only sound ; the pleasing moan of the breeze through the room.   He pulled off his shoes and fell heavily on the bed.

THE air was still when he woke up, and he sensed a deep tranquillity.   He looked out the window and saw that the sun was just going down.   Sharp pains followed each other through his head.   The quiet was broken suddenly by the sound of many people talking at one time ; the sound coming up the stairs in volume, when someone opened the door at the foot.   The noise came up the stairs like a draught of air. Chal heard unsteady steps on the stairs, and Peggy came in. Her eyes were very bright and she was very gay and excited. She rushed forward and threw herself on him with her arms around his neck.   "Hullo, honey," she said in his ear.   For a moment she almost smothered him, then he succeeded in pushing her away, and sat up on the edge of the bed with the sharp pains shooting through his head and making him surly.

"Whassa matter, honey ?   Sick ?"   She put her hand on his head and he threw it off.   "Whatcha need's a little drenk," she said gaily.   "A little drenky-drenky."   She smelled like a cocktail and Chal felt that he was being persecuted.   He put his shoes on hurriedly while she stood in front of an old, leprous, cracked mirror and applied lipstick. He started downstairs, and she bounded from the mirror and threw her arms around his neck.   He suffered her for a moment, then took both her arms away and went downstairs, while she followed with her hands against the walls.

He went straight to the jug and took a drink.   While Sim was trying to kiss Peggy, Chal walked over and picked up his coat from the floor, then went out the back door.

He climbed into his car and drove away.   He drove over

the prairie into the flaming, red west, then turned off the road, opened a barbed wire gate, and followed a twisting little trail over the prairie to a drab little shack.

The shack sat in the center of a bare space enclosed with barbed wire. To one side was an old cottonwood tree, and from one of the limbs a cable was suspended, supporting a castoff tire. Chickens picked crumbs around the doorstep. Back of the shack was a gray, disreputable shed, and against it and around it were piles of barbed wire, rusted farm implements, a junked car, and a tall manure pile. Stretching to the south was a field of corn, the tassels drooping and whitish with a sickly pallor. The long leaves were shriveled, and the bottom of the stalks were yellow as though some malady had crept out of the ground, and was slowly consuming them.

A wild-eyed little girl sat swinging in the tire ; swinging listlessly. When she saw Chal's car, the long, shiny car, she got out of the improvised swing and stared, standing there in her torn dress with her scabby, brown feet poised like some animal's. A dirty-faced baby crawled in the dirt, his bare bottom caked with mud. He crawled along picking up stones and pieces of stick like some clumsy, earthbound simian. The little girl went swiftly, gracefully into the house, and by the time Chal had stopped the car, there was a dirty, wild-eyed face at each window. A stooped, snaggle-toothed woman appeared at the door and stared. Behind her, clinging to her skirts, were three other children whose moon faces were without light.

Chal felt quite surly, and when he saw these people he became almost angry. When he saw people like these he felt vindictive toward the government, and the very impotence of the feeling contributed to its poignancy.

Chal approached the shack. "Howdy," he said. The

woman moved her head almost imperceptibly in affirmation, but said nothing. Then Chal said, "Where's your husband — is he here?" The woman turned to a barefooted, wild girl of about fourteen and said something which Chal couldn't hear. Then she turned to Chal and said, "No, 'e hain't." She hesitated, expecting Chal to go on.

"Well, he knows me — you remember, I was here last spring." Chal looked at her expectantly. He had one desire now, and he was afraid that something might go wrong, so he smiled. "Yeah," he continued, "I've done a lot of business with your husband — thought maybe he might have a little — a little sugar." The woman's face became suddenly very hard and she gave Chal a piercing look, then looked out intently at the car as though she would see if he were alone. He guessed her thought and said, "I'm alone," and he smiled again, because he had begun to doubt.

The woman came out into the yard, her bare feet crusty and splayed. She wiped the baby's nose with her skirt, picked him up and held him astraddle her hip. "Well, Ah don' hardly know — Jim hain't here an' Ah don' hardly know."

"That's all right," Chal said ingratiatingly, "that's all right — I know it'll be all right with him — he knows me, and he knows I'm all right."

The woman looked out over the prairie. The sun had gone down and the emerald grass had become dark and soft like velvet, and the distant hills were violet tinted. The whole prairie was sprinkled with grazing steers. She looked as though she were expecting someone. After looking long across the prairie, she looked piercingly at the car again. She shifted her eyes and looked up the line of barbed wire fence and said, "Reckon ya might find a jug under that there fur post tother side uh that rav-veen."

"Good, I'll go get it."

She watched Chal's quick step and his slim back for a moment, then she called to him, "Better take a sack." He turned back smiling, and one of the little girls came out of the house and handed him a sack. When he started up the fence line the second time, all the children came out of the house, and the whole wild group watched him walking along the wire fence. The woman was doubtful, but ever'one knowed them Injuns never said nothin' to nobuddy, hardly — so she guessed mebby hit was awright. A body always charged 'em more, too, and Jim had allus said that them Injuns never would tell nothin' nohow.

Chal came to the post indicated and catching the second string of wire, lifted it clear, and discovered the jug. He placed it carefully in the sack and came back to the house with it slung over his shoulder. He gave the woman five dollars, and she clutched at it with her dirty, talon-like hands, and the light in her eyes was wild and cunning.

Chal stopped the car on the trail and carefully filled a pint bottle, then took a long drink out of the jug. He looked back over the trail, but all he saw were the parallel lines crawling crazily across the prairie. The light was failing and the outlines of things were being magically softened. Even the shack, which was like a terrible scar on the prairie, was softened by the twilight. A plover whistled and he felt a distinct happiness. He took another long drink from the jug, lit a cigarette and drove out the gate onto the highway.

He saw dust ahead of him and he pressed his foot down against the accelerator. The great car sped ahead and he was filled with a delightful madness. He passed the car ahead of him so fast that the driver almost lost control ; almost drove his car into the ditch. Chal drove on, skidding around curves and rumbling across cattle-guards, the car seeming to float up the long hills. He had to slow down for some steers lying and standing in the road, but he maneuvered his car through them, pretending that they were a great obstacle to his flight. The lazy steers rose grudgingly, then turned quickly to face the car. Chal could hear the flies swarming and could almost feel the heat of the beefy bodies. The still, hot night was laden with the odor of cattle.

The nighthawks had already begun to settle in the road and he killed several of them as they flew up before the rush of his car. After darkness fell, the shafts of light from his headlights would shoot out across the prairie as the car followed the twisting road over the hills ; the shafts bringing out the hills in ghostly relief.

There were no other cars on the dirt highway that lay across the prairie hills, and the hum of the powerful motor was the only sound which disturbed the deep silence of the summer prairie. Chal looked at the speedometer and felt annoyance because it crept barely above seventy ; and only this on straight stretches. He believed he needed another drink, so he stopped abruptly and the rear wheels skidded crazily over the dirt. The motor idled as he reached into the car pocket and pulled out the bottle. He grimaced as he swallowed ; a thing he never did when anyone was watching. He sat for some time and emptied the bottle.

He was filled with a radiance and fire seemed to course through him. He put the car into gear and with a grinding noise again started a race over the winding road. Madly he raced, and he felt that he should like to whoop. It was very pleasing to see the cattle-guards appear for a moment in the bright lights, before the car plunged between the narrow opening in the barbed wire fences, and there was satisfaction in the rumbling noise when the car shot through untouched, because the opening looked so narrow.

The first blackjacks appeared like sentinel ghosts in the headlights, and they swam past and became indistinct in the darkness again. A ridge of blackjacks appeared, like a solid wall, and Chal thought of them as a barrier to his terrific dash through the night, and he was pleased and felt triumphant when the car roared through them, and they were left behind like a thwarted and defeated enemy, bowing to Chal the conqueror.

But it was not fast enough dashing through the night at terrific speed. He felt that he had to express himself in some bodily action ; to express the wonderful emotion that was dominating him. Without forethought he swerved off the road and drove along the top of a blackjack-covered ridge, dodging the ghostly trees as they appeared in the headlights. The tall blue-stemmed grasses made dry thumping noises on the front of the car. A bird rose in the headlights and fluttered away ; an unreal, moth-like spirit of the grass ; like everything else, ghostly and weird.

He stopped the car suddenly and climbed out and started talking to himself ; talking nonsense. He kept repeating to himself, "Extravaganza," without reason, as the word was not associated with any of his frothy thoughts. He reached in and cut off the motor and in doing so fell on the running board. He arose with difficulty, with an intense urge for action. Suddenly he began to dance. He bent low over the grass and danced, and as he danced he sang, and as he sang one of the tribal songs of his people, he was fascinated by his own voice, which seemed clear and sonorous on the still air. He danced wildly and his blood became hotter, and yet that terrific emotion which was damned up in his body would not come out ; that emotion which was dammed up and could not be expressed. As he danced he wondered why that emotion which had begun to choke him did not come out through his throat. He was an Indian now and he believed that the exit of all spirit and emotion was the throat, just as the soul came out through the throat after death.

He was in pain and he danced frantically for some sort of climax ; that sense of completeness that consummates the creative urge ; an orgasm of the spirit. But he couldn't dance fast enough, and his singing lacked the fire to release his dammed up emotion.

The dance became wilder and suddenly, in his despair, he broke the rhythm of his singing and yelled, but still the emotion was choked in his body. He wanted to challenge something ; to strut before an enemy. He wanted by some action or some expression, to express the whole meaning of life ; to declare to the silent world about him that he was a glorious male ; to express to the silent forms of the blackjacks that he was a brother to the wind, the lightning and the forces that came out of the earth.

He fell. His perspiration-soaked shirt stuck to his body and he felt the stinging drops of perspiration in his eyes, as he lay panting. Then he mumbled to himself the freighter's old phrase of impotence. "Goddamit," he said feebly.

He didn't know how long he lay there. He became uncomfortable with clammy cold, and he raised his head and listened for a long time. Funny, there wasn't a sound, he believed ; not a note from the grassroots and not a leaf stirring. The blackjacks were just dark outlines ; like plumes stuck in the earth. He had often wondered about the perfect patience of the blackjacks on still days ; perennially waiting for something. But tonight they annoyed him with their profound silence, and standing there as though they were accusing him of something. He was cold and he didn't like the way they stood there.

When he stood up there was no feeling of triumph or of dammed up emotion. He felt dizzy, and he was very uncomfortable. He went over to the car, and for some reason he thought that he ought to fill the bottle again. With trembling hands he filled it from the jug, but most of the liquid was spilled, and he just managed to fill the bottle with the last of the liquid in the jug. He swung the jug by the handle and threw it out into the grass where it would gleam in the sun and the moon of many days and nights, a symbol of man's effrontery to the great spaces. He held the bottle to his lips until he almost choked, then carefully put in the cork and placed it in the pocket of the car. He climbed into the car and sat, and warmth came over him again, but it was a calm and tranquil warmth.

Soon he held the bottle to his lips and took another long drink. After a while he lit a cigarette and by the light of the match he saw himself for a moment in the rear-vision mirror. He lit another match, and studied his face, then another, and another. The last time he saw his reflection he made a grimace, twisting his lips horribly and emitting a sound like an animal. He lit another match and this time he tried to look "mean"; trying several expressions to effect this attitude. He struck another match and attempted to light his cigarette, but he found that it was already lighted.

He closed his eyes and he seemed to be floating off across the prairie, but the pleasant feeling was disturbed suddenly by a distinctly unpleasant one in his stomach, and he opened his eyes and sat up quickly. His senses were dulled now, and he felt that he should like to go to sleep, but he was afraid to do so. He got out of the car unsteadily and took the blanket which he always carried with him ; he fumbled in the pocket and found the bottle, and drained it, but put it tenderly back. Then he wrapped the blanket tightly about him and lay down in the grass.

The early morning light was almost like twilight. A weak light, out of which came sounds that were sharp and clear ; disembodied voices. Sounds that ranged from the chirruping of the crickets in the half rotted logs, the many insects in the dew drenched grass, that sent up tinkling, rasping, sometimes mechanical voices, to the cawing of the crows. There seemed to be a sound of dripping, yet there was no dripping from the moist leaves, and the tall grass blades held their silver drops. It was a shut-in, intimate world, fresh and full of secrets and promises. At a distance the blackjacks, veiled in morning mist, seemed unreal and mysterious, and still farther, along the·ridges, there was nothing but a dark line made by the uneven tops ; a dark line which might suddenly become anything ; perhaps mountains.

Chal awoke to the yapping of coyotes which came from somewhere out of the breathless mist ; a jerky, whiney complaint which was not in the least like the drawn out howl of the hunting coyote. There was a vague shape a few paces away, made large by the mist. It looked much bigger than a steer, but of course it was a steer standing there with bovine, hazy curiosity, staring at that thing on the ground and that large red thing with the shiny eyes ; that large thing covered with beads of dew and so out of harmony here.

Chal lay there for some time just listening. He lay there until the tops of the blue-stemmed grasses began to move ever so little in the light breeze that had sprung up, then he carefully rolled the blanket down toward his feet so as not to get the dewdrops down his neck, and got up. He became aware of a slight ache in his head and his mouth felt dry.

He thought that the vague blackjacks just in front of him expanded a little as he looked at them, but he realized that this was only an impression.

The coyotes started another chorus with jerky petulance, and a squirrel joined them as though he had decided not to be outdone. Chal looked in the direction from which the chattering came, but saw only the strange, unreal shapes of the trees, like a stage setting, and the chattering seemed to come out of the unknown.

There was no romance left. The morning was cold and gray and held no interest. His new black-and-white shoes were spotted with the dew, and his trouser cuffs were heavy with absorbed water. He went to the car and started wiping the dew from the windshield. He stood there a minute trying to remember, then he fumbled in his pocket and produced a crumpled package of cigarettes, lit a match dexterously with his thumb nail, and after lighting the cigarette sent the match sailing off into the wet grass. He thought that the cigarette tasted the way damp straw smells when it burns. He climbed into the seat of the car and put his foot on the starter, and after a few coughs the powerful motor functioned smoothly and almost silently, and he allowed the motor to idle as he sat and looked over the drenched landscape.

The steer was still standing there looking at that queer monster with the big eyes. Chal looked at him and thought that he was very silly standing there, and he wondered what made a steer so stupid looking. He believed if he shouted the stupid thing would almost kill himself running. A sharp pain went through his head, and he put his hand up to his forehead as though he might ease it. He became annoyed with the steer, "Get out of it!" he shouted, but the steer remained standing there looking at the strange animal with the big eyes.   Again Chal shouted, "Damn you, hightail it," and he pressed his hand down on the siren button and held it there.   From the front of the car came a weird sound and the steer snorted and backed up several paces, looking at the car more intently and with an expression of surprise and doubt in his wide eyes.   The sound continued and the steer's nerves gave way ; he backed a few more paces, snorted loudly, then wheeled and clumsily galloped off into the mist.

Chal was not the least bit amused ; on the contrary, he felt very surly.   He put his hand to his head again, then crawled slowly out of the seat and started fumbling in one of the pockets.   He looked through both car pockets, then from the second one pulled out an empty bottle, threw it on the ground and searched again in the first one.   He found only a large powder puff, stained red and slightly soiled on the edges.   He looked at it for some seconds as though he were attempting to recall something connected with it, then threw it in the grass.

Chal sat down rather heavily on the running board and for several minutes held his head in his hands.   For some time after the sustained screaming of the siren, the voices were still, but soon from somewhere out in the mist a squirrel began barking again.   Out of nowhere a bluejay shot into the branches of a blackjack, cocked his eye on the quiet figure and the great red object, flipped his tail twice, and hopped to a lower branch, his body jerky with nervousness. When neither of the objects moved, he started screaming at the strange things there, hopping about from twig to twig. Soon others joined him, and like gaudy blue-and-white paper puppets, danced among the branches and screamed ; like puppets seeming to be whirled crazily by the wind as they danced.

Chal raised his head and looked at them, and when they saw that he moved, they flew to a more distant tree, but their scolding did not diminish. He felt that they were accusing him of something and he became unreasonably angry. He got up, picked up the empty bottle and threw it into the branches of the tree, and there were many streaks of blue-and-white floating away, each screaming "murder!" He stood for a while looking at nothing in particular, then looked carefully in each car pocket again but found nothing except tools. He climbed slowly into the seat, put his foot on the starter and was surprised to hear the whirring sound, then he realized that the motor was running. He threw it into gear then threw it out again and fumbled in his pockets until he found a crumpled cigarette. Then with the cigarette hanging from the corner of his lip and the blue smoke curling into his eyes and making him grimace, he backed over the tall grass and drove slowly toward the road.

XVI

THE black derricks had crept from the blackjacks of the east, slowly over the hills ; spreading to the south and north and on past the little town in the valley. They touched here and there, but climbed steadily west out of the valleys onto the high prairie ; across the treeless hills, and on across Salt Creek that lay like a silver ribbon across the prairie, fringed by elms. Then they crept to the very edge of the old reservation and lapped over into the Kaw country. There they stopped. At the tip of the westward movement, half a dozen little towns grew up ; not out of the earth like mushrooms, as they were not of this part of the earth ; they had no harmony with the Osage. Later they were like driftwood carried in from strange lands on a high tide and left stranded when the tide went out.

Riding on the wave of oil the little town of Kihekah grew out of its narrow valley and climbed exuberantly up its surrounding hills, then grew along the lines of least resistance ; along its elongated creek valley. The blackjacks moved back, stepping with dignity to protect their toes ; standing around the town and throwing their shadows across gardens and the green lawns that crept up to their feet.

Then one day something happened. It didn't all happen in one day, but it seemed that way. The all-powerful life that had come with the creeping black derricks began to recede to the east. The population of the little towns at the tip of the movement seemed to melt into the air, and the brick buildings stood empty and fantastic on the prairie ;

singing sad songs in the prairie winds. The roar of activity faded into the lazy coughing of pumps, and the fever brightness of the Great Frenzy began to dim.

The derricks stood black against the prairie horizon in rows, and became the husks of a life force that had retreated back along its own trail. The houses in the town of the little valley stopped their encroachments on the blackjacks, then they gradually became husks too ; like the shells of the cicadas clinging to the hillsides. The old trading store which had grown from primitive palisades into a domineering brick building closed its doors, and Ed Fancher took up a stand on the sunny corner of his old store, too old to believe what the more youthful were saying, that the oil would come back. The great store's empty windows stared out onto the streets like wondering eyes. Its owner expressing its surprised wonder when he said to a jovial, bankrupt mixedblood one day in the winter sun on the corner, that he "didn't see how 'Ye Shoppe' outfit across the street could keep goin'." As he and the mixedblood talked about the past they backed up against the empty, staring windows. Above them was an extravagant advertisement announcing the arrival of a circus which had folded its canvas and left Kihekah the summer before.

Mixedblood families came back to the old Agency from their large homes in the mountains, in California, and elsewhere. They dropped their golf clubs and lost their homes and came back to wander aimlessly along the familiar streets. They asked with the other citizens of the town, "S'pose it'll come back ?" All agreed that it would, but they wondered just the same.

One morning Jep Newberg was found with a bullet hole in his temple. Those who knew said that he sure was powder burned. He, with the sardonic humor of the hard-

headed business man, had elected to float out sentimentally
on the receding tide.

Doc Lawes, however, used a shotgun, and they said that
he did a good job, all right.

When the population had shrunk to a few thousand and
the citizens were still saying that times would be better, like
a boy whistling in the dark, Federal investigators made an
astonishing discovery. As a result, there was great interest
in the fact that a group of citizens in the Big Hill country
had been killing Big Hills for several years with the object of
accumulating several headrights into the hands of one Indian
woman who was married to one of the group. They were
preparing to put her out of the way when they were caught.
Running Elk had been the first relative to become a victim,
but his death had aroused little interest, and the other victims
were also disposed of in various ways during the roar of the
Great Frenzy, and naturally little attention had been paid to
the murders.

But now it was different. Here was an interest coming
up just when a lively interest was needed, and good citizens
rose early to be at the courtroom to hear the trial. House-
wives left their breakfast dishes in order to get seats so that
they might stare intently at the faces of the accused.

THE little cloud that had hung over the town in the valley
finally developed into a cumulus and spread over the sky.
But there were no lightning-thrusts of an angry Jove. The
senatorial committee came quietly and held their meetings
in the courtroom. The members sat at a table, and successive witnesses took a chair and answered questions.

It was a dull day. A monotonous questioning of witnesses, and the only relief was the evident embarrassment of
several guardians, and Roan Horse's speech. Chal sat in the

back of the room, and when Roan Horse was called, he felt a deep, vicarious shame. Roan Horse was an insurgent and he believed that everything was wrong. He was the leader of the east moon faction of the Peyote church, and believed that Me-Ompah-Wee-Lee, the founder, was a deity, much to the disgust of the conservatives.

When he was called, he walked with quick dignity to the table, but refused to take the witness chair, and Chal's heart sank. He walked proudly to the dais of the judge's bench and stood there like one who is preparing to make an oration. His long hair fell over his black coat in two braids which were interbraided with red cheesecloth. Some tribal instinct caused his hand to move to his right breast, as though he were holding the edge of a blanket under his right arm, then with his right hand he made a gesture and said, "Gentlemen of the senatorial investigating committee," then paused. The senator from the northwest Indian country sighed, and made a motion to the others that there was nothing to be done, then settled himself into a comfortable position. The others reared back in their chairs and pretended to be waiting.

Chal could see the anger in Roan Horse's face, and he looked down the bench where he was sitting as though he would escape if possible. Then again he heard Roan Horse's voice, "Gentlemen of the senatorial investigating committee : I am Roan Horse. I say this to you. You have come here twenty-five years too late." With a quick movement he descended to the table and shook hands with each of the members. When he came to the senator from the northwest Indian country, he stood at the senator's shoulder with his extended hand unnoticed. The senator was absorbed in some papers before him and apparently believed that Roan

Horse was still speaking. He turned, surprised, and took the long bronze hand.

People laughed about Roan Horse's speech, and said it was good, and Chal felt quite proud of him. His speech came at a time in the investigation when the citizens were beginning to believe that the affair was going to be tame, after all. They had hoped that the committee might stir up something which would be of benefit to them, but had experienced that childish injury which intensely acquisitive people feel when they have been thwarted. Thus they felt, in some vague way, that Roan Horse had been their champion.

Chal felt the atmosphere which was charged with depression, and he felt almost disillusioned at times. The representatives of civilization changed from jovial blackslapping, efficient people, around whom he had placed an aura of glory, to dour, reticent people who seemed afraid. The many ways which they had found to share in the wealth of the Osages, became less practical as the methods formerly used, now loomed in the quiescence, which before had been drowned in the frenzy. There was an attitude of waiting for something, and they told each other repeatedly that the Osage payments would become larger again.

The glamour was dimmed and Chal found that even corn whisky and home brew parties were of little aid in lifting his spirit from the effect of that strange atmosphere which had settled over the little town in the valley. He was annoyed with his mother because she didn't seem to understand that something had happened to the world. Fire Cloud would come with his wife, and the three of them would sit out in the shade under the postoak and talk as they had always talked. He thought they were like that postoak in a way. It had been standing there as long as he could remember ;

standing there in the shrill excitement of the frenzy, and
standing there now with the same indifference under the
pall of the dimmed glory.   Chal was annoyed with them
because they didn't seem to be aware that something important had happened to the little world of their blackjacks
and prairie.

One hot June morning Chal drove home.   He put the
car in the garage, making as little noise as possible.   Of
course his mother never said anything about his absences, but
he didn't want her to know that he had been drunk for the
last two weeks.

This morning he had come from the hangout of Pug Wilson and his gang, and he couldn't remember how he had got
there.   As he drove in he was wondering how long he had
been there and what he had done.   He had received his June
payment, which was certainly not much, but he didn't have
a cent left this morning.   As he rubbed his hand over his
chin his straggly beard seemed to be inches long.   He could
remember only snatches of the conversations at Pug's hangout, and he could remember vaguely that there had been
girls there.   He remembered Pug and the way he could
take his false teeth out and draw his cheeks in and pucker his
mouth so that he didn't look like the same man.   Pug had
boasted to him that he always did that before he went into a
bank.   He said he always put his false teeth in his pocket
and screwed his face up when he stuck the iron in their guts,
so they couldn't recognize him later.   He told Chal they'd
play hell catchin' him by the description of him with his teeth
out.

Chal walked slowly to the shade of the old postoak and
sat down.   He tried to recall some of the other things that
had happened at Pug's hangout, but he couldn't remember.
He was sure of one thing, and that was that he had not left

the house ; he was sure that he couldn't have accompanied
them on one of their "jobs." This assurance gave him a
pleasant feeling.

As he sat by the table this hot summer morning in the
shade of the old oak, he felt lazily indifferent to everything.
He slid back in his chair and watched a robin feeding her
young ; their quivering, jerky little heads reaching above the
nest with wide mouths. The mother robin shook herself
and flew away. A sparrow came hopping along the limb,
chirruped, and looked about, then hopped to the edge of the
nest. He cocked his head at the nestlings. They, hearing
the sound at the edge of the nest, reached for the expected
food. The sparrow looked quizzically at the little ones for
a while, with his head cocked. He looked around several
times, then reached in and lifted one of the nestlings out.
He hopped along the limb for a short distance, then looking
down at the ground, he let the little bird fall. Chal heard
it spatter as it hit the earth. The sparrow looked down at
it for a moment, then hopped back to the nest.

Chal was about to rise to scare him away when the mother
robin appeared, and with much scolding, chased the sparrow
away. When she came back she had a worm dangling
from her bill and began to feed the remaining nestlings.
She failed to realize that anything had happened to the
fourth.

The door slammed, and Chal's mother came out with
some coffee, and sat down in the other chair by the table.
For some time they sat silently, and as he sipped his coffee
Chal felt annoyed with her. He had felt antagonistic
toward her for some time, and he wasn't sure why. He
noticed that she had changed quite a bit. Her black hair
was parted in the center and brushed back and done into a
neat knot. Her long, copper-colored fingers played along

the arm of the chair nervously.   Her shoes looked neat on her very small feet, and she was dressed in a very attractive blue dress.   About her, as usual, as long as he could remember, was the odor of soap ; a simple, clean odor without the hint of perfume.   He noticed that her hair was still damp from the strokes of a wet brush.

The coffee in the pot grew cold.   Another sparrow came to the oak tree and looked about cautiously for the mother robin.   Chal watched him for a moment, then said, "The sparrows are still purty bad."   His mother looked at the ground in front of her, "Yes, seems like they're worse this year — I don' know why."

His antagonism left as a memory came back to him.   He turned to his mother.

" 'Member, I used to kill them with the arrows Uncle Fire Cloud made for me ?"

"My son was a great hunter — he killed many sparrows." A smile came over her face, then left quickly, and there was another long silence.   She looked straight ahead, then spoke softly, "Many white men are flying across the sea now."

It was only an observation, but Chal saw behind it into the Indian soul of his mother.   He became very angry and almost hated her for a moment.   An intense urge flooded him ; an urge to vindicate himself before this woman.   This woman sitting there was more than his mother — she was an Indian woman and she was questioning a man's courage. Suddenly he realized why he had almost hated her recently. She had been looking into his heart, as she had always looked into his heart.

As he sat there he was attempting to think of something to say which would vindicate him, but he was growing angrier in his futility.   Then suddenly he was warmed by a thought.   There was a primordial thing which thrilled

him and made his stomach tingle, and he felt kindly toward
his mother — toward this Indian woman who could see into
a warrior's heart. Under the influence of this thought he
got up from his chair and stood before her, instinctively
straightening his body.

"Ah," he said, "there isn't anything to flyin'. Flyin'
across the sea doesn't mean anything any more these days.
It's not hard. We didn't have these parachutes and things.
It was really dangerous when I was flyin'." He hesitated,
then a definite, glorious feeling came over him as he stood
there. "I'm goin' to Harvard law school, and take law — I'm
gonna be a great orator." The thought that had so recently
occurred to him for the first time, occurred to him the moment before, suffused him with glory, and he experienced an
assurance and a courage that he hadn't felt for years, and he
ended up with, "There isn't anything to flyin' any more."

As his mother looked at him standing there, she didn't see
a swaggering young man. She saw a little boy in breech
clout and moccasins, holding up a cock sparrow for her approval. She could see again the marks of his fingers on his
dirty face, and the little line of dirt in the crease of his neck.
As he held the bird up to her he had frowned like a little
warrior.

She thought that her heart might come into her face, so
she looked at the ground and said, "Huhn-n-n-n." She
got up quickly and went into the house.

Chal sat down again in the chair and slid down on his
back. He was filled with a calm pleasure. There was
nothing definite except that hum of glory in his heart,
subdued by the heat and the lazy tempo of life in the
heated yard.

His heavy head lolled back and he fell asleep. The leaf-
shadows made bizarre designs on his silk shirt, and moved

slowly to the center of the table, then to the edge, and finally abandoned the table to the hot sun. The nestlings in the nest above settled down to digest their food. A flame-winged grasshopper rose in front of Chal's still form, and suspended there, made cracking sounds like electric sparks, then dropped to the grass and became silent. The flapping and splashing of the mother robin, as she bathed in the pan under the hydrant, was the only sound of activity.

CPSIA information can be obtained
at www.ICGtesting.com
Printed in the USA
LVHW04s2205200818
587595LV00001B/10/P

9 780806 121604